A Novel

A Dancer's DRUG

Part One

MILLE ANNE

Purple Soul Publishing

Published by Purple Soul Publishing LLC
Los Angeles, CA

Cover Design by Acacia/Ever After Cover Design

Second Edition: June 2024
Printed in the USA

For more information, visit www.purplesoulpublish.com

For the solitary souls.

———— ♡ ————

Contents

CHAPTER 1
A Dancer

THE CITY BUS DOORS swing open, and I bolt out onto the street, hustling my butt up the block. I consider giving the driver a piece of my mind for never being on time, but I'll save it for a day when I'm not racing to work. Dodging late buses has become a sport for me over the years, so I handle it like a pro.

I can't afford to be late for this job again. Randall's patience with me is wearing thin, and I can't risk getting kicked to the curb for good. I work as a dancer at the Phoenix Fire, a hotspot where South Central's grit meets L.A.'s nightlife. I landed this gig when I was desperate, fresh off getting fired from my server job I worked at most of my high school career. I kept it from my daddy for as long as I could, but when he found out where I was slinging drinks and dancing, he kicked me out of his house without batting an eye.

"I ain't raise you to be a fool's toy, Chevonne. Get some sense about you," were some of his final words to me. Daddy passed earlier this year, battling sickness and heartbreak for years. Losing him hammered home the fact that I'm on my own out here. No one's going to take care of me. I couldn't even afford to take time off to mourn. But I swallowed those tears and kept pushing, because that's what Daddy would've wanted. If he were here, he'd probably tell me to suck it up and get back to work, anyway.

It's a bitter pill, but I've always felt like Daddy gave up on everything after Mama left us. Even me. He was tough on me, and I never got the chance to tell him how I really felt. But he's gone now, and I have a chance to heal from that pain alone. I'll just be damned if I ever treat my kids like that.

Outside the club, the crowd swells as we wait for the doors to open. In the dressing room, Tara's there, stretching with a cig in one hand and whiskey in the other.

"Randall's gonna catch on to you, Chevonne. And I'm getting tired of covering for you. You need to be here on time," she warns.

Tara's one of the few coworkers I can stand. She showed me the ropes when I started, but she's confident I didn't need much help. We've hung out a bit outside of work, and she's been helpful when she feels like it. So, I guess we're friends.

"I appreciate you covering for me, but you know I don't have a car, Tara. And the only bus close to where I live is never on time. I know Randall doesn't give a damn, but I'm doing my best," I shoot back, shoving my gym bag into a battered locker.

"I told you I could pick you up. You gotta give me gas money, but I'll do it. I don't get why you still don't have a damn car. You've been here long enough," she grumbles.

"I got other bills, Tara. I gotta finish paying off my old man's debts, plus rent and bills. And I ain't nobody's charity case. I'll get a car soon."

"You need to recognize when someone's trying to help, but whatever." Tara stubs out her cig, downing the last of her whiskey before flicking the ashes into the glass. She's got a killer bod, Randall's favorite long legs giving her special treatment around here.

"If you gonna stare, at least tip me, boo," Tara cackles, sauntering out of the dressing room. "Time to line up, so don't take too long. I'll see you out there."

The Phoenix Fire is lit tonight, no doubt about it. We're drawing in L.A.'s high rollers, married politicos, and even dope slingers. The club's vibe shifts with the night, and right now, it's electric.

I slide into line, waiting for my shot at the stage. Watching the current act, I stretch out my nerves, rolling my hips to the thumping beats. The crowd's energy pumps me up. Randall spares no expense to make our performances pop. We're his cash cows, and he expects nothing less than perfection. It's a fair warning, even if sometimes I feel like I belong in a Vegas show.

Randall didn't just throw me into dancing; I paid my dues as a bottle girl, then barkeep, before hitting the stage. I haven't even clocked a full year, but I rose up quick. Randall told me I immediately gave off the stripper vibe, and he could see me being one of his best. I didn't know what he meant by that, but I refuse to let him label me. He's got a twisted way of treating us women, so I don't take his words to heart.

"Chevonne, girl, it's your turn!" A coworker nudges me from behind, but I brush her off.

"Chloe, back off. You're crowding my space," I snap, making her step back. It's my time, and I won't be rushed. In this game, you gotta stand your ground. I'm not proud to say I've had to throw down a few times, but shit...

I'm all I got.

I strut to the pole, feeling the eyes on me. Nodding to the DJ, I let the music take over. I move slow, teasing the crowd.

Randall once encouraged me to focus on the fact that I have a big butt and to use it to my advantage so I can get more money, but I complained. He didn't like that at all.

"You're hoarding all that ass," he'd say, cigar hanging from his lips. "Pretty face is nice, but that backside brings in the bills."

The day we smashed on his desk was also the day he promoted me. Despite my efforts to brush it off like it never happened, I'm just glad I still have a job. Tara hasn't heard anything about it from me, and I don't plan on telling her. I'm not at my best when I'm feeling desperate, but that's no excuse. I didn't know he and Tara had a thing going before they called it quits. I'd hate to let her know that Randall probably made advances on all of us. It's just not my place to spill that. Tara might have been his favorite once, but good for her for not tolerating his player behavior anymore.

I wrap my leg around the pole, thankful for my strength. My body sways to the beat, drawing cheers and whistles.

But amid the spectacle, I remind myself to scan the room. The hunger in their eyes, the desire—it's intoxicating. Eventually, a regular with a beer gut approaches, eyes glued to my smile. He has cash clenched in his fist, and showers me with the bills.

As the music fades, I bask in the applause.

"Gentlemen, ladies, that was one of Phoenix's finest big booty strippers, Miss Chevy!" the announcer bellows.

"Dancer!" I mutter to myself, correcting the label. I gather the cash as the lights brighten, aided by a bottle girl, usually Sheila. Her naive excitement is always a contrast to the gritty atmosphere of the club., but she's also a friend, in her own way.

"That was great, Chevy, as always. The crowd was drooling over you!" I put my cash into the bag Sheila is holding and she murmurs, "You're such a natural."

"Thanks, girl. Maybe now, Randall will get off my back. I don't need to do all that extra stuff, you know," I respond and move out of the way of the ladies making their way to take their places in line.

"Of course, you don't *need* to. I believe you could stand up there without movin' a muscle and still get tips. But then again, what's the harm in that? It's your job. And you do have a great ass."

We both giggle as I softly prod her.

"Chevy, girl, you've been blessed. Shoot, I wish I was you sometimes." She helps me off the stage and gives my bottom a good pat as she does.

Sheila's only seventeen, our youngest on staff. Randall's got this thing where she can't dance until she hits eighteen, and I get where he's coming from. Sheila's this small, innocent thing, but she's dying for the spotlight the dancers get. I've seen how the crowd eyes her, waiting for her to step onto the stage. She can't wait to strut her stuff, and they can't wait to watch her do it.

I stash a few bills in my gym bag before lugging tonight's earnings to Randall's office. I earned every penny, and I'm not about to let him shortchange me. Randall's notorious for holding onto our cash until he feels like parting with it, so I try to stay under his radar. Unlike the other girls, I think ahead and squirrel away what I can to make ends meet until payday rolls around. I've dodged the cameras so far, but even if I did get caught, I'd grit my teeth and give Randall another lap dance if it meant keeping my earnings.

Dragging the box of bills to his office is a struggle, but I manage.

"I saw you sneaking a little extra," Randall grumbles, eyeing me like a hawk as he flicks his toothpick between his teeth. "But I'll let it slide this time. Good job out there tonight."

Phew. I breathe a sigh of relief. The last thing I want is to dance for him tonight.

"Thanks, Randall. Times have been tight lately, with rent and all. Hope you can understand," I reply, hoping he'll take pity on me.

He's chilling in his armchair, eyes glued to those camera screens like they're the latest episode of a drama series.

"I guess I'll head back out there," I say, keeping it cool, waiting to see what he'll say before I make a move to leave, but then I just shrug and start to open the door.

"Nah, hold up. Sit down for a sec," he says, pulling out another glass and pouring some scotch.

"Is that for me?" I ask, eyeing the glass suspiciously.

"Yeah, take it," he says, pushing it towards me. "Just knock it back. Don't overthink it."

I do what he says, but *damn*, that drink burns like hell on its way down. I struggle to keep a straight face, pounding on my chest to regain my cool.

Randall laughs. "You're somethin' else, Chevy. Shouldn't this be old news by now?"

"Yeah, well, it's not my thing," I reply, trying to keep my voice steady.

"Maybe it should be. Break out of that shell, girl," he suggests, taking a sip of his scotch, a smirk playing on his lips. "Heard you're still not feelin' my advice. That you want me off your back."

Sheila. That was fast.

I roll my eyes, firmly placing my glass down. I'm not having this conversation again.

"I'm just not into it, Randall. I have my own way of feelin' comfortable up there," I say back.

"Well, if you're not into it, maybe this ain't the right place for you," he retorts, his tone hardening. "Everybody else is on board. You should be too."

"What's with this obsession with my ass anyway?" I can't help but roll my eyes again. I really don't want to have this discussion again.

"Stop acting like you're all that. You ain't special, and don't forget, one of the reasons you're here is because of what you got back there."

"I think that's just *your* thing. None of the customers have a problem with how I do *my* thing," I gesture towards the cash box on his desk. "Hell, Amber out there with the long back still rakes in tips like I do. You ain't telling her to shake what she ain't got!"

"You need to watch your mouth, Chev, talking to me like that. If you don't want to play ball, then go back to bartending or find another gig You don't run anything around here."

"Fine, I'll go back to bartending," I mutter, arms crossed.

Randall glances over at me, shaking his head, clearly annoyed.

"Bartending it is. You're on bar duty for the rest of the night. And if you bail early, consider yourself out. Now, go," he says, his attention now back to the small security screens.

I'm seething with anger, but I hold back my words as I get up. I feel his stare as I make my way to the door.

"Or... you can swing by my place later, and you'll be back on stage in no time."

Hmph. The way he runs this place can't be legal. I'll have to look into it. Randall's on my radar.

"Goodbye, Randall," I close his door firmly, knowing I've stirred him up with my complaints. But he knows I'm frustrated too.

I head back to the main floor and settle in at the bar for the rest of my shift.

———— ♥ ————

I rummage through my gym bag, fingers searching in the darkness until they find the familiar shape of my apartment keys. Despite the lack of light, I'm accustomed to this routine, and soon enough, I lock the door behind me with a click, shutting out the noise of the world outside.

Inside, my cozy sanctuary awaits. My stomach grumbles, so I head straight for the fridge. I find last night's chicken ranch pasta, and my mouth waters when I eye that Tupperware. I'm so thankful I made extra.

I plop down at the table, surrounded by the silence of my small apartment. The TV flickers with nothing interesting, so I turn it off. The room settles into a peaceful quiet as I dig into my meal, each bite a comforting mix of flavors that I proudly put together myself.

As I finish eating, I feel the exhaustion creep in. I grab the soft, worn blanket from the sofa and wrap it around me like a cocoon. The thought of sinking into my bed sounds heavenly right now.

I'm grateful for the simplicity of my life. No drama, no complicated relationships – just the company of easygoing friends and a job that sustains me. It may not be glamorous, but it's enough and its mine.

———— ♥ ————

On our day off, Tara swung by to drag me along for some errands. I figured it was as good a time as any to stock up on groceries.

"You really oughta ask Randall to put you back on stage. The customers keep asking about you," Tara said between drags of her cigarette, filling the car with smoke that make my eyes water.

"I'm not about to beg to that man. He needs to understand that I won't do anything I don't wanna do," I reply, trying not to gag on the thick haze of cigarette and whiskey fumes lingering in the car.

"You're a stripper, Chevonne. The job's about showing what you got to the crowd 'cause that's what they're there to see. Stop complainin' about it."

"*Dancer*, not stripper, and I'm not even that anymore."

It had been a week since Randall bumped me down to bartender, and he'd been giving me the cold shoulder ever since. He even sent one of the other girls to hand me my pay. Surprisingly, though, he hasn't canned me yet. Tara wasn't wrong about the customers asking for me; a few had even approached me at the bar, offering to pay for private dances. But if Randall wants to play hardball, he'll have to deal with the consequences and miss out on that money. Sorry.

"He's just being stubborn. Maybe you should find another gig and stop tryna to guilt-trip him," Tara suggests, flicking ashes out the window. It was obvious Randall had put her up to this conversation.

"Well, there's more to it than that. He doesn't even feel bad. All he thinks about is ass and money. He'll manage."

"Obviously! What else is he gonna do? He's the big shot who signs your checks. You gotta stay humble, girl. It's not just about you. It's about keeping those paying customers happy and keeping us all employed," Tara lectures.

I lean my head against the window, watching the road signs blur past. She's got a point, especially when it comes to work. Tara's business advice usually hits the mark, so I trust her judgment. And yeah, I do miss dancing on that stage.

"I'll talk to him," I sigh, hoping she drops the subject.

We pull up at the wig store where Tara splurges on her collection. She's been pushing me to try them out, even offering to foot the bill so I wouldn't have to fuss over styling my hair, which is part of the reason I'm always rushing into work late.

Although I'm attached to my trusty mushroom cut, I experiment with a few wigs. Most look too tacky for me, but a couple catch my eye. Maybe I'll consider picking one or two for a change.

"So... I've been seeing someone on the down-low," Tara says, checking out her reflection while trying on a wig. Her gum-chewing is loud, and it seems to be bothering the cashier, who's waiting for Tara to make a decision.

"Oh yeah? Who's the lucky guy? And how long has this been going on?" I ask, not really in the mood for one of Tara's stories about her latest crush.

"Well... he's sexy, but he's also a dealer. Met him at the club a few months back, stopped me as I was heading to the stage. I gave him my number, and we've been hanging out since."

"And what does Randall think about all this?" I ask, absently running my nails across the countertop.

"I couldn't care less what Randall thinks. He never cared about how I felt when he was messing around with his strippers."

My head snaps up, meeting Tara's gaze in the mirror.

She shrugs. "I'm not dumb, Chevy. But it's whatever. Randall will find himself a new fling soon enough. He's not losin' sleep over me, so I'm just gonna do my thing."

"You know what I'm sayin'? He acts like he's above everyone just 'cause he's in charge. It's bullshit," I mutter, feeling irritated.

"But hey, he's the boss. Thing about Randall, though, he may like the ladies, but he's not forcing anyone into anything they don't wanna do," Tara shoots back, giving me a look through the mirror. "He always gives the option to walk away."

Once again, she's spot-on. I could've walked out of his office that night, but I went along with it. Wasn't even that drunk, just feeling... *you know*. Randall's got his charm, no denying that. Reminds me of my high school crush.

Okay, fine, I'll admit it. Randall's a good-looking guy, alright? But he irritates me so much, I hardly notice anymore. His freckles, though, are something else. The way they dance on his tan skin when he talks... it's kind of mesmerizing. And those lips? Plump and pink, always looking kissable. Plus, his hair's always clean. Probably one of the best-looking guys around here. Not that I'm paying much attention to guys these days. My mind's on my money.

"Anyway," I steer us back to the main topic, "Tell me more about this guy you're seeing."

"Not much else. I've heard about him around here, but his name is Omar and girl... He has a lot of money. He's a big deal. Told me he is building up an empire and could use a lady like me by his side. He knows I know my shit."

"You told me you wasn't gonna date any more drug dealers."

Tara takes off the wig and hands it back to the worker. She rips off her stocking cap and shakes her head, signaling she doesn't want it. "I know what I said, but that may be the move. Not just because he got money, but also because he teaches me good business and the man is damn good in bed."

I giggle. "Oh boy. Sounds like he has you whipped already."

"Girl, maybe I am. We bathe in champagne... *Champagne!* That's the kinda life I want for myself, and I deserve it. We all do."

I'll be straight with you, I ain't dipping my behind in no cold, fizzy champagne, but that's beside the point. He sounds like a real high roller, but hey, he's got money to spend. I wonder why I've never heard of him or seen him at the club if he's such a big deal?

"Who is this guy? If he's so damn good at what he does, why haven't none of us heard of him?"

"You haven't? He moved out here from one of those Carolinas a few years ago. I forgot which one. I guess shit started getting out of hand there, so he came out here and started some stuff up. His product is real decent." She hits me with an O-K hand symbol and a wink.

I immediately gasp at my dumb friend. "Tara! What kind of product? And why are you using it?"

"Just a couple of lines and some weed. Chill."

The employee taps her foot impatiently, and we both glance over at her.

"Girl, move along. We are paying customers. We are allowed to talk here. The hell is wrong with you!" Tara snaps at the lady.

My mouth gapes open in disbelief once more.

"Tara! Oh my Lord. Sorry about that, Ma'am. We're leaving now." I rise from the stool I'm sitting on and pull Tara up from hers. "Come on. Let's go."

"Whatever. I'm not buying shit from here ever again. Take your dusty wig back." Tara hurls another wig she had ready to try-on at the lady and clutches her purse, then pulls me out of the shop.

"Those folks be rude for no reason. I'm half of what that lady is in there, but I guess it don't matter. My own family showed me that."

"I understand your pain, girl, but you did just say—out loud—that you be on dope. And then you're yelling and smacking that gum like a cow. You would have to get the hell out of my shop too."

Tara shrugs and pulls out a pack of smokes. She draws one for herself before offering me one. I extend my hand to decline the offer and head toward her car.

"Where else do you need to go? We still have these groceries and I wanna be back home before it gets too late. I might not even feel like cookin' by the time I get back."

"Oh, bitch. Shut *up*." She takes a long drag and tosses the first cigarette, smashing it underneath her heel before getting into the car. "Making me not even wanna smoke."

Now she's just being disrespectful. I join her in the passenger seat and face her. "Excuse me? What are you callin' me a bitch for?"

"You keep running your mouth so listen to this: Your life is boring, Chevonne. You don't get out, drink, smoke, do lines, party, fuck, nothin'. Just sit at home cooking and watching cable like an old lady. But you're a stripper. You're not better than nobody."

Her car rattles loudly as she starts it up.

"There ain't one damn thing wrong with what I choose to do. I enjoy my time alone, and I don't give a damn if you think it's boring, thank you very much. Besides, Sheila is coming over later, and I'm gonna help her with some moves."

"You havin' a girls' night without me?" She frowns, looking in my direction before pulling off.

"I mean, she just wants me to show her some moves. You know she's about to be eighteen, and she's probably getting promoted soon..." At this point, I don't even think Tara is listening anymore.

She peers at her pager and sucks on a new cigarette, barely paying attention to the road. "All that means is Randall is about to have his new boo thang. Anyway, shit. I forgot my cousin is hangin' with me tonight. Maybe we can have a little girls' night at your place. What do you say, Chevy?"

"Sure. But you bring your own liquor and no cocaine."

"Ha-ha, *fuck you...*"

We giggle and cruise down the road to my apartment.

———— ♡ ————

Before my friends arrive, I tidy up my place because living alone sometimes makes me lazy. I've been catching up on rent and bills, and I'm trying to make my home look nicer by adding more furniture and decorations It's hard to choose between furnishing my place and saving for a car, but I'm okay with taking the bus for now. I also need to get my driver's license.

I put bowls of chips, soda cans, wine, and other snacks on the dining table. I also set out some fancy glasses since Tara is bringing her whiskey. Even though I won't drink with her, I want my guests to have a good time. I'm discovering that I enjoy being a host and I just might like having friends over.

Someone knocks rapidly on my door, surprising me. It's Sheila, smiling wide and holding a plate of homemade treats.

"Hey, you scared me with that knocking."

She hugs me and takes off her shoes. "Sorry, Chevy. I know you're not used to visitors. Here are some brownies my grandma made."

I smell them through the plastic wrap. "*Mmm...* I can't wait to try these, Sheila. Tell your grandma thanks."

"Sure, but she thinks they're for school tomorrow."

I sigh and put the plate down, then look at Sheila. She pauses, and we make eye contact.

"What's up? Chevonne, you know school isn't my thing."

"You still need to finish high school. That's the least you could do for yourself. I completely forgot you dropped out."

"Well, it's my life, and I have other plans. It's not like I'm stupid."

"You're not stupid, but you're being foolish. This would have been your last year, anyway."

She shrugs and takes her hair tie out, letting her relaxed hair fall to the sides of her head. "Okay, Mama Chev. What about you? How come you haven't found yourself a man yet?"

"That's not my priority right now. I'm focused on getting my life together." I scoff and head toward the kitchen.

"Well, I might be seventeen, but I know you don't have to have everything figured out at... how old are you again?" I hear her unzip her jacket and toss it onto one of the dining chairs.

"Twenty-one," I call out from behind the fridge door.

"*Mhm*. Find yourself a man with money, girl. That's my plan. Then you won't have to worry about school and work and all that stuff. He can take care of you."

"Well, that's not my life goal, Sheila. I'll find a man when the time is right, and I can take care of myself."

After a while, the other ladies arrived, and we spent some time chatting and getting to know each other. I felt it was time for more fun, and I had just the thing to liven things up.

I retrieve the Game of Life board game from my hallway closet, but it is covered in dust. I blow it away and notice the dust bunnies on the closet floor. I probably should have dusted before inviting people over, so my home looks more lived-in, but I'm learning. I can already hear Tara complaining with her high standards, and if her cousin is anything like her, I might have to ask them to leave.

"Hell no, Chevonne. Put that game away and come here," Tara commands before I could even suggest the next activity when I return to the living room.

"What? I thought we could play a game?" I ask, feeling disappointed that she isn't up for a regular girls' night.

"Girl, no. You need to relax. Come here and take this shot. Now," Tara insists, pouring a sloppy shot of whiskey into a glass.

"You might be the oldest one here, but remember, I'm a grown woman, Tara. And you're in my home."

Tara, at twenty-five, ought to be setting a better example for her fifteen-year-old cousin, Shannon. Shannon's too young to be knocking back shots like she is, but when she's with her favorite cousin, it seems she can do as she pleases. I glance at a giggling Sheila, who's clearly had too much to drink. I'm only feeling a buzz from my wine; I didn't plan on getting wasted with these ladies in my apartment. I don't know them well enough yet.

Feeling irritated that Tara is trying to take charge as host, I push my glass away and cross my arms. "I had plans to help this girl with her dance moves, like I said, so y'all need to leave."

"Chevy, why you gotta be so mean? And it looks like you won't be helping her with anything. She's gone," Shannon laughs, pointing at Sheila.

I frown as I watch Sheila roll around on the floor. I knew I should've stopped her after that third shot of whiskey Tara gave her. I'm surprised Shannon is still standing strong, especially considering her age. She and Tara took the most shots out of all of us.

I'm relieved to hear my phone ring and quickly get up to answer it. Tara gives me a skeptical look.

"Saved by the bell, huh?" she sneers.

I'm not a fan of talking on the phone, so I usually let it ring to gather my patience before answering.

"Hello?"

"Let me speak to Tara," the man commands. His voice has a smoky, smooth quality to it. But that doesn't give him the right to call my phone and make demands.

"Excuse me, who the hell is this? You're calling *my* phone."

I hear him chuckle before responding. "My bad, this is Omar. Let me speak to Tara, *please.*"

I don't say anything else; I just glance over at Tara and nod her over. She eagerly hops up and rushes over to me.

"Why does he have my number?"

She takes the phone and gives me a playful slap on the backside. "I gave it to him just in case he needed to get ahold of me. My bad, I forgot to tell you."

Shannon's annoying cackling immediately prompts me to start tidying up for the night. I hope they catch on because I'm ready for these bitches to leave. Sheila rolls onto her back and stares up at the ceiling. She's smiling, but I can sense a sadness in her eyes. I know that look.

It's the look of uncertainty, of not knowing what comes next or what to do next. That was me last night, wiping away the steam from the mirror after my shower, facing myself. Before bed, I practice posing and smiling in the mirror, afraid that without it, people will see the sadness in my eyes. So, apart from teaching Sheila to dance, maybe I should teach her how to hide the blues too.

I don't know why I get so down like that. Maybe it's because I'm young and alone out here, or perhaps it's because I don't even know what I'm doing with my life. I glance around my apartment and wonder what the point of it all is. What am I even working towards? Because if someone asked me right now, I wouldn't know what to say. I guess that's just life. It doesn't matter where you come from or what your past was like; you have to make the best of what you have until you can do better.

"Chevonne!" Tara's voice breaks through my deep thoughts, and I jerk my head up to look at her. "Girl, I wish I could see what's always going on in that head of yours. Anyway, Omar is having a get-together. You want to come with me?"

"Tonight? What about our girls' night?" I remind her, still secretly wishing these girls would leave my place.

"Yeah, tonight. It wasn't really a question, so... go put on something sexy and let's go," she insists, shooing me toward my bedroom.

"Tara, she's too drunk, and she's too young," I gesture toward Sheila, then Shannon.

Shannon stands up and yawns. "She wasn't talkin' about me and Shelia. I gotta get home before it's too late anyway, or I won't be able to hang out with Cousin Tara again."

Shannon heads to the snack table, grabs a handful of chips and brownies, piles them onto a plate, and slips on her shoes.

"Come on, Chevonne. Get dressed. I need to drop them off," Tara insists, shooing me with her cherry red fingernails.

"I don't want to go to this get-together, Tara," I complain. "Especially not to some drug dealer's party. Are you crazy?"

"I am crazy, but you knew that. Yes, you're coming with me. It's time to live a little."

"We have work tomorrow night. I don't want to be tired for work. So, no. Have fun. Get them home safely. Goodnight," I insist.

Tara folds her arms and gives me a stern look. I'm starting to think I'm her only friend because why else wouldn't she ask any of our other coworkers? Well, never mind. I know the answer to that since she's fought with almost all of them.

"You owe me. I haven't been asking you for gas money. And I'll talk to Randall for you tomorrow. I can probably guarantee he'll let you dance again after I talk to him, but you have to come with me," Tara bargains.

And that's exactly why I need to stop accepting her offers to drive me places and telling her my business.

"Fine, I'll go, but I'm not getting involved with all those drug dealers and stuff, Tara. If I see anything suspicious, I'm walking home. Got it?" I point at her.

"I love it when you talk dirty to me," Tara laughs, joined by Shannon. Sheila groans, and I roll my eyes as I drag my feet to my bedroom to get dressed.

———— ♡ ————

I'm not exactly sure why I allowed Tara to talk me into coming here.

As we pull up to the party, it's clear that most of the folks here are already deep into the party scene, whether drunk or high. I stick close to Tara, silently daring anyone to test my patience. They'll be carrying these junkies out in body bags, messing with me.

"Hey, don't worry, we're with Omar. He's got us covered and these are his people," Tara reassures me as we navigate our way towards the kitchen.

Omar's house is something else, I mean it's massive. And once we head down to the basement, it's like stepping into a whole new dimension of the party. I find myself constantly pulling down my skirt, making sure it stays in place. The last thing I want is to draw unnecessary attention to myself and my behind when I'm not getting paid for it. But thankfully, I manage to make it down the stairs without any mishaps.

"There he is..." Tara gestures towards a strapping, solid-built man approaching us.

It's pretty dim down here, so I can't see his face well from here, but you can't miss the sparkle of the jewelry he's wearing. He carries himself with this aura of authority, like he owns the place—which I'm sure he does. And I catch a whiff of his cologne from across the room. It's familiar. Slightly musky, slightly sweet, like...

Sandalwood. It feels like saying hello to an old friend. Daddy always kept a small satchel of sandalwood shavings in his drawer. He said it was for protection, but I never quite understood what he meant. I just recall the scent every time he opened it and how it brought him comfort. I placed the pouch in his coffin, so he'd always have it with him.

"Tara, who's your friend?" Omar's voice cuts through the music as he approaches.

"Omar, meet my friend Chevonne. Chevonne, this is Omar," Tara introduces us.

I try to remember to be polite when I shake his hand, but I still remember how he answered that phone earlier. I don't care how good he looks. "Nice to meet you. Just make sure you show some respect when calling people's phones."

Omar meets my eyes, a grin spreading across his face. Tara laughs beside me, like she's in on an inside joke.

"Sorry about her mouth. Chevy's a little upset because girls' night got cut short."

Honestly, I'm not mad about that at all. I'm mad that I'm here.

"It's all good, I get it. I'm sorry about girls' night, but welcome to my place. Make yourselves at home. What can I get you to drink, baby girl?"

His voice, it's... hate to say it, but captivating and sexy. Even more so than I imagined from our phone call. Tara may have hit the jackpot with this one.

"You know how I like my whiskey," Tara teases.

Omar winks at Tara, then shifts his gaze to me. "Yeah, I know what you want, baby. I'm asking about her. What'll it be?"

Tara nudges me, urging a response.

"Hmm? Oh, I'm good. I had some wine earlier, and it's still doing the trick, thank you." I brush him off, scanning the room to avoid staring at him.

Tara and Omar exchange glances before bursting into laughter once more.

"She's a fuckin' riot, isn't she? Give her the same as me, babe," Tara suggests on my behalf.

"You got it. I'll be right back..."

Mm. I'll have to find a way to speak up for myself next time. I keep quiet and steal one last glance at him as he heads upstairs.

Only thing is, he's peeking back at me too.

CHAPTER 2
Baby Girl

T ARA KEPT HER WORD and talked to Randall. I knew he'd give me a hard time about dancing again, but after a private lap dance and a few shots of scotch together, he finally let me back on stage. I thought if I agreed to shake my booty more, he'd lighten up, but he still seemed in a bad mood, so I knew I wasn't the only one annoying him. He bugs me more than anyone, but I still wanna know what's going on in his head.

"Randall... I know you're my boss and all, but if you need to talk, I'm here." I nudge his hand to snap him out of it.

He seems lost after our last drink. "Is it Tara?" I ask, figuring he's upset about her dating someone else.

"You never know what you got till it's gone or someone else's. That's the truth, Chevy," he chuckles to himself, trying to pour another drink before realizing the bottle is empty. *"Damn."*

"You don't need that stuff, Randall. I don't get how you guys can live drunk and high all the time. How do you do it?" I seize the bottle from him and fling it in the waste bin next to his desk.

He winces, then sinks back in his chair. "Maybe none of us are really living, just getting by. Booze helps with that," he says, suddenly sitting up. "Who's getting high? One of my girls?"

"No, Randall, I'm just mentioning it because you're aware of how popular that stuff is around here," I explain.

"Thank you for bringing that to my attention, Chevy. I'll have to check y'all out. You all know it's a strict no-no in my business place. Cops keep trying to push me out of here anyway. Other folks too."

I should warn Tara against trying her man's product anytime soon.

"Well, I'm sure you don't have anything to worry about. And as far as Tara, it's mature of you to let her go. She seems happy."

"What do you know about anything? You, what... twenty, twenty-one? What do you know about love and all of that?" He spits.

Ugh. "Never mind. You should talk to someone your own age then. I'm about to head home and prepare for work tonight. Thanks for letting me back on stage, and sorry we drank all of your scotch."

He tugs on my arm as I turn to leave. I have to release a sharp breath and consider how I'm going to reject him without jeopardizing my position... again.

"Randall... you should stop tryna sleep with every girl you bring in here. It's probably why you lost Tara in the first place." I pull my arm away and face him.

He drags his hand over his face and sighs. "I mean, I love the girl, but she's an opportunist. She goes where the money is, so it was always going to be temporary until she found the next fool with more wealth."

"Okay, but I saw you two together, and I do believe she loved you for who you are. You hurt her, Randall. She might have her preferences, but that doesn't give you the right to disrespect her. At least she's not some crazy ex, and at least you're still sort of friends, and she still looks out for you."

Randall glances over and raises an eyebrow. "How old are you again?"

"I'm twenty-one. But that's beside the point. It's common sense not to hurt someone you love."

"It's more complicated than that, Chevy. We hurt the ones we love the most, even if we don't mean to."

I watch as his eyes assess my figure once more.

"Are you planning to come over to my place after your shift tonight? I've got more scotch stocked up there."

"No, Randall. I'm not going to sleep with you. We shouldn't be doing that, anyway."

"Says who? This is my establishment, baby."

"Listen. You can't have me anymore. And if that's a problem, then go ahead and fire me." I glare at him in disgust and without another word, I turn to leave his office.

Tara whirls in late, her aura vibrant as she enters the room, and I return to the changing area to gather myself. As she strides toward my station, some women roll their eyes while others ignore her. I'm surprised she's showing up so late; it's not typical for her to be the last one to arrive for work.

"Look at you... glowing and all. You better not be high," I tease, searching for any signs of intoxication in her eyes.

"The only thing I'm high on today is love, girl. I'm just feelin' good. I think I met my one, Chevy," she beams, unbuttoning her jacket to reveal love bites.

My eyes widen at the markings, but I continue with my makeup.

"Wow, girl. Y'all nasty," I remark, glancing at the marks again as Tara lets out a loud shriek and blushes. I don't think she should be calling him 'the one' just because of some silly hickies. With the way he's got her skin looking, she should be asking him if he even likes her ass.

"You better cover that up before Randall notices. He is not happy with you moving on. Don't throw it up in his face if you're still gonna work here because that's not right, either" I caution.

"Chevy, shut up, damn. Let me have my moment. Always tryna talk sense into somebody. You ain't nobody's mama in here," Tara snaps back.

"I feel like I have to talk sense into everybody. Something is wrong with all of y'all in this place," I mutter with a sigh.

Tara's fingers move quick over her makeup palette, trying to cover up the hickey marks scattered all over her neck, chest, and belly. Each dab of concealer feels like she's trying to hide more than just the marks — it's like she's trying to bury the drama bubbling under the surface.

"Did you talk to Randall or something? How you know he's mad at me?"

"Yeah, I did. And trust, it's written all over his face. And if you're gonna still work here, you should consider tellin' your man not to mark you up like that. That's gonna set him off, Tara. It's like you're asking for drama." I turn to her, squinting in disbelief.

"Well, that's on him. Watch how he hits rock bottom soon with his gambling problem. I dodged a bullet by leaving his sorry ass, and I ain't looking back. Let him mess with whoever, I'm done with his drama." Her words drip with bitterness, but it's clear she's hurting deep down. "You hoes can have him."

Even when she drops the 'hoe' bomb on me, I don't bat an eye. It's just another part of the drama in her messed-up relationship with Randall. My heart goes out not to her insult, but to the chaos he's caused. And now, she's finally getting the guts to walk away, leaving behind a whole lot of hurt and disappointment. I admire that.

"Well, if you're happier now, then I'm happy for you. My dad always said guys like Randall... they're weak and they don't know themselves, chasing after every woman they see. That's why I'm taking a break from dating. It's too much drama. I've heard too many horror stories that messes with people's heads and emotions and stuff. They end up drowning themselves in booze and drugs. And if I'm going to get hurt anyway, it better be by someone worth the trouble," I vent, mulling over my own standards.

Tara places her hands on her hips, observing me as I apply my makeup. She's dressed in a sheer two-piece thong with no nipple covers, exposing her brown nipples and the curve of her body. I catch her scanning me from head to toe.

"Damn. I didn't even realize you were in stripper gear. Randall finally let you back in, huh?"

"It's dance attire, not stripper gear, 'cause none of this is coming off. And yeah, thanks for talking to him for me."

She scoffs, rolling her eyes. "I'm sure it took more than just me talking to him to get you back on that stage. Maybe that booty did most of the talking."

Maybe it did.

"No. All he needed was someone to listen to him, honestly. He's going through a lot, Tara."

"Well, I couldn't care less. I'm falling for a guy who keeps me flying high. Randall ain't ever gonna be worth a damn, and I don't want him anymore."

With a muttered curse, she strides over to finish styling her new wig.

I shake my head, perplexed. It's beyond me how people in love wouldn't want to put in the effort to make things work, and how Randall believes love always comes with pain.

Maybe I'm just too young to get it because the solution lies in common sense, if you ask me.

But didn't nobody ask me.

———— ♡ ————

After clocking out from my shift, I shuffle back to my apartment, collapsing onto the couch with a sigh of relief. All of the dancing I did tonight has drained me, but at least

I've pocketed decent cash. Randall seemed satisfied with my performance, though I secretly hoped he'd bring up his offer to spend the night together again before I left.

But I shouldn't even entertain those thoughts, should I? Sleeping with my boss, especially with the regret lingering from before, is a messy road to wander down. I think I'm just lonely. I've never wanted to give in to someone so easily, but it's the allure of being wanted, desired, that draws me in—maybe that's why I love dancing so damn much. For a moment, I can be someone's everything, the focus of their attention, and it feels good to reciprocate that pleasure.

But I push those thoughts aside. Randall will find his company for the night, no doubt.

After a refreshing shower, the clock ticks closer to four a.m., but sleep isn't quite ready to claim me. Before I retire for the night, I jot down a list of groceries I need to pick up. Without a game plan, I might oversleep and miss my next shift—I have responsibilities, even if they're boring.

And then what? Tara's words about my supposedly dull life linger in my mind. Maybe it is time for a change, nothing too drastic, just a subtle shift in my routine.

As I grab some cash from my gym bag and slip it into my wallet, the phone starts ringing.

Who could be calling at this time of night?

I bet it's either Tara, Randall, or maybe even Sheila. I don't really talk to anyone else, and I definitely don't give my number out.

Letting out an annoyed sigh, I let the phone ring a few more times before reluctantly answering. Amidst the chaos, the sound of "I Need Love" by LL Cool J blares through the receiver. That's my jam too.

"Hello? Who's this?" I ask, already considering hanging up.

"It's Omar. I'm tryna reach Tara," his voice crackles through the line.

Ah, right. I almost forgot Tara gave her man my number. "She's not here. And why are you calling me so late? It's four in the morning."

"My bad, baby girl. Just tryna find her."

"She's got a pager. Use that instead of blowing up my phone at this hour. What if I was sleeping?"

A chuckle ripples through the line. "My bad. I won't bother you again."

"Thank you," I reply, relieved.

"So... you really don't know where she's at?" he probes further.

"No clue. Last time we talked, we were leaving work. She mighta had a few drinks before heading home, but she's probably knocked out by now," I explain.

Omar lets out a sigh and murmurs to some people in the background before returning to the phone. "A'ight. I'll check there. Thanks for pickin' up, though."

It hits me all of a sudden—the significance of him calling me at this time. His worry makes me wonder if she's in some kind of trouble. I feel bad for coming across so harshly when all he wants is to find his girlfriend.

"You don't think... she's gotten herself into some kinda mess, do you?" I blurt out, feeling a bit worried. Tara doesn't care if she's sober, high, or drunk—she'll drive regardless.

"Nah, we had a little heated conversation earlier. She stormed off mid-convo, so she probably just off somewhere upset," he explains.

"*Mm.* Just don't go hurtin' her. Deep down, she's still a good person."

"How you even know what a good person is? You think you one?" he challenges.

"I believe I'm decent, at least real. And if Tara wasn't decent people, I wouldn't be hangin' around her," I reply, twirling the phone cord before stopping myself.

"Huh. I like that. You do seem decent, got a mind of your own. Word on the street is you ain't big on drinkin', you sound smart, and you're damn beautiful," he adds.

I pause, caught off guard. *Should I say thank you?*

It's amusing that I'm being talked about in the streets for who knows what reason. I don't even know these people, so how are they going to speak on me like they know who I am?

"Well, I'm gonna let you go. Thanks for watching out for Tara... Being a good friend and all that. Hit me up if you need anything, a'ight?"

"Yep. Good night," I reply.

"Take care, baby girl."

Baby girl.

Is that his go-to for any woman he meets? With a shrug, I hang up the phone. I stand there for a moment, debating whether to check in on Tara. But something tells me she's okay, so I figure I'll give her a buzz when I wake up. I get it—sometimes you just need space, especially when you're pissed.

Letting out a subtle yawn, I leave my grocery list on the table where I won't forget it. After glancing at the bus schedule, I finally crawl into bed.

———— ♡ ————

For the past few stops on this crowded bus, I've been practicing holding my breath. A homeless man boarded earlier, and with no one offering him a seat, I moved my bag to make room. He's just going about his business, not bothering anyone, but damn it...

He *stinks*.

My thoughts are suddenly interrupted by a buzzing vibration in my bag. I check and find Tara's pager. *Why do I have her pager?* I search further and find her handbag inside. *Oh no.* I just remembered her locker broke last night, and she asked me to keep it for her. We both forgot about it.

I slump back in my seat, frustrated. If she knew I had her handbag, why didn't she swing by to pick it up? Looking at its contents—a whiskey flask, wallet, and cigarettes—I know for sure she can't live without those things.

The pager displays a code, followed by a phone number, likely Omar's. I have no clue what that number means, so I decide I'll call him once I get off the bus and inform him about my latest discovery. Come to think of it, I should've just called Tara earlier; this isn't typical of her.

After finding a payphone, I queue up behind two people already waiting. The pager buzzes in my hand once more, prompting me to scrounge for change to use the phone while I wait. Finally, it's my turn. I feed the payphone with coins and dial the number.

"Tara?" Omar's voice seethes with frustration.

"No, it's Chevonne. I didn't even realize I had her purse and pager until I checked my bag."

"Why do you have her shit?" His tone is sharp. I know he's frustrated but I don't care about his feelings right now. I'm worried for my friend and I'm not about to tolerate this sassy attitude.

"Because she asked me to hold onto her *shit* for her last night, that's why. You need to calm down," I retort.

I hear him making an effort to control his temper before responding, "A'ight, my bad. I'm gonna head over to her place and check if she's home. You wanna come with?"

Not really. Especially not with him. "I guess, if my friend might be in trouble."

"Where are you right now?"

"I'm just outside this supermarket, near Randy's Donuts. Had to grab some groceries."

"I'll come over there. Take your time, get what you need, and I'll take care of you, baby girl."

There's that *baby girl* again.

"Okay."

We end the call, and I enter the store to pick up the items on my list, all the while keeping Tara's well-being at the forefront of my thoughts. Tara isn't one to get tangled up with the law. She somehow manages to avoid it, and that's a skill, if you ask me. So, I won't jump to conclusions that she's in jail.

Despite his foul mood, Omar is kind enough to assist me in loading the groceries into his car. Speaking of his vehicle, it's very clean—fits his vibe—and I'm looking forward to riding in it.

"What kind of car is this? It's nice," I ask as we speed through a stoplight.

"El Camino."

"I guess selling weed, cocaine, or whatever it is you do pays off, huh?" I tease, offering a slight smile.

Omar ignores my joke, his smug demeanor intact. That's fine; he doesn't need to respond because I already know the answer. What I don't get is why he's driving so fast.

"Okay, you need to slow down. I'm not tryna die. I have things to do. You just ran that light back there, by the way. I saw that."

"You're safe with me," he asserts confidently.

"Slow down, I said. Seriously. Your car is nice, but you don't want to wreck it, do you?" I feel the speed of the car decrease and glance over at him.

Lost in thought, he gives me a moment to observe him.

And *wow*.

My eyes check out his fresh chinstrap beard and the clean fade lines. They match his sharp cheekbones real nice. His bling game is a bit much for me, but he didn't ask for my opinion, so I keep that to myself. Tara's description of him painted him as pompous but seeing him in person confirms it. He seems like he can't step out without decking himself out in jewels. His scent, that familiar smell of Sandalwood, is pleasant to bask in, though up close, it's very strong. I remind myself not to be judgmental, though. He's spending his hard-earned money on what he wants, and I respect that.

I can't shift my gaze away from him fast enough to avoid our eyes meeting. A sly smile spreads across his face, revealing a few gold caps on his teeth. Instantly, I look away, feeling my cheeks flush.

"You like what you see?" Omar quips. He could've just let it slide and spared me the embarrassment.

"I didn't mean to stare you down like that," I mumble. That's all I got for him. No excuses. I should be ashamed for eyeing my girl's man like this.

"Don't sweat it. I know it's hard to resist checkin' out a brother like me," he replies, his tone oozing with confidence.

"Okay, don't let it get to your head. You're just flashy, that's all. So yeah, it's hard not to look if that's your aim."

"You got a mouth on you. Not always necessary, but I can see you don't take shit from nobody," he acknowledges, flicking on his left signal and waiting for his turn to go.

"Exactly. I don't care who you are. I speak my mind, no matter what," I assert.

"I feel you," he grins. "You from around here?"

"I was raised in Inglewood, been an L.A. native all my life. And you, Mr. Flashy?"

"South Carolina, baby girl. Born and bred."

"So, what brings you to L.A.? Oh, wait, let me guess," I say, a hint of sarcasm in my voice. "You're here to contribute to the dope crisis. And not in a good way."

"What makes you say that?" he asks, intrigued.

"'Cause that's what drug dealers do," I reply bluntly.

Omar chuckles and turns to me. "That's the truth. I came up rough and wanted better, so I hustled and started my own thing. Might not be your cup of tea, but it pays the bills."

"And then some," I interject, nodding towards his flashy jewelry. "So, you crossed the country just to sling drugs? That's the whole story?"

"To live the dream, baby girl. Build my empire. I'm one of the few from back home willing to come out and make some shit of myself."

"Mm. It's cool, but it ain't all that for you all to be flocking here and making things worse. But maybe I'm a lil' one-sided about that 'cause I know this place like the back of my hand," I say, tracing my fingers over my palm. "Never been anywhere else."

"Tara mentioned you don't have much family around. So, it's just you?" Omar probes.

"Yeah. My dad passed last year. Mom split when I was young, and that's pretty much all the family I had. No siblings or nothing."

Omar nods, and as I gaze out the window, I sense his eyes on me. "I'm sorry to hear that, baby girl. I can relate. Not much blood family on my end either. But I respect that you're makin' moves for yourself."

"Got to. I'm not one to sit around and cry forever. Living on the streets isn't my vibe. I have to get my shit together so when I have my own kids, they'll be alright, with a family to come home to."

"I feel that. That's real deep. I'm makin' moves too, just in a different lane. You enjoy stripping?" he asks, bluntly.

"Dancing... And yeah, I do."

"Alright, Miss *Dancer*. I might have to catch one of your shows sometime. Heard you're skilled with your moves. And you look good too."

"Thanks."

Hmm. I shouldn't be grinning like this, should I? *What's gotten into me?* And he should know better. "Anyway, your girlfriend's street is coming up, so don't miss that turn. It's a small street."

——— ♥ ———

Tara swings the door open with a drunken grin plastered on her face. I could tell she was alright, just hungover bad.

"Good to see you're okay. I grabbed your purse and pager," I say, handing Tara her belongings as we step into her place, Omar trailing behind.

She gives me a hug, plants a sloppy kiss on my cheek, then turns to face her man.

"Why didn't you pick up the phone?" he grumbles, irritation creeping back into his tone.

"I was out cold, baby. My bad," Tara replies, stumbling a bit.

I watch as she shuffles over to Omar, trying to hug him, but he steps back. That must have been one hell of a fight.

"We'll talk later. Go grab your shit so we can bounce," he instructs, pointing her towards her room.

"You guys..." she hiccups. "Were worried about me?"

"Yeah, girl. You gotta answer your phone and let someone know where you're at, if you're alive. Too many weirdos out there doing who knows what," I chime in, concerned.

She steals a glance at Omar, who stands with his arms crossed. They share a look loaded with meaning, but I simply shrug and settle onto her sofa.

"Come on, Tara, I've got groceries in his car to stash in the fridge," I urge, grabbing a nearby magazine.

"*Aww*, thanks for taking her to the store, babe. You're so sweet," Tara coos, batting her eyelashes at him.

"He just gave me a lift so we could track you down. No biggie," I interject with a nonchalant shrug.

"Get your stuff together so we can roll. We got things to do," Omar insists, nodding towards her bedroom once more.

As she heads to the back, she stumbles over clothes strewn across the hallway floor. I glance at Omar, still simmering with anger but lost in thought as he steps out.

I get his frustration, and it's clear he cares deeply about Tara to be this upset with her. Relationships aren't always smooth sailing from what I've heard, but as long as he remains patient and understanding with her, that's all I could wish for my friend.

No matter what line of work he's in.

----— ♥ ——----

After a few days, I find myself happily indulging in some of Sheila's birthday cake, a homemade delight courtesy of her grandmother. I suggested a cozy movie night at my place for a low-key but cute celebration, so she brought me a slice. It's just the two of us—no Tara, no Shannon, and definitely no whiskey.

Despite her unchanged demeanor from when she was seventeen, it's heartwarming to see Sheila brimming with excitement over officially turning eighteen. She still seems eager to rush into adulthood, in my opinion. But she didn't ask for it.

As a gift, I got her a new outfit for her stage performances, complete with her initials bedazzled on the bra cups, a personal touch from me.

"You're the sweetest, Chevy," she says, hugging me tight as she admires her dance attire.

"You're welcome, Sheila. Try it on whenever you can, just to make sure it fits right. I was worried it might be too snug."

"I'm trying it on now. And tighter is better. *Duh*," she laughs before heading to the bathroom.

The pile of dishes in the sink isn't going to clean itself, so I start tackling them while I wait for Sheila to finish. My phone rings just as I dip my hands into the soapy water, so I quickly dry them off and answer the call.

"Hello?" I sigh as I answer.

"Hey, baby girl. It's Omar."

"Hi, Omar. Tara's at work. She grabbed an extra shift today." I balance the phone between my ear and shoulder while I continue scrubbing dishes.

"I know," he says. "Actually, I called for you."

Why? Why does he want to talk to me? I hear something clatter in the bathroom, and Sheila quickly apologizes before I refocus on Omar. "Okay, what's up? I've got company here, so I can't chat long."

"No problem. I had been thinkin' about our conversation, about family and all. Thought we could hang out, grab some food or whatever. You could use more friends out here."

Did this man seriously just ask me out? "You're not asking me on a date, are you, Omar?"

"It don't gotta be like that. If I'm gonna let you and Tara kick it around me, I need to know you better. Plus, not havin' family don't mean you can't find one," he explains.

Sheila emerges, striking a pose to flaunt her new outfit. I give her a thumbs up and move deeper into the kitchen so she can't overhear. "Okay... Well, I hadn't planned on hanging out with you and Tara like that, especially with the lifestyles y'all lead."

Omar laughs a bit before replying to me. *What's so funny?* "My business is my business, and that's somethin' you don't need to worry about. You a good friend to Tara, and since she wants you around, I want you around... for her."

I ponder Tara for a moment, wondering how their conversation went the day we picked her up. She didn't mention anything about it or their prior argument at work. She seemed cool, so I assumed they were okay.

"Speaking of Tara, I don't think she'd appreciate it if you took her friend out to eat," I point out.

"She made the suggestion. She said she wanted me to get to know you better, and I agreed with her," he explains.

"Oh..."

It would be nice to have dinner paid for once. Assuming he'll foot the bill with no strings attached, because I hate having things held over me. I'm almost debt-free, and I intend to stay that way once I reach that point.

"Don't you have work to do? You seem to have a lot of free time," I ask, curious how he manages it all. I know I watch too many movies, but I always thought dealing drugs was a demanding gig.

"I make time for what I want to make time for, baby girl. I'm the boss."

The response was straightforward, but it puts a grin on my face. "Alright then, boss. If Tara's really cool with it, when were you thinking of hanging out?"

"I'm thinkin' later tonight. Got some shit to handle, but I can swing by your place and pick you up after," Omar explains.

Sheila strides into the kitchen once more, hands on her hips, and silently mouths, "Who is that?" I wave her off and turn back to the conversation.

"Okay. Just so you know, I'm still running this by Tara because I'm not about to get caught up. That girl is wild," I caution Omar.

He chuckles. "I know she is, but I get it. What's your address again, baby girl?"

After giving him my address, I eventually hang up the phone and fidget for a moment. I'm trying to understand why I'm so nervous. Maybe it's because he's a drug dealer, and if someone who doesn't like him sees us, we could both be in serious trouble. Or maybe the cops might think I'm involved with him, guilty by association. I've been around long enough to understand how these things work. My favorite movies also offer some insight into the dope game, so I'm fairly informed about that world.

Shaking off my thoughts, I let go of my worries and return to the living room to join Sheila.

She's giving me a smirk. "Who was that? You were all smiles on the phone, whispering... You got a boo, Chevy?" She nudges me until I respond.

"No, no boo. It was Tara's man. I guess he wants to get to know me better since he and Tara are getting serious, and I'm her closest friend," I explain.

"*Hmm.* That's... interesting. Tara's cool for that because you're a catch, Sis. I couldn't have my man around someone with that face and that booty. Nope." She grabs her cake and takes a bite, making a cringe-worthy sound as she scrapes the fork with her teeth.

"It's not like that, Sheila. He's cautious about who he lets around him, especially with his shady business. And even though he said Tara was cool with it, I'm still going to check with her," I say, grabbing my plate of cake and settling beside her.

"So, you're going on a date with Tara's boyfriend? They might be into some wild stuff," she jokes, and we both laugh as I try to push her off the couch. "Maybe she's tryna rope you into their bedroom fun. I've seen the way she looks at you, Chevy."

"Nope. Stop right there. You need to stop watching all that nasty stuff. Cleanse your mind for once," I retort, snatching the remote and flipping through channels.

I can tell her curiosity is piqued.

"When are you two hangin' out?"

"I guess he's coming to pick me up later tonight," I reply with a nonchalant shrug, though inside, I'm a bundle of nerves.

"Okay, who is this guy? Tara mentioned something about him bein' in the game, but she never tells me anything, and I've never seen him before," she presses, leaning forward expectantly.

"His name's Omar. Spence or something. That's about all I know, babe."

Sheila's eyes widen, her mouth dropping open. "You're kidding! Tara's with Omar? *Omar*, Omar?"

I shrug again and glance over. I don't see why it's such a big deal; I'd never even heard of the man before meeting him. "Yeah, so? You know him?"

"Girl, who doesn't? He's a big name around here. Made a reputation for himself and been at the top ever since. I know about him because my friend from school bought from his crew a few times. Word on the streets is, you don't want to cross him," Sheila explains, her tone serious.

I suddenly feel like I've been living under a rock for not knowing. Guess that's on me for not getting out much.

"Chevy, he got money! And a lot of it! Make sure you have him take you to a fancy ass spot. Don't be no cheap hoe tonight, sis," Sheila advises with a mischievous grin.

"Something's off with you, Sheila. It's not a date. He's still with Tara, and I respect that. I need to call her anyway," I reply, trying to stand up.

Sheila pulls me back onto the couch, her grip firm on my arm. I give her a puzzled look. "What?"

"If he says Tara's cool with it, why stress? Get us in on that. You feel me? I don't want to be broke and stripping forever. You gotta look out for us," she urges.

"What's this got to do with you, Sheila? The guy wants to get to know me. That's all."

"Look... I know I'm younger than you, and you drop wisdom bombs sometimes, Chevy, but you need to loosen up and live a little," she pleads, still holding me back from the phone.

Her too?

"I still don't see how that changes the fact that I need to call Tara and make sure she's cool with this. It's about respecting my friend, Sheila. That's what friends do."

"Is she really your friend? Or is she just keeping tabs on you, playing both sides? Keeping the enemy close? Tara's all about her business, and she's only cool with you 'cause you're bringing in that money and business to the club. We all know you're Randall's new favorite. And now she's sending you to chill with her man while she's out doing who knows what?" Sheila's words hit me like a brick. It's messed up hearing this kind of talk behind my back. I'm finding out things about myself I never knew existed. I try to keep my own lane and stay clear of drama, so it's hard to believe Tara would keep someone she's not feeling close. Otherwise, she'd be tight with Sheila and the rest of the girls at the club too.

"I don't think so, but I'm not going to sit here and entertain that nonsense. Eat your cake, enjoy your birthday, and bask in your day off from work," I reply, attempting to steer the conversation back to the celebration.

Sheila takes another bite of cake but gives me a hard look. I sigh and sink back.

"Fine, I won't call Tara... yet. I'll just enjoy hanging out for the night. With a dope dealer."

———— ♡ ————

I'm perfectly content with Omar deciding on the restaurant since I don't eat out much. While I do enjoy cooking, it's a relief not to worry about washing dishes now and then.

As we approach a tavern, a line forms at the entrance, but Omar takes my hand, and we slide past everyone like we own the place. I feel kind of bad because I know the struggle of waiting in line just to see others breeze by like celebs.

"Omar, why are we cutting in front of these people?" I ask, acknowledging the disapproving stares of those waiting.

"We got a reservation and paid for it," he explains. "I have a good relationship with the owners and have supported the business several times."

"That's nice of you. You must receive VIP treatment all over L.A., based on what I've heard."

He glances at me as we approach our table. "I'm curious to know what you've heard about me."

"Don't expect much, because it ain't a lot. I seem to be one of the few around here who had no clue who you were."

"That's probably for the best," he replies.

We're sitting across from each other, and I can't help but notice his smooth skin. It's obvious he takes care of himself. Just like Randall, I like a man who knows how to look after himself.

"I'm glad you decided to hang out tonight. You hungry, huh?" His interruption snaps me out of my thoughts, and I realize I've been staring. I quickly divert my gaze to the menu, thinking I should grab an appetizer before I keep ogling him.

"Yeah, I had some cake a while back, but that's been it for today."

"Is that why you so little? 'Cause you don't eat your meals?" He raises an eyebrow.

"I'm just naturally this size, like my mama was."

"Didn't mean to step on toes if I did. You got a nice figure. And those curves..." He shoots me a wink, his gold watch catching the light above our table and hitting me square in the eye.

I scoff, half expecting him to mention my body. "How about you focus on your girlfriend's body instead of mine? Being on this date is already bad enough."

"Date?" Omar arches an eyebrow once more.

"No... Not a date. You know what I mean. Cut it out." I roll my eyes and focus back on the menu, while Omar chuckles.

A server comes over, and Omar orders himself an old-fashioned and picks out some cocktail I've never heard of for me. It's nice that he knows I'm not a big drinker because I wouldn't have had a clue what to order. I hope the cocktail suits my taste, but I'll hold off on complaints for now, especially since he's paying for it.

"I've got a question," Omar interrupts the quiet.

"What's on your mind?"

I hear him scratching his beard as the waiter scurries off to fetch our drinks. I'm still scanning the menu, debating what I'm in the mood for. The center-cut sirloin sounds tempting.

"Your eyes. They natural?"

"Yeah, Omar, they're real. Got them from my mama's side," I say, meeting his gaze before shifting my focus.

He nods, checking out my eyes like they're some kind of mystery.

"They look good on you," he comments.

"Thanks."

"No problem." Leaning in, he adds, "With those green eyes, it's gotta make it easier to spot your family out here. At least on your mom's side."

"Sure, but there's probably plenty of folks with green eyes around here, Omar. I haven't ran into nobody that looks like me yet."

"It narrows down the search is all I'm sayin'," he says with a shrug.

Closing my menu, I slide it to the edge of the table, and our eyes meet. This time, I notice the deep amber hue of his eyes, and I'm not the first to look away.

"I already told you; I don't have any family left. Drop it. But I got a question for you now," I say.

"Shoot, what's on your mind?"

"Are you ever worried about being so out in the open, especially with what you do?"

"This is my turf, baby girl. Ain't nothin' to fear," he says, shrugging again.

"Okay, not only are you flashy, but you might be a little too into yourself. Seen enough movies where guys like you get taken out because they let their guard down, thinking everyone's cool with them. I'm telling you, those people we cut in front of back there had that look in their eyes for you."

Omar chuckles at my response, and I shake my head. "Yeah, maybe I should watch my step more carefully, huh? Thanks for the advice, but we're cool, I promise, baby girl."

"Sure thing. But you're throwing around 'baby girl' like we go way back. You barely know me. Save that for your girlfriend. Don't get it twisted. I was planning to tell my friend everything about tonight. You're not gonna use your reputation to juggle multiple women and pit them against each other. I don't care who you think you are."

Omar clicks his tongue and watches as our waiter sets down our drinks. "You're really into those movies, huh? You need to get out more."

Hearing Omar say what everyone's been saying lets me know that I do, indeed, have a boring life.

Deciding to drop the subject, I take a sip of my cocktail, enjoying the taste as the straw touches my lips.

"This is delicious," I remark, taking a few more sips. "By the way, what was that argument with Tara all about? If you don't mind me asking."

For someone who claims to mind her own business, I sure do pry into matters that aren't mine to know.

"Not a big deal, just Tara being a bit too friendly with folks sometimes... Gets herself tangled up. I had to set her straight, and she didn't take it well. Surprised she didn't mention it to you."

"Oh... 'cause of Randall, huh? I can understand how that might stir up trouble. She still cares about him, but Randall's not exactly over her yet. Tough for him to see her moving on and being happy with someone else. But that's on him..."

I catch myself mid-sentence, realizing I've said more than I intended.

Can't blame it on the alcohol; it hasn't hit me yet. Omar nods, intrigued. He plucks a curly orange peel from his drink, takes a sip, and scrunches his face at the taste.

"Yeah, he's still hangin' on, baby girl. But I'm not sweating it."

"I've been told I'm his new favorite, so he might start directing that energy more my way. He's already started, so Tara won't be bothered for long, don't worry."

Omar sips again, silent for a beat. "Well, just give me a heads up if he crosses the line with you. I know a thing or two about him."

"He's not all bad. Just into sex, money, and women. Probably drugs, too. I mean, the guy owns a strip club. You two might have more in common than you think."

"Never."

He says nothing more, only watching me across the table. As the waiter comes to take our order, he finishes his drink, sliding the empty glass to the edge of the table.

———— ♡ ————

It's sweet of Omar to walk my tipsy butt up to my apartment. Throughout dinner, I had managed well until that sneaky cocktail caught up with me.

"I really shouldn't drink like that. Look at me," I admitted, stumbling over my own foot, only to be saved from a potential tumble down the stairs by Omar's swift reflexes. "I can't even see where I'm going."

"I ain't think one drink would get you, but I got you," Omar reassures, shadowing me closely. "It's okay to unwind every now and then. You work hard."

"How would you... How do you know that I work hard?" I ask, while rummaging through my bag for my keys. I retrieve them and search the ring for my front door key.

"I just do. We're alike in some ways."

"Not really, 'cause... If I were in your shoes, I'd have bodyguards! Too many people know you. How can I trust you with my friend if you don't protect yourself?"

"We're covered, trust me. I'm always a few steps ahead," Omar reassures once more, taking charge and swiftly unlocking the door as I struggled under the dim porch light. "There you go, baby girl. Home sweet home."

He managed to find the right key out of the ten on the ring before I could. *Why does he have to be so smooth with everything he does?* After quickly recovering from admiring the way he smells, I step inside and turn to face him, trying not to stumble too much.

"Okay, thanks... thank you for dinner. It was fun, but it's never happening again out of respect for my friend. I don't care how many times she says she's okay with it. Okay?"

"Okay. You welcome."

I move to shut the door, but he remains in the doorway.

"Alright then. Goodnight, Omar."

A smile spreads across his face as he steps back onto the balcony. "Just waitin' for you to shut the door and lock it. Wanna make sure you're safe."

I know the alcohol is to blame for my behavior because I genuinely don't want him to leave just yet, and my hand continues to hold the door. It's the loneliness speaking again, even when the company is pleasant. I don't know him well enough to be thinking this way, but despite feeling like I'm in front of the *lord of the cokeheads*, I still feel safe.

As my gaze meets Omar's, his tongue glides over his lips. He's now scanning my body.

"I dance on weekends, Mondays, and Tuesdays, so you can get a better look on those days. Goodnight, Omar."

"Good to know. Goodnight."

"Oh, wait, hold on."

He pauses and pivots slightly, biding his time until I say what I need to say.

"Do you... trust me? Now? I know that's why you took me out to dinner tonight... Because you want to see if you can trust me around you and Tara."

"Yeah, you not bad, baby girl. You stay safe, a'ight? I'll see you around."

I watch him turn to leave and head down the steps. Glancing back, he gestures to a car parked across from his. Apparently, a few of his buddies were keeping an eye on him after all. Good stuff.

Always a few steps ahead...

CHAPTER 3
4 A.M.

TARA STARES AT ME in shock, her eyes widening as she clutches a pregnancy test in her hand.

"I'm pregnant, Chevy. Oh my God..."

My jaw falls open, and instinctively, I reach for the test to double-check. After comparing the result to the box, I confirm the positive sign.

"Tara, you need to see a doctor to know how far along you are," I tell her as she flushes the toilet. "Especially with all that smoking and drinking you be doing."

"Well, it explains why I've been feeling weird lately."

She's been a lot more irritable recently, more so toward Omar than me or anyone else. I only know this because he called to chat for a few nights after we had gone out to dinner. He would come to me for advice and complain that Tara was getting on his nerves, but I would tell him it was probably just her period and to give her some space. Turns out it was not because she was having a period, but because she had missed one.

"Are you gonna tell Omar? Is it his?" I ask, scrubbing my hands in the sink after realizing I touched the stick she pissed on.

"Um, he is my man. Of course, it's his baby... I think."

"You *think*? Tara, what the hell do you mean?" My mouth gapes open, but I try not to pass judgment. "Whose else could it be?"

"It doesn't matter 'cause Omar is the one I'm with, like I told you, Chevy. I'm pretty sure it's his, so I'll let him know he's gonna be a dad soon."

Soon after she does, I'm sure Omar will call me about it. I appreciate that he listens to me and asks me about my thoughts, but I want no part of the drama that is about to unfold because of Tara's doubt and dishonesty.

"Tara, you know that if Randall finds out, you might end up on the cutting board. He's never gonna let it go. What will you do about a job then?" Sincere concern drives me to ask.

"You must have already forgotten who I might be pregnant by." She smirks at me through the mirror, and I roll my eyes. *Might.*

"No, the fact that you don't know if it's your man's baby is even scarier. You still need to be careful. Just make sure you confirm it first, then tell Omar as soon as possible."

"Yeah, I'll do that, Chevy. Thanks for sticking around while I dealt with it. My nerves have been shot," Tara says, hugging me tightly before loosening her grip slightly, her arms still draped around my waist. "I know I've been distant lately, so I'm sorry about that. I meant to ask how your dinner with Omar went. He said you had fun."

"Yeah, it was cool. But it's not happening again, Tara, so quit settin' me up without giving me the heads up. Not cool," I reply.

"To be honest, I just wanted him off my case for a bit. He's still mad at me over Randall," Tara admits.

Wait, something actually went down with Randall? I'll have to ask Omar. Or I'll just ask Tara directly. Before I can ask, she continues.

"And I told him your booty was big, so I knew he wouldn't mind being seen out with you while I got myself together. So, thanks for doing that for me."

"I thought it was 'cause you wanted him to get to know me better so he could trust me since we're friends?" I question.

"Yeah, that too," she says casually.

Classic Tara—full of it, not even considering me. Why I'm even a little hurt by that is beyond me. It was weird she suggested it in the first place, but being used isn't right either.

Tara adjusts her wig and heads for the door. I consider telling her how I feel but decide against it. She's clueless. And if she ever asks, I'll tell her straight up.

And if I'm doing the math right, Poor Omar. He seemed to really like and care about Tara while she was sneaking around behind his back, messing with someone she claimed to be over.

I thought she found 'the one'. *Is love really this complicated?*

"You coming? I wanna see Sheila embarrass herself on stage," Tara urges, her impatience clear as day while I stand there, arms folded.

"You were new to it once too. Cut her some slack," I reply, trying to ease the tension. Tara lets out an irritated sigh.

"My bad. I didn't mean to diss your lil' work-daughter. She's still cute and has a nice rack. Randall already adores her; I'm sure of it," Tara says, gesturing towards the hallway as we head out. "She's perfect for the fool, anyway. They're both grimy as hell."

At least Sheila wouldn't use me as a distraction while she cheats on someone. Then again, I don't really know any of these women well enough to be sure.

I'm wrestling with what friendship means among these types of women. Tara has her moments, but she usually puts herself first, even if it means using a real friend now and then. I understand self-preservation, but people should still have some decency.

It brings back Sheila's comment about Tara keeping me close for her own reasons, which I'm starting to believe more as I get to know her.

And now, I don't feel nearly as guilty as I did for having drinks and dinner in public with her man.

---- ♥ ----

Some nights fly by, but the atmosphere in the audience tonight is just plain bleak. Since I didn't rake in as much as usual, I didn't bother stashing any tips; I'll just wait for the payout.

Arriving at Randall's office, I notice the door shut, blinds drawn. Normally, unless he's in a meeting, he keeps it open so we can breeze in with our hard-earned cash. Knocking softly, I press my ear to the door, only to catch faint groans. No reply, just more groaning. I decide to push the door open and peek inside.

"Yes, daddy!" Sheila's voice pierces the air with a loud scream.

My jaw practically hits the floor at the sight of Sheila sprawled out on his desk, with Randall busily slugging it out between her legs. He pauses and looks up.

"What the hell, Chevonne? Can't you see I'm busy?" he snaps.

"Oh, Chevy, oh my God," Sheila stammers, hastily pulling up her panties. "Hey, girl... Um, I got promoted!"

Dropping my box of cash to the floor, I cross my arms, shooting them both looks that could kill. An unexpected surge of annoyance washes over me. I already knew Randall would put Sheila on that stage - after taking her innocence - once she turned eighteen. He wasted no time.

But I'm more disappointed in her. I warned her not to fall for it like the rest of us, and yet, here she is.

Randall sighs, pulling up his pants.

"Go clean yourself up, Sheila. I need to talk to Randall," I say firmly, watching Sheila's guilt-ridden expression as she scurries out of the room and disappears from sight. Randall pours himself a scotch and sinks into his chair.

"Come in and close the door," he orders.

"No, Randall. I'm not doing either. I'm heading home after I say what I need to say because this is too much for me to handle right now."

"What's on your mind this time, Chev? You're supposed to be working," he counters.

"I am working. I was bringing my money to you. But why are you messing around with Sheila? She's barely of legal age. Couldn't you wait to mess with her?" I fire back, my frustration is bubbling.

He smirks and glances over. "Someone's feeling a bit jealous, I see."

Jealous? Never. "I'm not jealous. I'm worried about my friend."

"Listen, she came in here offering something. I was just planning to do a performance review with her before officially giving her the new role. That's it. Then we had a few drinks, one thing led to another, and... Here we are," he explains casually.

Blah, blah. I know all about his "performance reviews".

"Why are you so upset anyway? You did the same thing. All of you have," he counters, trying to deflect.

"You shouldn't be messing around with any of us, Randall. I've said that before."

"Who do you think you are? You're *my* employee. I'm not asking for your suggestions on how to run my business. If you don't like it, you're free to leave," Randall retorts, his tone sharp now.

I can feel my attitude taking a turn for the worse, and it's too late to hold back what I really want to say to him.

"You must be in your feelings about Tara again. Upset because Omar makes her happy? Is that why you're fooling around with Sheila now?" I smirk as I pose the question, and Randall's expression shifts.

"How can you be open to hearing me out one day, then throw it all back in my face the next? Just like all the other women out here. You're only good for two things—sex and money. Get out of my office," he commands. That's cold.

"That's low, Randall. I just want you to be better. Sleeping with Sheila is uncalled for."

"Get out, or the next thing you'll hear is that you're out of a job," Randall threatens, tossing back his scotch and wiping a stray drop from his chin.

I frown at him and rise from my seat to leave.

"I'll let you make it up to me," he says as I crack the door open.

"No. I'm not sleeping with you—"

"Sheila mentioned you're gettin' real tight with Omar these days. Is that true?" he interjects.

Damn it, Sheila. Can't even trust her with my personal business. I really need to start keeping a diary.

After a brief pause, I decide to entertain the conversation, so I shut the door before turning to face Randall again. I'm not sure where he's going with this, but I also want to make it clear that I know about the possibility of him and Tara still fooling around. "Alright, and? Tara's already aware. We're all good with it. But I've heard a few things about you, too."

"I know, and fuck what you've heard. I just need to ask you for a favor."

"What's the favor, Randall? After the way you just spoke to me, you don't deserve anything from me," I say, tapping my foot impatiently as I await his request.

"This stays between us, Chevy... But Omar's tryna meddle in my business affairs. I can't let that happen, or the money you all take home might be a little short, you catch my drift?"

"What's the favor? And what does this have to do with me?" I ask, genuinely puzzled but intrigued. I walk back to the chair and take a seat.

"I need some help. It's good to have you on the inside now, and you could help me get some of the stuff he's dealing out. I hear it's top-notch. That's why he's running around L.A., tryna control everything. This fool is from South Carolina, coming into *our* city, tryna take over. So, I need some intel on what he's up to. What do you think?"

"I'm not doing anything like that! Are you out of your mind? First of all, I don't mess with cocaine or whatever he cooks up, and I sure as hell won't steal it from him for *you*. He's actually a decent man... I wouldn't dare to think about it." This man must have lost his damn mind to even ask me something like that.

I thought he was gearing up to ask me to talk to Omar for him, not rob him blind.

"I know it sounds insane, but Chev, I need someone I can trust—someone loyal. Look, I actually do respect your feedback when it comes to running my club. I was gonna ask if you wanted to work as a sort of house mom for these girls... You know, lend a hand? You'd be running the club right alongside me," Randall says, tracing the rim of his glass with a finger, attempting to muster up puppy dog eyes that fall flat.

"No, ask Tara to do it. Bye. I don't even care for these girls like that," I reply firmly, standing to leave.

He exhales heavily and leans back in his chair as I turn to go. "He threatened to kill me, Chev. He wants a piece of the action, and I can't allow that. This place is all I've got. I'd die for it; you know what I'm saying? If I'm not safe, none of you are safe. And we're all fucked if I let that happen. I mean, come on... Some fool from South Carolina? That doesn't bother you?"

I spin around, studying his face. It's etched with sadness unless he's a master at putting on a show. "He said he's gonna kill you? Why? You don't deserve to die just because you won't hand over your business. That's messed up."

"Exactly..."

———— ♡ ————

My phone won't stop ringing. I've picked up twice to find Sheila on the other end, crying and apologizing. I tried to reassure her that I wasn't upset with her, that it wasn't my business. But she keeps calling, so I let it ring and retreat to the shower.

Sitting on the floor of the tub, water cascading down around me, I can't shake the thought of Omar threatening Randall's life over something as stupid as business. It makes me wonder if Omar's jealousy of Randall having Tara first is driving his actions. Or maybe it's because Tara is still seeing Randall. I can't understand why Tara, after enduring so much heartache from Randall, remains so close to him when she has someone like Omar. She should've been more careful, especially if she was going to be jumping back and forth and getting pregnant, even if she enjoys the attention.

Threatening someone over Tara is crazy, and Randall's not worth it anyway. I'd never treat Omar like that, but he's not my guy, and I'm staying out of their mess.

As I leave the bathroom, the phone continues its relentless ringing. Glancing at the time, I see it's four in the morning. I sigh, feeling irritated that Sheila's persistence has disrupted my peace.

"Sheila, stop blowing up my damn phone—" I start to say, but I'm cut off.

"Hey, baby girl... It's Omar."

Omar and I haven't spoken since before I found out was Tara expecting, but after what Randall just told me, I'm not thrilled to hear from him.

"Why are you calling me this late?" I ask, my tone sharp.

"Just checkin' in to see how you doing."

"Why do you care anyway?" I shoot back.

"Aren't we friends? Can't I care about my friends?"

I take a moment to collect myself before replying, "Thanks for checking on me, Omar, but I'm good. How's Tara? I haven't seen her."

"She's doing a'ight. I guess she's comin' down with the flu or something, so she's gotta stay home until she's better. Can't risk gettin' me sick."

"It's probably just morning sickness, Omar."

"Morning what?" he asks, confused.

Damn it. I'm assuming Tara hasn't told him about the pregnancy yet, and now I've just stuck my foot in their business.

Scrambling for a way to change the subject, I blurt out, "Never mind. I'm kinda mad at you though, so I don't really wanna talk."

That should do it.

"Why you mad at me? For not callin' sooner? You know you can hit me on my pager if you need anything," Omar asks, his genuine concern starting to make me feel a bit guilty, even though he's still in the wrong.

"No, not that... It's nothing I really want to get involved with anyway, so I'm just gonna leave it there. I'll get over it," I reply, trying to brush off the issue.

"You gotta say what's on your mind, or I won't know," he insists.

"It's nothing..." I trail off, not wanting to delve into it further.

There's a brief silence, interrupted only by some R&B playing in the background. I wonder what he's listening to; it doesn't sound like his usual crowd noise.

"Are you by yourself tonight?" I finally ask, breaking the silence.

"Yeah. I had to kick everyone out of my place. I'm too damn spent to be hosting anything right now."

"If you're that tired, go to sleep. You calling my phone, but you could be knocked out right now."

"I knew you'd be up."

It's difficult to hold onto my anger right now because he sounds like an ordinary guy, not a flashy dealer or a potential murderer. But Randall's words echo in my mind. No matter how much he annoys me, I still care for Randall, and he doesn't deserve to be threatened for defending what he's built.

I wonder if there are others who have had similar experiences with Omar that we don't know about. I've witnessed him stroll into places like he owns them. That's the part I can't wrap my head around. I understand the need to sell to survive, but Omar's got enough money now. He doesn't need to muscle into businesses he didn't build. *What drives him to do that?* It feels greedy to me.

As annoyance washes over me again, I stifle a yawn and lean against my kitchen wall. "I'm too tired to chat, Omar. Go call your girlfriend."

"I'm still waitin' to hear why you mad at me," he persists.

"Not tonight."

"What you up to tomorrow?"

"Working, as usual."

"Since you don't start until late, give me a shout when you're up, and I'll swing by. Help you run errands and stuff. I know you need to. I'll even drop you off at work," he suggests.

His offer is thoughtful. I do need to grab a few things from the store, but I don't necessarily need a ride from him. Yet, the idea of avoiding the bus to work is tempting, even if I'm not entirely sold on it.

"I'm good, Omar. I got everything I need," I reply.

"A'ight. You mind helpin' me out with something then? I'll still take you to work tomorrow night," he counters.

I know I should decline, but curiosity gets the better of me. "Help you with what? Just so we're clear, I'm not getting involved in any shady business. If that's the case, we're done. Got it?"

"That's cute. You sound like my girl. But a'ight. I'll be by in the morning to get you. Enjoy the rest of your night, baby girl," he says before hanging up.

I bite down on my lower lip to curb any hint of a blush. There's no way I'm allowing myself to feel giddy about this. I should be mad at him right now.

What is he doing to me?

———— ♡ ————

The scent of sandalwood fills the air as we zip through my neighborhood. I must admit, I slept on Omar's offer, but waking up in a decent mood made me open to the idea of a free ride around town.

We're blasting Al B. Sure!'s "Just a Taste of Lovin'!" and surprisingly, I'm not bothered by the speed. It's actually kind of exhilarating seeing people wave at us as we pass by. If Omar was really as dangerous as some say, I doubt people would be so friendly.

We cruise right past my apartment complex, and I shoot Omar a puzzled sidelong glance. "Hey, Omar, you just passed my place."

"Yeah, I know. You was helpin' me out with something, remember?" he responds.

Help with what? I vaguely recall him asking for a favor, but I don't remember agreeing to anything. At least, I don't think I did. Omar looks over at me, a smile playing on his lips as he adjusts the volume on the radio.

"Don't you remember our phone conversation?" he asks.

"*Mm*, I remember. But this is why I'm wary of accepting offers from people. There's always something they want in return," I reply, crossing my arms.

"Relax."

"Don't tell me to relax. I might just open this door and run home to relax. Where are you taking me? And where's Tara?"

Omar leans forward and twists the dial to crank up the volume again. *Very rude.* I reach over and shut the music off completely. He shoots me a quick glance, but this time, there's no smile.

"I don't know you well enough for you to be taking me places and having me do favors, especially with you, Omar," I assert.

At this point, all I can do is settle back and enjoy the silent ride because I get no response and decide not to push it. I find myself pulling my keys out of my purse and slotting them between my knuckles, just in case. As I do, I start to regret ever getting involved with this coke dealer.

Omar's focus is on the road, so I know I'm ready if anything happens. He eventually pulls up to a sprawling, Spanish-style house, with tall palm trees lining the driveway. His laughter snaps me out of admiring the home, and I look back to see him pointing at my hand holding the keys.

"That's cute, baby girl. But come on. Let's go," he says, striding toward the house.

I don't blink as I follow him. The house stands two stories tall, with a front balcony that could fit my entire kitchen. It seems carefully designed for a large family. I might be jumping to conclusions, but it doesn't seem like the kind of place Omar would live. His other house didn't look anything like this. That one had a more vintage feel, with lots of woodwork, which suits him better.

Omar comes to a stop and turns around. "I promise you safe with me."

I steal a quick glance at the row of homes lining the street, all resembling the one we're standing in front of. I'm faced with a decision: follow this man into the house and let my curiosity take over, or bolt down the street. But since I'm already here, I figure I might as well see what this is all about.

As I approach, Omar extends his hand to me, keys still clenched in my other hand. I hesitate for a second before taking his hand and following him inside.

"*Wow...* This is beautiful, Omar. Is this yours too?" I ask, taking in the spacious interior.

"Mhm. Take your shoes off and follow me," he commands, slipping off his boots.

I comply, glancing around as I follow him. It's a pleasant space, with rich, homey browns in the wood flooring that match the banister at the foot of the stairs. The walls could use a fresh coat of paint; I've never been a fan of the standard off-white, though they're nicely adorned with shelves of plants. And the furnishings? Omar clearly has great taste. This is exactly the kind of home I'd want for my family.

"Did you design it yourself? Or did you hire someone?"

"I did it," he replies, taking my hand once more and leading me into another part of the house. I didn't expect him to admit to being the designer, but it makes me reconsider who he is beyond his drug-dealing persona.

We end up in the kitchen, but it feels like a tiny factory compared to the grandness of the rest of the house, throwing off the overall atmosphere. Bags of what looks like pot, measuring instruments, and stacks of cash clutter the dining room table.

"What the hell? Is this what I think it is, Omar?" I blurt out, unable to conceal my shock.

"What do you think it is?" He turns to face me.

"I think you brought me to your drug-making spot."

He smirks at my observation. *How can he be so casual about this?* I don't see any security measures, and what if someone followed him here?

"Omar," I press, my arms folding across my chest as he opens a window above the sink, dismissing my worries.

"No hard stuff here. I promise," he reassures me, but I'm not convinced.

"What if someone followed you?" He ignores my question, instead calling out the window, "Aye, Eddie! Get in here, man!"

A dark, wiry man saunters in through the back door moments later. He looks older than Omar, maybe in his forties, though it's hard to tell with all the wear and tear. Drugs have a way of aging people prematurely. Not that I'm implying anything about him. I just can't help but notice the shotgun slung over his shoulder. It makes me gasp, and I instinctively press myself against the wall.

"Eddie, this is Chevonne. Chevonne, meet Eddie. He's been with me since Carolina. My right-hand man," Omar introduces.

Eddie extends his hand, and I reluctantly shake it before retreating back to my spot against the wall.

"Nice to meet you, pretty lady. Heard some things about you," Eddie remarks.

"Thanks, nice to meet you too. What things have you heard about me?"

"You friends with O's lady, right? You a stripper too. Haven't made it to the club yet, but I'll swing by to see what the buzz is about," Eddie replies, his gaze wandering over me momentarily. I notice Omar eyeing me too as he leans against the counter.

"Okay, I usually dance on weekends, Mondays, and Tuesdays, so feel free to stop by. Are you a drug dealer too?" I ask, my curiosity getting the better of me.

"A drug dealer?" Eddie seems taken aback by the question, shooting a glance at Omar, who merely shrugs. "Why would you think that?"

"'Cause I'm not stupid. You live here, right?"

"Yep, pretty lady, this is my crib. We call it the family house. Not just anyone is invited here, only the special ones," Eddie declares with a grin, shooting Omar a knowing look. Omar returns the gesture and focuses back on me.

The family vibe of the home makes a lot more sense now.

"I thought you said you didn't have family, Omar?" I ask, genuinely confused.

"I built my own family, just like we talked about... Eddie's part of it."

"Do you have kids too?" I ask.

"Nah, no lil' ones running around... Yet. Word on the street is there might be one on the way, if you catch my drift," Omar reveals casually.

His acknowledgment of Tara's pregnancy catches me off guard. My earlier comment about morning sickness might have gotten through to him after all. But I do hope Tara finally came clean about it first; that would be a relief.

Omar signals for Eddie to leave the kitchen, and he bids us farewell before disappearing outside. I try to catch a glimpse of what he's up to before the door shuts behind him. "What's he doing out there?"

Omar remains silent for a moment, busy pouring flour into a metal bowl and whisking it. Finally, he responds, "Eddie helps out around here."

"I gotta say, it seems like a waste to have such a beautiful house just for making drugs. Do you spend a lot of time here? Or is it really for the family?"

"Your mind's always buzzing, huh?" Omar says with a casual grin.

"Well, what do you expect? You bring me into your family business and act all surprised when I start asking questions?"

He reaches for the oven door, checking the temperature with a casual flick of his hand before tweaking the dial.

"Oh, and by the way, congrats. Are you excited?" I ask, trying to focus on something good amid the whirlwind of other people's drama. Having friends is a lot to deal with, and it makes me grateful for my simpler life.

"Not really," Omar replies nonchalantly. His lack of excitement catches me by surprise.

As he cracks eggs into a measuring cup, I admire how he's this smooth at everything he does, even baking. I have a lot of questions for him. The question about his dreams of running L.A. lingers, but his indifference to his own possible child takes precedence. Our eyes meet briefly, and I quickly shift my gaze, realizing I'm lost in thought again.

"You tryna learn how to make what I'm makin'?" he asks, breaking the silence.

"Hell no. I'm steering clear of this," I assert. "And I already know my way around baking."

"What are you scared of, baby girl? We're just makin' brownies," he teases, his tone light despite the underlying seriousness of our conversation.

What am I scared of? I'd say it's the fear of being tangled up in something I never signed up for. I could easily tell Tara and him to back off and mind their own business because I have that power. But the truth is, I'm just plain curious.

And I'm starting to care more.

"Anyway, why aren't you thrilled about becoming a dad? You seem mature enough," I ask, trying to break the tension.

"It's not that I don't want kids. I just got doubts that baby she havin' is mine," he admits, nonchalantly stirring the brownie batter. I wonder how that conversation played out between them.

"Why do you say that?" I already know the answer, but I'm careful not to let on that I'm privy to more than he thinks.

"Things just don't add up," he replies cryptically. Then, shifting gears, he throws me off with a new question. "So, what's the deal with your boss? He been givin' you trouble?"

Bringing up Randall makes me feel that he knows very well why things don't add up. However, I'm glad Omar mentioned him. I still had this very bone to pick with him. "No, but I'm ready to tell you why I've been mad at you."

Omar pauses, giving me his full attention. "I'm all ears."

"Well, Randall told me that you threatened to off him to take over his business, and that's not sitting well with me."

He chuckles to himself, pushing away from the counter. "That's the story he spun, huh? But he conveniently left out the part about owing me money. That fool right there is a lousy businessman, baby girl. He's a snake. I bailed him out of a tight spot not too long ago."

I blink, processing. "Oh... Well, killing him still seems extreme. How much does he owe? I could probably scrape something together and pay you back for him."

Omar sizes me up for a moment, his gaze lingering on mine. "Nah. The debt's on him, not you."

"Why does it matter who settles the debt, though? As long as you get your money, right? Besides, you'd be messing with all our jobs and yanking a business from a local guy who busted his butt to build it. This isn't your city—"

"He owes me, not you. It's about principle," he interjects, a glimmer of irritation in his eyes. "And this city? It's mine now."

"Okay... But couldn't you ask for something like a private dancer party or lifetime VIP access or something? Taking over the whole club seems excessive, Omar."

He has to know he's doing too much, standing here looking stupid. He makes stupid look good though with his fine self.

"Maybe if you were the one givin' me a private—" He's cut off by his pager.

Good timing because I was about to give him a reality check. He checks his pager and then looks back at me. "Tara wants me to call her. You know your way around the kitchen, right?"

"Yeah..." I see him glance at his pager again as it buzzes.

"A'ight, here's where I need your help. Grab that saucepan over there, put in a quart of water, and set it to boil. Then add a couple of sticks of butter and let 'em melt. I should be back before it's done, a'ight?"

The pager interrupts again, and I let out a sigh. Can't believe I'm agreeing to this, but I grab the saucepan. "Okay. Just make sure everything's cool with her. I got it."

He gives me a smile and heads out of the kitchen. "Thanks for the assist, baby girl."

Yeah, whatever, fool.

CHAPTER 4
It's Just Business

I ARRIVE AT WORK earlier than usual tonight. Omar dropped me off, but it felt like he was in a rush, weaving through the late-night traffic like a cat on the prowl. I'm sure he went to see Tara after we baked those brownies. I haven't heard much from her, so I hope she's holding up okay.

He left me with a bag of those goodies, tempting me to share with the few girls I can stand. But I decide against it, knowing Randall would flip if I passed out pot brownies, even though I'm low-key proud of my baking skills.

As I slip on my heels, the door to the dressing room bursts open, and Tara storms in, her presence riled with distress. She collapses into a chair opposite me, breath ragged and eyes swollen.

"Tara, what's wrong? Why did you come all the way here?"

"Omar knows I'm pregnant and thinks it's Randall's. I don't even know how he found out. We got into it bad. I think he's ready to bail."

"Wait, why did you come all the way here?"

"Who else can I talk to, Chevy? Most folks ain't worth a damn, and you never pick up anymore when I call. But I knew you'd be here." Tara's eyes are red, tears threatening to spill. "He... he hit me."

"He what!" Shock pounds through me as Tara reveals a bruise on her chest, evidence of Omar's rage.

"He laid his hands on me. Said he can't trust me anymore 'cause of Randall. Someone told him I still care about him and got feelings for him, which doesn't make sense when all I've been talking about is how happy I am with Omar."

Oh damn. That was probably me. I didn't mean to blow her cover. I can't blame Omar for being pissed if Tara's been playing both sides. *But Omar hitting her? The same man I chilled with today?* I can't wrap my head around it.

"We've been going at it a lot lately, but I thought today would be different after I shared my good news about work. He seemed proud when I called him earlier. I bring in good business, and he appreciates it."

That must've been the call he took with her while I was with him. I won't be confessing that to her.

Tara continues, "And then he got mad because I waited too long to tell him about the pregnancy. You know who I think is stirring all this up? Makin' him mad at me?"

I brace myself for the storm. "Tara, I'm sorry—"

"Randall and Sheila. I found out they're together now. Remember how mad he was when he found out I moved on? I didn't tell you, but he fired me. In our last conversation, I told him I didn't want him anymore, and he got mad. I didn't even get to tell him about the baby, and now I don't want to. But he keeps calling and hanging up. I know it's him. And that *bitch*, Sheila... you know how I feel about her."

"Tara, I'm sorry about your job, but I don't think Randall and Sheila told Omar."

But she's not listening. As she rummages through her purse for a cigarette, I decide not to press further. She's here for a reason, and I don't want to make things worse.

Tara gives up on finding the cigarette and slumps back, defeated. She looks at me, mascara streaking her face.

"I think I love him, Chevy. I don't wanna lose Omar over my stupid feelings for someone else that I don't even want. I fucked up, and I don't wanna lose him."

"I get it, but you shouldn't be with someone who lays hands on you. And you shouldn't have to lie about your child. If you were truly happy with him, you wouldn't have gone back to Randall. It's a tough situation, but you have to own your part in it."

She sobs, "I want it to be his. God dammit I'm so fucking *stupid!*"

Yeah, Sis. *As hell.*

"But I understand why he's upset. I've been distant because I'm not ready to be a mom. I didn't know how to tell him or Randall. I've been thinking about not keepin' it. But since he found out, he doesn't trust me. Now he might leave me. I'm losing everything."

I kneel in front of her, wiping away her tears. She's torn between two men she loves, and I don't envy her position. But I can't confess my part in this mess just yet.

Tara brightens for a moment, "Can you talk to Omar for me, Chevy? He might listen to you now. Tell him it's his baby and to stop listening to Randall. Tell him I wouldn't lie about something like that."

If I talk to him, I might tear into him for hitting her. I won't lie for her either.

"I'll talk to him, but it won't be pretty. No man should lay hands on you, Tara. I don't agree with what you did, but I don't agree with his actions either."

"Thank you, Chev! You're such a good friend, even when I'm not. I'll do better. Just help me fix things with Omar. I love him."

Love? Yeah, right.

———— ♡ ————

It's the dead of night, 4 a.m. I'm back home, freshly showered, craving the comfort of my bed. My gaze shifts between the phone and the piece of paper Omar gave me, now crumpled, resting on the kitchen counter. Maybe he'll dial me up first and spill about the fight with Tara. But as impatience gnaws at me, I snatch the phone off its hook, punch it in the pager number, and wait for the callback.

"First time for everything. You wanting me to call? At this hour?" he answers, sounding wide awake, R&B vibes humming in the background. "Everything cool, baby girl?"

"No. We need to talk," I reply, my voice quivering with anger.

"Want me to roll through? Sounding serious."

Him rolling through? That's new. I pause before passing on the offer, "No, we'll talk right now, over this phone. Did you hit Tara?"

He sighs, silence hanging in the air. "Yeah. By accident."

"Accidentally hitting a pregnant woman because you're mad!" Hand on my hip, I feel a surge of protectiveness. "How does that make any sense?"

"I ain't mean to, Chevonne." His use of my government name feels off, like it's reserved for everyone else but him. *Strange, right?* "Tried pushin' her off, needed space. She kept rushin' me. I ain't mean to hit her. That girl is crazy as hell, you know that."

"How you leave a bruise like that from just a push?" I press.

"Dunno, baby girl." He yawns.

"You sound like you don't care. Your girl—my friend, you hurt her. If you love her, you wouldn't hurt her. She doesn't want Randall. This is happening 'cause of me anyway. You need to think and stop letting your temper control you."

"So you're mad because I listen to you? What reason do you got to lie? You know stuff about your friend that I don't," he counters, cool as ice.

"You're a big dummy. You believe everything I say? What if I set you up? You'd believe me then, like a dummy?"

"Hey... I'm not one to mess with," he warns.

"Neither am I. Hurt my friend again and see what happens." After slamming the phone on the dialer, I lean against the wall.

What am I really going to do? This is why I didn't want to get involved.

Before it could possibly ring again, I unplug the phone, and then proceed to push the dining table against the door, just in case. I might be paranoid but I'm prepared.

I should have probably left it available for Tara, in case she needs to reach me, but I'll call her tomorrow. I'm too wired right now to deal with her.

Sitting on the table, legs swinging, I ponder. I might have to follow through on my threat if things go south. He sounded like he didn't care, though.

I was starting to like him. *Why am I disappointed?* He's not mine, but maybe I liked him for Tara. *Does he even love her? Care about her more than his business? Does he care about anyone other than his stupid business?*

Then a thought dawns on me. *The brownies...*

I rush to the fridge, grabbing the bag. They're cold to the touch as I stare, and they hold one of Omar's products...

And now I know what to do.

———— ♡ ————

The brownies hit Randall's desk with a thud. He glances at them, then shoots me a look.

"Thanks?" he mutters.

"Omar's special brownies. They're infused with his stash—well, in the butter or something. I whipped them up myself," I explain.

"Where'd you even get the pot from?"

"I was with Omar when I made 'em. He showed me the ropes."

Randall digs into the bag, pulling out a piece. They look damn good, dark, and perfectly cut. He takes a bite, leans back, and chuckles.

"So..." He chews, thinking. "Nice effort, Chevy, but I needed the real deal, not baked into a brownie. But damn, these are good. Nice work."

"I wasn't gonna swipe the buds straight up. I'd get busted for sure. Omar was eyeing me like a hawk," I explain, dodging the fact that I didn't think it was because he didn't trust me, but because he was eyeballing me like I was the prey.

"The pot wasn't what I was after though. I'm talking about the stuff that puts him on his throne over L.A. The stuff that gives him real power," Randall clarifies, licking his fingers clean.

"The white stuff?" I ask.

"Yeah, that's the one. But hey, good try. Appreciate the effort," Randall nods, finishing his brownie.

"First off, I'm steering clear of cocaine, and second, our friendship is over anyway," I retort, hands on my hips.

"Why's that?" Randall leans forward.

"He laid his hands on Tara, so I let him have it."

Randall's smile fades, concern replacing it. "He hit Tara? What do you mean?"

"I mean he hit her hard enough to leave a bruise. I don't stand for that, so I gave him a piece of my mind. Might've thrown in a threat or two," I admit.

Randall shakes his head, then leans back. "Well, she chose him. Guess grass ain't always greener in the yard of a kingpin, huh?"

I grimace as he laughs. *What's so funny about someone else's pain, especially someone he claims to love?*

"You know what," I say, grabbing the bag of brownies off his desk. "Forget it. I'm taking these back. You don't deserve my help, Selfish."

"Come on, Chevonne. This could be our way of getting back at him for hurtin' Tara, you know?" Randall reaches out, but I pull away.

"No. How about you just pay the man back and handle your own business. I'm taking these with me," I declare, turning to leave. Randall grunts, but I don't give a damn. I need to stash these and hit the stage anyway.

Something is wrong with these men.

The air fills with that familiar mix of sandalwood and musk as I bump into Omar and his crew heading into the club. Eddie is here too.

My eyes widen as Omar locks eyes with me, and I swiftly hide the bag of brownies behind my back.

"Hey, baby girl," he drawls.

I glance past him, and Eddie flashes a smile and a wave.

"Omar? What are you doing here?"

"Just here for some business... And a good time."

"Oh, well... Hope you all have a blast," I try to sidestep him, but he's too quick, grabbing my arm from behind.

"I figured you woulda passed these out by now," he teases. "Made a lil' money for yourself."

"Oh, I, uh... forgot them in the fridge overnight and was grabbing them for later. They're pretty damn good though. Just had one," I stumble through the lie. I've never been good at lying, and Daddy always said I should stick to the truth to avoid making things worse.

Omar studies my face, probably trying to figure out if I'm lying or thinking about our chat earlier. I catch Randall sneaking a peek from the balcony. Omar follows my gaze and spots Randall too.

"Well, you better get to your meeting, so you don't miss out on the show," I suggest, trying to usher them along.

"When you hittin' the stage, pretty mama?" Eddie asks, stepping closer and resting a hand on Omar's shoulder.

"Um... supposed to be up there now, but suddenly not feeling too hot. It must be the brownies," I say.

Omar chuckles and releases my arm. "That's a shame. I was thinking about takin' you up on that offer and checkin' you out on that stage."

"Even after I threw threats your way?" I question, puzzled by his lack of retaliation.

His crew chuckles, and he grins down at me. "Oh, those were threats, baby girl?"

Relieved yet annoyed, I realize he didn't take me seriously.

Our silent exchange is interrupted by Randall finally speaking up. "You fellas wanna let my stripper through? She's got work to do, money to make for me."

Omar glances up, but it's not a friendly look. I wonder what they're here to chat Randall up about—probably the money he owes Omar. He seems like the type to seek revenge this way.

"Sounds like he thinks you're stickin' around to work. Hope you'll still be here when I'm done up there, but if not, feel better," Omar says, brushing his finger against my chin.

"We're feelin' generous tonight, baby. You might wanna stick around," Eddie chimes in.

I head toward the dressing room, feeling their eyes trailing me. Of course, I'd pick the G-string today.

I catch a *"gaaah damn"* but don't bother looking back. I don't know how I'll muster the courage to hit that stage with Omar lurking around.

After a bit, I finish up a call with Tara. I decided to stay at work, but I wanted to check on her. She's alright, just a bit under the weather and still upset about Omar being mad at her. She mentioned Omar apologized for hitting her, so I'm glad about that. She thanked me for talking to him, but I doubt he let it go. No amount of talking can save someone who may be pregnant by somebody else. Or got somebody else pregnant. At least for me, there wouldn't be.

Maybe he does listen to me. It's good they are talking it out. Seeing her down like that, especially with a baby on the way, hurt me.

I wonder about Sheila, though, but she must've switched her shift. She's still too green, even though I'm not that much older. It would be nice to vent, but I probably shouldn't share my business with her much anymore and risk it getting out into the world.

The clock reminds me I've got three hours left in my shift. I might as well hit the floor and rake in some cash. I touch up my makeup and check myself out in the mirror. After admiring how good I look, I snap the string on my thong and giggle to myself. Time to cash in on Eddie's promises of a fat stack tonight.

———— ♥ ————

The pole feels icy against my grip. I quickly scan the crowd, spotting Omar's crew but no sign of Omar himself. It's a little relieving, to be honest. *The thought of dancing in front of that man?* No thanks. Maybe he's still hashing it out with Randall.

"I see you, baby!" Eddie winks, making it rain with bills. Other people chime in too. Feels good to have some support.

Lost in the rhythm, I let myself flow onstage. The pole becomes my dance partner, steady as I work my moves. The music flows through me and I'm feeling good.

Eddie wasn't lying about the cash flow. I scramble to scoop it up before hopping off, but the other girls are already swarming Omar's crew, eager to get their share of the generosity.

Suddenly, a hand grabs my arm, and I drop the cash as I'm yanked into the hallway leading to the private rooms. "Omar? What the hell? Let go!"

We're in a dimly lit room now, and he shoves me against the wall. His gun drawn, pressed against my lips. Tears well up in fear, blurring my vision.

"Omar, please... don't..." I plead, my voice trembling.

He's fuming, I can feel it. *What the hell happened between now and our last encounter?*

"You played me once, baby girl. Never again." Tobacco stings my eyes, speeding up my tears. "You tryna double-cross me?"

"What? No... I... I didn't," I stammer, the weight of the gun on my lips making it hard to speak.

The pressure of his grip around my neck intensifies, and he taps the gun against my teeth.

"Omar, stop..." I beg, my heart pounding in my chest. "I'm sorry."

"I didn't expect this from you, but you warned me. You were right. That's what I get for trustin' you too damn easily, huh?"

He releases me, and I gasp for air, my whole body trembling. I've never had a gun to my face before, and he's still holding it to me, his eyes burning with fury.

"I didn't mean to... I was trying to help my friend, okay?" I choke out, my voice barely above a whisper.

"Help your friend by stealin' from me? You know what I do to folks who steal from me?" His voice is cold, sending chills down my spine.

I have a damn good idea.

"I just didn't like that you wanted to off him over some stupid shit and that you hit Tara. I was pissed."

Randall must've snitched about the brownies while I was onstage. Omar lowers his gun and stands opposite me, his expression now unreadable.

"Now, you owe me."

"Owe you? What? I said I was sorry."

"Sorry don't mean shit when you're tryna fuck with my business."

"I took the damn brownies back. What's the problem?" I shoot back, frustration bubbling up inside me.

He looks crazy as hell... I won't lie.

"The problem? So you told him you was gonna snoop around my operation and report back?"

What? That's not how it went down. *Randall's lying on me?* That's what I get for helping his sorry ass.

"That's not true, Omar. Randall wanted me to get closer and bring stuff back. I didn't offer jack."

"The point is you brought my shit back to him. You were planning to sell me out, baby girl. That's cold," he says, his voice dripping with venom.

He's seething, blocking the door, so there's no running. I probably wouldn't make it anyway.

"Now, I don't trust you, but I ain't killing you. You work for me now. How's that?"

"What do I have to do? I don't wanna owe nobody."

"Too bad."

The tears dry as I wipe my face. I feel so stupid. It was never meant for me to get this deep in that lifestyle, but it's on me to know better.

"You and Randall gonna push for me. Right out of this club. Then you report it to me. Every damn day. Miss one? Fuck up? I put one in your head. You got it?"

I don't like this side of him. Must be the one folks warned me about.

"Okay. Whatever. Just keep it cool." Now my gut's twisted, and I'm scared I might puke.

"Go get your shit. Meet me out front. I'll take you home." Omar stands, gun tucked away, and opens the door. He glances back. "You hurt?"

I shake my head, waiting for him to leave. Only now do I notice the mirror shards at my feet, reflecting the shattered fragments of my shattered reality.

---- ♡ ----

The neon lights of the club fade behind us, replaced by the dull hum of the city at night. Pulling up to my apartment building feels like a damn relief and a getaway from the chaos that I probably started anyway. I scramble to pop the car door open, feeling the cool breeze hit my face. Now that I'm involuntarily roped into the dope game, I'm itching to get away from Omar as fast as I can.

"Sorry 'bout all that, baby girl," Omar says, his voice gravelly, reaching over and tugging me back into the seat. He eyes the gash on my arm, his expression softening with concern. "You want me to patch that up for you?"

I hadn't even clocked the cut until I was packing up my bag at the club, blood gushing like a damn faucet. "No, I got it," I brush him off, pulling my arm away.

He shuts off the car with a tired sigh, the engine's hum dying down. "I'ma help you with your stuff then."

I'm too drained to protest. All I want is a hot shower and my bed. The gun-to-the-face ordeal tonight drained me more than climbing that pole. I'm still hoping it's some twisted dream.

Omar's already ahead, keys in hand, unlocking my door with ease. His movements are smooth, practiced, but something about the way he handles my keys sets me on edge. His comfort with it pisses me off. I'm changing my locks pronto. Maybe even ditching this place altogether so he can't track me down.

He dumps my bag on the dining table, eyeing the place like he owns it before turning back to me.

"Let me see that arm," he insists, his voice low, reaching again. I slap his hand away.

"No. Just get out."

"That cut's bad. Lemme patch it up for you. It's the least I can do."

The sight of blood makes me queasy, so I relent, and we head to the bathroom.

I wince as he tends to the cut. He then wraps it up with some gauze he found in a first-aid kit, his touch surprisingly gentle against my skin.

"There you go, baby girl."

"I'm not your baby girl..." slips out before I can stop it, my voice hoarse. "How long do I gotta hustle before I can go ghost on all of y'all?"

He chuckles a deep rumble, wiping the counter before responding to me. "About a month should do it."

"A *month*? Are you nuts? I am not working as a dope dealer for that long. I'm out. Go ahead and shoot me, I don't care."

Omar grabs me before I can dip from the bathroom, his grip firm yet strangely comforting, although I truly hate being petite sometimes.

"You don't gotta do much. Just cook up at the family house like I showed you, push it for me. That's it. And you keep half of what you make. Fair deal for the risk."

Why's he cutting me in? I thought I owed him. The air in the bathroom is thick with unsaid tension until I speak up.

"Why? You just want somebody to owe you something."

"Nah, 'cause you deserve compensation for the risk. I'm still a businessman, baby."

I peel his hand off me and slink off into the living room. This whole setup is messed up, and I want out.

"I *never* thought I'd be slinging drugs. I didn't sign up for this. I just wanna live my life and build my own family. Now I'm in deep 'cause I got a soft spot and trust too easy. I regret getting this job, knowing Tara, helping Randall, and meeting *you*."

I didn't realize he was waiting for my last word before locking his lips on mine. I didn't even notice that he followed me out of the bathroom so closely. Omar pulls me in, and *damn it*, I can't stop kissing him back.

Omar eventually removes his tongue from my throat and moves down to my neck. He sucks, *hard*. Now I see why Tara has all those marks on her like that.

Oh shit, Tara!

I pull back as hard as I can and shove him off. My feet barely hit the ground in time, but I catch myself. Omar stumbles back and shoots me a confused glare. "What's wrong?"

I didn't know I was still crying until I open my mouth to speak, and my words come out in trembles. "This is so fucked up. You are my friend's man. What about Tara, huh? She is pregnant and everything. She told me she loved you, Omar."

He wipes his mouth with the back of his hand, then sighs without taking his eyes off of me. "I ain't know you was only twenty-one. You got an old soul like me. I like that about you."

What? What the hell is he talking about?

We are standing opposite each other, thinking. He didn't seem to hear anything I said, and I don't think he wanted to. One thing is for sure: if I sleep with this man, I will be a damned fool. I should have known better than to have let Tara's shadow cause me to develop feelings for him. Just an hour ago, he had a gun in my face, and now I'm standing here wishing that he would stay with me for the rest of the night.

I *feel* him wishing the same.

Without taking his eyes off mine, he steps closer to me, and the next thing I know, I'm up against the hallway closet. He reaches over my thigh to the roundness of my ass, and he clutches, and I forcefully swallow.

With his lips, he pulls on my neck once more, and I groan softly. I finally cave and grip his back, putting my legs around him. He guides us to the bedroom and peels off his shirt, revealing inked skin. *Sexy as hell.*

I wince, remembering the cut, but his eyes on me make it fade. He's scanning, searching. *What's he looking for?*

"Take that off," he whispers. "I wanna see you."

I comply, but he rips my G-string before I can get to it, making me want to protest.

"I'll get you another one," Omar says, eyes locked on mine. "Can I have you?"

"I'll answer if you keep me out of the dope game."

He shoots me a glare. "That's business. This is pleasure. I'm the one that ultimately got played, anyway. Tara, Randall... *you.*"

I'm scared. Scared of liking him, scared of hurting Tara. Scared of him. But damn, I want him.

"I'm scared, Omar. Of all of this."

"You ain't gotta be scared. I won't hurt you. I won't let you get hurt."

"What about Tara?" I ask weakly about her again, hoping he would come to his senses for the both of us. I'm too far gone at this point.

"We'll figure it out." *And so is he.* "If you don't want to do this, say no."

But saying no means stopping. And I don't want that.

"I want you," I admit, my voice barely above a whisper.

He smiles, moonlight hitting his face. The clock reads 4 a.m.

"I know," he whispers, moving closer. "I knew I wanted you since we met that night. Just bein' real."

That's real.

I recline and let go of everything in my mind. Every concern I have... and choose to spend my night with Omar Spence.

CHAPTER 5
Afterparty

S O, IT'S BEEN A whole month, and things are cruising along just fine. Tara, Sheila, and I are heading to the family house to whip up more of that stuff for Omar. It's kind of surprising that Tara and Sheila are getting along, but I guess when money and drugs are in the mix, anyone can become best buds.

Yep, I'm still in the drug game. I asked Omar if Tara and Sheila could join the party, so I wouldn't be flying solo. He hesitated a bit, but eventually gave the green light to have them part of the family house team. We're using Randall's club as a front, just like Omar wanted. But I'm keeping it low-key, only selling to the other dancers who I know can cough up the cash. Don't want to be making a name for myself on these streets.

I could have quit by now, but the success and making Omar proud are giving me a good feeling. And I noticed when Omar is in a good mood, everyone is doing well. Even Tara's cheating ass. The extra cash isn't too shabby either. I share the wealth with the ladies, and we're living large. I've spruced up my apartment, got some new furniture, and still clock in at the club.

Talking about Omar, we only had that one wild night together. It was incredible, and I wish it didn't have to end, but I had to pump the brakes. Seems like it hit him in the feels or something because now he's keeping our conversations short. As long as I'm pulling in the work for him, he shouldn't be complaining, especially since he's *still* in a relationship.

Sheila's in the back seat, belting out tunes along with the radio while Tara's behind the wheel. She's still puffing on those cigarettes. I tried telling her to quit, especially with a bun in the oven, but she swears it helps with the stress. Whatever floats her boat. Feel bad for that baby though.

I'm going through my stack of mail, and I open one to find a letter from my landlord. Turns out, I've paid off the rent for the rest of my lease. *"What?"* I thought I was whispering, but Tara catches wind of it.

"What's up?" She glances over, unintentionally blowing smoke my way.

"Um... I don't owe rent for my place anymore. It's all taken care of."

"Woo! Good for you, Chevy!" Sheila gives my shoulder a squeeze.

"Yep, that's good news, Chevy. Bet working with Omar helped you save some extra cash," Tara remarks, exhaling her smoke out the window this time. It dawns on me that I didn't settle this bill; it has to be one person.

"Now, all you need is a car," she suggests.

I definitely do, and I need to act fast before Omar beats me to it. While going through my mail, I find a letter from the funeral home that handled my dad's service. Same story – paid off, with a note of gratitude.

I cover my mouth, keeping my thoughts to myself this time. Omar must've covered the expenses, and while it's a kind gesture, it irks me. *Why?* I could've handled it myself. I don't like owing anyone anything.

"Hey, party tonight, huh?" Sheila's voice chirps from the backseat. "I've got a few girls comin' over to give Omar and his crew some love for lookin' out for us, you know?"

Tara rolls her eyes. "Just make sure none of you bitches get too close to my man."

Too late.

I'm still kicking myself for what we did behind Tara's back and how clueless she is about it. But what annoys me most is that Omar is still with her, and I say that because if he felt the need to step out on her, *why drag her along if he knows that's not what he wants?*

Maybe it's because she's pregnant. Or maybe he truly does love her. Either way, I'm not going behind her back again. He's got to choose to find someone else to step out with or stay faithful.

Omar's throwing a block party for Eddie's forty-second birthday. I always knew that guy was much older than us. I just never knew how he and Omar clicked, especially with Omar only being twenty-five. Eddie's been a real gem, always hanging around the family house with us. He's a breath of fresh air, not all serious like the rest. And I dig his goofy side—his and Sheila's.

"I gotta swing by my place real quick, make some calls... bills and stuff. You two cool with dropping me off, Tara?"

"You're still coming to Eddie's party, right?" Sheila gives me a concerned look.

"Yeah, I'll be there."

"You better be, or we'll come drag you out ourselves," Tara adds with a smirk, Sheila nodding along.

"I will." Before hitting the party, I have to call Omar and ask if he's the one who paid off my bills. And I need to make sure he knows I'll pay him back.

As soon as I step through the door, I reach for the phone and dial Omar's number. No answer. I try again, but my pager buzzes in my purse. Got myself one of those pagers because they say it's handy in the drug scene. Can't believe I've gone this long without one.

I grab the pager from my pocket and glance at the code glowing on the small green display meaning "see you tonight.". Omar must be tied up, so I'll just catch him at the party later. With Tara and the crew around, though, I'm not sure how I'll manage to snag him alone long enough, but I'll figure something out.

I'm glad I skipped out on Tara and Sheila until later. I needed a breather and some time to decompress before diving back into that crowd. Eddie's gift still sits on my table, untouched, so I'd better wrap that up. He's been talking about getting himself a camera, and I thought a 35mm would be a sweet gift. Took a few test shots with it earlier, now I want one for myself.

After wrapping Eddie's gift, I take a look around my apartment. It definitely feels more like home, thanks to the extra cash flowing in. Guess I'll have even more now that my major bills are covered. *Sigh.* I can't decide if I'm actually mad about that or not. Daddy always said to count my blessings, but having a dope dealer pay my debts feels... off. I remember how he dealt with Randall after bailing out his club.

Oh, shit! I forgot about work. I rush to call Randall, and thankfully, he picks up. "Hey, Randall, it's Chevonne. Am I on the schedule for tonight?" I ask, hoping I got my dates mixed up and its actually next week I'm thinking about.

"Hell yeah, why?" his voice comes back sharp.

"I forgot, alright? I was doing some stuff for Omar and then heading to this important party later. Can you please call somebody in or let me make up for it on a different day?" I implore Randall, hoping he'll cut me some slack.

Randall stays silent on the other end for a few moments before responding to my question. "That ain't my problem, Chev. You don't get any special treatment. I already made that clear."

"Okay, but it's for Omar and his crew. I can't miss that either. You know how that is," I press, trying to make him understand the situation.

"Not my problem. Make sure you're here on time," Randall retorts, hanging up the phone before I can even respond.

"Ugh!" I grunt, frustration boiling over as I slam the phone back on the dialer.

Why does this man make shit more difficult than it has to be? I'm sure he hates my guts since I admitted to Omar that he asked me to steal his drugs for him. I have no clue what happened, but I have barely heard from Randall after that besides us coming together to sell Omar's product out of the club. That shit pissed Randall off all month because that is one thing he did not want to happen in his club, but his dumbass did it to himself. He's in the clear now though. Well, for now, until he does something else to piss Omar off.

I gotta call Tara and tell her I can't go tonight. I'm sure it will disappoint Omar and Eddie to hear that. I know Sheila will be disappointed too. Or I could just skip work and go to the party. It's not like I'm short on cash. I'm mad at myself because I could skip work, but that would be dumb of me because I'm not even supposed to be selling anymore. My debt is paid, and I still love to dance; I just can't stand working for Randall anymore.

Maybe I'll ask Omar to back me up so that I'll still have a job tomorrow. I just don't want to rely on that man for anything or, once again, owe him anything. It's just a party, anyway.

With a decision this hard, I'll decide what I want to do after a few hours of much-needed, quiet time alone.

————— ♥ —————

We pull up to one of Omar's houses and park in the back. I ended up telling Tara about my shift, and she called Randall and somehow got him to cave. So, it looks like I still have my job, and I get to party with my newfound coworkers. I did not know that her and Randall were still cool like that, but I have also learned to mind my own damn business.

The place is packed. I recognize some regulars from the club, a few local business owners, and a slew of women. Omar's crew is massive too. I only recognize Eddie and his crew; the rest are strangers to me.

Sheila spots some friends and lets us know she'll catch up with us later. Tara takes my hand that isn't holding Eddie's birthday gift and squeezes. She is grinning hard as she looks around.

"Everybody loves them some Eddie, huh?" she asks.

"Yeah, him and Omar," I answer and shrug as I allow her to lead me into the house.

Too many guys whistle and mutter slick remarks as we pass by. I'm used to it, being a dancer and all, but they act like they've never seen ladies in short dresses and high heels before. Some folks are already wasted, doped up and drunk as hell and I realized they wasted no time; the party's barely kicked off.

It doesn't take us long to spot Eddie. He's so tall and loud so it's hard to miss him. Plus, they've got him decked out in a birthday hat and ribbons. I chuckle as we make our way over.

"My favorite ladies came to visit the old man on his birthday. How y'all doin'?' Eddie greets me and Tara with a hug. He carries a strong scent of tobacco, pot, and cognac, especially when he talks.

"Eddie! Happy birthday! Can't believe you're forty-two. Time flies,'" Tara says to him.

"You've seen a lot in your time. It's impressive 'cause life isn't easy," I add.

"Yeah, I've been around for a while, but you two are already doing much better than I was at your ages, that's for sure."

Not entirely true. I'm not exactly where I want to be. But then again, I'm only twenty-one. My bills are paid, I have clothes, food, and a bed. So, I'm doing alright, I suppose.

"Oh, Eddie, here's your gift. Hope you like it." I hand him his present.

He plants a wet kiss on my forehead. Tara whispers a *yuck* and leans in to watch him open it.

"I wonder what this is..." he says as he tears off the wrapping paper. "Well, would you look at that... A camera. You're too kind, Miss Chevy! Thank you."

"You're welcome, Eddie. Remember we were talking about it, so I figured you'd appreciate one. It's got autofocus and all," I say, giving him another hug, catching Tara's glance.

"Chevy always comes up with some decent gifts, I'll give her that much," Tara remarks, not too impressed.

Eddie nods in agreement. "We could use more of that around here," he says with a smile as he unpacks the camera.

Tara asks about Omar, and Eddie mentions he's in a meeting downstairs. She rolls her eyes and mutters under her breath as she walks away. I trail close behind.

"A meeting? At Eddie's party? That's messed up," I comment as I catch up to her. We head down to the basement.

"I don't care about that. It's the fact that he's in one without me."

"Since when do you get to sit in on meetings with Omar?"

"Since I'm his woman. He wants me by his side; that's what he said, and I happily accepted."

It's typical Tara, always aiming to be the queen by the kingpin's side and in on his operations. I thought I could be jealous, but I'm not. It just makes me pity her because all it takes is one slip-up to get in trouble, and then everyone's messed up.

Down here, it's not as crowded, but the vibe is more laid-back compared to upstairs and outside. Following Tara, I enter a room deeper in the basement where a couple of guys sit by a door, guns in hand, passing around a joint.

"Hey, fellas. Is my man in there?" Tara asks.

I hang back a few feet because I'm not about to get close to anyone packing heat.

The door swings open, and Omar steps out. Two sharply dressed white guys follow, one carrying a briefcase. *Huh, alright.* I wonder who they are and what kind of meeting that was?

Omar exchanges handshakes with them, and they head towards the stairs. I turn back to Omar and Tara.

"Babe, why are you holding meetings at your right-hand man's birthday bash? Don't you think that's kinda shady?" Tara asks, her hands on her hips, confronting Omar. Funny, that's exactly what I was thinking. I thought she didn't care about that.

"Relax. Eddie knew I had some business to handle real quick. Y'all look good," Omar replies.

I watch them kiss and can't help but look away. *What's with this burning sensation in my chest? Why does that make me so uneasy?* They're a couple, after all. But I've never been one for public displays of affection. I even cover my eyes when I see that stuff on TV... and yeah, that's coming from someone who dances half-naked to entertain folks for a living.

Finally, Omar glances up at me. A faint smile tugs at his lips. I look away again and fidget with my feet to ease the awkwardness.

"Y'all havin' a good time?" he finally asks, still looking at me.

"We just got here. Chevy got Eddie a camera, and he's probably upstairs messing around with it," Tara replies.

"Eddie's always talkin' about snapping pictures of everything. I never understood why he didn't just buy one himself, but he's got one now," Omar says.

I finally muster the courage to glance up and speak, feeling like I need to stop acting like a nervous child. "Did you guys get him anything?"

"Yeah, me and babe got him a Rolex and that Cadillac... I think it's the Fleetwood he was eyeing," Tara says. "Brand new, too."

She didn't even mention she got him anything, or I would've put more thought and money into my gift. A measly 35 mm camera. *Seriously?* It doesn't stand a chance against fancy cars and watches. That's how I know I don't belong with these people.

Omar must have sensed my embarrassment. "Gifts like that, they're more meaningful, you know? They linger in memories a bit longer. Shows you pay attention. Eddie's gonna cherish that."

I give him a smile as Tara adjusts her berry-colored tights. He throws a wink, and we both quickly avert our gaze before Tara catches on.

"Alright, babe, let's hit this party. Chevy, you gonna stick with Sheila, right? She needs a babysitter," Tara says.

I completely forgot about Sheila. I better go track her down before she drinks and smokes everything away. "Yeah, I'll just stick by her and Eddie. Oh, by the way, who were those guys you were just talking to, Omar?"

"Allies," he says, taking Tara's hand as they head towards the main area in the basement.

I glance up at the stairs, pondering for a moment about the way this stuff is straight like the movies I like to watch. *Allies? What kind of allies?* I wish he'd be a tad more specific. *Damn.*

But then again, why should I care? It's got nothing to do with me.

——— ♥ ———

Sheila's currently heaving her guts out, and I'm right by her side, ensuring her hair stays clear. I can't stand seeing her like this, but I'm relieved I only had a couple of shots of tequila earlier in the evening so I could play babysitter. It's been a few hours, and as the night winds down, so does my buzz.

I made a point to steer clear of Omar and Tara for most of the night. They were all cuddled up, and I didn't want to dampen the mood or face the memories.

Sheila kept her promise and brought in a few dancers for Eddie. It seems like he had a blast on his birthday, and I'm all for it. Everyone deserves to go all out on their special day. I sure plan to do that with my own future family.

Once Sheila empties her stomach, I wipe her mouth and help her out of the bathroom. She's dead weight, and it takes all my strength to support her and guide her along.

"Damn it, Sheila. You really need to handle your liquor better. This is getting out of hand," I mutter to her.

We bump into Eddie before we can make it outside to Tara's car.

"O's looking for you, Miss Chevy," he says, concern flickering in his eyes as I struggle to hold Sheila up.

He ends up scooping her into his arms, and I'm grateful.

"Thank you so much, Eddie. I could barely keep her up."

"No worries. I'll find her a guest room and keep an eye on her until you and O are finished. He's in his room... on the third floor," Eddie offers.

I lift my head to look at Eddie, and he flashes a smirk.

"Finished... *talking*. Got it. Thanks. I won't be long. Just need to have a quick chat with him and then grab Tara so we can head home. Hope you had a great birthday."

"One of the best I've ever had," Eddie responds.

Sheila groans but rests her head on his chest as he carries her off. I dash to find a bathroom, checking my appearance before heading up to the third floor of this massive house.

Oh, he wasn't letting anybody up here. The third floor is immaculate. Not a trace of the party below, and the familiar scent of sandalwood fills the air. Several closed doors line the hallway, but there's a soft glow emanating from one at the end. As I approach, I hear soul music drifting out.

Just the two of us... we can make it if we try...

I tap the door lightly, assuming Tara's probably inside with him. It's cracked open, and I hear Omar invite me in.

His bedroom is like the size of my entire living and dining room combined back home. I'm struck with awe as I take in the thick comforter on his king-sized bed, the plush carpet that seems untouched, the paintings adorning the walls, all in shades of gold, brown, and red. My favorite piece is the jeweled elephant painting. Omar sure knows how to decorate.

"Like what you see?" he interrupts my silent admiration, stepping out of what appears to be a connected bathroom.

"Omar, it's stunning in here. This room alone is massive," I reply, still taking it all in.

He chuckles, leaning against the door frame. "I know you called earlier, but I was out handling some business. Then there was this party. Everything okay with you?"

"Yeah, so... Why did I find my rent and my dad's funeral expenses paid off in the mail today? Was that you?" I ask, crossing my arms and awaiting his response.

"Who else would it be? Randolph? You know he couldn't care less about you," he retorts bluntly.

Ouch. "His name is Randall, and damn, I know, but you don't have to say it like that."

"The truth stings, baby girl," he says, motioning for me to follow him into the bathroom.

I follow without hesitation. "Why'd you pay those bills? Are you trying to make it seem like I can't handle my own stuff?"

"Just say thanks and let it be. What's done is done. And nah, you don't owe me anything for it, so ease up on those thoughts. I know they're running wild right now."

He seems to understand me better than I thought he would. But I still can't shake the feeling that him doing this for me might be held against me one day.

"Well, thanks, I guess," I reply, trying to keep it casual.

I pause when I notice a bathtub brimming with bubbles and surrounded by candles. There's also a bottle of champagne and two flutes. I glance over at Omar, and he chuckles.

"Um... what's all this? Is it for you and Tara?" I feel a knot of nerves forming because I know this setup isn't for him and Tara. "Omar, where is Tara?"

"She left... probably about an hour ago. Wasn't feeling too great. And she had an attitude with me most of the night, didn't want to be bothered, I guess."

Wow. So, she really bailed on us without a word. She's not the best kind of friend. But shit, neither am I.

"I'm kind of annoyed because she knows Sheila and I came with her, and she was our ride. And no one bothered to mention anything? Damn."

"Relax, baby girl. You and your friend can crash here at my place for the night," he offers, dipping his hand into the water and swirling it around.

"Okay, thanks, but... what's all this for?" I gesture to the tub, waiting for an explanation.

"It's for you."

My heart races, and I struggle to hold a foolish grin. I can feel heat creeping into my cheeks as I try to collect myself. Omar stands, his gaze wandering over me with hunger.

"We shouldn't... we can't be doing this, Omar. We talked about this," I manage to snap out of my daze and regain my composure.

"Look, baby girl, I didn't feel right about putting that gun to your head, making you hustle for me when I knew you hated it, and leaving you hanging all night tonight. You deserve this," he says sincerely.

"Well, you didn't leave me hanging 'cause you're in a relationship, and that's what you're supposed to do. You and your girl should be together like that."

"You didn't like it."

"It doesn't matter if I like or don't like. She's your girlfriend."

Omar nods, appearing indifferent to the conversation. "So, are you getting in before the water gets cold or what?"

I pause, shifting uneasily as I contemplate my choices. The idea of sinking into that tub and indulging in some much-needed relaxation is tempting. "I don't want to leave Sheila by herself. I promised to look after her."

"I'll go check on her, and you just worry about getting in this tub, alright?" he offers, his tone reassuring.

I glance at the water, then shift my gaze back to Omar. "That's not champagne, is it? 'Cause Tara mentioned something about y'all bathing in champagne, and I'm not up for that nonsense."

Omar chuckles and gestures towards the tub as he makes his way to the door. "Get in."

———— ❦ ————

We got water *everywhere.*

Candles flicker around us as we lay together in the tub. We were so exhausted, we couldn't even muster the energy to climb out, so I just leaned back against Omar's chest.

He's unusually quiet. I've tried to start a couple of conversations since we finished, but all I get are "mhms."

"Omar... what are you thinkin' about?" I finally gather the courage to ask. I don't need to see his face to know he's lost in his thoughts; I'm a professional daydreamer myself.

"Just my plans for the day," he answers, surprising me, as I didn't expect a response.

"Okay... Do those plans include checking on Tara?" I ask, feeling the weight of guilt settling in. I know I should probably shut up; I shouldn't be in this tub, naked, with him. What a lousy friend I am—sleeping with my friend's man more than once, or at all, and leaving my other friend to sleep alone in this massive house while I got frisky in hot bathwater with bubbles.

"Yeah, I'll check up on her. What are you up to later today?" Omar asks.

"Probably just clean up and get ready for work. I don't feel like making drug brownies today, sorry." I finally turn and look up at him.

He's peering down at me with that half-smile, making me bow my head a bit.

"That's cool, baby girl. You've been doing your thing. So, you can have a break..." He lifts my chin with a wet finger and plants a kiss on my lips.

I kiss him back but then pull away almost immediately. Omar clearly doesn't like that and sighs.

"Omar... this isn't right. We shouldn't be doing this. It's messed up. Why are you with Tara if you're just going to cheat on her?" I confront him, locking eyes with him, but there's no indication that he's going to answer my question.

"We're not doing this anymore, okay? I need to find my own man, not my friend's man," I assert, trying to make my point clear.

Omar chuckles and gently moves me off him as he stands to get out of the tub. I'm too preoccupied watching him dry his chiseled body to notice his irritated demeanor.

"Get out of the tub, and don't make a mess on the floor," he instructs.

"There's already water on the floor..." I retort.

He shakes his head and strides over to the door. As he opens it, Sheila stands on the other side, wide-eyed with her mouth agape, as if she was about to knock.

"Sheila, oh my God!" I gasp, instinctively ducking further into the tub.

Omar smiles and glances back at me.

"Oh... my... God..." Sheila breathes out, her eyes fixed on Omar's physique. He doesn't seem fazed at all, walking past her into his bedroom. She watches him for a moment before turning back to me, her jaw still hovering near the floor.

"Sheila... you have to let me explain," I plead, the cool air causing me to shiver as I reach for a towel and step out of the bathtub.

"You... I aspire to be you *so fuckin' bad*, Chevy," she whispers.

Laughter echoes from the bedroom, cutting through the awkward tension. I'm grateful Omar finds this amusing because I feel like a complete mess. I dry myself off and hurriedly grab my clothes to cover up. Sheila's gaze shifts from the bedroom to me and then back again, a wide grin spreading across her face.

"How long has this been going on, huh? I knew something was different about you, Chevy! You've been glowing and walking like you're on air!" she exclaims.

I hear the door close, signaling that Omar has probably left the bedroom. He left me here to face the consequences alone.

"Sheila, this should never have happened. I know I messed up big time, but please don't say anything to Tara. I need to be the one to tell her, okay?" I murmur, my head dropping in shame as tears threaten to spill over.

Sheila comes over and envelops me in a tight hug. "I won't breathe a word of this to Tara; you can count on that," she reassures me, though I'm not entirely convinced, given her history of sharing my business with Randall. "Besides, Tara's been messing around with Randall behind Omar's back anyway, so I see this as her karma. And who better to serve it to her than someone as fly as you? I *knew* that man was into you!"

I brush off her hands and cross my arms. I had no idea Tara was still involved with Randall, but I wouldn't put it past her. I wonder if that's why Omar didn't hesitate to get involved with me.

"How do you know about that?" I raise an eyebrow, genuinely curious.

"I can see the way he looks at you—" she begins to explain.

"No, I mean about Tara and Randall," I interject, shifting the focus of the conversation away from Omar and me for a moment.

"Oh, because she tried to throw hands with me a few weeks back when she showed up at his place and found me in his bed," Sheila shrugs casually.

I roll my eyes; we've discussed her involvement with Randall before. I've told Sheila that I don't care what she does with him, but she needs to be cautious, especially considering the gambling mess he always finds himself in.

"You two seemed alright yesterday," I remark, my lips tightening. I had hoped Tara and Sheila had smoothed things over, but it's clear that Tara's resentment toward Randall and Sheila hasn't faded.

"Girl, because she knows if she starts something with me, it'll blow up in her face. She doesn't want her man finding out," Sheila scoffs, glancing around the bathroom. "This man really got money and good taste. *Damn...*"

A wave of relief washes over me, although I realize I shouldn't be feeling so satisfied about being with Omar. Given this newfound information, I'm no better.

"I don't understand why Omar and Tara won't let each other go, then. I'm confused," I admit, sifting through my thoughts for an explanation but coming up empty.

"Maybe he still cares about her. I don't know, but that could be it. You already know why Tara won't leave him alone. Look at his crib. The man got money," Sheila remarks casually, leaving my heart sinking.

"Plus, I talk to Randall all the time, and he says Tara tells him things like how much Omar claims he wants her, but who knows," she adds nonchalantly.

I can't help but feel sorry for Omar; he probably doesn't know about Tara's conversations with Randall, or he wouldn't be holding on to her.

"I'm backing off 'cause I messed up by getting involved with him. I knew from the start that this was all kinds of wrong," I admit, my voice tinged with regret.

"Do you have feelings for him, Chevy? How long has this been going on between you two?" Sheila asks, placing her hand over mine to still my nervous twiddling.

"I... It happened once before, but it's not happening again. I do have feelings for him, a lot, but he's not mine, Sheila. So, I know I'm in the wrong for this," I confess, my gaze shifting past Sheila to the doorway, where Omar stands. *Uh oh.* I wonder how much of our conversation he overheard.

"You both ready to leave?" he interjects, his eyes locked onto mine.

Sheila jumps a little and whirls around. I nod, gathering the rest of my belongings. I know I need to have a conversation with him about this later.

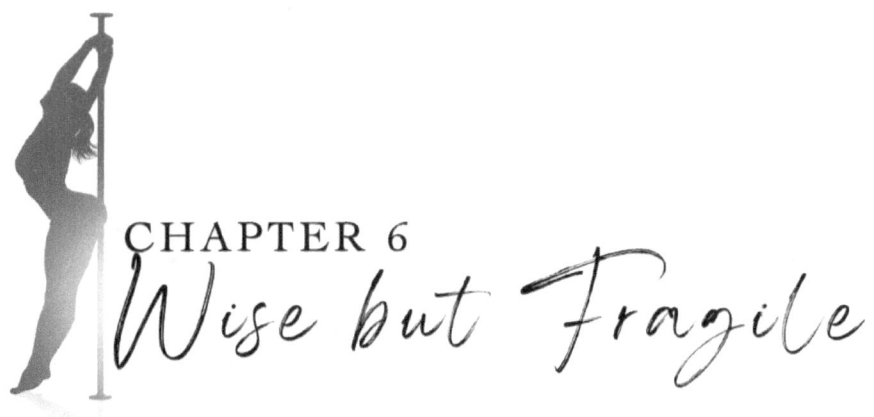

CHAPTER 6
Wise but Fragile

Later that day, right before I had to head to work, Eddie came up to me with his shiny new camera, all excited for me to model for him. I wasn't really in the mood, but Eddie's enthusiasm was infectious, so I agreed. I mean, I'm not afraid of being in front of the camera, but I was more focused on getting my hands on some cheesecake-flavored ice cream. Eddie said he'd treat me afterward, so I went along with it.

We found a cozy spot outside the ice cream parlor, soaking up the typical LA vibe - warm air, a bit of smog, and kids buzzing around for their sweet fix. It's moments like these that make me appreciate this city.

Eddie, with his camera clicking away, teased about making a collection of LA's finest ladies and including my photos. Cheesy, but kinda cute.

As I savored my ice cream, Eddie casually brought up Omar and Tara. Eddie and Omar are pretty tight, so I figured he might have some insight into their situation. Time to dive into the gossip, I guess.

"Eddie, I have a question," I say.

"Ask away, pretty lady," he says as he tosses an empty wine cooler bottle in the trash can near our table.

"What's up with Omar and Tara? Like... Are they alright?"

He lets out a heavy sigh and digs a cigarette out of his pocket. After a few tries, his lighter finally catches, flickering long enough to ignite the tip of his smoke. "They play the perfect couple in front of everyone, you know? But behind closed doors, it's more like a business deal."

I wave away the smoke drifting my way, courtesy of him and Tara and their never-ending cigarettes.

"What do you mean?"

"When it's just them two, things ain't all smooth," he explains. "I try not to get too deep into it, but O sometimes opens up to me. He ain't the talkative type, so if he's spillin' to you, it means he trusts you."

"Got it," I say, not wanting to pry too much, but I can't help wondering if Omar's ever mentioned me. "Does he... talk about me? Not like that, you know, but 'cause I work for him?"

Eddie gives a quick nod, exhaling smoke. "Oh yeah, Miss Chevy, you come up a lot."

A warm, fuzzy feeling spreads through me, and a smile creeps in. *Easy there, Chevy. Don't get too carried away.*

"So... why's he still with Tara if it's not all lovey-dovey? I mean, he doesn't even know if he's the one that got her pregnant, right?"

"You mean... Why he's with her and not you, right?" Eddie smirks.

"Well, no, not just 'cause of me. Just in general," I quickly reply, clarifying my question.

"You might not like hearin' this, but she looks good on his arm, you know what I mean? She street smart. She know the business well. They complement each other real well. That's just my take. I'm not sayin' you don't have it, 'cause I believe you do, but think about it."

"Tara's got that fly girl vibe, plus a killer body. She's confident and well-connected out here. It makes sense," I acknowledge with a shrug, polishing off the last of my ice cream before it turns into a puddle.

Eddie shakes his head, avoiding eye contact. "A lot of the powerful folks, like O, know the importance of the type of partner they got by their side. Certain qualities she gotta have. I can't say if he thinks you got it or not 'cause I'm not in his head, but Tara is a woman who does without question. You might be a lil' too fragile for this kinda thing here, lil' mama. I know that's one thing O believes about ya."

Oh. I get it. Fragile, like not tough enough to handle this wild lifestyle.

Eddie puts out his cigarette, casually flicking it to the ground. Standing up, he extends his hand for me to grab. "O is young, but he's got wisdom. I can see him waking up. He just a lil' torn between love and business, baby."

"What do you mean?" I ask as I take his hand, letting him pull me up.

"He's not gonna stick around with her much longer. O plans before he acts, and he's been cookin' up some changes. I won't knock Miss Tara's hustle, but... I'm rootin' for you and O."

I shoot Eddie a smile, but beneath it, there's a lingering sadness. Despite feeling like I'm kept in the shadows when it comes to Omar and his true feelings, I appreciate Eddie sharing why Omar's been acting so strange about this whole situation. But even if Omar isn't feeling Tara anymore, it doesn't justify how quickly things escalated between us—no matter if she wronged him or not.

"I feel like shit for messing with him, and she's supposed to be my friend."

Eddie arches a brow and glances over as we stroll down the sidewalk toward his car. "Love doesn't always play by the rules, Miss Chevy. Y'all are still young, figuring out what you want. You really don't know if somebody is your person until you meet your person, you feel me?"

I let out a sigh, nodding in understanding. "Even if he does break things off with Tara, it would be messed up if I kept seeing him. That would be so wrong. So, I hope that's not his plan. I won't go for it."

"You sure about that?"

I cross my arms, keeping my thoughts to myself. I'm not sure, but I also have morals.

"None of us got where we wanted by givin' up what we want. Not one of us. And O is a master at gettin' *everything* he wants," Eddie opens the passenger door for me, and I slowly hop in.

What's his angle? I don't want to be labeled as some man-stealer. And even if I like him, I don't need Omar, his lifestyle, or his money.

Maybe Omar just needs to be single and find himself, just like I was trying to do before I got caught up in this mess. If he's worried about having a street-smart woman by his side because that's the standard in that world, then I don't want any part of it.

I'm too *fragile* anyway.

———— ♡ ————

Work is dragging tonight. I can't tell if it's just me feeling this way or if I'm just getting fed up with the whole dancing scene right now. Probably just saying that because

Randall's managed to tick me off again, but I try not to let him get under my skin too much. He's annoyed because I didn't show up last night, but honestly, who cares?

Omar called me before my shift, offering me a ride home later, but I brushed him off, saying I had it covered. Truth is, I wouldn't mind the walk back home. Gives me some time to clear my head.

In the dressing room, a few of the girls are whispering and shooting looks my way. "Got somethin' to say?" I shoot back at them. *Silence.* They roll their eyes and skedaddle. "That's what I thought."

I wish Sheila and I had the same shift tonight. She'd be good company right about now. Well, maybe not, because she'd just want to chat about Omar and encourage my questionable choices, which is probably what those girls were gossiping about now that I think about it. Okay, maybe I'm being paranoid, because how would they know?

Why's everything gotta revolve around that man? Glancing up at the clock, it's almost time to punch out. I've already handed my earnings to Randall, no longer needing to skim a dime, so I figure I'll leave a bit early tonight.

I've only walked home from work a few times before, during daytime shifts, so it wasn't as dark as it is now, but still, it didn't feel unsafe. And it doesn't feel unsafe now either. It's peaceful, just chilly at this time of night. Although, these chunky heels I'm wearing might make people mistake me for a streetwalker.

Now that I think about it, I should have changed shoes in case I need to bolt it for any reason. I won't jinx myself, though. Daddy always warned me about wishful thinking.

I'm a few miles from my place when I spot Omar's car parked outside a bar. I can pick his ride out from a lineup, because there ain't many that shine like his does. But the timing seems too good to be true. *Maybe I accidentally wished to see him since I couldn't get him out of my head?* Anyway, being the nosy chick I am, I saunter toward the bar to see what's happening. He's probably out with his crew. I have no plans to make my presence known, though.

The bar's windows are plastered with posters and unfolded newspapers, so I keep on moving until I catch muffled screams coming from a garage right behind the joint. I see lights and windows and decide to peek in. Even with these heels, I gotta stand on my tippy toes to get a good look.

I see two dudes on their knees, tied up with black bags over their heads. They're squirming, and I can hear them yelling or something, but there's probably something covering their mouths too. Omar's crew surrounds them, and I watch as they all turn to their left while Omar picks up a gun from the table and walks over to the guys. Eddie's right behind him.

"Only one of you is gonna make it out of here alive tonight. I expect whoever it is to take this message back to whoever's in charge. It won't be looking too good for the other one though."

I watch as Omar passes Eddie a glass filled with amber liquor, then raises the gun toward one of the men's heads.

Oh my God... My heart races, but I can't tear my eyes away. I just hope I don't witness anything crazy tonight, so I'll carry on about my business. But before I can back away, Omar fires a shot into the guy's head, and I scream as I see blood hit the pillar, and the guy crumples over, lifeless. Everyone, and I mean everyone, turns towards the window, so I sprint away as fast as my legs can carry me, almost forgetting I'm wearing heels.

I hear a door open and footsteps pounding behind me. I'm scared out of my mind, but I don't stop running. I must have spoken this mess into existence.

"Aye, homegirl! Get your ass back here!" one guy calls out. I recognize his voice - he's one of Omar's close friends, seen him around Omar a lot, but his name escapes me.

I can't tell if I'm flying or what, but I feel the adrenaline pumping through me. I spot a convenience store a block away and plan to run in, hoping whoever's inside will help me escape these people.

I really witnessed him kill somebody... Has Tara ever seen anything like this? Maybe that's why she isn't always around him? Or maybe she has, and it doesn't faze her. Either way, I'm beyond bothered.

I reach the sidewalk right in front when Omar's El Camino speeds up and screeches to a stop, cutting me off from reaching the store. Omar and Eddie hop out and start coming toward me. Luckily, my ankles are real strong, and I manage to cut to the right and run up the hilly street. I used to play basketball at the park with the neighborhood kids growing up and was known for breaking ankles. Yep, me, the petite black girl with the bony arms and legs used to give all those kids a run for their money.

It's dark around here, and I can feel my body slowing down, even though I don't want it to. My heart's pounding like crazy as the running footsteps catch up to me. My last resort is to fight, and I don't want to waste all my energy by running, so I fumble for my keys. It hits me—I must've dropped my bag when I took off, so it's just me, my fists, and maybe my heels.

With tears streaming down my face, I turn to face the danger, ready to fight. I reach down, yank off a shoe, tearing the strap that held it to my ankle, and swing it around since my vision is blurry from the tears.

"Miss Chevy. It's Eddie. We ain't gonna hurt you, pretty lady, but you gotta relax and let us talk to you."

I hear Eddie, but I don't give a damn and keep swinging my shoe to keep some distance.

"All of you step the *fuck* off from around me! Or I'm gonna mess you up!" I shout at them.

But then, like a fool, I stumble over a raised piece of sidewalk as I back away, losing my footing and crashing to the ground with a thud. Before I can react, someone snatches my shoe away, and another hand clamps over my mouth, muffling my scream.

Eddie and another guy pick me up and carry me back downhill. I'm bawling my eyes out, thinking about how I shouldn't have been so bold to walk home alone at this time of night. *What made you think you were invincible, girl?*

Omar is posted by his car, waiting, as the guys put me inside. I try to kick, but my legs are pinned down, and Omar gets in the back seat with me.

"Eddie, roll us over to the family spot since it's close," Omar finally says, holding me down.

"You got it, O," Eddie responds, his voice calm.

"Baby girl... take it easy," he whispers to me, his hand gently moving over my trembling body. "Why you out here all alone? You coulda called me, I woulda picked you up."

I can't respond. My body must be in shock because not a single part of it will budge. *Is this even real?*

———— ♥ ————

Still trembling, I watch Omar and Eddie share a joint during their hushed conversation. Each moment feels haunted by the image of the man falling to Omar's gunshot. He doesn't show any sign of remorse, confirming my suspicion that he's done this before. It's insane.

"So... you be killin' people?" I mutter, the words slipping out unplanned. I hadn't meant to say anything to him.

Omar glances over at me, then back at Eddie. Eddie hands him the joint he rolled and gets up to leave.

"I hope you can calm yourself enough to listen to what O gotta say, Miss Chevy. Remember what we talked about earlier? Ain't none of us perfect," Eddie says, squeezing my shoulder before closing the door behind him. *Damn.* He left us alone.

I hear a lighter flick a few times and look up to see Omar lighting up. He rises and crouches down in front of me, offering the joint to my lips.

"Here... smoke this. It'll help you relax," he says.

I shake my head and purse my lips tightly. He persists, holding it to my mouth for a while before flicking off some ashes and offering it again. He's patient, I'll give him that.

"I did what I had to do to protect myself and my people. Those fools were sent to cause trouble. We caught up with them and handled it," he explains, taking a drag and extending the joint to me once more.

"I know that scared you, and I ain't mean for you to see me like that, baby girl," Omar adds, gently lifting my chin with his other hand.

I know I must look like a complete mess with mascara streaks running down my face from the tears. God knows how my hair must look. All I'm certain of is that I'm only wearing one shoe.

"I just want to go home. Please, take me home," I eventually plead.

"... I want you here with me. I need to make sure you're okay," he insists, shaking his head and taking another drag.

"I understand. You had to do what you did to survive. I won't rat you out, Omar. You can let me go."

"Ion' want you to leave."

I glance at the joint he's holding, and he notices, offering it back to my lips. I give in and take a drag, but I must have taken too much because I immediately start coughing. It earns a chuckle from Omar, who pats my back.

"Yeah... I gotta teach you how to do this," he remarks with a grin.

"No..." I manage to say between coughs. "I don't want any more."

"Try one more time but take it slow. Relax and inhale."

With some hesitation, I bring the joint to my lips once more and take a cautious puff. I do what I think is right—inhale and blow it out.

"There you go, baby girl. You got it."

I squint my eyes at him through the smoke. "You're still a murderer."

"I'm a survivor. Always been one, and I'll do whatever it takes to protect mine. Whatever the hell it takes. Whether that means putting bullets in people or greasing palms with cops. When you passionate enough, you can accomplish things you didn't think you could." Omar flicks the ashes and holds the joint back up to my lips.

"How can you be passionate about drugs?" I continue to narrow my eyes and take another hit or two as he chuckles.

"I'm passionate about building my empire. And like I said, I'll do whatever it takes."

"Even killing people but doing it like they do in the movies. On their knees and all. Who do you think you are?"

Omar shrugs. "I'm sorry you had to see that, baby girl. I was sending a message. You don't need to know none of that, though."

"Am I high?" I lean forward and ask him.

"Probably gettin' there. I can tell you've never done this before." He takes the joint from me and stands up. "I'ma get you somethin' to snack on. You probably hungry. Then we can shower up and get you cleaned up."

"Go shower with your *girlfriend*."

Omar halts in his tracks and pivots back toward me. I keep my gaze fixed on the ground.

"I don't got a girlfriend. Not anymore," he announces abruptly.

Well, that was unexpected. "Huh?"

"Yeah, you heard me," he confirms.

I can't help but feel a twinge of irritation. I feel bad for Tara, and I hope it's not because of me, but because he realized staying in a relationship they both didn't want was unhealthy.

"Okay. Well, good for her, I guess. She doesn't need this kind of stress anyway. When did this happen?" I ask.

"After I dropped you off."

"How did she take it?"

"Not too well. But Ima let her be with who she wanna be with. Who am I to get in the way of her and your boss?"

I frown at Omar. So, he heard the conversation with Sheila earlier, unless he already knew.

"I guess it's true what they say, you can't help who you love. Maybe that's why they can't leave each other alone," I comment.

"I can agree with that." He opens the door. "You run fast as hell, baby girl. That had me crackin' up."

"Well, y'all were chasing me. And then you really blew the guy's head off like it was nothing," I remark, feeling fantastic from this stuff I smoked. *Is this the same stuff I put in the brownies?* No wonder we get a lot of sales and repeat customers.

"I'll be right back, though. Don't go anywhere," he instructs.

He's so demanding, and strangely, I like it. Not being bossed around like a child, but the way he does it makes me not feel like one. I'm still stuck at the thought that he ended things with Tara so quickly. I'm so curious about how that conversation went and if she admitted to still seeing Randall. Why would she get into a relationship with Omar in the first place if she knew she wasn't going to leave Randall alone? And then get mad when Randall moves on, like she wasn't throwing her whole fake relationship in his face to hurt him back? The concept of revenge is wild to me, but the best thing anybody can do is just save their energy and move on. Then again, I've never really been in a situation that would warrant the act but I hope to never be put in that position.

I glance down at the joint burning away in the ash tray and stare at it for a moment. This thing has my mind racing. *Damn*, where did he get this stuff from? I wonder if it's from his hometown. I'd like to visit there one day.

After a few more hits, I cough again, nearly hacking up my lungs. I snub the joint out and push it away from me. No more of that. It did its job. I'm relaxed now.

I sprawl out on the bed, gazing up at the popcorn ceiling while rubbing my belly. Omar was spot-on; I am starving. I hope he brings back something satisfying and delicious, or else I might just ask him to take me home so I can whip up something myself. But deep down, I know he won't take me home without a fight and I don't have the energy.

I mull over what Eddie mentioned earlier about going after what we want. Then there's Omar and his whole "passion" spiel. They're kind of right. Life doesn't often favor those like me, who are too kind, unfortunately. Or maybe that's just my mindset because of the people I'm surrounded by—Omar, Randall, Tara—they navigate life as takers, hustlers, and it seems to work for them. At least, that's how it looks.

Before I met them, I was struggling, always trying to do the right thing, working low-paying jobs, dealing with my grumpy dad, and taking care of him while he was sick. But look at me now. I have no worries in the world because my bills are covered. I'm even considering quitting my job and working for Omar full-time. I know money doesn't buy happiness, but it sure does pay off worry, and right now, I don't have much to really worry about, I won't lie.

Omar returns upstairs with a bowl of potato chips, another bowl of buttery popcorn, some licorice, brown liquor, and two cans of Coke. I sit up eagerly, drooling over the snacks, and snatch a handful of popcorn to munch on before he can even set everything down.

"You too cute, Miss Chevy," he chuckles, wiping butter from my chin.

"Thanks..." I manage to mumble with my mouth full.

I'm stuffed to the brim after chowing every single snack he brought up. I don't think he got much of it, but he doesn't seem annoyed that I didn't share, more amused.

"What are you looking at?" I question, chugging back the Coke. I turned away that liquor he brought up because I'm already high. I don't need to be drunk too.

"Just wanna know what's on your mind?" He must know I was lost in my thoughts again. We have that in common.

"*Mm*... I was just thinking about how my daddy died lonely, sick, angry, and broke. It makes me sad 'cause he worked his ass off all his life and had to get through my mama leaving us and raising me all by himself. And that's how life repaid him..." I don't want to cry, but I feel myself choking up.

"Your pops walked so you could run, baby girl." Omar reaches over and wipes a tear struggling its way down my cheek. "You in control of your life. You real young too. Got a good head on your shoulders. You got time. You can have whatever you want."

I shake my head. "Why do we gotta do bad shit to be happy though? Like... I'm happy my bills are paid down, but it took me doing something I said I would never do. Why does it seem like life never works out for people like me and my daddy?"

"Ion' know. I just think sometimes, the reward is worth the risk," Omar says. "Why repeat that kinda miserable cycle when you got the means to escape it, feel me? The means don't gotta last forever, it can just serve as the way out, if you want it to."

Eddie was right about this man. He seems wise, and he seems really confident that what he says is true. I like this side of him.

"Yeah, I guess that makes sense 'cause I didn't stop worrying until I took the risk of selling drugs for you. It's not like I have to do it forever."

I don't know why he keeps laughing at me. Maybe I sound stupid.

Omar casually traces his chin with his fingers before responding, "I'm glad you understand what I'm saying, baby girl. But taking risks can apply to anything, not just drugs."

"Yeah, right. 'Cause if I stop pushing your stuff, you're gonna handle me like you did that poor man back there."

"I'm not gonna hurt you. You do what you want. I'm glad I could help if I did. Just know the job is yours if you want it," he shrugs.

I'm not so high that I can't see through his game. I understand he doesn't want me to walk away, and he made it clear. He's talking about tonight, but it's also a subtle plea for me not to leave altogether. He doesn't want me to.

"What happened between you and Tara? Was it because of what Sheila and I said?" I press, my tone firm.

Omar pauses, reaching for his can of Coke and offering it to me. "You want this second can?"

"I want you to answer my question. Why do you always dodge the Tara talk? Feeling guilty?" My frustration seeps into my words.

"I don't feel guilty about shit, and I don't regret a damn thing," he replies, taking a sip of the soda. "And neither should you."

"Well, I do. I called her my friend, and I did this behind her back. We're both in the wrong. At least I'm owning up to it."

Omar's gaze sharpens, and a chill runs down my spine.

"If you didn't wanna do it, you ain't have to. Just be honest. If you really cared, you wouldn't have gone through with it," he states bluntly.

"That's why I feel bad, though."

"Your face lit up when I told you we're not together anymore. Just like it did when you saw I made you a bath. Just like it did when you confessed to your lil girlfriend earlier that you were into me. You bring up Tara 'cause you feel guilty for bein' happy, not because you care about her feelings. Let's keep it real, baby girl."

He's right, but I don't want to hear it. What we did was wrong, and here I am still sitting in his face instead of checking on Tara. I do care about her feelings. She's probably blown up my phone and pager too. Damn. *Where's my bag?*

Omar waves his hand in front of my face. I must have spaced out again, but I snap back to reality.

"Okay, so you don't regret sleeping with me?" I ask him.

"No."

"Why didn't you break up with her before cheating on her, Omar? I don't understand that."

"I never said I wasn't feelin' Tara. If I ain't wanna be with her, then I wouldn't have been."

My heart drops. So maybe he loves her. Or did. Omar looks over and watches my face.

"Shower... Let's get to it."

I look at his hand, then back up at him. If I go to this shower with this man, I know damn well what's gonna happen. *And he's single now?* ... I need to be thinking about how I saw him kill that man. I cannot just let that shit go. That still has me spooked, no matter how high I feel.

I slap his hand away and meet his eyes. He frowns slightly while shooting me a confused glance.

"I said no more. I'm showering by myself. Move." I hop up and grab the towel on the bed. As I leave the room and head for the bathroom, I glance back to see him in his thoughts again, eyes still on me while rubbing his lip.

I hope his wise ass is feeling stupid.

CHAPTER 7
Half Truths

TARA'S EYES ARE LIKE dark shadows. They're all red and watery from crying so much. And I can't help but join in with her tears. It sucks seeing her like this, and the whole situation is just plain sad. She's been gripping my hand like her lifeline ever since I walked into the hospital and parked myself next to her bed. We've been sitting in this room for a while now, in silence, after finding out she's no longer expecting.

It's been a week since I last talked to Omar, the same week I watched him off someone. He also dumped Tara during that time. Eddie told me Omar was out of town on some "business" when I asked about him, but I'm not too happy that he's not here for Tara.

Tara turns to me, still holding onto my hand. "What's going on in that head of yours?"

"Thinkin' about you," I say. "I'm sorry about all this. I can't even imagine what you're going through."

"It's not the physical pain that's killin' me, it's my heart," she says, tears streaming down her face and soaking into her pillow.

"Are you ready to talk about what happened, Tara?" I brace myself for the inevitable question, "Did he hurt you again?"

I knew Omar wasn't thrilled about the pregnancy, and he refused to accept that he could be the father. It wouldn't surprise me if all of that resentment finally boiled over.

Tara shakes her head. "No, he ain't do nothing wrong. It's all on me."

"What happened?"

"I decided to get rid of it, Chevy. I just couldn't go through with it... Not knowing was killin' me."

"You had an abortion?" I ask.

"Yeah."

Silence fills the room again, and I'm at a loss for words.

"Oh, Tara... I don't know what to say."

"You don't have to say anything, Chevy. I know. I messed up. I lost him because of this. And if that baby looked anything like Randall... I don't know what I would've done."

"What do you mean? It's still your baby, no matter who the dad is."

Tears keep falling, but she doesn't acknowledge my words. Instead, she asks, "Do you think he'll take me back?"

"Who? Omar?"

"Yeah. We don't have to worry about 'what ifs' anymore. We could start over, him and me."

Even if I hadn't crossed that line with Omar, I'd never encourage that mess to continue. I'm thinking that may be another reason she didn't keep the baby, hoping to change Omar's mind. but I'll try not to pass judgement. I don't know how that feels and would never want to know. "Doesn't matter, Tara. Look where you are, and neither of them are in this room with you."

She rolls her eyes and turns away, facing the ceiling again. "Can you just try calling him again for me?"

"Yeah, I can if you want. But I don't know what else I can do for you right now."

"You're here. That's all that matters."

I start to get up to find the phone, but she stops me. "Never mind, don't call him again. He got the message. Omar moves when he wants to."

I sit back down, still unsure of what to do for her. It seems like she has a lot she wants to get off her chest, and I'm here to listen. It's the least I can do.

She goes on a rant. "I'm so pissed about how this turned out. What really gets me is Sheila actin' all *buddy-buddy* with me but plottin' on Randall. She never listened to you or me when we told her what kind of loser Randall was. Lil' hoochie. I don't want him no more, but damn, don't act all friendly if you want my ex. Bitches kill me."

I try to swallow, but it gets stuck, causing me to start coughing. Tara looks over and hands me her cup of water.

"You okay, Chevy?" she asks as I take a sip.

"Yeah, I'm listening. Sorry about that."

"When Omar started actin' like he ain't care anymore, I knew I was losing him. I asked him if we could try again, and he just shook his head and looked me in the eye when he did it. It messed me up, Chevy. I really loved that man. It was the best five months of my life."

"I'm sorry, Tara. Did he say he'd still help you if the baby was his?"

"He didn't say anything, but I knew he wouldn't. Now that I think about it, I think he's seein' someone else. That was the last thing I asked him before he left my place. He didn't admit to anything, but I'm not dumb. I knew what I was getting into with him. Women are always throwin' themselves at him."

I realize I need to come clean with her, right now. It doesn't sit right with me that I'm here, comforting her, and not owning up to being involved with Omar.

"Okay, Tara..." I start, hesitating to find the right words. "I need to tell you something—"

"Hey, Tara," Omar interrupts me. *Figures.*

We both look at him standing in the doorway. He strolls in, making eye contact with me. *How long was he standing there? And why didn't he let me finish?*

I sit back and pout as I watch him lean in to kiss Tara's forehead, ignoring me completely. I've been ignoring him too. All of his calls. All week. And I plan to keep doing that.

"What happened?" he asks.

"I lost the baby. The doctor said it might've been from stress," Tara tells him, wiping her tears.

I thought she said she ended it. Now it's a miscarriage?

Yeah, I can't do this shit anymore.

I get up, grab my purse, and head for the door. "I'm gonna leave you two alone. I'm sorry, again."

"Thanks for being here, Chevy. Love you," Tara says weakly.

"Feel better, Tara."

Omar looks like he wants to say something, but he stays silent. I roll my eyes and leave.

It sickens me that Tara's lying to him about ending the pregnancy. And it makes me sick that me and Omar are still lying to her.

———— ❧ ————

I'm standing in this sketchy used-car lot, more like someone's messy backyard than a real dealership. But hey, my coworker told me her cousin sells cars here, and she got hers from this place. So here I am, listening to the salesman jabber on about their selection. I can't help but glance across the street at the fancier dealership. Their cars are way nicer, but they're out of my league. I shake off the temptation and focus on these beat-up cars on this lot.

Finally getting a car feels like a relief. It's crazy I've gone this long without one, especially with my late-night shifts. The salesman hands me a pen.

"Alright, Miss Bleu, just sign right here on the dotted line, and I'll hand your keys over."

I scribble my signature and practically snatch the keys. I'm grinning ear to ear, clutching them to my chest.

"Thanks, sir. Appreciate all your help."

"You're welcome, Miss Bleu. I suggest you get licensed soon, though. But that can be our little secret." He winks and shuffles the papers.

Okay, so I slipped him some extra cash to let me walk out of there with a car and no license. I don't really know about the laws and stuff, but it's true what they say—money talks. It's opening doors for me, getting me things I never thought I could have.

I slide into my cute little Toyota and grip the steering wheel. The car kicks off kind of rough when I turn the key, but this baby is gonna take me places.

I have to admit, my driving skills aren't the best. I know the basics, though. Daddy used to toss me his keys and send me to the store, which was just a few blocks away from our place. Oddly enough, he never actually sat with me in the car to teach me the ropes. I had to figure it out on my own.

I'm cruising down the road, enjoying some tunes, when I notice a cop tailing me. *Great.* I pull over, turn off the engine, and after rolling down my window, I lean back in my seat, bracing for the cop's approach.

"License and registration, please," the cop says, leaning in as I drum my fingers on the steering wheel.

His coffee breath hits me, and it's a struggle not to gag.

"Um, I'm kinda on the other side of town from my place and left my stuff there. Sorry, officer." I know I can't lie, but maybe a little understanding might help.

"You're driving without a license on hand?"

"Mhm, yeah. Just left the dealership and—"

"How'd you get a car without your license? Did you have a licensed driver with you?" The cop interrupts.

"Um, no, they said it was okay to do that," I mumble.

He stands up firmly and steps back to look at the car. "Sit right there."

I glance in the rearview mirror and see him getting back into his cop car. Panic sets in—I may have to come clean with this guy. But that means admitting to the drug money I handed over to that salesman. And that's not an option.

I could maybe play it off, say it's money I saved up from tips and maybe give him a lap dance. Or set up something for him and his boys at the club.

The officer returns to my car, cautious with his hand near his holster. "I need you to step out of the vehicle slowly. Now," he instructs, signaling for traffic to go around us.

I step out, trembling with nerves. This is my first run-in with the law, and I'm hoping the officer will let me off with a warning or something.

"You're driving a stolen vehicle, are you aware of that?" he accuses.

"Huh? Officer, I just bought this car from a guy named Fred up the street. He's got a car lot and sells to people. It can't be stolen. I've got the papers right here in my car," I explain, gesturing toward it.

He doesn't seem interested in my side of the story, and I can't blame him—I don't even have my license. Before I know it, I'm at the police station, waiting to make my phone call. I wonder if that salesman is in trouble. He really should've known better than to sell me a stolen car like that.

———— ♡ ————

Tara showed up to pick me up, and I hadn't seen her since we left her and Omar in the hospital room last week. Surprisingly, there's no trace of sadness on her face. Instead, she keeps chuckling every time I glance her way.

"Sorry, Chevy, but I've never heard of someone losing their car as soon as they drive off the lot," she says between laughs. I don't see the humor in it. I was genuinely hyped about that car and about the fact I got it for myself.

"Yeah, well, turns out they pulled me over for driving too slow. I didn't even know the car was stolen. I was just caught up in the moment."

"Well, at least they only got you for driving without a license," she says, sounding cheerful. I wonder how things went down between her and Omar.

"So, what's the deal with you and Omar?"

Her smile disappears instantly, replaced by a look like she's seen a ghost. *Oops,* spoke too soon.

"He handled the whole pregnancy thing really well. I'm glad he was there to support."

"Tara, why did you tell him you lost the baby? Why not just tell him the truth?"

"The truth isn't always necessary, Chevy. I told him what he needed to know—that I'm not pregnant anymore. How it happened doesn't matter."

I turn away and sigh out. I can see her getting worked up a bit, so I'm letting it go for the sake of us not ending up in a ditch somewhere and back in that hospital room. "I'm sorry for intruding on your business like that. I was just curious."

"I know you noticed. I can tell you the truth 'cause I know you won't go run your mouth like Sheila would."

I drop my head. "Are you both working on things again?"

"We are just gonna do our own thing. We talked some stuff out and was honest with each other. After I apologized about Randall, he admitted that he was datin' somebody else too. Like I said before, I'm not surprised about that. I just don't know how to feel about that but I'm really not in a position to feel any kinda way, after what I did. I got too comfortable."

Oh no. I don't know how I feel to Omar only admitting half the truth. At least he was honest with her. Part of me feels like I owe Tara the other half of that truth. I'm debating opening my mouth about my truth. I don't want to put more on her right now than she can handle, and maybe that's why Omar stopped me from speaking up. I'm torn, though.

She continues. "But he said we ain't have to end on bad terms or nothin', which is cool 'cause our last fight was crazy, and we are better than that. I am happy that he still wants to do business with me. Maybe one day we'll make it work."

"Well, I'm glad y'all still cool. You still gonna be helping him out?"

"Yeah. We still got business to take care of together, but I miss dancing too, so I was gonna talk to Randall about letting me back on."

"Tara... if you wanna get back with Omar, don't you think you should just apply somewhere else?" She is confusing me.

"Girl, I know Randall will give me my position and pay back. I'm still single, so if Omar wants me, he's gonna have to come get me. I'm doin' what I wanna do."

Wow. The way she thinks never fails to amaze me. She's very dumb to do that if she wants him back, so maybe she truly doesn't want him back. I wouldn't dare go back to working for my ex if he's the reason for the breakup, especially if I want to get back with a man like Omar. But then again, he cheated on her too, with *her friend*.

I shake off my thoughts as we pull up to my place. Tara reaches over and smacks my ass as I get out.

"Besides, I miss working with Big Booty Chevy."

"Oh, miss you too, girl."

My attitude is still pretty messed up from losing all that money I had saved up, and still don't even have a car, then ended being laughed at in my face.

I wave to her as she drives off, but instead of going home, I march toward the family house. I may as well go make that money back.

———— ❧ ————

Eddie's in the kitchen as I stroll in. His face lights up, and he stretches his arms out for a hug the moment he spots me.

"Miss Chevy, we missed you. How you been?" he greets me warmly.

"Hey, Eddie, missed you too. And obviously not too great if I'm back here," I grumble, returning the hug and dropping my bag to wash my hands.

"O is gonna be happy to know you back."

"I don't care about him. I'm using him and his drug business to make my money back."

"What's eating at you, young lady?" Eddie asks, concern flickering in his eyes.

I take a deep breath before responding. "Got a car today. Lost it because turns out I bought a stolen whip. Ended up back where I started, laughed at, and hassled by those stank breath cops. Feels like there's always something going wrong in my life, like I can't catch a damn break. Then there's people like Tara, lying through their teeth but getting everything handed to them on a silver platter. I care about my friend, but I just can't wrap my head around that."

"I feel you on that, Miss Chevy. Seems like the worst folks always luck out, you know? When you feelin' up to it one day, I'll share my theory on why that happens."

I'll definitely take him up on that offer because I need some clarity before I go off the rails. "Alright, I'll be looking forward to hearing your take."

Eddie pulls me into another tight hug. "I'm real sorry about your car, though. How you end up over here?"

"I just walked to blow off some steam. I don't live too far from here," I explain.

"You know you can always call me if you need anything," Eddie says, smiling warmly as he gives me a reassuring pat on the back. He's such a kind soul.

"Thanks, Eddie. I'll remember that."

"But are you sure that's all you upset about?" he asks, raising an eyebrow as he faces me.

"Um, yeah, I think so. Why do you ask?"

"No reason," Eddie replies casually, taking the bag of flour from my hands. "O's upstairs."

Oh. I hadn't noticed Omar's car, so that catches me off guard.

"You should go talk to him, tell him what's goin' on. I'm sure he will help you. He misses you, Miss Chevy," Eddie suggests.

"I'm not sure about that, Eddie. I'm not askin' for any handouts. If I'm doing anything illegal, it's because I'm doing it on my own terms. I don't like people holding things over me. It's a big pet peeve of mine."

"I get that, but go up there and at least show your face," Eddie insists.

I think I like Eddie because he reminds me of the dad that I kind of wanted my own to be. I miss my daddy though.

I sigh, dragging my feet up the steps. I'm not exactly thrilled about talking to Omar. Especially since we haven't exchanged a word since the night I found out he's got a murder streak. But it would be downright rude to be in his house without at least acknowledging him. After all, he's the reason I was able to save up for my car in the first place.

I knock on the master bedroom door, and I'm welcomed inside. Omar stands by the window, a glass of one of those dark liquors they all seem to favor in his hand. He turns around, but his expression remains unchanged. Maybe he's not as pleased to see me as Eddie thought. I close the door behind me and take a step forward.

"I'm just comin' up here to say hello 'cause it would be rude to be all in your place and not say anything. I didn't know you were here anyway."

He's about to take a sip, then stops.

"Eddie made you do it, huh?" he asks.

"And if he did?"

Omar shakes his head and proceeds to taste his drink. "Nasty attitude you got."

"Well, whatever. I'm here to get my money back. I shouldn't have to march up here and greet you every time. I know that's how your crew operates, but I'm not one of them. Well... after today, I won't be. But that's not the point."

"You ain't need to march up here and do nothin'. I saw your lil' mad ass stroll into the house. If I felt like talking to you, I woulda come down when you walked in," Omar says. Alright, so he's upset with me too, and that's fine.

"Anyway, bye," I mutter, turning around as he puts his glass down.

"Why you here if you don't wanna be here? Ain't nobody holding a damn gun to your head," he spits out, and I turn back around.

"Oh, you mean like you didn't hold a gun to my head and force me to work for you, Omar?" I retort.

"I'm talkin' about today. Right now. You here 'cause you wanna be, baby."

"Whatever. I'm here 'cause I need to make my money back. Like I said," I reply, my frustration building.

His head shakes are starting to get on my nerves. "You must not know how to manage your money. Where'd it all go?"

"I can manage my money. There are just snakes out here getting away with shit, robbing people like me, all for the damn money. But don't worry about me."

"Calm down. Tell me what happened," he says, moving in closer. For a moment, he seems genuinely concerned. But I'm not falling for it.

"I got a car today, and it got snatched away from me today. That's all I wanna say about it. Back up," I tell him, throwing my hand up in his direction.

"Well...sorry to hear that," Omar responds, returning to his spot to pick up his glass for another sip. This time, he adds a shrug.

I hang for a moment, waiting to see if he's got anything else to add, but nope. He just continues like I'm some invisible presence in the room with him. Eddie fed me some lines; Omar clearly doesn't give a damn about me.

"Alright then, bye," I mutter under my breath. *What an asshole.*

"How you mad at me? You wanted me to tell you I got you? What happened to you wantin' to do things on your own? Now, it's a problem when I don't offer my help. Make up your mind."

I spin around. "I don't need your help! If I did, I would have asked!"

He chuckles and tosses back the last of his drink. "A'ight."

Here it comes. I just can't help myself.

"You know what? I'm glad Tara is going back to workin' for Randall. I'm glad y'all are not together, 'cause she deserves better. While she was carrying that baby, you were busy fuckin' on me!"

He shrugs, as cool as a cucumber. "Wasn't mine. And I like you."

"Wow, Omar. So, why did you stop me from telling her the truth?" I demand, frustration bubbling up.

"Is that what you're mad about?"

"Answer me!"

"That ain't the time to drop no shit like that, that's why. You wasn't thinkin'," he explains.

"I was thinking. I was thinking about what a lousy friend I am for crying with her, knowing what I did behind her back!"

"Aye, don't nobody need to hear shit like that when they already down. She just lost a baby, regardless," he reasons.

"Mhm."

He squints at me. "Right?"

"Yeah, Omar. That's between y'all, though," I respond, breaking eye contact so he doesn't catch on that I'm covering for Tara. I don't believe it's my place to spill anything like that to him.

I glance up, and he's still staring me down. *Oh God.*

"Anyway, I'm not happy with you right now, so don't keep calling me 'cause I will continue to ignore it," I assert.

"A'ight."

"You don't care, got it," I add with a tinge of frustration.

"Ion' know what you want from me. If you wanna go tell your homegirl the truth, go do what you gotta do. I already told you Ion' regret shit. But you not finna keep comin' at me and think I'm finna keep taking that shit. And you ain't even my bitch. You gotta be crazy."

He scoffs as he slips on his shoes, then his watch.

"Yeah, you're absolutely right. I'm not your *bitch*. And I don't wanna be. I'm too *fragile* for you, anyway."

Omar twists his face when he looks back in my direction.

"Fragile?"

"Yeah, that's right. I heard about what you think about women like me. That's why you chase after women like Tara. She's not fragile, right? I'm just here for a good time. Those kinda bitches get the long time."

Silence hangs thick in the air for a moment.

"Where is this shit comin' from, baby girl?" he asks, breaking the quiet.

"Stop calling me your baby girl!"

He shakes his head and turns back to the window. "So... what's the point in all of this? You just came over here to scream up in my damn face for what? You need some money? That's all you gotta say, baby."

As Omar reaches into his pockets, I march up and stand right in his face. "I don't wanna see or talk to you again. That's what I want. That's what I came here to say."

"That's how you feel?"

"That's how I feel."

I bite down on the inside of my cheek, feeling a pang of disappointment in myself for lashing out like this. But it's necessary to make things clear, so we can both move forward. I'm too fragile for him, and it's not just me who knows it—Omar does too.

We stand there, locked in a silent gaze for a moment, before I turn away, hiding the tears that threaten to fall. I'm not sure why I'm so upset.

Or maybe I do. Maybe I want him to just finally be able to read my mind without having to say it.

Without exchanging more words, I slam his door shut and head straight down to grab my bag. I tune out Eddie's attempts to comfort me and offer a ride. It's not fair to him; he didn't do anything wrong. But my attitude is beyond my control right now. I glance back up at the window and catch Omar watching me. Without a word, I turn away and stroll down the street.

CHAPTER 8
Ethereal

I DON'T WANT TO be on stage tonight. I'm just feeling more exposed than I want to right now. I know it's because I'm in my feelings really bad. There's a lot swirling in my mind, from being a bad friend, to being labeled fragile to being kept hidden although I shouldn't really be upset about that. It really hurt my feelings when Omar said what he did, but I know why. I like this man more than I should, and it's good that I made that clear.

Maybe I should apologize. The idea echoes through my mind as I effortlessly swing around the metal bar. I'm glad the club isn't as hype tonight. It's one of our couple's night, so nothing but smooth R&B and some intimate lighting. I find it funny that couples visit strip clubs together. I just never thought that was a thing before I started working here, but it's cute.

We're understaffed tonight, so I'm stuck here longer than usual. And to top it off, Randall's giving me a hard time, even after I told him I didn't want to be up on stage too much tonight. It sucks that he's acting like this. He should be thanking his lucky stars that Omar didn't go all gangster on him for trying to swipe his dope recipes. He should also be grateful he made enough to pay Omar back and keep his business safe. Tara's single now, so you'd think Randall would be feeling good, but nope, he's stuck on being bitter.

In the background, Zapp & Roger's "I Want to Be Your Man" sets the mood as I keep moving on stage. *Love this song...* And thank goodness I wore my new two-piece tonight. The lights are hitting it just right.

Scanning the room through the fog, I spot couples cuddling, lap dances happening, and some folks eyeing me while their dates try to get their attention. I shift to the other side of the pole, humming along.

The VIP section is almost empty, except for a man fixated on the stage. I can only see his silhouette until he leans forward.

"Omar?" I whisper, forgetting to dance.

I wish I hadn't seen him because now I'm too nervous to keep going. Our eyes lock, and I can't tell if he wants me to come over or not, but I need to get off this stage.

Luckily, the next girl's ready to take over as I hop down. I'll probably catch hell from Randall later, if he even bothers to watch the tapes since it's so slow tonight. I make my way over to Omar, his eyes tracking my every move.

"Didn't expect to see you here, watching," I say, trying to sound casual.

"Well, how would you know if I ain't tell you?" He grins, then his expression shifts. "Why you stop dancin'?"

"Uh, I guess I was just done. Wasn't really feeling the stage tonight," I reply, toying with my fishnets.

"Looked like you were feeling it to me. Maybe 'cause you saw me sitting here," Omar says, tilting my chin to face him.

I fidget with my thumbs, scrambling for another excuse, but come up empty. "I'm sorry for acting weird earlier. I was just pissed about other stuff, took it out on you."

He nods, tucking his lips, sitting back, hand in his pocket. I watch him pull out a wad of cash, holding it up to me.

"I can't take that, Omar." I gently push it away.

"You workin', ain't you?"

A smile I try to fight sneaks onto my face, and I use my hand to cover it. I reach my other hand out for the cash, and he sets it in my hand. "Thank you."

"Now, I think you really meant what you said to me earlier. You kinda mean, baby girl." He sits back again, leaving one leg propped out. I wonder if he wants me to sit on him.

"I'm not mean. I was just mad, like I said, and real embarrassed after what happened to me," I explain to him.

"So you got your stuff taken 'cause you were riding around in a stolen car?"

I nod, then glance away. He chuckles a bit, then stops. "That's funny. I'm not laughing at you, just the situation."

"You can laugh. I don't care anymore." I shrug.

Omar reaches out and pulls me onto his lap. Knew it. His scent is getting to me again. I have to squeeze my thighs together.

"I didn't know something as small as 'fragile' would get to you like that. I didn't mean to upset you."

"But you said it? That I'm fragile?"

He doesn't say anything.

"Is that what you call an apology?" I tilt my head slightly, letting him know I'm not feeling it.

"I'm sorry." His lips brush against mine, making me shiver. "You are fragile though."

I push away from Omar and stare into his eyes. "Omar, cut it out. I ain't fragile. Why you keep saying that?"

"To me, you are. It ain't a bad thing, so chill out."

"It is a bad thing. You're calling me weak."

"Nah. We all know you ain't weak. Not after the way you attacked me earlier."

I cover my mouth and giggle a bit. "I didn't attack you, Omar. But I'm not fragile."

"A'ight, I thought of a better word anyway."

"What word?"

"Ethereal..."

"*Ethereal?* What does that mean, boo?"

"It means that you just might be too good for this world, baby. Too delicate. So, you're fragile and need to be handled with care. That's why you met me."

Our eyes lock for another moment. I feel like I'm getting lost in them as his words start to make sense.

"What time you out of here, baby girl?"

"Shoot, now," I respond with no hesitation, making him chuckle. "I can't worry about Randall right now."

We both stand up, and he takes my hand, leading me away from the bustling part of the club so I can grab my stuff. I haven't checked the time yet, but I already know I'm not off duty yet. And when I said I wasn't feeling work tonight, I meant it. Randall isn't going to fire me; I'm one of his best performers anyway.

The hallway is dimly lit and quiet. Our hands remain intertwined as we make our way towards the dressing room. With each step, the sound of my heels clicking on the floor fills the space. Just as we're about to reach the door, it swings open abruptly, and in walks Tara.

Damn.

She freezes on the spot, her eyes darting from me to Omar, then down to our joined hands.

"What the hell is this?" she finally blurts out.

I try to speak, but it's as if the words are trapped in my throat. I steal a quick glance at Omar, who's just standing there, watching Tara with an unreadable expression. Not only is he still holding onto my hand, but he's tightened his grip and subtly moves in front of me.

"Omar! Why the hell are you holding her hand? And where do you think you're going?" Tara's voice rings out, dropping her bag as anger flashes in her eyes.

"Tara... we need to talk," I stammer, feeling overwhelmed. I never wanted her to find out like this. "Just calm down, okay?"

"Are you messin' around with him, Chevy?" Tara's voice grows louder, echoing down the hall.

Omar releases an exasperated sigh and finally lets go of my hand.

"Go get your stuff, baby girl. Tara, don't start with that crazy shit," he says, sounding far too composed.

I inch towards the dressing room as Tara shoots him a furious glare. "Is this the bitch messin' with your head?" she snaps.

Hold on. "Now, wait a minute, Tara. I messed up, but I still care about you, and I always tried my best to protect you, even when I didn't agree with you. I knew this was wrong to keep it from you, and I'm sorry. I never wanted you to find out like this."

"Did you sleep with him while I was with him? While I was *pregnant*, Chevy?" Her yelling seems to draw a crowd, whispers swirling behind us.

"You not explaining shit else right now. Get your stuff. Let's go," Omar repeats, his voice strained.

I watch tears well up in Tara's eyes as she gazes at him in disbelief. My heart sinks. This isn't a good situation, and I'm disappointed in myself for developing feelings for him behind her back. I couldn't help it. I reach for the dressing room door handle, but before I can touch it, Tara charges toward me. I really don't want to get into a fight with her.

Clenching my fists, I drop the cash Omar tipped me, preparing myself to block her punches as she heads straight for my face. Omar steps between us, shielding me. All I see are her arms flailing around him, trying to reach me. She's losing control, swinging wildly, and I dread to think what will happen if she manages to land a hit on either of us because I'll definitely fight back, whether it's right or wrong. But he's doing a good job of keeping her away from me.

"Aye, calm down!" he shouts in her face, still blocking her path to me.

"Get off me! I'm gonna fuck her up!" she screams.

The crowd has doubled in size now. I'm pretty sure everyone in the building is watching us, just waiting for Randall to show up. *Ugh.*

"Tara, I'm sorry, but do you really think throwing hands with me is gonna solve anything? Let's calm down and talk like grown-ass women," I say, hoping she'll consider my suggestion.

"Fuck you, Chevy! I trusted you; you skank ass hoe! I should've known you were gonna open your legs up to him!"

"We not even together anymore and you the one who fucked up that shit for real... so you need to relax," Omar says to her, then glancing back at me and nodding for me to grab my things again. "Hurry up."

Tears sting my eyes as I finally stumble into the dressing room, slamming the door behind me. I collapse to the floor, burying my face in my hands. I can't believe Tara caught us like that. This is not how I wanted her to find out. I knew if things kept going with Omar, I'd have to talk to her eventually, but this is way too soon. Now, I'm not even sure if I want to keep this whole thing going.

And then there's Omar. He's acting all cool, and I can't tell if it's just a front or if he genuinely doesn't care. They haven't been broken up for long, and here I am already tangled up with him.

Hell, I was in bed with him before they even split.

Randall's voice jolts me from my thoughts, and outside, I can hear arguments and banging on the door.

"Chevy! Get your ass out here! You scared or something?" Tara's relentless. She probably won't quit until she gets a piece of me.

I'd say she's out to beat me down, but I won't let it come to that. I'm already embarrassed enough for stealing her man. Why add more shame by letting her rough me up?

I jump up from the floor and head for my locker. The door swings open as I grab my bag, and a few other dancers rush in. No sign of Tara, though.

"Damn, Chevy," Whitley, one of the dancers, chimes in. "I gotta hand it to you. Didn't think you'd be the one serving her karma, but this is juicy."

The girls burst into laughter, and I quickly turn back to wipe my eyes. "Just shut up. You don't know shit, so keep your mouths shut."

The hallway stretches empty as I finally step out, my senses on high alert, fists clenched and ready in case Tara reappears. *Where did everyone vanish to?* They must've cleared out, knowing Randall wouldn't tolerate any drama in his club.

"You ready?" Omar's sudden appearance startles me as he emerges from the lobby.

"Yeah... Where did everyone go?" I ask, moving towards him.

"I flashed my piece, and they scattered like roaches," he chuckles, and I'm annoyed that I can't help but smile back.

"That's not funny, Omar. Did Tara leave too?" I ask, feeling worried.

"Nah. She's in Randy boy's office; he tryna calm her down," Omar replies, taking my bag and draping his arm around my shoulder. "You okay?"

"Not really... She caught us," I choke back tears, remembering Tara's expression in that moment. "She didn't deserve to find out like that."

Omar shrugs, kissing my forehead. "She'll be okay. Tara ain't fragile at all."

I nudge him with my elbow as he chuckles.

"You shouldn't take pleasure in this. She's in pain," I chide gently.

"The pleasure I'm getting is movin' the hell on with my life. Didn't nobody really consider how I felt about all this shit, really. "

I stop and turn to look up at him. "Oh, boo... I'm so sorry. You're right. Are you okay?"

"I'm smooth. That's just how shit goes, baby girl. I'm glad you free from that burden now. She knows, and I couldn't care less. Neither should you, so cut it out with the apologies. It's all in the past."

I exhale deeply and remain silent as he guides me out of the club.

I'm not sure if *ethereal* accurately captures the essence of who I am in this moment. But I do appreciate him handling me with care.

———— ♡ ————

Some days fly by, and I've pretty much been hermitting myself. After Tara blew up that night, Omar dropped me off at home because I wasn't up for talking or doing anything. I even ditched work to avoid the embarrassment. I'm crossing my fingers that by the time I go back, folks will have forgotten the whole mess.

My phone's been blowing up, but I only pick up if it's Omar or Sheila. I make them send me a pager message first. The day after the drama, my phone rang like crazy, four or five times in a row, and each time I answered, the line just went dead. No doubt, that's Tara being weird. Surprisingly, she hasn't shown up at my place yet. Maybe she's lurking outside, waiting for me to step out. But I haven't left my apartment since that day. I'm not too proud to admit; I'm a little jittery that she might be hiding, ready to jump me, so I'm not taking any chances.

Suddenly, there's a knock on my door, and I jump out of my seat, almost falling over. I peek through the peephole before unlocking the door.

"It's me, Chevy," Sheila announces, still knocking.

I open the door a crack and let her in, quickly closing and locking it behind her.

"You can't keep hiding in here forever," she says with a kind smile.

"I know that. I'm here 'cause I'm embarrassed and feeling guilty. I hate that she found out the way she did," I confess, pursing my lips as I guide her to the living room.

As she flops on the couch, Sheila grabs a magazine I'd been flipping through out of boredom. She also spots the trashcan filled with crumpled-up tissues beside the couch.

"Chevy... I don't think you're completely in the wrong, and you shouldn't let Tara make you feel that way. Own up to it. You took her man, but who cares? If he wanted her, he'd be with her, not calling your damn phone," Sheila asserts, her voice firm. "She feels some type of way about me, too, but I don't care. Me and Randall have a good thing going."

"I never wanted to be a homewrecker, Sheila. I've seen what it does to people. It's messed up," I reply, feeling a scratchiness in my throat. I get up from the couch to pour myself a glass of ice water.

"Okay, but you acting like they were married, and you came in as the other woman. They ain't even make it six months. She couldn't stop fucking on Randall but wanted to run back to love up on Omar when Randall got with me. And to top it all off, Tara set you up, even if she didn't mean for you to end up with her man. So what? Maybe he wanted you anyway. Have you talked to him since then?" Sheila questions.

Wow, Sheila.

"Yeah. He called and asked if he could come see me. I said no 'cause I'm not sure if I even like him that much to deal with this mess," I admit.

"You're getting on my nerves, girl. This isn't the Chevonne I'm used to seeing. If I were you, I'd walk my butt out of here and meet up with Tara to settle this once and for all. She's going to have to get over it eventually. And you do like him. Stop fooling yourself," Sheila says, following me into the kitchen and gesturing for me to pour her some water too.

She's right. I do look like a coward hiding out in my apartment. I'm missing out on work and life being cooped up here. I also miss Omar.

"I'll think about it. Have you been at the family house lately?" I ask as I pour her water and return the pitcher to the fridge.

"Not really. I've been hanging out with Randall more, so he doesn't want me over there like before. You know how he feels about Omar and them. Plus, Omar said I can't work under him if I'm messing with Randall like that," she explains.

It makes sense. Those men hate each other.

As I finish my second full glass of water, I feel pressure building in my belly, prompting me to set it down and lean against the counter. My toenails are screaming at me for a redo, and my nails definitely need a fill. I can't believe I've been neglecting myself like this because I can't face up to my actions.

Sheila wraps her arms around my waist and holds me there. "What if you come out with me and Randall tonight? He's taking me to this little secret nightclub he and his friends go to. Are you down?" She looks up at me, resting her chin on top of my chest. "Please, Chevy? I'll stick with you."

I guess I should go. I wonder how Randall would feel about me joining them. If he's still hanging out with Sheila and inviting her to his "secret" spots, then maybe he and Tara aren't as tight as they seem.

"Okay, I'll go," I agree, feeling a sense of reluctance.

Sheila squeals with excitement and bounces on her feet. "Yes! Now, let's find you something sexy to wear," she exclaims, pulling me towards my bedroom.

I'm actually looking forward to getting out and having some fun tonight. It's surprising how I'm taking advice from an eighteen-year-old who hasn't been through much. I guess I'm rubbing off on her, hopefully in a positive way.

——— ♥ ———

I've never heard of this club before. BlueSpace seems like the place to be. I guess it's no surprise I haven't heard of it if it's exclusive to the high rollers. I wonder if Omar knows about it.

The dance floors light up in vibrant blue hues, and the multicolored walls add to the energetic atmosphere. I'm captivated by the industrial-warehouse theme. Sheila keeps tugging at my arm, urging me to keep moving, but I'm too busy taking in the interior of this place. Randall could learn a thing or two from here and step up his club game.

Speaking of Randall, he didn't seem to mind me tagging along. He just wanted to know how I could party but not show up for work. Sheila told him she practically dragged me out, so he dropped the subject. I get the feeling he's pretty high anyway, so he probably doesn't mind much about having two women on his arm.

"Would you ladies like a drink or something?" Randall leans in between me and Sheila to be heard over the music.

It's loud in here, but not loud enough for him to be pounding on my eardrums like that.

"Yeah, babe. Me and Chevy will have those Long Islands," Sheila replies.

I don't mind Long Islands. I just know they can sneak up on you like wine. I hope they don't make mine too strong because I won't be able to finish it. Not all of it.

Randall nods and heads towards the bar, leaving us near the dance floor. Sheila tugs at my arm again, pointing towards the floor. I shake my head. "What about our drinks?"

"Randall will find us. Come on. Let's dance."

I stash my cash in my bra and hit the dance floor with Sheila. The beat is thumping, and even though I don't know the song, I'm feeling it.

Sheila smacks my ass. "Shake that moneymaker, Chevy!"

Well, why not? I carve out some space, put my hands to my knees, and start popping my booty. Cheers erupt around me, and it feels good. And to think, I'm doing this without a drop of alcohol in my system.

"Woo! That's right! Show 'em why Omar chose you, Sista!" Sheila's comment prompts me to playfully shove her.

She laughs just as Randall shows up, handing us our drinks.

"Thanks, Randall," I mumble, immediately taking a sip through the straw. Whoa. This stuff is potent as hell. It burns on the way down, and I had the audacity to gulp it down quickly. My face scrunches up as the liquor settles, and I have to fan my mouth.

Randall laughs. "I forgot you can't handle any kind of drink, Chevy. And don't waste it."

"I'm not wasting it. Chill on me" I retort. Once I adjust to the taste, I give it another shot, and it goes down smoother the second time.

He gives a thumbs-up, and I didn't even realize he was watching me drink.

Slow jazz starts flowing through the speakers, and I observe couples coming together, swaying to the music. I'm leaning against the bar, a bit tipsy. I should've known better than to down that whole glass of Long Island; it's making me feel queasy just thinking about it.

I drag my third-wheeling self over to Sheila and Randall, who are all cuddled up, and I cup my mouth to speak only to them. "I'm... I'm gonna hit the bathroom... be right back."

Sheila gives me a thumbs-up, and I notice Randall whispering something to her as I turn and head down the red-lit hall toward the ladies' room.

"Hold up, Chevy. You doing okay?" I hear Randall call out, and I turn around before entering the bathroom. *Why the hell does he care?*

"I'm good. Just wanna be in here by the toilet... just... just in case." I say between hiccups.

Randall shakes his head and pulls me back. "I think you'll feel better stepping outside for some fresh air. C'mon."

He grabs my hand and leads me outside, past security. They nod at us as he explains that I need a moment. He's right. This is already making me feel better. Being drunk in that place with all those people, the sweat, the heat, and the smell of liquor just wasn't a pleasant combination.

"Why'd you leave Sheila in there like that?" I finally ask, leaning over the grass, preparing for a potential upchuck.

"She's getting us more drinks. She's okay, been here before. We didn't want you to be alone for your first time here," he explains.

Aww. That's sweet of him. I didn't think he was capable. I'm sure it won't last long.

"I'm surprised..." I start but have to pause. "Oh... okay. Never mind. Thought it was coming. But I'm surprised you're not mad at me." My head turns in his direction, and he walks over to stroke my back.

"I am, but I can understand why you wanna hide. I wouldn't want you embarrassing yourself by getting beat down on that stage," Randall says, a chuckle escaping him as he lightly nudges me. I playfully shove his arm away.

"That's not funny, Randall."

"I'm just messing with you. But you gotta make those hours up anyway. I know you're tired of being broke," he says, his hand now resting on my back.

I'm torn between feeling offended and just accepting that Randall is always going to be Randall, even when he's trying to help.

"Why did you lie... to Omar about them brownies? You lied on me, and I was trying to look out for you," I blurt out, the question weighing heavy on me since that night Omar threw me against that mirror.

"It ain't like he wasn't gonna forgive you. I knew that," he replies, his fingers digging deeper into my back. I straighten up, realizing I won't be throwing up as I had feared. The fresh air really helped. Confirmed.

"Well, I'm done drinking 'cause I'm already too gone. I can't have no more, so I'll just head home." I wonder what time it is. I barely glanced at the clock all day now that I think about it.

Randall steps in front of me and wraps me in a hug. My shivering calms down. I hadn't even realized it was happening.

"Hey, sorry 'bout tossing you into the lion's den like that. Knew you'd be safe though. How 'bout you come crash at my place with Sheila?" Randall squeezes me tight, still.

"Like a sleepover?" I mumble, too drained to lift my head to see him.

"Yeah, exactly. Figured you wouldn't wanna be alone tonight."

I really don't. Can't even pretend. Plus, Sheila being there should make things chill. No need to deal with my creepy boss trying anything. "Alright."

"Gonna grab Sheila and your stuff, then we'll bounce. Got a long night ahead," Randall says, giving my butt a playful pinch before heading inside.

Scratch that. Nearly forgot who I was dealing with. Randall probably thinks he's in for a two-woman showdown tonight. Not happening.

I shake my head and the thought as I continue to wait for them to bring my stuff out. But seriously, what's taking them so long? *You know what?* I'll just grab my stuff myself. No point freezing out here for no reason when I need to turn down the sleepover offer anyway.

The club entrance feels like it's miles away, but I'm determined to get there. I barely make it halfway when I hear a car screech to a stop right beside me. Both the driver and passenger doors swing open.

"Chevonne! Get your ass over here!" Tara yells as she rushes around the car.

Oh, crap! And she's got her cousin, Shannon, with her. *Are they about to jump me?*

I spin around, fists clenched, as they both pounce on me, and we crash to the ground. A fist connects with my cheek, and someone yanks my hair, but I'm swinging wildly, hitting whatever I can.

"You damn hoe! Sleeping with my man, bitch! I trusted you!" Tara's knee digs into my chest, pinning me down. *How the hell did she find me?*

"Get the hell off me!" I shout, kicking Shannon with my foot. Thank goodness I still have my heels on; that probably got her attention. I hope I left a mark on her chubby ass. She's too busy jumping someone in the middle of the night when she should be in bed, thinking about school in the morning.

Tara is yanking my hair like there's no tomorrow, so I grab hers, only to realize it's a wig and it slides right off. Security finally calls out for us to stop, and they rush over. I can hear Sheila too.

"Chevy!" Sheila shouts, sprinting to my rescue.

I watch as she tackles Tara to the ground, giving me a moment to kick off my heels and wipe the blood oozing from my eyebrow.

"Get the hell off me, you *bitch*!"

Tara punches Sheila in the temple, and she falls off. Randall rushes over with security to separate us as I lunge toward Tara. My knee connects with her back, sending her sprawling, but I'm pulled away before I can unleash on her. Then Shannon charges at me, landing a punch on my chin. I'm seething because the bouncer has my arms, leaving me defenseless.

"Let me go!" I scream, feeling my leg being yanked. I glance down to see Tara trying to drag me from under the bouncer's grip. I shake her off and kick at her again as he tightens his hold, spinning me around until we're facing the corner. Tara is still trying to leap over him, grabbing some of my hair, but he shifts to push her back.

"Sheila! You got Shannon?" I shout over the chaos.

I catch a glimpse of her on top of Shannon out of the corner of my eye. "Yeah! You good?"

"I'm good! Just need this fucker to let me loose so I can finish this!" I reply, still struggling to break free from this guy's grip. *What's his deal?* Damn.

"Come on, Chevy! Thought you could hide forever, huh, bitch!" Tara's restrained by someone, probably another bouncer.

"I can't, damn it! This guy's got me in a vice grip, but give me a sec, I'll get to you."

The only thing that comes to mind is biting the man's arm, and it works. He loosens his hold just enough for me to slip out. I swiftly dodge from under him and make a beeline for Tara, who's pinned to the ground by Randall. I leap to kick her but accidentally hit Randall instead, and he lets go.

He groans in pain, and I'm not even sorry because he deserves it, but Tara's charging at me with those damn sharp nails. I swing my fist as hard as I can before she can scratch me, landing a solid blow to her jaw.

"You wanna jump me! I said we could talk, you stupid bitch!" I shout, landing another punch to her throat, causing her to stumble back. Before I can go at her again, I'm pulled away.

I wish that the security would let us squash this shit once and for all so we both can move on from it. But it seems like reinforcements have arrived because more of them are here now, and we're all being separated. I scan the area for Sheila, and she's spitting blood from her mouth.

"You okay, Sheila?"

"I'm good. They can't handle us even off guard, huh?" We share a giggle.

"Not at all."

As the wind picks up, I wince as it hits the sore spots. *Damn*, they really got me good. I keep my guard up until I see Tara and Shannon being dragged toward the car they came in while the rest of us are ushered back inside the club.

CHAPTER 9
The Best Drug

I 'VE BEEN CRASHING AT Omar's place for the past week. He wasn't too happy when he found out about the fight and didn't want me out of his sight until things died down. My eyebrow needed stitches, and my lip was busted up for a bit, but it's all good now.

"You got any idea who told to her about you bein' out that night?" Omar asks, tending to my small bandage and cleaning the stitched wound. I keep picking at it, which makes it bleed again. But he's patient, always there to patch me up. "That shit smells like a set-up to me."

"I don't know. Maybe she followed us. I was thinking maybe Randall told her, but then again, why would he set me up if he wanted me to go home with him and Sheila?" I should watch bringing up Randall around Omar. He got hurt once because of him, and I know it bothers Omar, even if he won't say it. He gives me a sharp look before turning away to grab a new bandage.

"I wasn't planning on going home with Randall, I was just waitin' outside for my stuff," I explain, but Omar stays quiet, just shrugging. Maybe I shouldn't worry about it. I'm still single and he actually claimed Tara at one point. I might be ethereal, but if he's only looking at me as someone to protect, that's not good enough.

"Ion' understand why you were hangin' out with that fool, then actin' like you ain't wanna be around me or nobody else," Omar raises an eyebrow, giving me a puzzled look.

"I actually went out to hang with Sheila, but she was with him. That's why. I really wanted to be by myself anyway."

We are at the family house today. I agreed to help out while I stayed with Omar since I wasn't working at the club right now. We didn't want to risk me getting jumped again, and Randall is also still pissed at me for kicking him in the head. I'm not apologizing for it either just in case he did set me up.

Omar continued with his business as usual, while I stayed cooped up at his place, but as long as I had some snacks and some cable, I was fine while he was out. I haven't even seen Eddie all week because Omar had me up under him.

Eddie pulls me in a tight hug and kisses my cheek as we come out of the bathroom. "My pretty lady had to fight. I'm sure you was gettin' them hits in, wasn't ya? I woulda liked to see them girls' faces, barely a scratch on yours."

"I know I got some hits in, and I saw Tara's lip was bleeding, but that's all I know. Oh well. Let's hope that she isn't still plotting on me 'cause I'll be ready next time." I pick up a bag of flour after washing my hands and dump it into a bowl for sifting. Omar is sitting behind us, so I turn to see him checking me out.

"You okay?" I ask.

He nods and looks at his watch. "Get those started and then I want you to come with me."

"Okay. To where?" I ask, placing my hand on my hip.

He considers me for another moment before standing and walking toward me. "I wanna show you something." His favorite thing to do is swiping at my chin with his finger.

We hold gazes for a moment before I start to feel nervous and turn back to help Eddie. "Show me, what?"

"Don't worry about it. Let me know when you finished with that."

"Okay. This shouldn't take long."

Omar leaves the kitchen, and Eddie chuckles to himself.

"Is he alright?" I whisper to Eddie, noticing Omar's quiet demeanor lately.

Eddie glances towards the kitchen entrance, checking if anyone's around before responding. He lowers his voice, "He might be feelin' a tad guilty about what happened to you, Miss Chevy."

"Guilty about me getting jumped?" I hand Eddie the bowl of egg yolks, and he nods, pointing for me to start cutting the cooled brownies.

" He wasn't too pleased when he got that call. I'll tell ya that much. Now I ain't seen too many things that make my O boy lose it, but you happen to be one of 'em."

Me? I watch him chuckle to himself. "Ion' know what you've done to him, but good on you both. For as long as he's breathing, you safe, I'm sure of it. And as long as you safe, it will make him content. And we all good with that over here. When O is happy, everybody is taken care of."

The thought of being under Omar's protection is comforting, but it still leaves me feeling a bit peeved.

"That's nice and all, but Tara had every right to be upset, you know? She told me she loved him. I can't blame her, Eddie. I didn't wanna get jumped, but I get why she didn't wanna talk. I probably wouldn't wanna talk either."

"All I can say about that is, whatever's meant to be will happen if you let it flow. Not everyone's gonna like it, but it ain't your job to worry about how someone reacts. People always gonna think about themselves first, so you gotta consider yourself first at some point."

I need to work on that. It's tough because I don't want to justify anything hurtful just for my own peace. I still care about people's feelings, but I'm going to start putting myself first more. I try to watch out for others and still end up in the same mess I wanted to avoid.

Eddie leans in. "Besides, you two need to talk more. Stop assuming what the other is thinkin'. Just talk."

"It's not my fault he tells you everything and me nothing."

"You gotta let him in too, Miss Chevy." Eddie helps me bag up the brownies and puts them in the fridge. I wash my hands once again, give him a hug, and head out to meet Omar.

Let him in? I already have. Twice.

———— ♥ ————

We arrive outside a large warehouse, and I figure this must be where they craft the dope. It definitely has that look, like something out of a movie. It's the kind of place cops would hit first if they wanted to bust a dope dealer.

Omar turns off the car, and we sit in silence for a moment. I find myself sinking into the seat, taking in our surroundings. It feels like we're in the middle of nowhere, so now I'm wishing I paid more attention to the turns and street signs.

Omar chuckles softly. "Why you hiding?"

"If this is where you make your dope, then it's probably being watched. This is risky, Omar. Why choose the most obvious spot? That's where they'll look first," I turn to him, concern etched on my face.

"I like your thinking. Thanks for lookin' out for me and my business, but don't worry. Come on," Omar takes the keys and gets out of the car.

I hesitate to leave the safety of the car. Omar walks around to my side and tries to open the door, but I've already locked it. He looks at me, questioning. I shake my head and mouth, "No."

I watch as Omar stuffs his hands in his pockets and sighs, leaning against the car. *What is he thinking?* Why bring me here, knowing how cautious I am about places like this? The cops could show up any moment, and it would be game over. They must know who Omar is. They have to because I don't understand how he can operate without consequences.

It seems Omar has waited long enough; he heads towards the warehouse without me. I tap on the window with panic because there's no way he's leaving me out here. I imagine all sorts of sketchy folks lurking around, and that worries me a bit.

Omar disappears inside the building, and I quickly make my way to catch up with him. There's no way he's leaving me out there, especially after I've already been in one fight; I have no desire to tussle with any junkies. They possess a different kind of strength. I've seen things.

The door is heavy, but I pull it with all my might. I expect to see bright lights and maybe some unsavory scenes, but when I peek inside, it's just an empty warehouse with old, rusted scraps of metal scattered around. Omar is nowhere in sight.

"Omar! Where are you?" My voice wobbles as I call out.

"I'm over here, baby girl," his voice finally echoes from behind another door.

"I don't like this spooky stuff. What are we doing here? Are you finally gonna leave me for dead?" I ask as I trudge towards the sound of his voice. All I hear in response is his laughter.

What's so funny, anyway?

I open the other door and freeze as I watch him pull a cover from the top of a car. "Oh... wow, Omar. Is this for me?"

He nods and gestures for me to join him. I hurry over with excitement, a wide smile on my face.

"Thank you so much!" I wrap my arms tightly around his waist, and he hugs me back.

"You welcome, baby girl. Like I said before, I know you work hard, and I see that. You deserve it. I know you not one to ask for things, but I did it anyway. And no, you don't owe me shit."

I bury my face into his side, holding back tears. I can't help but think about all I've been through in my life, all on my own. It feels amazing to know someone sees me and cares about me like this.

Omar gently lifts my face and wipes away the tears with his thumbs. "I hope these are happy tears," he says.

"They are. You're very kind for this, so I really appreciate it. Thank you, Omar."

"You got it. Go ahead, take it for a spin."

I release him and wipe away the remaining tears as I gaze at my car. I love the navy-blue color, and it's just the right size for me. I let my fingers glide over the waxed exterior before opening the door and sinking into the gray cloth seats.

Omar reaches in and hands me a key. "Turn it on."

I slide the key into the ignition and turn it on, shooting Omar an exaggerated grin. He responds with half a smile, and we share a moment of silence.

But soon enough, the thoughts creep in. *What makes me so special that he'd do this?* I can't help but think of all the other girls he could have surprised with a car. *What's the message here?* Does he see me differently? Or is he just helping out of pity? Maybe he senses my loneliness and thinks it's an easy way to keep me close.

I finally tear my gaze away and switch off the car. Omar helps me out, and I close the door behind me. "I really appreciate this, Omar, I truly do... but I'm not sure if I can accept it."

"I won't hold it against you. It's yours, even if you told me you never wanted to speak to me again. You could drive off in this, and there'd be no hard feelings."

But he's lying through his teeth. This is the same man who dragged me into the weed business because of some supposed debt. And the same one who keeps me on a tight leash because of Tara.

"I think we need to talk about... *us*. What's really going on between us? I'm grateful for the car, and I could use it, but are you giving it to me as a friend, like charity, or... something more?" I confront him, watching as he nods and leans against the car, lost in thought. Besides the wind rattling against the old building, there's nothing but silence between us for a moment.

"I kinda figured that's why you been actin' all weird lately," he finally admits, still avoiding my gaze. "Ion' know how to answer that, I'm just figuring out the best move to make, if I'm being real."

"What does that mean? You said you didn't regret anything. It's better if you just admit that you still feel guilty about Tara, too. That's why you're still keeping me hanging down here," I say, lowering my hand to the ground.

"When you gonna let go of Tara?"

"When are you?"

"I already have. It's you who's still feelin' guilty. You can't expect to move forward with you if you still holdin' onto her."

I let out a scoff and start pacing back and forth before turning back to him. "Why are you doing all this for me, Omar? I'm so damn confused," I finally blurt out. "If you know why I've been upset, then why dodge the issue?"

"I don't mean to confuse you."

"But I am confused. You do all these things: cheat on your girlfriend, buy me stuff, give me a job, sleep with me, pay my debts, and now suddenly, you're unsure?"

"So, you want me to tell you that I wanna be with you, right? Is that what you're waiting for?"

"Yeah, Omar, that's exactly what I'm waiting to hear," I respond, my heart racing as I stand there, tapping my foot nervously. I can't believe I brought myself to finally admit that, but I suppose it was about time I said what was weighing on my heart.

"I've already shown you I wanted you. Plenty of times," he insists, his voice steady. "I'm waitin' on you to realize you good enough."

"But you just said you were tryna figure out how to go about this," I say.

"I'm not talking about Tara, though. I mean, if I made you my girl, I'd have to figure out how the hell I'm gonna keep the stuff you don't like about me away from you," he explains, his words hanging in the air.

My head shoots up, and I meet his gaze. "There's nothing I don't like about you, Omar. You shouldn't say that."

"You don't like what I do. And I can respect that."

"But that's not a reason to not try to make things work... right?"

"Ion' know. That's what I was tryna figure out."

Leaning against the car, I let his words soak in, replaying my talk with Eddie in my head. Keeping an open mind is the plan until I figure things out.

"I don't wanna be confused anymore," I admit, my voice barely audible, hoping he'll get where I'm coming from.

"No need to be confused, Chevonne. I've been showing you. You doubt yourself, think you don't deserve this. Question *why me*, right? When there are plenty of others I could be doin' this for, right?" Omar's words hit hard, and tears start to flow. Maybe I've been too tough on myself, thinking I was doing it all right.

His touch brings warmth, and he's right. I've been judging myself just as much as I've been judging him. In a tight embrace, Omar's holding me close.

"We haven't known each other for long. How do we know this is right?" I ask, gripping onto him.

"We've known each other long enough to feel something. Let's give it a shot. We can just say, 'fuck it,' and do the damn thing," he suggests.

I really love this side of him. This is probably the most I've heard him speak at once, and I know he can get deep. I love the way he thinks.

"Okay...fuck it. Let's try."

A half-smile spreads across his face as our lips meet. I feel him lifting me gently, carrying me until I'm lying on the hood of my brand-new car.

He stands tall over me, positioning himself between my legs to keep me from sliding off. His hands trail over my stomach, lifting my tank top until my braless chest is exposed.

"Omar, what if someone catches us here?" I murmur, instinctively covering myself.

He presses a finger to his lips, silencing me, and moves my hands away. "Who cares," he murmurs, his tone low and determined.

I purse my lips, allowing his touch to roam freely. It's exhilarating to feel desired, to know it's not just in one way. He truly wants me, and he's making it known.

With a gentle tug, he helps me shimmy out of my jeans. Leaning in, he kisses a slow trail down my stomach, igniting the desire in me. I hope he doesn't ruin this thong—it's one of my favorites, and he still owes me a replacement for the last one. It's almost as if he reads my mind; he removes it with care, tossing it aside.

Our eyes lock, and I see hunger in his gaze. It's electrifying, and I can't resist teasing him. With a playful gesture, I snap my legs shut and pull away.

"Why'd you do that?" His voice is husky, filled with longing.

"Tell me you want me," I tease.

He places his hands on my knees and gently spreads them. "You know I do."

"Say it."

"I want you, baby girl," he says, and his words make me squeal with excitement.

Omar ditches his jacket and starts unbuckling his belt. I'm squirming underneath him, feeling a mix of nerves and anticipation. I'm acting as if it's our first time, but in a way, it kind of is—no guilt hanging over us.

Omar takes a moment, that intense staring thing again, his smile fading. I catch him focusing on my smile.

He leans in closer, asking, "Ready?"

"Ready," I reply with a mix of nerves and excitement.

He pulls me by my thighs, and I slide down to his waist. My heart races, but I'm ready for whatever comes next. *Is this for real?* I can't believe that this dope dealer, this successful and attractive dope dealer, wants *me*. I find myself holding him admiration as it all sinks in, and now that he's my man, I can truly enjoy the moment.

Tara had her fight. I tried to make amends, so what more could she possibly want? I know this will hurt her, but we can't avoid it. Not right now, we just can't.

As he enters, Omar teases playfully, then thrusts forward in one smooth motion, and we're completely connected, my back arching in response. "Oh *shit*, Omar..." I gasp.

Omar's gaze lowers, and he grips my sides to steady himself as he moves his hips against mine. Unsure of what to do with my hands, I grasp onto something, anything, as the intensity escalates.

Grabbing onto Omar's chain, I pull him closer, urging him to sink deeper. Our lips part, and our breaths mingle with our moans. This is the kind of high I want to relish forever. We should package this up and sell it because we could change the world with this kind of drug, in all the best ways.

"You're the best drug, Omar..." I smile up at his focused expression.

He closes his eyes briefly, shaking his head. "Keep talking like that..." he groans.

"I will, as long as you don't stop..."

CHAPTER 10
In Too Deep

"**G**IRL, I CAN'T BELIEVE you're moving in with him!" Sheila squeals, her voice filled with excitement as she tapes up another cardboard box and sets it aside.

I've barely been spending time at my own place lately, mostly crashing at Omar's, and now he's asking me to move in after just a month of being together.

"I know, right? It's kinda wild," I reply, glancing over at the boxes piled up on my kitchen table. "I just hope we're not jumping the gun too much."

"You're not. But the fact you're not giving up your place? That's bold," Sheila chuckles, pouring herself some lemonade. "I can't believe you told him to get with the program or kick rocks."

"Well, he needs to understand that I can't keep all my eggs in one basket. My dad always said to keep my independence," I explain, taking a sip of my drink. "But Omar seems to dig it. He knows I'm not playing games."

"Your dad's advice is solid. And let's not forget that Omar got you that sweet ride, Chevy! That's a big deal," Sheila points out, her eyes wide with admiration.

I pause, realizing the weight of it. "Yeah, it really is a big deal."

Suddenly, my head starts spinning. I drop the box I'm carrying onto the dining table and plop into a chair, holding my head. Thankfully, it's not filled with anything fragile, but Sheila's giving me a weird look.

"Chevy? You all right?" Sheila sets her lemonade down, her concern noticeable. "What just happened?"

I pinch the bridge of my nose, shutting my eyes tight. Hunger pangs shoot through me – I haven't eaten yet today, and the morning's been a whirlwind. I hadn't even realized I forgot to feed myself.

"Yeah, I'm okay. I think I just need some food," I mumble.

"No problem. I'm starving too, babe. We've been at it all morning. Let's grab something." Sheila leans down in front of me, her voice filled with care.

I still haven't opened my eyes.

"Chevy? You listening?" Sheila's voice is gentle, but I can feel the queasiness swirling inside me, worsening at the mention of food. I take a deep breath and place my hand on Sheila's shoulder.

"Man, I'm feeling really off, Sheila. I might need to lie down."

"Sure thing. I'll help you to the couch and then grab us some grub. Come on." Sheila wraps her arm around me, guiding me up. I hate how suddenly this has hit me. Must've caught something.

Sheila settles me on the couch and drapes a blanket over me. "I'll get you some water."

"Thanks, Sheila. Sorry about this," I mutter.

"No worries, babe. Just rest up," she says, disappearing to fetch the water and food. I hope I'll have an appetite when she returns, but for now, I'll just close my eyes and wait it out.

———— ♡ ————

I wake up from my nap to darkness outside, squinting at the clock. It's been a couple of hours. *Where's Sheila?* My pager sits on the kitchen counter, blinking with missed calls from both her and Omar.

I grab the phone and decide to call Sheila first, just to check in. The number on the pager doesn't look like her home number, but I dial it anyway.

"Hey, Chevy. Feeling any better?" her voice comes through, mixed with faint music in the background.

"Yeah, I'm good. What happened to you? I thought you were bringing back our food?" I ask.

"I swung by Randall's 'cause he wanted to chat. Sorry about that. I figured you were probably knocked out. But hey, I can swing back with some grub if you want," she offers. I'm not sure how a solid plan turned into an offer instead, but I shrug it off.

"Nah, it's cool, Sheila. Don't want you making that drive back from Randall's. It's way across town. I might just crash at Omar's tonight."

"Alright..." I hear her chuckle and hush someone in the background. "I'll be around if you need anything, though. Just holler or beep me. Oh, wait, Randall's asking if you wanna join us?"

I shake my head, even though she can't see me. Randall's confusing. I thought he was pissed about me quitting my job, but now he's acting all friendly. Probably just wants to hook up.

"I'm good, thanks. Talk to you later. Stay safe, okay?" I say before hanging up. *What is it about Randall that has these women sprung like this?* I could never be sprung on him, and I've had him too. He's decent, but not worth all the trouble he comes with.

As I stand there, contemplating my dinner options, I find myself gripping the wall for support as that dizziness creeps back in. Hot food would've been a dream, but reality slaps me: *I'm all I got.* Grabbing my purse and keys, I shuffle out the door, aiming straight for a burger joint then to Omar's place before he starts to get worried. Fingers crossed the dizziness doesn't hit me mid-drive; I really don't need another run-in with the cops.

I stop at a drive-thru and order myself a double cheeseburger with a fry and a lemonade slushy—all large. The food smells so good that I just have to park in a nearby lot to eat. The way I am scarfing this down my throat lets me know that my body was mad at me for not feeding it. My pager vibrates in my purse, so I check it and see Omar's name. I should probably get over to his place so he doesn't worry.

But as soon as I start the car, a wave of nausea hits me like a ton of bricks. I barely have time to throw open the car door before everything I just ate comes rushing out. It's so much that tears well up, and I struggle to catch my breath. It's a mess. None of it makes any sense to me.

After I close the door, my pager goes off again, but I'm so drained from emptying my stomach that I can barely move. My body's angry at me, I get it, but did it really have to waste my dinner like that? I slump back in my seat, trying to gather some energy and catch my breath before hitting the road again. But exhaustion takes over, and I find myself drifting off. So, with what little strength I have left, I lock the doors and surrender to sleep.

——— ♡ ———

There's a persistent tapping on my car window, jolting me awake. I blink groggily and find Eddie's concerned face peering in. Panic sets in as I realize I've spent the whole night in my car.

I roll down the window. "Hey, Eddie..."

"You okay, Miss Chevy? O's worried, got us scouring the streets for you. Some shits goin' down. It's a lil' dangerous for the family to be out and about right now. You included," he says with a concerned look.

I glance around, taking in the daylight. "Damn. Where's Omar?" I ask, recalling how I abandoned my plan after last night's set of circumstances.

"He out here lookin' for you too. He stayed up all night waitin'," Eddie replies, his gaze shifting from me to the ground beside the car. "You alright? Is this your artwork?"

I nod slowly. "Yeah. Ate too much, too fast. I'll tag along to the house, wait for Omar there. Don't worry about me, Eddie."

Eddie gives a nod before turning back to his car, and I start mine, trailing him to the family house. Guilt gnaws at me for not keeping Omar updated. I don't want him to worry about me or think I'm bailing on him. However, now I'm starting to worry about what danger Eddie is referring to.

After a refreshing shower, I find Eddie's whipped up scrambled eggs and toast. He settles beside me on the couch, his presence is comforting as his hand rests lightly on my back.

"If you feel like you're gonna lose your breakfast, there's a bag right there by the couch." He points to the plastic grocery bag, and I manage a smile.

"Thanks, Eddie. I don't know what hit me yesterday... I was packing with Sheila, then started feeling sick. I think it's 'cause I didn't eat anything. It's happened before."

Eddie presses the back of his hand to my forehead. "Maybe you comin' down with something, Miss Chevy. You a bit warm."

Before I can respond, the front door creaks open, and Omar strides in. I flash him a smile, but it fades when I see the look on his face. He's clearly not a happy camper.

"I'll leave you two to talk..." Eddie stands, making his way toward Omar. Lowering his voice, he says, "Found her sleepin' in her car. I think she's sick."

Once Eddie's out of earshot, Omar crosses the room, his gaze fixed on mine.

"Sorry I didn't swing by last night. Didn't mean to leave you worried like that," I finally say, watching Omar's jaw clench. Looks like he's grinding his teeth.

"What was you up to? I called your place, even your homegirl, and you was nowhere to be found," he probes.

"I spent the whole day packing, started feeling sick, took a nap, then went out to grab some food and accidentally knocked out in my car."

"All night?" Omar shoots me a skeptical look.

I take a moment, blinking it through. "Yeah, all night. I didn't even realize until Eddie found me. I know I should've called you before I left, but I really was on my way."

He nods, leaning back, still studying me. "If you didn't wanna move in with me, you coulda just said it. No need to disappear to get the message across.'

"How did I disappear if I'm right here, Omar? Did you get any sleep? Eddie said you were up all night," I reach over, smoothing his cheek with the back of my hand.

"If my girl is missing, and I ain't heard from her, how the hell do you expect me to sleep?" Omar's words linger in the air, and I smile softly, appreciating the way he calls me 'his girl.'

"Okay, my bad. I really was packing all day, boo. Everything I explained is what actually happened. I'm sorry.." I glance away, reaching for my fork. "You been keeping busy with work?"

"Gotta lay low for a bit. One of my guys fucked up on a job, so I been sortin' things out before diving back in," Omar explains, taking the fork from me to scoop up some scrambled eggs from my plate. He offers it to me, and I take a bite.

With my mouth full, I try to respond, "Oh... that's not good. A fucked up job? Are the cops after you? Are you nervous?"

"Don't talk with your mouth full, baby girl. You'll choke," Omar interrupts gently.

It's a new experience for me, having someone look out for me like this. He's sweet, even though he still seems a bit skeptical about last night. I don't blame him after what he went through with Tara. I'd probably be concerned too if the roles were reversed, but I understand that building trust takes time. Especially for somebody like Omar. I chew and swallow my food.

"Nah, not nervous. No cops involved. Just some folks who weren't too pleased with how the last job went down, so we're keepin' a low profile," Omar explains calmly.

"You're really good at this, you know. I admire how you're taking care of your business, being careful after someone else's mistake. You've worked hard for it, and you don't deserve to see it crumble."

"I'm surprised to hear you say that baby girl. Especially since you seem to think I'm some kinda terrible motherfucka for real," Omar responds, his tone softening.

"If I thought you were a terrible motherfucker, I wouldn't be sitting here as your girl, lettin' you feed me eggs," I retort.

A slight smile tugs at Omar's lips as he rubs my chin affectionately. "You feelin' okay?" he asks, concern flickering in his eyes.

I shake my head and grab the plastic bag beside me. "Eddie gave me this 'cause he saw I threw up last night's dinner. Got some on the side of my car too."

"Yuck. We're gonna have to deal with that later."

I grin at him and lean against his chest. He plants a gentle kiss on my forehead before lifting my chin up.

"You brushed your teeth, right?" he asks, his stare lingering on my lips.

"No, 'cause I knew you were gonna kiss me, and I was saving these lips just for you. Hope you catch whatever I've got," I tease, even though I did actually brush my teeth.

He chuckles softly. *"Yum..."*

Our lips meet, lingering for a moment. "I think... we should go take a nap. You get real grouchy when you don't sleep, and I'm still feeling a little sleepy," I suggest.

"Still? You ain't get enough of that yesterday?" Omar teases.

"I only took two naps. It's not like I slept in a bed with my *boyfriend*," I reply, shrugging.

Omar glances at his watch, then back at me. "A'ight, that's cool. Just a short one, though, 'cause I got some stuff to take care of, and we still need to get your stuff moved into my place. Finish your food first though," he adds.

I nod and lean forward to eat as he continues stroking my back. I'm relieved Eddie didn't pile on too many eggs; I really don't want to embarrass myself and throw up in front of Omar.

———— ♡ ————

I should've known better than to think this nap would actually be a nap. Omar and I can't seem to keep our hands off each other as we roll around in the bed. I can feel the love marks he's left all over me; the man sure loves to suck on skin.

"You must've thought I really went missing, Omar," I moan as he moves on top of me.

"Nah, I think you tried to run away from me," he murmurs, nipping at my neck.

Run from him? I feel his hand tangle in my hair, and he pulls back.

"Um, ow. Do you have to pull my hair like that?" I wince, noticing he's gone still and quiet.

He gazes down at me, and I can't quite read his expression. "Why are you looking at me like that?" I ask, trying to break the silence.

Still no response.

I reach up to untangle his hand from my hair and gently push him back. "Omar?"

"My bad. Did I hurt you?" he finally speaks, moving to sit beside me.

"It didn't actually hurt, but you ain't have to pull my hair like that. What's wrong?" I ask, now concerned.

He props his knees up, resting his elbows on them before turning to face me. "Don't pull that shit again, Chevonne. You coulda easily picked up the phone... hit my pager... done something," he chides.

"I didn't do it on purpose. Chill out," I retort, rolling my eyes as I scan the room for my T-shirt and panties. There's no time to rehash why I didn't call him. That's ridiculous, and if he wants to be mad about it, then so be it.

After a while, I notice him turning his head away. He must have been watching me, as he often does.

"Omar, I wanna do something today. Can we go see a movie or something? I don't want to just lounge around watching cable all day," I suggest.

"I thought you were sick," he responds.

"I mean, I feel better now that I'm with you. I just don't want you to leave me right now," I admit.

"Yeah, well, I do have some things lined up to take care of today. But I got you covered. Just relax and get better, 'cause you're not about to be throwing up all over my damn car," Omar says with a smile, and I playfully nudge him from the side.

"Don't do me like that... Quick question, but have you heard from Tara? I haven't, but I ain't expecting to," I ask.

Omar leans back, scratching his head. "She called me a couple of times last week, crying and shit, but I ain't really feel like dealing with that."

A pang of sadness hits me upon hearing that, mixed with annoyance. Sadness because I feel like her heart is broken, both by me and by Omar. Annoyance because she's not the type to talk anything out. I'm relieved I haven't seen her since I've been with Omar; that would be a disaster waiting to happen. I wish I could talk to her without expecting a fight, just to wish her happiness. I would genuinely mean it.

Back to reality, Omar's eyes are fixed on me, trying to read my thoughts. "You don't gotta worry about that, baby girl. I'll make sure she can't reach you again."

"I appreciate that, but I wish I could have one good talk with her. Like I could have with my daddy. Maybe she needs that to help her move on," I confess, leaning back on my elbow. "I'm just tryna help."

"Help with what? You was part of the damage done, so that's just comin' from a place of guilt, baby girl. We all gotta move on and that don't always mean havin' one last conversation with somebody. Some folks can't accept that never hearing from someone again is the answer they need," Omar explains.

I genuinely enjoy listening to him explain things; I always end up learning something new. The way he speaks tells me he's been through a lot, probably had to mature early, just like I did. It's something I could bring up over dinner one of these days.

"You talk about your dad not caring for you much, but you mention him a lot."

"He was just always so mean and angry. I don't think he liked me much 'cause I reminded him of my mom. He just tolerated me after she left us," I explain.

"Sounds like he cared, in his own way. Maybe he had to be tough on you to prepare you for life, especially since you didn't have anyone else to look out for you," he says, rubbing under my chin. "He probably knew he wasn't gonna be around long for you, baby."

I hadn't considered it from that angle. Maybe he's onto something.

Omar gets up, pulling on his boxers and then his pants. "We can finish this later. I gotta get out of here."

"We could've finished now if you hadn't been pulling someone's hair," I retort as I pull my T-shirt over my head.

He flashes me his cute half-smile and shakes his head. "I'm going to shower real quick. What are you gonna do while I'm gone?" he asks, scanning the room for his bath towel.

"I need to get my damn license. Maybe I can look into that," I muse aloud.

"Hmm... Ion' know if that's a good idea right now. With all this shit goin' on, I don't want you caught up in anything," Omar cautions.

I tilt my head to the side. "What do you mean? You said y'all were just laying low because of a slipup. I shouldn't have to worry about anything, right?" My mind flashes back to Eddie's comment about "some shit" happening. Maybe that's why Omar is genuinely concerned but not sharing all the details.

"When I say lay low, I mean all of us, including you," he clarifies.

Damn. Dealing with the consequences of dating a dope dealer wasn't something I was looking forward to. Now, everything he does affects my life. But I knew what I signed up for when I agreed to be his girl. I can't just back off now, or he might question my commitment.

"I wish I could see what's goin' on in that head of yours, baby girl," Omar sighs, shaking his head again as he walks toward the door. "Tryna join me?"

———— ♡ ————

Feeling uneasy about the need to "lay low," I opt to stay indoors at the family house, cocooned with snacks and magazines. Omar left a few hours ago, and since then, I've been alternating between glancing out the window and checking my phone and pager. I chide myself for acting so needy, considering I just saw him. I miss him too much right now, but I know I need to chill and get a grip.

"You would have a life if you hadn't quit your job," I remind myself. But I did quit my job. Omar asked me to, so I did. That's why it caught me off guard when Randall wanted me to swing by last night. I miss dancing terribly, but Omar insists I don't need to do that anymore. I'm not easily taken in, so I understand it's because he doesn't want me dancing for other men, or worse, Randall.

Suddenly, the crack of gunfire pierces the air, jolting me from my thoughts. I instinctively duck, the sound uncomfortably close. Gunshots were a common occurrence in my childhood neighborhood, but it's been a while since I've heard them. This time feels different, more encoded, and I wouldn't be surprised if it's targeted for...Omar.

The back door swings open, and Eddie rushes in, his handgun drawn, followed by a couple of Omar's men.

"Eddie! What's happening?" I blurt out in a panic, jumping to my feet, but he swiftly pulls me down to the ground. The gunfire continues, and I watch as one of the men turns back, brandishing his weapon toward the source.

"Eddie!" I cry out, fear gripping me tightly.

"Stay down, Miss Chevy!" he urges, holding me close to the floor as chaos unfolds outside.

As the gunfire intensifies, I shield my head, feeling my heart pounding against my ribcage. Tears threaten to spill, but fear holds them back. *What the hell is happening?* I want to ask Eddie, but I can sense he's in no position to answer questions right now. As long as we avoid getting shot, I'll keep my questions to myself for now

Eddie's gun brushes against my leg, making me jump. The sound of shattering glass near us prompts me to push Eddie away and scramble to my feet.

"Where's O at?" A voice from outside shouts. "Tell him to bring his ass out here! We here now!"

Fuck this. I'm not about to risk my life over drug deals gone wrong. Grabbing my purse from the entrance, I bolt out the front door. Adrenaline courses through me; I'm flying, barefoot, and terrified. I don't even glance at my car. Eddie calls after me, but I can't afford to stop. I wish him the very best, and sincerely hope he makes it out of this alive, but this life was his choice.

The gunfire ceases, and the silence is deafening. I don't hear Eddie either. Lost and disoriented, I realize I'm probably near my apartment. It hits me – I haven't even officially moved in with Omar, and here I am, on the verge of losing my life. It feels like a sign, a clear indication that I shouldn't be involved in this dangerous world.

As my sprint slows to a stop, nausea creeps back, and I struggle to hold it at bay while catching my breath. I may not understand what just transpired, but one thing is certain – this is not the life I want to be a part of.

The distant wail of police sirens pierces the air, breaking through the eerie calm that follows the chaos. Slowly, I become aware of the figures on their porches, peering down the street, their gazes landing on me. An older lady's voice cuts through the tension, calling out to check if I'm alright. I offer a feeble wave and nod, assuring her that I'm fine.

As the adrenaline subsides, a sharp pain shoots through the back of my leg. I twist to inspect the source and find blood trickling down my thigh. Panic sets in as I collapse to the stained ground, realizing I've been shot. *There's a damn bullet hole in my leg!*

"Miss, are you okay?" A young guy cautiously approaches, and I grit my teeth against the pain while covering the wound.

"I think... somebody shot me," I manage to say.

He kneels down, gently moving my hand aside. "Looks like you got grazed. Want me to call an ambulance?"

Uncertainty clouds my mind as more people gather around us, their murmurs making me want to hide. "Um... I think I'm okay. It doesn't hurt that bad. Thank you," I reply weakly, trying to downplay the severity of the situation.

"What do you want to do, ma'am?" he asks, his voice gentle but insistent.

What do I want to do? I wrestle with the options swirling in my mind. I could leave it all behind, start afresh, and Omar would understand. Or I could go back, confront the reality I've chosen to embrace. My gaze flickers right, then left, torn between two paths.

"Miss?" he prompts again.

"I... I want Omar," I finally admit, my words weighing heavy with dilemma but commitment.

CHAPTER 11
Unexpected

"BIG WHOOP, YOU'RE SEVEN weeks in," the doctor deadpans, nonchalantly removing her latex gloves and chucking them into the trash can beside the sink. The news of my pregnancy hits me like a gut punch, right after having my thigh patched up from the close call with a bullet. I spilled out some symptoms, half expecting her to dismiss it as a mere fever, but instead, she hands me a cup, and surprise, surprise—I'm pregnant.

"Okay... so what now? I've never been pregnant before," I mutter, struggling to digest the reality that I'm about to become somebody's mama.

"You haven't?" Her disbelief is as clear as day.

"No..."

"Well, do you even know who the father is?"

I shoot her a sharp look, holding back the urge to snap. "Yeah, I know the father. He's my boyfriend."

"Alright, well, I advise you to let him know, and then you both can figure out what you want to do from there." The doctor stands up, making her way to the sink to wash her hands, leaving me alone to grapple with the weight of her words and the uncertain road ahead.

"Is that all?" I raise an eyebrow, the doctor's dismissive tone taking me by surprise..

"Well, if you're dead set on this pregnancy, come back, and we'll hook you up with vitamins and whatnot." Her words sound more like an afterthought, and I can't help but wonder if she treats everyone with the same indifference.

I can feel her judgmental gaze piercing through me as she continues, "Think long and hard about your decision, Miss Bleu. Consider the environment you'd be bringing a child into. You stroll in here with a gunshot wound, no father in sight, and a neat note on your sheet proclaiming unemployment. Twenty-one... or twenty-two, I don't really care. Can you honestly care for a child right now?"

Her words cut deep, and I can't deny that she's got a point. I already knew it, but her condescending attitude rubs me the wrong way. I recognize her type, though – the judgmental, holier-than-thou sort. I won't let her see me crumble under her ignorant assumptions. But damn, I never pictured myself dealing with motherhood at this stage in my life, especially not with a man deep in the drug game.

I flashback to that moment in the kitchen when Omar casually mentioned that having kids wouldn't alter his lifestyle or choices. *Is that a good thing or a bad thing?* I want him to be true to himself, but a safer lifestyle wouldn't hurt either.

"Get dressed and meet my nurse outside to sign some papers before you leave. Take it easy on that leg for a while, and you should be fine," the doctor orders, casting a final disapproving frown my way before exiting the room, leaving me alone with the weight of the revelation settling over my hand on my now pregnant belly.

After the chaos of the shooting at the family house, I crossed paths with Omar before one of his henchmen, Curtis, dropped me off at the hospital. Tears streamed down my face as I overheard Omar discussing Eddie's ambulance ride with the cops in hushed tones. It was shady, the way he dealt with them, probably greasing their palms with dope or cash to keep them from probing too deep into the house. It felt like a scene ripped straight from a movie, except this time, I was living it.

Omar approached me, concern etched into his features as he assured me he knew who was behind the attack and promised to handle it. I didn't protest. Instead, I simply nodded, letting his forehead kiss serve as a reassurance that he'd pick me up from the hospital later.

Now, here I am, fidgeting at the entrance, the weight of unexpected news settling in my stomach as I wait for an El Camino to pull up. Omar assured me he'd be here soon when I called him, so I'm keeping my eyes on the street, expecting him any moment.

The thought of checking on Eddie crosses my mind, knowing he's in the same hospital, but guilt gnaws at me for fleeing the scene and leaving him behind. I can only imagine the agony he's enduring; my own gunshot graze feels like a fiery branding iron against my skin.

It's all a whirlwind of confusion. I went from being fiercely independent, commuting to work solo, to this tangled mess. I haven't been with Omar for long, haven't even moved in with him, and yet, here we are. The realization that I'm pregnant adds another layer to the chaos. I made a choice to be with Omar, to weather whatever storms came our way, but now I question if this is a test of loyalty or if I'm scrambling for more to justify my decision. No one lost their life, and Omar couldn't have predicted the shootout... *right?* All I crave are answers, and I'm prepared to demand them from Omar when the opportunity arises.

After waiting for what felt like forever, I couldn't take it anymore and headed inside to call Sheila. She sounded frantic on the phone, promising to come get me soon.

I hear her beat-up car rumbling down the road, and she jumps out without bothering to close the door. "Chevy! Oh my God..." She wraps me in a tight hug, and I let her. "Are you okay? What happened?"

"I got shot in the leg. Kinda. It's just a flesh wound," I mumble, feeling utterly drained.

"I'm so sorry, girl. Where's Omar?"

It's like Sheila summoned him with that question because right then, we see his car pulling up next to hers. He steps out, hands stuffed in his pockets. "Hey, baby girl..." His voice is soft as he reaches out to touch my chin.

I'm torn. *Should I cry? Should I yell at him? Should I just get in Sheila's car?* I don't know what to do.

"What happened, Omar? Chevy got shot, and I wanna know why she's here alone?" Sheila's voice is shaky but determined as she confronts him.

I watch Sheila swallow hard, her demeanor shifting slightly as Omar's gaze falls on her. I've told her a hundred times not to shrink in front of him, to stand tall, because he can sniff out fear like a bloodhound. *Me?* Well, I don't fear folks who bleed red like me, not even Omar, unless they're pointing a gun at my head. That's a little different.

"Some shit went down, and Chevonne got caught in the middle by accident. She good, though. I'm here to get her," Omar finally speaks up, his eyes fixed on Sheila in a way that makes me uneasy.

"Oh... got it. Well, she's a bit shaken, so I can—"

"I said I got her," Omar cuts in sharply, and Sheila nods, sensing the tension thickening the air. I'm so tired, I couldn't care less about talking. Whoever gets me in the car first wins at this point. Sheila turns to me.

"Alright... you just holler if you need anything, okay, babe?"

"Sure thing. I'll catch you later," I mumble.

"Love you, Chevy. Rest up." Sheila gives me one more squeeze before heading back to her car.

I glance up at Omar as Sheila drives off, and his expression darkens. "I don't trust her," he mutters, pulling me closer to him.

I let out a big yawn before speaking up, "Why not? That's my girl, Omar. She ain't the one who shot me."

"Just keep an eye on her," he warns.

"Well, I called her 'cause you were taking forever," I shoot back.

"I'm sorry about that, baby girl. You ready to head home?"

"I am not going back to the family house. You might as well leave me here if that's the plan."

"Nah, we're heading to my place. The one you're moving into. The family house is gonna be off-limits for a while," Omar explains, pulling me into a hug. I melt into his warmth, his scent wrapping around me like a blanket. He plants another kiss on my forehead.

"I'm sorry about all this, baby girl. I'm glad you came back. Thought you might have given up on me by now, the way Ed said you took off."

Yeah, if only he knew the struggle behind making that decision.

"I just want to know what went down, why, and if you had any idea something was coming. You and Eddie were acting weird earlier," I say, another yawn escaping me.

"Some young fools thought they could mess with my operation. They didn't succeed, though. I took care of it."

What the hell did he do? Did he... kill them? I wouldn't put it past him. "I don't even wanna know. I'm glad Eddie is okay but I'm ready to go. I might just fall asleep right here."

We pull away, and he bends down to check out the back of my thigh. "You're officially initiated, baby girl. First bullet, congrats."

"Not funny. Let's bounce before I punch you for putting me through this stress."

Omar laughs and stands up, wrapping his arms around my shoulders, still grinning.

Guess I'll drop the pregnancy bomb after my marathon nap. Almost forgot about that, so I need to wrap my head around it myself before breaking it to him.

———— ♡ ————

You know, there's this fluttery thing happening in my belly every now and then. It's like a tickle, but I think my little one's trying to remind me they're in there, and it's about time I spill the news to Omar. I've been holding off because I wanted us to be sure of my decision before dropping the baby bomb. Luckily, I haven't been as sick as I thought I'd be. But, man, I'm not sure how he'll take it. I can't shake off the memory of how he treated Tara when she was pregnant, but I also haven't been with anyone else for him to question me about. And seriously, I can't believe I got knocked up this fast. I could have sworn I told Omar to be careful with that.

But despite all that, Omar and I have been having a blast. He even let me give his place a makeover, so it feels more like home. After we got the news that Eddie was going to pull through, we went all out, partying hard for weeks after the incident.

Omar's been throwing house parties left and right, even organized something for Eddie at one of the hottest clubs off the Sunset Strip. It's been surreal being by his side. He takes me everywhere, loves flaunting me like some kind of trophy. I feel like royalty, with people always showering me with gifts, snapping pictures—it's like living a dream.

I've even made a couple of girlfriends—Janay and Rita. They're chill, and they're part of Omar's crew. The only thing is, they've been in the game longer than me, so there's some slight disconnect as far as common interests goes. Janay's pushing thirty, and Rita's probably Omar's age. Sometimes, though, I can't help but miss Sheila. We only catch up every now and then, and Omar's not a fan of it. He really doesn't trust her, and I'm dying to know why.

"Girl, you've hit the jackpot," Rita says, her hand gently rubbing mine as we settle into our booth at the bar. "Omar treats you like a Queen, Chevy. We ain't never seen it before."

"He does," I reply, signaling the server for a glass of water with lemon. Maybe I shouldn't be sipping on booze anymore, but truth is, I've had a few lately. Just didn't want folks raising eyebrows or giving me the third degree.

Janay adjusts her drooping bra strap and takes a drag of her cigarette before turning to Rita and me. "That's beautiful... You think he's gonna put a ring on it?"

"Girl, we've only been a thing for a couple of months. Marriage ain't exactly on the agenda for either of us," I shoot back.

Rita and Janay exchange a glance before looking away, and a flicker of unease ripples through me. *What do they know that I don't?* My heart starts thumping. Marriage hasn't even crossed my mind. *Isn't that rushing things?* Or maybe this is what Dad meant when he said I'd just know. That the right man would just know. I love Omar, sure, but we haven't even dropped the L-bomb yet, so the marriage talk feels too soon.

"What's the big difference between what we're doing now and tying the knot anyway?" I ask, genuinely curious.

Both of them sport some pretty sparklers on their fingers. If I had something like that on my finger, I'd be staring at it 24/7. Just the thought of a man slipping a ring on my finger as a declaration of his love feels downright magical. But the whole institution of marriage? I'm not sold just yet.

"I forgot you still young so you don't understand yet. It just makes it official, I guess. People say we live longer, get richer, and overall happier when we're hitched," Janay explains, shrugging as she takes a sip of her sweet, red wine, coughing a bit afterward.

The light overhead is starting to make me sweat, but I keep my cool. I ponder as to why they put marriage on a pedestal. They both don't seem too thrilled about their marriages, so I'm not quite getting it.

"That's not cutting it for me. I need time. We're still getting the hang of each other. People change, you know? What if we decide, after really knowing each other, that this isn't our thing anymore?" I throw it out there.

Janay shoots me a side-eye. "You ain't into being tied down, huh? Might be onto something, Chev."

"It's not like that," I clarify.

Rita chimes in, "Or look at it this way: you'd have his last name and probably half of everything he's got. We're talking about Omar here. Better lock that down, honey. You won't be young or look this good forever."

They're getting under my skin. But maybe it's not just them; it's the fact that I never really thought about any of this until now. I mean, having a baby on the way is making me rethink a lot about my life.

Rita continues. "And your babies would be set if you two tie the knot." She reaches over, tapping my glass of water after giving me a pointed look. *Does she know? And if she does, how?*

"Well, Omar and I haven't even talked about marriage and babies. We're just focusing on each other right now," I say.

"That ain't bad at all. You're only twenty, right?" Janay asks.

"Twenty-one."

"Since you haven't even hit that second puberty yet, I'm sticking with the idea that Chevy doesn't wanna be tied down. I can get behind that... Keep yourself a backup in case Omar starts acting up," Janay adds.

"Nah, that's not my style. Cheating's cheating. If I can't commit to one guy, then I shouldn't be in a relationship at all," I declare firmly.

Janay crushes her cigarette into the ashtray, grabbing her second drink and taking a sip through the straw. I should probably let her know she's got lipstick on her teeth. "What's the big deal? You really think Omar ain't already doing that?"

Rita scoffs, checking her makeup in her compact mirror, then handing it to Janay. "Exactly. They all do it, so why can't we?"

I glance between Janay and Rita, feeling myself shrink in my seat. I hadn't even thought about that. *I mean, why would a man like Omar only want me?*

"Chevy, you might as well accept it. It comes with the territory. Just remember, you're still his number-one lady, especially if you end up marrying the man. Those other bitches don't even matter," Janay says, resting her bony hand with chipped, red fingernail polish on my shoulder.

I glance across the room at the men. The air is thick with cigarette smoke, but it's easy to spot Omar. He just has that kind of presence in a room. Then again, maybe it's because he's the only one I'm looking for.

I watch him mingling with his crew and a sting of sadness hits me. *What if he's already got someone else on the side?* Those late nights and the times when I don't see him for half the damn day—it's hard not to wonder if he's really out there building his "empire." Then again, why the hell would he ask me to be his girlfriend if that's the case? It's messing with my head. I mean, he pulled the same move on Tara with me.

Omar must've caught wind of my thoughts because our eyes lock, and here he comes, making his way over. *Damn.* I'd better pull myself together.

"Hey, baby girl, you doin' alright?" he asks as he reaches our table.

Janay and Rita purse their lips and deliberately look away. Why do these girls act like he's going to break them or something? That's got to sting for him. Maybe I should bring it up sometime.

"I'm good, Omar. Just getting a bit tired," I say.

"Let's bounce, then." He digs some bills from his pocket and leaves them under a wineglass on the table. "Ladies..."

"Thanks, O," Rita chimes in.

"Yeah, y'all have a good night. Catch you later, Chevy," Janay adds.

Omar extends his hand, and Rita slips out of her side of the booth to let me out. I give a little wave to the ladies, and we make our exit from the club.

"So, we're just gonna dip from the party like that? Not even gonna say bye?" I glance back at the crowd still streaming into the bar.

"What they need us for? We showed up, had a bit of fun, now we're out," Omar replies, his tone casual.

I appreciate the fresh air outside. The smoke and the noise inside were starting to get to me. But damn, why's he gotta walk so fast? His strides are huge, practically dragging me along behind him.

"Hey, slow down, boo. I'm feeling a bit lightheaded," I tell him, swallowing hard as I start to feel queasy.

Omar eases his pace and turns to face me. "You pregnant, ain't you?"

Well, damn. Should I even be surprised he figured it out? He's like a human lie detector. It was only a matter of time, I guess.

"Um... Why do you say that?" I stall, knowing I can't keep denying it.

"It's pretty obvious, baby girl. You've been sick, tired, and ain't been hitting the drinks or the smoke."

"Oh..." I thought I was hiding it well, but I guess not, if Rita and Omar can see right through me.

But at least he's been paying attention to me. That's kind of sweet too.

"Yeah, I am. Sorry I didn't tell you sooner. I just wanted us to be solid before dropping the bomb," I admit, feeling a weight lift off my shoulders.

"I ain't mad at you," he says, opening the passenger side as we reach the car. "I kinda figured it was just a matter of time with the way we've been all over each other."

I can hear him chuckle as he closes my door and strides around to the driver's side. Well, there goes my surprise. But he's got a point. We can't seem to keep our hands off each other. And we sure as hell haven't been careful about it. I'm talking barely stepping through the door before our clothes hit the floor or waking up in the morning and getting busy before even brushing our teeth. And don't get me started on showering together—that's a whole other level of risky business. I swear, watching those water droplets slide down his sculpted body does something to me.

The one thing that gets on my nerves from time to time is how he lets his crew come and go as they please. They mostly hang out in the basement, but still. Can't they give us some damn space once in a while? I'm not used to having people invade my personal bubble, and I'll have to bring it up with him. The only person I'm cool with always being at the house is Eddie.

The family house still isn't ready, so Omar let Eddie crash here. I've barely said two words to him since the incident. *What can I even say to a guy I left hanging like that?* He could've been killed, and all I was thinking about was saving my own skin. Omar keeps telling me I'm overthinking it, that Eddie's not holding it against me like that, so maybe I'll talk to him soon.

Omar gives some of his crew a dap as we enter and head upstairs. I flop onto our—yes, *our*—massive bed without even bothering to take off my jacket. He smiles and pulls off my shoes.

"You must've been real tired," he remarks, gently sitting me up and helping me out of my jacket.

"I was just tired of chatting with those girls. I mean, I like them and all, but they can be a bit much sometimes," I explain.

"They still better than your lil' friend Sheila," he mutters as he lights a few candles.

Alright, it's time to address the elephant in the room. And not the painting of the one he has hanging on this wall. "Omar, why do you have an issue with Sheila? What's going on that I don't know about?"

"If she's messin' around with your old boss, she ain't good news either. They both sneaky as hell, and I on' want you getting tangled up in that shit and whatever else her desperate ass be doin' out here."

"I couldn't care less about Randall's business. We've known for a while that he's shady, but Sheila just got caught up and fell in love."

"And that's the dangerous part. It means she'll do anything for him. The only reason he ain't try anything with you is 'cause he knows I won't stand for it. He knows I on' fuck with him or his type," Omar explains.

"You don't think you and him are cut from the same cloth? He's into drugs, money, women, *me*... Just like you," I challenge, sitting up to meet his gaze.

He gives me a side-eye, and I can sense his irritation. "You really think I'm just like that fool, huh? That bothers me, baby girl," Omar shakes his head and takes off his jacket. "I'm nothin' like him."

"I don't mean it like that. Just help me understand how you're so different, Omar? Convince me," I urge, searching his eyes for answers.

His smile carries a hint of intrigue. "For one, I got you."

"You got me? So, what, your goal was just to hit and quit?" I tease, wanting to see his reaction.

"Nah, it's more like... You mine now. He couldn't snag you," he explains, his tone softening. "I win."

A slight blush warms my cheeks. "You make me sound like some kind of prize. I'm not that damn special."

"You are a prize. You are special. I haven't met a lady like you, someone who thinks the way you do. So, the fact that we crossed paths, I couldn't let you or the opportunity pass me by," he admits.

Omar disappears into the bathroom and starts the bath. He is so thoughtful, and it sends a warm flutter through my belly. His presence alone causes all sorts of sensations through my body. But hold on. *Is it the baby?* I think it's the baby that's causing those flutters too.

I hold my hand over the lower part of my tummy and let out a deep sigh. Omar is casually leaning against the door frame between the bathroom and our room when I glance up.

"We gonna be a'ight, baby girl. I know we just starting this thing between us, and it might be a lil' early for us to be havin' one, but it'll work out," he assures me.

"How can you be so sure?"

He might say all the reassuring things, but he has to realize that with his growing status and influence, it'll only draw more attention, whether from enemies or the law. *And what if something happens to him?* It'll just be me and our baby, alone.

Omar flips on some R&B music and comes closer, bending down to place his hand on my tummy. The sadness leaves instantly as he locks eyes with mine.

"We both know what this world can be like... being abandoned out here and havin' to rely on ourselves to get through. But the way our minds are set up, how strong we are alone... How much stronger we are together.... this is the goodness we about to bring into the world, and the world could use our combination. What you think?" he says, his words hitting me in all the right places.

Oh, he's so sweet. He has this way with words that makes everything clear. Tears tease the brim of my eyes, and I bite my lip.

"I agree with that..." I smile, placing my hand over his. "Did you feel the same about you and Tara?"

And just like that, he withdraws his hand and straightens up. *Damn it.* I had to go and ruin a perfectly good moment. "I'm sorry, boo. I didn't mean to bring that up right now."

"You good, baby girl. Tara admitted to me that she just ain't know for sure. So, she ended it."

Wow. I'm glad that she fessed up to the abortion but now I wonder if Janay and Rita got into her head about that foolish side-piece stuff. "I'm sorry to hear that, Omar. I had no idea she was still doing stuff with Randall behind your back."

"I was doing stuff behind hers too," he says, shrugging and winking at me.

Right. He was doing me behind her.

"Well, word on the street is that I'm not the only one you might be doing either," I say, raising my eyebrow as I await his response.

His face remains unreadable. "Sounds like word on the street came from a hater."

I collapse to the floor in laughter, rolling over onto my back. Okay, that was funny. Omar joins me on the floor, laughing until we're both staring up at the ceiling. This rug is so plush and cozy. I could easily fall asleep on it.

"Nah, but seriously, baby girl. I don't want nobody else. You rare, and you real to me. I like how you not afraid to be yourself out here."

"Thank you. But yes, I'm not afraid, and I'm gonna teach our baby the same thing one day."

"I like that. I'm okay with that. You shouldn't be afraid. It seems like everybody's tryna be like somebody else these days. So it makes you stand out against the rest."

"Oh yeah? You think so?"

"Hell yeah. It's like... when we in a room full of people, I always find you."

My mouth parts slowly, and I turn my head to look at him, in awe watching him stare up at the ceiling.

"You gonna make me cry, Omar. That's the nicest thing somebody has ever told me. I always find you too," I respond, moving my forefinger to catch a falling tear. "It's easy to spot you though. You can be real flashy sometimes. And you smell real good."

Omar chuckles, then turns his head to face me. "You trust me?"

"I trust you. You trust me too?"

He nods calmly, moving his finger under my chin. "I trust you, baby girl."

We push our lips together, and I surrender my mouth to his.

———— ♡ ————

The Phoenix Fire is still jumping, just like old times. Honestly, I didn't think it would be after Randall ditched me and a few other dancers. But hey, I gotta check my ego because this joint was booming before I even set foot in here.

Tonight, I'm here to see Sheila do her thing — well, watch her dance, that is. She asked me for some tips because apparently Randall's got his eyes glued to some new girl, and Sheila's determined to keep his attention on her. It's sad, really, but if she wants to play that game, I guess I'll let her. I can't be an enabler, but she'll figure it out soon enough. We all know how Randall rolls.

My baby bump is starting to show, but only if I'm wearing a dress that's tighter than a drum. Lately, I've been squeezing into those whenever I'm out with Omar. He's always saying nobody can tell because my ass distracts them. I just remember playfully shoving him when he cracked that joke. And let me tell you, he's all about that booty. But hey, that's my man, so it's all good.

"Check you out, Chevy! You're getting thicker, mama. Omar's treating you right, isn't he?" Sheila gives me a knowing wink before pulling me in for a hug. "You know what I'm saying."

"Yeah, I know what you mean, and it's true. Look at this." I tug my V-neck down just a bit to reveal the hickey on my chest.

Sheila covers her mouth, trying to stifle her giggles. "Y'all are wild, ha-ha. But you look happy. Glowing and all. Hair touching your shoulders. Come on, sit with me and let's catch up." Sheila guides me over to a table near the stage, and we settle in. "So, spill the tea. What's new with you?"

"So, um... I've just been hanging out with his crew a lot. Partying, doing all that girlfriend stuff, you know? Like wearing his clothes and sniffing his shirts all day... waiting for him to show up. Talking on the phone when he's not around," I tell Sheila.

"Well, at least he's claiming you, girl. I'd give anything for that," she sighs, her gaze drifting up to the balcony.

I follow her eyes and spot Randall chatting it up with some girl. Must be the one Sheila's trying to outshine. I give her hand a little tap.

"Maybe you should just ditch him, Sheila. You know how he is. It was just a matter of time before he moved on," I suggest.

"That's easy for you to say, Chevy. I fell hard for him," Sheila replies, her voice heavy with emotion.

"I know, but you're young, girl. There's more out there. Fuck Randall."

"You're young too, and you've got someone. Why do you always have to bring up my age, Chevy? You hate it when people do that to you," Sheila retorts, frustration evident in her voice.

"I'm not saying it like that. I'm saying I don't want you wasting your life on some jerk like Randall. You don't deserve someone who can't keep it in his pants," I explain firmly.

Sheila pushes a curl away from her face and rests her head on the table. I watch her for a moment before turning back to glance at the balcony. Randall catches my eye and smirks. I roll my eyes and turn away.

"Sheila, seriously, if you keep messing with him, your heart's gonna keep getting torn up. I don't want that for you," I caution.

"You say that, but you're messing with somebody you said you never would. Isn't that the same thing?" She raises her head, waiting for my response.

"It's all about how the person treats you and makes you feel. The way Omar loves me outweighs the messed-up stuff I thought about him at first," I explain.

"You act like you know it all, but Omar's still one dangerous cat, Chevy. I don't think you realize that. At least Randall isn't out here killing people and slinging dope," she retorts.

I can tell she's feeling some type of way. *What did I do to make her go off like this?*

"How's your leg doing?" She changes the subject, probably noticing my expression.

"It's cool. I have a scar, but it doesn't hurt anymore," I reply.

"You're talking about me and protecting myself, but you really got shot at, and you didn't even do anything wrong," she points out.

"Omar has made sure I don't have any connection to that part of his life, and he promised to keep me safe from it," I explain.

"See? You sound like me, Chevy, and you don't even know it. Both these dudes ain't no good for us, and deep down, we know it. But we don't wanna believe it 'cause we want them," she says with a sigh.

Damn, she's really hitting me where it hurts. I hate to admit it, but she's got a point. I just don't know how to make her see that she deserves better treatment than what Randall's dishing out. It's hard for her to take me seriously or my advice seriously when I'm involved with Omar. Although, I still believe my situation is completely different than hers.

"He must be hiding it from you real well, Chevy, 'cause you must not know how dangerous your man really is."

"He's not dangerous. And if he is, it's towards people who wanna hurt him or mess with what's his," I respond, rolling my eyes.

"But he's the one getting involved in all these businesses and trying to take stuff that isn't his. How is that protecting what he's got? No, he's just greedy," she counters.

"You don't know him, Sheila—"

"You don't either, Chevonne."

"You've got this preconceived notion about him 'cause you're messing with Randall, and you already know Randall doesn't like Omar like that. Think for yourself."

Sheila shakes her head. "Okay. Well, I see why he wants to mess with you now. You're so blind to his bullshit, and you want to be ignorant. That's what he wants. Somebody gullible by his side, and before you know it, you're gonna be popping out his kids and bowing down to everything he says."

How is she getting to me like this? What is she even talking about? I can't stand it when people make assumptions about my relationship just because Omar is who he is. The thing about her last statement is that Omar could really get with any naive chick, but I'm not naive. I'm not gullible, and I'm definitely not weak. He knows that, so if that was his goal, then why did he pick me? Sheila doesn't know what she's talking about.

I let out a heavy sigh and reach for my purse. I refuse to just sit here and take her belittling because Randall has already moved on to the next girl.

As I stand up, she reaches out and grabs my wrist. "I'm sorry, Chevy. I didn't mean to say that. I'm just jealous," she confesses.

"It takes a lot to admit that, but you could have just said that before going off on me like that," I reply, giving in to her pull and sinking back into my seat. "I get what you're saying, but I understand that nobody really knows Omar beyond the rumors and what they've seen. He's a decent man who came from messed-up circumstances like most of us, and he wants to ensure he and the people around him never have to go through that again."

"I know, okay..." Tears trickle down her face, and I reach over to wipe a few away. It's too late; she's already fallen for this man.

"Your heart's in a rough spot right now, and it's only going to get worse before it gets better. But for that to happen, you have to let go of Randall," I advise.

"Chevy... how do you know so much? Sometimes, I can't believe you're the age you say you are," she admits.

I don't really have an answer for her. Besides my dad's words from when I was growing up, I just rely on my intuition and a thing called common sense. Plus, I live in my head, always thinking and piecing things together.

"It doesn't really matter if I'm telling you all this if it's just going in one ear and out the other," I respond.

"I... I want to give him one more chance. Just one more," she pleads.

"Why? If he cared, he'd be down here with you instead of up there cozying up to her," I point out.

"I know what he wants, and if I can give it to him, everything will be fine again."

"Okay... What is it?" I ask, trying to decipher her expression as she grabs my hand.

"He's all I have, Chevy. I don't talk to my grandma anymore. She kicked me out. I don't have my own place, so I stay with him. And you're too busy for me now, so all I have left is this job and him. And if I lose him, then what?" she explains, her voice tinged with desperation.

Dumb. I told her to finish school. "Okay, you didn't tell me all of that. That makes me sad," I respond, squeezing her hand gently.

"I know... so I'm saying that I know what he wants, and if I can do that for him, we'll be good."

"Okay, so what does he want?"

She hesitates. "He... um, he wants you, Chevy. I told him I would get you into bed with us, and he promised not to put me out on the street."

Mm. I should have seen this coming. I've been nothing but selfless to this girl, and she wants to sell my body to beg a man to stay with her.

I snatch my hand away and stand up again. "So that's why you really called me here. You're a sick person, Sheila. Omar was right about your sneaky ass," I accuse.

"Chevy, don't be mad or take it like that. It's not like you haven't been with Randall before," she counters.

"Don't bother calling me again. Good luck out there in the streets, Sheila," I snap, turning away from her.

I hear the sound of her head hitting the table in tears, and my heart sinks. I feel guilty for leaving her like this, but I'm furious that she would offer me up like that, using me for her own gain. *What's wrong with these women out here?* All of this drama over a man who couldn't care less about her. It's not just disrespectful to me, but to Omar and our relationship as well.

"He was right about her, Chevy. She'd do anything for Randall," a voice whispers in my head.

CHAPTER 12
Concrete Confessions

I MADE SURE TO call ahead and place an order for breakfast at a nearby neighborhood café. This place is always bustling, especially at this hour, and Omar couldn't understand why I insisted on having their breakfast. They whip up some of the best waffles and scrambled eggs, according to me and many other locals. Besides, I'm on good terms with the owners, and I don't need Omar's status to speed up my order. I'm looking forward to treating myself after the disappointing chat with Sheila last night, anyway. I'm just relieved Omar could join me.

"I can cook up something better than this," Omar declares, shoveling eggs and a somewhat soggy piece of waffle into his mouth.

"I gotta admit it, boo. These are some of the best waffles I've ever had. I'm always willing to wait in line for these. And the eggs."

"No, they not. If they soggy before I even drown them in syrup, somethin' is off back there. Probably over-stirring the ingredients and shit."

"That's pretty bold to say in a place that's packed every morning, and people are okay with being late to work for a plate," I remark, shrugging and adding a few sugar packets to my coffee.

"I'll be bold then. I challenge these waffle spots in town to a throwdown."

I'll give it to him; his waffles are top-notch. I once sat in the kitchen and watched him in action. He makes them crispy and fluffy with his secret ingredient – corn starch. And he prefers a light dusting of powdered sugar with just a bit of syrup.

"You can't be the best at everything, Omar."

"Why can't I?" he asks, his eyes blazing as I peek over my coffee cup at him.

"I'm just saying... leave some stuff for other people to be good at. You'll be fine, boo," I tease, giggling as his waffle bit falls from his fork.

We sit in silence for a moment. I playfully toy with his foot under the table, lost in thought about my next question. He notices my contemplation.

"What's on your mind, baby girl? You feeling sick?" he asks, breaking the silence and dabbing his mouth with a napkin.

Before I can utter a word, I notice a few people glancing at our table. Some wave at Omar, and there are a couple of giggling ladies at the front counter. They seem to be admiring my man.

Omar acknowledges the waving folks and follows my gaze behind him. "Nah, I ain't messing with any of them. Ion' even know them," he assures me.

I chuckle. "That's not what I wanted to ask you."

"What do you wanna ask me? And be careful 'cause you don't wanna ask questions you ain't ready to hear answers to," he warns.

"Well, I was wondering if I could spend a day with you? I mean, like a workday. See you in your element," I blurt out, hastily picking up my coffee mug after the question slips out.

Alright, I gotta admit, I slept on Sheila's comments from last night, and now I'm curious why she keeps insisting that I don't really know him. But I do. I know him well enough. I understand why he does what he does; he's just trying to avoid the struggle. Heck, most of us do things we never imagined just to avoid that struggle. I became a dancer, and now, I'm pregnant as a girlfriend. Not a wife.

Omar thinks about my question, leaning back in his chair, flattening one of his hands on the table. "No."

Oh. I wasn't expecting him to straight-up say no. I guess I thought he'd at least ask me why first.

"Ready to bounce, baby girl?" he asks.

Squinting at him, I question, "Wait, why can't I spend the workday with you, Omar?"

"'Cause I don't want you to."

"I thought you trusted me. I know I messed up with those brownies and tried to give them to Randall that one time, but I would never do that shit again. I won't spill your secrets or anything," I insist.

Omar looks around before leaning in. I hope I'm not being too loud.

"I trust you, but Ion' want you to be part of that. I know how you really feel about what I do, and I think it's better to keep you where you comfortable," Omar explains.

Is he genuinely thinking about me, or is he hiding something? I furrow my brow and shift in my seat. "I'm not a little girl, Omar. I know I can handle it."

"I ain't say you was a lil' girl. I said that I know how you feel, and Ion' think you should have to see that side of what I do."

"I have before. Are you scared I'm gonna look at you differently?" I question.

Omar rubs below his chin and sighs.

"Can we just get up outta here? I don't want you to be late for your lil' nap," he suggests.

I playfully kick his shin under the table, and he winces with laughter. He makes me sound boring. Maybe I am boring, like Tara used to call me. Or maybe I'm just bored. Well, I'm not bored. This is one of the most exciting times of my life, living all in love and shit like that.

"The reason I've been sleeping like this is 'cause of the kid growing in my belly. Thanks to you."

"It ain't just my fault. You was the one telling me, 'don't stop, don't stop, Omar.' So, what the hell did you expect me to do? Stop?" He leans back, chuckling.

I giggle softly. "Well, don't make fun of me because we can't help what we say or do in the moment sometimes."

"Yeah, okay. You clawed the heck out of my back, baby girl. I felt that when the water hit it in the shower. You a lil' wild," he teases.

"*Me?* I'm the one with lip prints, suction holes, and chunks of skin missing. I think that might be you," I counter.

He throws his head back, laughing heartily. I love making him laugh.

"You silly. I meant to ask you, how was your time out last night? You got to see your homegirl?"

Great. I was hoping he wouldn't ask about that because it makes me sad just thinking about it. But I know he won't let it go unless I tell him what happened. I can't share with him what Sheila said about him and me though. That might hurt his feelings. I also can't tell him about that arrangement Sheila was trying to set me up in. There's no way in hell, especially because he already doesn't like them. I don't want to think about what he might do or say right now.

"Baby girl?"

"Oh, uh... yeah, it was cool. I watched her dance and gave her some pointers. Stuff like that," I reply.

Just as he's about to respond, his pager goes off. *Saved by the pager.* I didn't even realize that thing had been quiet this entire time. I guess I should be grateful because now it's time for us to go. There are just so many things I want to discuss with him, though. But we have plenty of time for that. We have so much more to learn about each other.

———— ♡ ————

As I step through the front door, Eddie is limping down the stairs. Omar had to drop me off while he tended to his usual business. Already, I miss the man, but I'm grateful for the morning we spent together.

"Oh hey, Eddie. Need some help?" I offer, watching him navigate each step carefully.

"Aye, Miss Chevy. Nah, I'm alright. I gotta get there on my own," he assures me.

I hang up my jacket on the coatrack and slip off my shoes.

"How was breakfast with O?"

"It was nice. I'm glad he had some time for me this morning,"

"Well, yeah... He's always gonna make time for you anyway. You got our boy in *love* love," Eddie remarks fondly.

Aww. I really wish I could be a fly on the wall when Omar talks to Eddie. I know he's the only other person who knows Omar on a deeper level. I'm getting there... Trying to.

Finally, Eddie reaches the bottom of the steps and waves me over. "On second thought, let me use your shoulder, Miss Chevy."

"Of course. I got you, Eddie," I assure him. Together, we make our way to the dining room, and I help him pull a chair to sit in it. "You didn't want to sit in there and watch some cable?"

"I wanna sit in here and chat with ya. We ain't been talkin' much," Eddie says.

He's right. I've been avoiding him, and it's time I offer my apology. I can't hide from him forever.

"I know, and I just want to say that I'm sorry for leaving you to get shot up like that. I feel so bad, Eddie. I didn't know how I could face you again," I admit.

"Missy Chevy. You never gotta apologize for savin' yourself. I'm glad you thought fast. That mighta been what saved my life," Eddie reassures me.

"How?" I ask, intrigued by his perspective. "You still got shot."

"Well, if you savin' yourself, Ion' have to worry too much about you. I would be dead anyway if O saw me come out alive without you." Eddie laughs to himself, adding in a headshake.

"He would never do anything to you. Not over me? He's known you longer anyway," I argue.

"How you think I got this hole in my leg? The one in my back came from the enemy. But this one..." Eddie trails off, and I look down at his leg in shock.

"What! Omar shot you!"

"All jokes, my dear," Eddie chuckles, holding his hand to his face.

That wasn't funny. I actually believed it for a second.

"I'm sorry if you didn't like that joke, Miss Chevy."

I release a quick sigh of relief. "No, it's all right. It's funny now that I think about it, but I'm mad at myself for even entertaining the thought, even for a second, that he would do that."

"He would though. Probably not to me, 'cause I don't got any reason to wanna hurt you. Anybody else gives you hell? You know who to go to. When O says he's gonna handle something or somebody, he follows through. Always," Eddie asserts.

That's both comforting and concerning. Comforting because he's a natural protector, and I appreciate that about him. Concerning because he has a temper, a bad one, and he won't hesitate to act on it. I have a scar on the back of my arm to prove it, although that sounds bad.

"Anyway, I heard you got a little bun in the oven. I'm happy for y'all," Eddie remarks, pointing at my stomach, and I instinctively place my hand over it.

That reminds me I have to take my vitamins; I didn't remember this morning.

"Yeah, thanks, Eddie. I'm scared as hell, though. I also think me and Omar moved a little too fast with this," I confess.

"Don't think like that. There's no timeline for any of that. Things just happen how they're meant to out here, Miss Chevy. Let's hope you're popping out a healthy one instead, eh? O's gonna make sure y'all are okay at the end of the day," Eddie reassures me.

Once again, he's right. I love talking to Eddie. He always knows just what to say, and now, I'm not so nervous anymore. "Okay. I hear you. I should probably stop moping around about it and get myself ready. I always knew that I wanted to be a mama, so I'm excited to meet my little baby."

Eddie smiles and nods, but another question pops up in my mind.

"Hey, Eddie... I asked Omar if I could spend the day at work with him, see what he does, but he said no. I'm kinda bothered by that 'cause I don't wanna think he's hiding something from me. Do you know why he probably said no?"

"Well, what was his reason? I know he gave you one." Eddie turns his head to the side.

"He said he knows that I don't like what he does, so he wants to keep me away from it. But Eddie, if that's the case, then why did he have me staying at the family house and making those brownies and shit?"

"Brownies ain't nothing compared to what else he got going on, Miss Chevy. You was able to get yourself together 'cause of it and that's how O is with the people he cares about. He wants to look out for you. That's love. I ain't never seen him like this with no other lady in his life," Eddie explains.

Not even Tara? It seemed like he loved her to me. "So I shouldn't worry about other women and shit like that? Did he have other girlfriends before me and Tara?" I ask Eddie.

"I don't think you gotta worry about that, Miss Chevy. From what I've seen about O, he don't get caught up in women all like that. He used to tell me they were too distracting for him, but he... well, the ladies loved him, and he let himself have a quite a bit of fun before he pulled back. So the fact he's spending all this time and energy on you is a good thing," Eddie reassures me.

Sounds good but sounds like Omar used to get around. "Was Tara his first girl-friend?"

"Nope. But it takes some time to find somebody good for you. You can't worry about that or you might drive yourself crazy. You his woman now and that's what you gotta focus on," Eddie offers, adjusting his posture in the seat.

I notice him wince a bit. "How come you don't have a woman or kids yourself?"

I don't think he was prepared for that kind of question. Eddie looks off and out of the window in the dining room. He just stares out, contemplating like the question I asked him is too heavy. The lingering silence in the room makes me feel a little awkward, and I'm thinking about just getting up and leaving him with his thoughts and hoping I didn't go too far, with my nosy ass.

"I had a woman. Ain't loved another one since. I got two kids though. I met them once."

"So, wait... what happened to her? And why have you only met your kids one time?"

"She left. Was scared away by this life after a job gone wrong one day. This was years ago. She never looked back."

Damn.

"Neither one of my kids are by her though. I wasn't the most loyal man to her." He scratches his ungroomed beard. It has gray hair all throughout.

I don't think I want to hear any more about this story because it doesn't seem to have a happy ending. If so, they would be here with him. Then he admits to cheating on her, and it had to be more than once if he got two kids that aren't by her. *But he loved her?* All the things I am afraid of with being with Omar.

"That was years back though. Back when I was in the street gangs in the south. Nothin' too bad but bad enough to make me wanna leave it alone," Eddie says, his voice carrying the weight of those memories.

"I'm sorry to hear about that, Eddie. That makes me so sad. Is that how you met Omar?"

"Yep. He was holdin' his lifeless mama when I found him. He sat there on that concrete and wouldn't let her go until he absolutely had to."

Immediately, I'm taken aback. Then, my heart completely shatters. My poor Omar. "What... What happened to her?"

"Her boyfriend at the time had killed her. She was tryna leave him, and lil' O was already out runnin' the streets at that age. I think he was about fifteen years old, Miss Chevy," Eddie explains, his voice heavy with sorrow.

I quickly catch the tears that fall from my eyes with a folded napkin from the table. Eddie sits quietly, his expression filled with understanding, as I try to compose myself.

"So, he was on his own since he was fifteen?" I ask, feeling a mix of admiration and concern for Omar.

"I mean I was there, and he had his crew. The boy was already mature for his age. He just struggled with finishing up school, but he did. He finished that shit, and I was proud of him. After that, he would tell me he wanted to leave home and go west, wanted me and the family to go with him. So we got our shit together and moved this way a few years back," Eddie explains, his voice tinged with pride.

I'm trying to piece together why I've never heard of Omar until I met him through Tara if he had such a significant impact on our city over the last few years. Okay, let me scale it back. I was probably too preoccupied taking care of daddy and in school while it all happened. Daddy never really talked about gangs and drugs, just said to stay away from them. So, before meeting these people, I only knew what I did from watching movies and cable shows.

My pager buzzes, and I take a moment to get up and retrieve it. Eddie is already in the kitchen, fixing himself a snack, providing me with a convenient excuse to step away from the heavy conversation we just had. Even though it was somber, I find myself grateful for the insightful revelation about Omar's past.

"Alright, Eddie, I'm gonna go see who this is, and then I'ma take a nap or somethin'," I inform him, making my way to the jacket where I left my pager.

"Alright, pretty lady. Let me know if you need anything. I'ma be down here for a while," Eddie replies, and I appreciate his understanding.

I glance at the pager's display, recognizing the number—Janay. *What could she want?* Probably just to hang out. The cordless phone feels weighty in my hand as I dial Janay's number, not really eager to chat but ready just in case it's urgent. She picks up.

"Hi, Chevy. You busy?" Janay's voice comes through, slightly muffled by the sounds of children in the background.

"Um, not really. I was probably gonna take a nap. Why? What's up?"

"Well, save that nap. You wanna do somethin'? I need to get away from these damn kids," Janay suggests, her tone suggesting she's in need of a break.

Damn it. I was really counting on catching some Z's, but I don't mind helping out my new friend. It could be a chance for us to bond and get to know each other better.

"Okay yeah, we can chill. Where do you wanna go?" I hope she doesn't suggest hitting up a bar.

"Let's do some day drinking," Janay proposes.

"I don't really wanna drink right now, Janay. I need to slow it down 'cause it's been makin' me sick," I reply, recalling the importance of a swift "no" when dealing with these situations.

"You buy, and I drink for the both of us. Curtis is out, and he ain't tryna spend time with me anyway, so I thought to call my girl, Chevy."

"Fine, but who is gonna watch your babies?"

"Oh, his mom is here. She said I should get out."

"Okay. I'll come get you soon," I agree, resigned to the idea of setting aside my nap for a chance to support Janay and spending time with her, even if it means playing the booze babysitter for a while.

❦

Janay can't resist exploring every nook and cranny of my car, and although it mildly irks me, I'm relieved I'm the one behind the wheel. Since she plans on drinking, I'll be the judge of when it's time for us to head home. Despite how touchy she's being to my vehicle, I can't deny that Janay is cute. With her big, fluffy curls and stylish ensemble – parachute pants, a small V-neck top, and a high-waist belt – she exudes a Lisa Bonet vibe. I notice that her makeup might be making her look older, and I suspect her smoking habit might be speeding up the aging process. However, I decide not to mention it because her comfort is more important to me than picking at her.

"Chevy, I love your lil' car. It fits you so perfectly," she compliments, glancing at herself in the visor mirror and absentmindedly using her index finger to wipe her teeth.

"Thanks. I really shouldn't be driving it a lot 'cause I still don't have a license, but I'm a careful driver."

"I don't got my license either, and I'm haulin' kids around all day in mine. I be having to reach back and pick up bottles and shit... Stop them from fighting each other and jumpin' outta windows while I'm driving. I'm surprised I ain t get ticketed yet."

Is that what it's like driving around with babies? I guess I will find out when I have mine. "What bar you tryna go to?"

Janay hesitates before answering, and my raised eyebrow prompts her response. "Actually, I only had said that on the phone 'cause Curtis's ma was in my face and my business."

Oh, no.

"I wanna... go check on Curtis 'cause I think he seein' somebody."

"Janay, I'm not tryna do this. Why ain't you call Rita or somebody else?" I protest, not eager to get involved in relationship drama. *Again.*

"Rita's probably floating in the clouds right now, so I figured I'd count on you."

I groan internally. *How did I become the go-to confidante?* It's like I have a neon sign on my forehead that says, "Talk to me about your drama."

"Anyway, where is he? I'll just drop you off, Janay. I'm tired and not really in the mood for drama. Sorry."

"No worries, girl. I get it. He's either at the office or the Lab." Janay taps her cigarette pack before lighting one. "Let's try the Lab first since that's where he spends most of his time... and where everyone else hangs out too. The favorite hoes included."

The Lab? I wonder what that is. Omar seems to have so many places, and I still have a lot to learn about him and his operations – if he allows me. "Where is that? What is it?" I ask Janay.

She looks over slowly and blinks. "How are you dating the man who runs the show and don't know shit about it? It's where they handle the major stuff. Where do you think he probably is right now?"

"He doesn't want me too involved in his operations, so, no, I don't know where or what that is 'cause he didn't tell me."

"I can understand that. Okay, it's right over there, off Rosecrans Avenue, near that old church."

"That close? I thought it was off in the middle of the hood somewhere."

Janay laughs while blowing out smoke. "You would."

I roll my window down, letting the lingering smoke escape, so I won't have to endure the smell for long. It seems like I'll have to reveal my pregnancy soon to keep them and their unhealthy habits at a distance.

"How long have you and Curtis been together?" I steer the conversation toward Janay's personal life, feeling like I need more context for the detective work we're about to embark on.

"Been about five years. We tied the knot right before O brought us all over here. Curtis was different then. We both were," Janay responds, her voice drifting as she gazes out of the window.

"What do you think changed between you two?" I prod gently, sensing there's more to her words than meets the eye.

"Kids happened, and then Omar promoted him. I had to suck it up 'cause why rock the boat when we got everything we need? But still, it wouldn't hurt to have a loyal husband," Janay admits.

Questions start popping into my mind like fireworks on the Fourth of July. "When did you find out he was messing around?"

Janay nonchalantly shrugs. "Girl, that man never kept it in his pants. But, like I told you the other night, I'm the number one lady, baby. I got the ring." Yet, there's a hint of disbelief in her tone, as if she's trying to convince herself of something she doesn't quite believe.

I'm confused. "If you already know he's been fooling around, why choose today of all days to investigate? And why bring me along?"

Janay falls silent, her gaze shifting away from her ring to meet mine. "You need to see what you're gettin' into, Chevy. Up close and personal. The Lab is where it all happens."

A part of me wants to turn back, respecting Omar's boundaries. He was already against my request to delve deeper into his work, and I don't want to betray his trust. Yet, there's an undeniable allure to this mysterious "Lab," where apparently...

It all happens.

CHAPTER 13
What Lies in the Lab

THE LAB TURNS OUT to be nothing like I imagined. It's just an ordinary office building that blends right in with the rest of the neighborhood. I've probably driven past it countless times without even noticing. Who would have thought that this unassuming place is where Omar runs his operations? There's a large brick warehouse attached to the main building, with a couple of smaller office buildings nearby. It all fits in so well with the surroundings. I can't help but feel proud of Omar for keeping things low-key.

"Ladies, can we help you with something?" One of the burly guards inquires, his presence intimidating. They look like they could lift dumbbells for breakfast. I've never encountered these men before, or perhaps I've overlooked them amidst the throngs of people at Omar's gatherings. The sheer number of people in Omar's network is unbelievable, leaving me to wonder about the true magnitude of his power. It's just surreal to think of him as *my man.*

Janay doesn't miss a beat. "O and Curtis are expecting us. You don't have to let them know, though. They said to come right in," she says confidently, though I can tell it's a bluff. The security guys exchange a doubtful look before focusing their attention on me.

"We know you, but... who's this?" One of them gestures, his stubby finger pointing in my direction.

I keep quiet, fully aware that I shouldn't be here in the first place. If the guards decide to escort me out, I won't put up a fight. Omar explicitly told me this morning to steer clear of all this, so what business do I have strolling into the very place he orchestrates his supply chain?

"This is Chevonne," Janay responds confidently. "We came to see our men, like I said."

"Oh yeah... Miss Chevy. O's girl," one of the guards acknowledges. "It's nice to officially meet you."

"Yeah, I'm Chevonne, nice to meet you too. I'm with Omar, but I didn't come here to see him. I'll catch up with him later. I just brought her to see *her* man," I explain honestly, gesturing toward Janay, who rolls her eyes and nudges my hand down.

I can't help but feel a slight swell of pride that they already know me by name, and their intense stares seem to soften a bit after I speak. Omar must have told everyone about me, which feels oddly touching and makes me realize the reality of being with him.

"Okay. We weren't expecting anyone outside the workers today, but if O and Curt had you come out, we ain't gonna stop you," another guard says, easing the tension.

I don't feel right barging in like this. I definitely don't want to upset Omar. I'm sure he wanted to show me this place himself when he felt the time was right. A wave of nausea hits me suddenly, but it's manageable.

I turn to Janay. "Let's just go, Janay. I'm exhausted."

"Just give me a minute to handle what I came here for, and then we can go. Won't take long, hon," she insists, grabbing my wrist and pushing past the guards.

They shoot us confused glances but decide not to intervene. Clearly, Janay's popping up doesn't seem out of the ordinary for these guys, and I'm tempted to have a word with Omar about tightening up security – petite women shouldn't be able to push their way past his guards.

Janay continues her relentless pull, leading us through what feels like a labyrinth of doors, stairs, and more doors. I'm tempted to snatch my arm away, annoyed at this ridiculous journey. As we approach another door, she turns to me, placing a finger with a French-tipped nail against her lips.

In a hushed tone, she says, "You gonna see everything from in this room here. Don't nobody really go in here, so I like to come and see what Curtis is up to sometimes."

I give an indifferent shrug, waiting for her to open the door. Despite my irritation, I can't shake the sudden feeling of queasiness.

Upon entering, a distinct smell, like burning rubber, fills the air. I shake off the thought and follow Janay into the small, dreary office. The space is cramped, cluttered with cardboard boxes and miscellaneous items. Two enormous windows offer a view of the warehouse below, the same one I spotted attached to the building from the outside.

"Wow..."

This isn't like the crime scenes you see in movies. Well, some elements are familiar, like the topless women wearing face masks and the multitude of men stationed around, guarding the doors and overseeing operations. I notice piles of opaque, white powder neatly lined up on scales and tables, workers meticulously cutting up blocks and adding them to the heaps. It's all so clean and organized, but it's overwhelming for me. Omar was right to shield me from this. I might faint.

After giving me a moment to absorb the scene, Janay steps in front of me. "How you holding up, Chevy? I know it's a lot to take in since you ain't seen this before."

I continue to peer past her, unable to tear my eyes away. It feels surreal. "This is... all Omar's?"

"Mhm. He's got a whole setup, Chevy. And this ain't the only place, but it's the main one."

"How can none of you be afraid of this? It's too risky. Anyone could find this shit!" I press my hands to each side of my head, feeling overwhelmed.

"You know how long they've been at this? Since their days in Carolina," Janay explains, guiding us away from the window. "You shouldn't worry about that, Chevy. Omar's got the whole city wrapped around his finger, including the cops. The whole damn city is on your man's payroll."

"I understand that, but don't you think someone might wander in here one day, only to be confronted by a bunch of big guys in black and start asking questions?"

"Take it easy. That's not why we're here... You don't need to get worked up about something you already knew was happening."

"Janay, I'm sorry, but I couldn't care less about what's going on between you and Curtis right now. I'm trying not to pass out. I'm really dating a drug dealer, and he's way bigger than I thought. This is beyond anything I could have imagined!"

Janay lowers my hands to my sides and presses her finger to her lips once more. She glances out the window and then back at me. "I lied. I didn't bring you here to spy on Curtis."

All I can do is lower my eyes in annoyance. *What's wrong with this girl?* I jerk my arms away from her grip.

"Chevy, remember when we talked about having backup? Like a side thing?"

"Yeah?" I grumble, my head turning toward the door. I should just walk out of here and go home. I don't want to hear anything else from this liar, and I probably won't be hanging out with her again.

"Well, look out this window and down to the right. The far right."

"Janay..."

"Just do it."

I shake my head at her and roll my eyes as I approach the window. My forehead hits the glass a little too hard, but it's not loud enough to worry about being spotted, so I cautiously peek. My eyes search in the direction she indicated, and I see Omar, a few of his friends I recognize, and—

"Tara?" I whisper sharply.

Janay nods her head. "I knew you wouldn't believe me if I didn't show you. Curtis had told me, but don't say that I said anything, 'cause I don't want him mad at me, and I don't want Omar mad at him."

I'm not paying attention to a word she says. My heartbeat is too busy pounding in my ears. I watch them smile toward one another. He is tracing her jaw with his fingertip, and they're all up on each other. My nausea worsens as I see her hand run down his chest.

"I already know about the whole situation with Tara. I ain't never like that bitch, so I was happy that O moved on to you, but it ain't sit right with me knowing what I knew, and you were thinking that he was just on you."

The queasiness teases at the center of my chest, but I hold it back. It was too good to be true. My tears fall as I realize my feelings for Omar at this moment were deeper than I thought they were. Why would he do all of that just to get me, had me and this woman fighting because of him, got me pregnant, asked me to quit my job and move in with him, just to turn around and still be with Tara? *Am I seeing this right?* It's noticeably clear they're still involved just by their body language alone. This is the actual reason he didn't want me around this shit, and I think Eddie knew it too.

Janay eventually pulls me so I'm facing her and tugs me into a hug. I feel so foolish to let this man really convince me I was something special to him. He had me convinced that I was the only one he wanted and that I didn't need to worry. He wasted no time.

"Why the hell didn't he just stay with her?" I cry into Janay's shoulder. "Why did he pick me and do all that for me and still see her? I don't get it?"

"Tara knows the game real good, Chevy. She got her own connections, and they make a good team."

This must be the partnership that Eddie was referring to. I didn't know much about Tara's connections, though. I remember her mentioning she came from a family of business owners and people in the game, but I didn't delve into it further.

"But one thing all these men want, especially Omar, is a woman that will take care of the home and have the kids while they're away. They keep girlfriends though. Curtis got him one, but I know that. They keep us happy enough, so we don't bother them. That's what I was trying to explain to you, babe. You're so young entering this game, and O knows that."

"So he picked me 'cause I'm young and dumb."

"No, you're not dumb. You're good as hell for him, Chevy. You make that man happy. The happiest we've all seen. You're strong enough to stand by him in all of this but could love him just a little too much to just walk away and he needs that. That's what you mean to him. Tara wasn't that woman for him. I'm just telling you now, so you have some time to take it all in before things get deep, and you really end up hurt. I wish I had somebody to ease me into it a few years ago."

I appreciate Janay for this but cannot thank her at this moment. This answers my question about why Tara suddenly went so quiet after our fight. I haven't seen or heard from her, and I figured she just gave up and moved on or something. Now that I'm thinking about it, Omar told me he had spoken to her, and it went right over my head.

"I'm... pregnant, Janay." I finally let the secret out as she rubs my back to comfort me.

She pulls back and sighs, taking my hands in hers. "It was kinda obvious. I won't lie to you," she responds.

Great. No one is surprised.

"You love O, don't you?"

"Yeah... I guess. I thought he loved me too, but now this all makes sense 'cause we really just started going together. So there probably ain't no way he loves me back like that."

"He does, girl. I've seen the way y'all connect. It didn't take O long to realize that you make sense for him. That's deep, sis."

I use my sleeve to wipe my face. "Thanks for telling me this shit. I don't think I can do this, though."

"Listen... being the wife or the main girl is always gonna be better than some washed-up hoe on the side who don't no man wanna be with. It's a compliment."

I was once that hoe on the side, so can I really be this upset?

"No, it's not a compliment. I'm not gonna be okay with knowing that my man is fuckin' me and someone else. And especially the woman that I helped him cheat on. That don't sit right with me, and I'm not doing this. If he wants Tara, he can have her."

I pull myself away and head for the door, but Janay stops me.

"Chevy, you bring in a fresh outlook on shit. We need you here, girl. It's really not that bad once you get past this first shock. And Omar seems to be in real high spirits since you've been around."

"No. You need to love yourself better."

"Excuse me?"

"I said you need to love yourself better. There are people out here, in love, that don't do this shit. We don't deserve this!"

"How do you know there are people out there not doing this? And what does that gotta do with me loving myself? I love my life, my man, and my kids. It's real secure and—"

"It's secure 'cause of the money. That's it, but you really not secure with yourself. If Curt got locked up or shot dead right now, you wouldn't be saying that shit, Janay. It's not safe; it's stupid. I have been shot and thrown up against glass already and barely been here long. What do I look like giving years of my life to this shit or Omar, especially if I'm not even enough for him? That's you, but it's not me, and it's never what I wanted for myself. Young or not, I know I deserve better than this. Move, Janay. I'm about to go."

"But Chevy..."

"I heard your side of it, and I don't agree with you, so I'm leaving. You can come with me so I can drop you off, or you can stay here." The anger boiling inside causes my vision to go red.

"Matter of fact..." I run back over to the window and slam my hand against it a few times until I catch the attention of the room. Everyone jerks their heads up in my direction quickly, and I can see the guards get their guns ready.

"Chevonne! What the hell are you doing!" Janay calls from behind me in a panic.

This ain't it for me. I'm not about to sit quietly like the rest of these women and allow myself to be disrespected by someone that couldn't leave me the hell alone in the first place.

Omar's eyes grow wide as they meet mine. He gestures for his men to drop their guns without looking away. My tears cannot stay inside of me, and they fall as I smack the glass again. I finally look behind Omar, at Tara, who has her arms crossed over her chest, flashing a nasty grin up at me like the bitch she is.

"Chevonne! You're crazy! Let's get outta here!" Janay's frantic voice pulls at my senses, urging me to retreat from the window.

My gaze flicks back to Omar, but he's already bolting out of the room. *Oh no, baby.* I need to leave before he has the chance to stop me from walking out of his life.

Relenting to Janay's pull, we race out of the room and thunder down the flight of stairs. Echoes of voices ring out at the stairwell's bottom, but we burst through the front doors of the office building and dash towards my car before anyone can stop us.

Enough of this shit. We peel away, leaving Omar, Curtis, and their crew dumbfounded in the swirling dust.

———— ♥ ————

I figured Omar would be waiting for me at the house after dropping off Janay, but he wasn't. Surprisingly, I'm glad because it grants me the space to pack my things and hit the road. My pager was buzzing like crazy, but in a fit of anger, I chucked it out the car window on my way back. When I'm that angry, I'm a force to be reckoned with – a trait inherited proudly from my daddy. It's not always something to be proud of, but damn, it works for me more often than not.

The front door slams with a resounding bang as I push it closed, locking it behind me with a heavy hand.

Eddie glances over from the living room, concern etched on his face as he mutes the TV. "Miss Chevy, you good? Somebody out there?" He wastes no time grabbing his piece and positioning himself to peer out the window.

"Nah. I'm outta here, Eddie!" I holler while shedding my jacket, the heat of the moment threatening to make me faint. "It was nice knowing you!"

"Hold on a sec. Calm down for a minute. O called, asking where you were and if you were home. I told him you changed your mind about your nap and you hadn't returned yet. What went down, Miss Chevy?" Eddie limps over to me slowly.

I shoot him an accusatory glare, baring my teeth. "Why didn't you tell me the truth when I asked, huh? Have me looking like a fool 'cause nobody wanted to tell me that Omar was still messing around with Tara!"

Eddie raises his hands in surrender, his expression falling. "Miss Chevy. Talk to me. O needs you—"

"I don't give a damn! He didn't need me when he let that woman lay her hands all over him!" I wipe my tear-streaked face and make my way towards the stairs, my footsteps heavy with anger and hurt.

I don't have the patience to entertain Eddie's attempts to rationalize why being cheated on is acceptable in this circle, just like Janay tried to do earlier. As I hear the screen door creak open and the front door handle jiggles, I begin to believe that Eddie is only stalling.

Oh, hell no. I hustle up to the third floor of the house and dart down the hall to Omar's bedroom. And let's be clear, it's Omar's room now—it stopped being mine about an hour ago. I slam the door shut behind me and turn the key, securing myself inside. Scanning the room, I search for my suitcase, but it must be stashed away somewhere else because it's nowhere to be found. Instead, I grab the nearest bag and start cramming it with my clothes. The bedroom door handle rattles, and I pick up the pace, stuffing clothes in with more force.

"Baby girl…" His voice filters through the door, its smoothness momentarily tugging at me. But I can't let Omar sway me with that charm.

"Step off! I'm done with this!" I shout back, using my feet to stomp down the overflowing bag.

"I just wanna explain something to you. Then I'll let you go. I promise." His words sound sincere, but I've learned not to trust promises that come too easily.

I watch the door handle move and glance at the window. Knowing he has a key; I realize I need to hustle if I want to make my escape. Struggling to open the window at the front of the bed, I discover it's locked. After unlocking it, I yank it up. Just as I turn to grab my overstuffed bag, Omar is standing beside it, the door wide open behind him. I gasp sharply, freezing in place.

"Ayo, what are you doing?" Omar's face registers confusion as he looks from me to the open window. "Chevonne, I know you not stupid."

"I must be stupid since I believed all that crap that came out of your mouth!" I shout, moving back to put some distance between us.

Omar steps forward. "I'm glad you did, 'cause I meant it."

I watch him skeptically through tear-filled eyes as he extends his open palm. I'm cautious; he might try to snatch me up. I quickly bring my hands to my neck, holding my throat as if I'm choking. I can tell he's struggling to suppress laughter but I'm trying not to faint from this heartbreak I think I'm experiencing.

"It's not funny!" I shout at him. "Liar!"

Omar exhales and takes another step forward. "I ain't lie about nothing. I just ain't tell you everything. Come over here so we can talk about what you think you saw."

"I know what the hell I saw! I'm not gonna let you talk to me like I'm the crazy one. I saw both of you. I saw the way you looked at her... Why don't you go be with Tara, huh?" Another tear or two falls as I force out the last bit.

"I don't want Tara. I want you. I been tellin' you that, and I'm sick of saying that shit." Omar takes a few more steps to close the distance, but I back away to the window and throw my hand up to gesture for him to stop.

"Well, I don't want you. I might be 'good for you,' but I'm not gonna sit here and turn the other cheek just 'cause you run the city and bring home a lot of money. I'm not gonna keep getting pregnant for you just for you to be all up in someone else's bed. And I damn sure won't give my loyalty to you if you can't respect me enough to be just for *me*."

I can tell he's listening intensely, his eyes never leaving mine. Omar nods and steps forward again. "I respect that, baby girl, and I agree with you. If you let me tell you that ain't shit going on with me and Tara, I can let you know what the real deal is right quick. But you gotta get away from that window and come sit with me."

He must think I'm going to jump.

"I'm not gonna hurt myself. I'm leaving out this window 'cause I won't make it past you or out that door. I already know," I assert, my voice firm.

"You not gonna make it out that window either." He finally stops and seats himself on the edge of our neatly made, California king-sized bed. I mean *his*.

"You can't force me to stay here with you."

"You right, and I won't. I just wanna talk to you, baby girl. Can I at least get that much before you make a final decision?"

My shoulders relax slightly at his reassuring tone, and I exhale. "Fine, but don't touch me. You hear me?"

He nods slowly and watches me sit down at the other end of the bed. The tension here is thick as hell, making me want to just leave now, but I owe it to myself to hear what excuse he has for me.

"Me and Tara met through some mutual friends, and then we ran into each other again when I visited that club, so we linked up. She's got family in the business out here in LA and had been helping me out with some of my work. After everything had cooled down with all of us, she came back around and said she still wanted in. She's only around to work. That's it, baby girl," he explains, his words eliciting an eye roll from me.

"You're so full of it. She's here to work, yet you're all cozy in each other's faces, and she's touching you. Just be real," I retort, not buying into his story.

"She knows what this is with you and me and is respecting that. I can't help any leftover feelings she might got or if she still feels some type of way because of us."

"You can help it. She doesn't need to be around you or touching you. Stop flirting with her, and maybe she can lose whatever feelings she has!"

"It ain't like that."

"Omar... I don't understand this. If you both do good business together and you both still got feelings, go be with her. I won't be mad or stop you. I'm the reason y'all broke up anyway."

"You not the reason we broke up. We broke up 'cause we wasn't supposed to be together. You ain't got shit to do with that."

"Well, I can't be mad if you realize that you made a mistake and want her back. But what you're not gonna do is make me look stupid out here and expect me to stay. I'm not gonna put up with it. I'm not sharing *my* man."

"I know." Omar is facing away from me, hunched over with his elbows propped on his knees. He drops his head and leaves it hanging.

"Why is it so hard for you fools to stick with one woman though? Why does Janay have it in her mind that that shit is okay? She's pushing thirty, thinking like a dummy, and I can't even blame her. You men are the ones to blame."

"So, it was Janay you were with? She brought you out there?"

Oops. My big mouth just got her and Curtis in some trouble; I already know. Time to lie. "No. I haven't seen her in a few days. That's not even the point though, so don't try to get off the subject. I know you men play mind games and shit."

I'm good at this. I'm prepared for this. I don't have a long dating history, but I've got a brain. Daddy always said if I've got that, common sense, and trust my gut, then that's all I need.

"A'ight, so what you about to do? I'm getting a lil' frustrated about this. I won't even lie to you, baby girl."

"For what? *I'm* the one that deserves to be frustrated. You're just mad 'cause I see right through your bullshit. You got caught up, and you can't think of any excuse that I don't already know about."

"Okay," is all he says.

"So, before I make my final decision, answer this one question..." I hold up my forefinger, noticing I broke a nail. Mental note: gotta get that redone.

"What's that?"

"Did you mess around with her anytime we were together? Be real."

Silence fills the room, and I already know the answer. I feel rage bubbling up, spreading through my head. I might even throw up. I'm so mad.

Omar finally lifts his head and turns it in my direction. "It happened once, by accident. She doesn't mean the same to me as you do, though. I know there really ain't no reason to justify that shit so I'm sorry, baby girl."

I've heard enough, so I stand up quickly and grab the bag next to his leg. "Okay, well, I'm about to 'accidentally' leave your lying ass. You just tried to lie to my face, talking about nothing was going on! You are so... like... how you put in all that damn effort with me just to throw it away? You thought I was a damn dummy. No, baby. You really made me believe you care and love me, setting me up to believe that this life is gonna be good, and that we are gonna be our best selves together with our lil' baby. But I don't even believe that anymore."

Omar stands up and moves toward me, snatching the strap of my bag from my shoulder. I freeze in place because I don't know what he is about to do if he is about to throw me out of this window or what, but he picks me up by the waist and lays me on the bed. I squirm under him as he kisses all up on my neck, eventually pulling my shirt down until my chest is exposed. *It feels good, damn it.*

I press both palms against his chest in an attempt to push him away. He wraps his lips around one of my breasts, his touch surprisingly gentle, almost soothing. Despite my anger, part of me wants him to continue, but my frustration prevails, and I just want to leave.

As tears of anger stream down my face, I can't help but wonder how this man has such power over me. *How did I allow myself to become so deeply involved with him, so quickly? Is this kind of shit really normal for others?* We've spent so much time together, getting to know each other intimately, sharing deep conversations, and yet he's willing to risk it all with a woman he claims to no longer want.

Omar pulls back, his gaze fixed on me from above. I must look a mess, my face wet with tears, my eyes strained and puffy. He sits up slightly, reaching out to wipe away the tears cascading down my cheeks.

"I ain't mean to hurt you. I'm sorry. And I do love you, baby girl..." he mumbles against my mouth.

The "L" word. He actually said it. I squeeze my eyes shut, trying to block out the sight of his pleading eyes. Part of me wants to believe him, to believe that he truly loves me and is genuinely sorry, but I can't shake the feeling that his remorse is only because he got caught. *How long would he have kept this secret? Would he have made Tara his girlfriend behind my back, all while I thought he was committed to me?*

While I want to believe in his love and his apology, he would be a fool if he thought offering me security and treating me like royalty to keep me content would be enough to turn my cheek. But not for me, baby.

Not for Miss Chevy. My daddy ain't raise me to be a fool's toy.

CHAPTER 14
Let's Call It Even

MY BABY BUMP HASN'T changed much in size for ages. I guess packing on some extra pounds helps in keeping it under wraps. I've got this feeling that I'll be one of those moms who stay small for a while and then suddenly pop, or maybe just stay small till the end. Honestly, I'm cool with that. I gotta keep this pregnancy on the downlow until I land another job.

I'm back at Phoenix Fire now. Getting back in wasn't a cakewalk. I had to pull some lap dancing moves to sway Randall into letting me back. He was relieved I dumped Omar, but I didn't let him revel in it for long. I've barely held a conversation with him, and he keeps his distance as well.

Thankfully, I kept my apartment, moved back in, and Omar even asked me to keep my car, buying me a new pager for contact. Leaving him was tough, but I had to show him I had self-respect. No matter how much love we had, I couldn't tolerate his disrespect and lies. He was angry, and put up a fight, but didn't stop me when I left.

My last words to him were, "Hope you learn better for your next girl." I could tell it hit him hard. His amber eyes said it all. Money and power don't mean squat if you don't value what you have.

Omar checks in with me a couple of times a week, trying to be sweet and all, but I keep our chats short and to the point. I miss him, sure, but he just needs to know I'm safe, eating, and the pregnancy is going fine. That's the extent of it. I haven't even told him I'm working for Randall again, but I know that he knows. And however he may feel about that is just not my problem anymore. My focus is on making money, not dealing with jealous drama.

The dressing room is packed tonight, bustling with all the ladies ready to work. It's overwhelming, especially since I'm not used to it, just getting back to work and all. Sheila's still around, but we're like two ships passing in the night—no words exchanged, just keeping our distance. I catch her eyeing me through the mirror sometimes. If she's still with Randall, I bet he's spilled the beans about me and Omar. But honestly, I couldn't care less about her opinion. If she comes at me with some "I told you so" nonsense, she might just get the first punch since I got pregnant.

"Chevy, you're filling out! What's your secret, girl?" Keyera, one of the seasoned dancers, calls out to me.

I roll my eyes before glancing her way, aware that the entire dressing room's attention is on me.

"Omar's been feeding you good, huh? Still treating you right?" she continues, her tone dripping with curiosity.

"That's none of your business, boo," I reply, turning back to finish running the hot comb through my bangs.

"Just surprised to see you back here after quitting for 'your' man. Did he move on to a model or what?" she persists.

I shake my head, brushing off her question, and focus on getting ready for the night ahead.

"Typical cycle with cats like that. They drop you just when you're getting comfortable, then snatch up the next bitch willing to play their game. Bet he already had someone else lined up, huh?"

"Keyera, shut up. What's going on with me ain't your business, like I said." My sharp retort draws a few gasps from the ladies nearby.

"Yeah, she thought she hit the jackpot when she stole him from Tara. Now look at her, getting chubby and back where she started. Meanwhile, he's probably treating the next girl to bubble baths and all that," Keyera laughs, joined by a few others. They sound like a bunch of haters to me, but her words still sting, and I feel myself getting emotional.

I turn away, blinking rapidly to hold back tears. Just as I reach for my lipstick, I feel a gentle touch on my back.

"Don't pay them any mind, Chevy. Keyera's just jealous because Omar never even looked her way," Sheila says, her hand resting on me as she speaks to my reflection.

I'm surprised by her kindness. She's been quiet in the corner since I got here.

"Thanks, but I'm good. I try not to let stanky-breath girls like that get under my skin. She's been stuck here for too long with no other aspirations," I reply, struggling to maintain eye contact as I fight back tears.

"You look beautiful, Chevy, and you're glowing. I don't know if anyone's told you that," she says, removing her hand and nervously twiddling her thumbs.

I haven't forgotten our last conversation, so it's hard to let down the walls I've built up with her.

"Thanks, girl," I manage to say.

I watch as Sheila nods and retreats to her corner of the room. I can't shake the feeling that I should just let go of the past, especially considering we're all dealing with our own struggles, and I haven't even checked in on her. I hope she's doing alright, maybe back living with her grandmother if not with Randall. She was right about me not fully understanding Omar, so I should probably talk to her about it when I'm more in control of my emotions.

Feeling a bit rusty, I make my way to the pole, but I don't hold back. Randall made it clear that if I'm not on my game, he won't give me another shot. So, I pull myself together, close my eyes, and give it my all, swinging around as best as I can. The club is packed tonight, business booming at the Phoenix. It's good for me—means more tips.

Suddenly, a tease of sandalwood tickles my nose, and I quickly open my eyes, scanning the room. Is he here? I keep dancing, scanning the crowd, expecting to catch a glimpse of Omar. I even peek over at the VIP section, but he's nowhere to be found. It's not the first time I've caught whiffs of his cologne in the club, but each time I've looked, he's been absent. Maybe I'm just imagining things.

God, I miss him... *a lot.*

Although we speak often, I barely saw him since we split anyway, but we need this distance. I recall one of our last fights, when I stormed out and he watched me dance from that exact spot. So, it stings to see another woman there instead, smoking a cigarette and watching the stage intently. When I snap out of my daze, I realize I'm staring right at Tara. What the hell is she doing here? She doesn't work here anymore. She works for Omar.

My set finishes, and I head straight from the stage to where Tara is seated. If she's here to start something, I'd rather it play out in the open, where everyone can see me put her in her place.

"What are you doing here, Tara?" I ask, hands on my hips.

"I can't be here? Last I checked, I'm not banned from this place," she replies, taking a drag from her cigarette before exhaling a cloud of smoke.

"If you're here to pick a fight with me, then let's do it. I don't have time to be caught off guard, so I'm right here."

A few heads have already turned in our direction, and I can hear whispers behind me. The thought of my baby shoots to the forefront of my mind, so I'm hesitant about the follow through of my threat, but I won't let her punk me or hurt my child.

Tara scoffs and stubs out her cigarette in the ashtray. "I want to talk to you, Chevy. Woman to woman."

"Oh, so now you wanna talk? Why? So you can gloat about sleeping with Omar to get back at me, right?" I cross my arms over my chest.

"Listen, what you did to me was messed up, and I don't regret what I did. But no, I'm not here to rub it in your face."

"Then why do you want to talk to me?"

"I'm here because I want to see how you're doing."

I can't help but roll my eyes. "For what? I'm fine, Tara. I'm back at work and taking care of myself. I don't need to be checked up on."

"Well, I want to make sure you have someone to lean on because I didn't, and I know how it feels."

I don't understand where she's coming from. We haven't been friends in months, and I don't feel right being buddy-buddy with someone who attacked me and made me fight.

"Why? I'm fine. Omar and I ended things smoothly. It was tough at first, but I can rely on myself. You can have him back."

"Chevy, I miss my friend, okay? I'm willing to overlook what happened to rebuild our friendship. You're a good person deep down, and I just want to be there for you like you were for me."

"I don't know, Tara. I don't really trust you. I'm sorry. You knew exactly what you were doing when you pulled that stunt."

"Just like you knew what you were doing when you pulled that stunt on me, right? Are you serious, Chevy? Did you forget that you did the same thing with Randall too? But that one didn't sting as much as with Omar, 'cause Randall fucked every hoochie he hired. So, let's call it even. We both screwed each other over, and neither of us ended up with Omar."

There it is. She wants to bond over the fact that Omar isn't in the picture for either of us anymore. That sneaky side of her just can't help itself. Unlike her, I actually care about Omar's feelings.

But she's right about the Randall thing too, which I hadn't even thought about in a while, so I still feel a little dirty. It's a damn shame because I never meant to hurt her like that.

I shake my head and turn away. "No, I'm good. It's weird that you want to be friends now. I wouldn't want to be cool with someone who did me wrong, so you're different for that one, Tara. Besides, you wouldn't even be here talking to me if I was still with him."

She reaches for my wrist. "Chevy, chill. Come back here and sit down with me, please? Let's talk for a second, and then you can go about your business."

I glance up at the balcony overlooking the main floor, checking if Randall is lurking around. He's not, and his office door is closed, so I figure I can hear Tara out before getting back to work. I'm supposed to be working in the private dance rooms after my stage performance, but we have plenty of girls here tonight anyway.

Tara takes a seat and pats the space next to her. Her long, neon-pink nails catch my attention. I sit a few inches away, just in case. I don't trust people who catch others off guard. Plain and simple.

"Are you still helping Omar with his business stuff?" I ask immediately.

"Yeah, but we don't really talk much unless it's about just that. He's been acting really mean to everyone since you left," she replies.

Damn. I'm not exactly surprised, though. I spoke to Rita last month and she told me Omar went on a rampage, but I don't know why I didn't consider it was only because of me. I also didn't bother asking him about that because I saw it as him throwing a fit for not getting his way.

"Oh. Well, that's not cool. I hope he gets over it soon, 'cause nobody deserves to be treated like that just 'cause he messed up."

"Right," Tara forces a smile, but I can see right through it.

I need to make sure I'm not spilling all my secrets to her, because that's probably why she's here in the first place.

"So, I wanted to check on you and see how you're doing 'cause I heard he might have a new girl to distract him. You can't be surprised, though."

Pause. Did I hear that right? I snap my head back towards Tara. "What? He didn't tell me that, and we talked on the phone a couple of days ago."

"He's not gonna tell you that. Why would he admit he's messin' with someone else if he wants you back? And if it's not one, he's definitely fucking around. He's still a man. Surprised you didn't know that by now."

My heart sinks. "You came here to stir up trouble, Tara. I see right through you. You don't give a damn about me. You just want to see me upset."

Maybe he is dating to get over me or something. I know that's what many people do—rebound—and he must not enjoy being alone if he wants another female companion so soon.

"No. I don't want to see you upset, and I do care about you, or I wouldn't be here, girl. I'm just giving you some insight on the game. And the men in this game. Oh, and he also kicked out Curtis and Janay. You could say they're out right now."

"Out? What do you mean?"

Could be why I haven't heard from Janay. I tried calling her a few times, but I thought maybe she didn't want to talk to me anymore since I left after she tried to plead with me to stay.

"Like he kicked them out of everything, Chevy. He was furious and held a gun up to Curtis about controlling his woman. Seems they were the reason you left."

No... it's not their fault. Tara continues. "I was at the Lab the day that shit happened." She throws back a shot. "Omar had everyone tightened up."

I drop my face into my hands, leaning towards my knees. I didn't even think about them or that he would do that. It makes me feel so guilty because it's not their fault. Janay was trying to help me, and Curtis didn't even know about Janay doing what she did. For Omar to put out one of his best friends makes me think about what Eddie told me. Omar would really do something like that over me, and it makes me sick.

"They have kids and everything. That's messed up." I grab the black napkin that Tara was using and dab under my lower lid to catch a few tears. "I'm gonna have to talk to him. I don't even care about him seeing somebody else."

Omar needs to grow up. Throwing a fit because he got caught up is so stupid. I was considering going to lunch with him this weekend because he asked, but no, sir. He's acting like a twenty-five-year-old toddler.

Tara notices the distress on my face and reaches out, placing her hand on mine. "I'm sorry to bring you all this bad news, but you gotta know what's goin' on out here. Just in case you ever need to save yourself."

I pull my hand away abruptly and stand up. "Okay. Well, thanks, I guess. I don't know if I believe you about the other girl, but I need to call him about Janay and Curtis 'cause that's not right."

"You don't have to believe me, Chevy. I'm not gonna lie to you. You know me and you know I know the game." Tara lights another cigarette, signaling that it's time for me to leave her and her unwanted news behind.

I was managing just fine, but now I have to worry about my friend and her partner because of something that wasn't even their fault, and deal with the crushing blow of finding out he's with someone else. I hope neither of those things are true and Tara is just stirring up trouble, but deep down, I know better.

"If you do go back, just don't get too comfortable, okay?" She says, blowing out smoke as I turn away from her. Whatever that means.

I bid Tara farewell and make my way down the hall to the payphone. I dial Omar's number and wait for him to answer. It rings a few times before he picks it up, but there's only laughter and music in the background at first.

"Hello? Omar? It's Chevy," I say into the phone.

"Omar's busy with his party. Want me to take a message?" A young woman's voice responds.

My blood boils. When does Omar ever have a bitch answering his phone?

"Who is this? Why are you answering his phone?" I snap back.

"Who is this again?"

I hang up and slam the phone against the wall, then leave it dangling. I'm furious, but I can't help crying. How could he move on so quickly? Maybe I'm selfish. Maybe this is my karma.

A few people pass by; their drunken faces showing concern as I lean against the wall, holding my baby bump. I try to compose myself before heading back into the dressing room full of jealous women. I don't want to go back to Tara either. She definitely doesn't need to see me like this, but I hate that she was right about me needing someone to lean on. I'm just out here by myself again, and it feels a lot lonelier this time around.

My thoughts drift to Randall, and I glance towards the stairs. It would be foolish to rely on him, but I trust him more than these girls I work with.

Then I think of Eddie. I should reach out to him.

Eddie is usually a good listener, but as I glance back at the phone I left dangling from the booth, I realize I can't remember the family house number anymore. Omar mentioned they fixed up the house last month, and Eddie was back there. That's a relief. But I'm pretty sure he's at Omar's party right now, and I'll be damned if I call the house and Omar's new girlfriend answers again. I shake off the thought.

Starting up the stairs, I have to force myself up each step. The fact that I have to make this effort makes me question if it's even worth it. But the anger boiling inside me overpowers any hesitation I have about confiding in Randall.

Randall's door is closed when I finally reach it, so I knock.

"What?" Randall's voice comes from behind the door.

I open it enough to peek my head in and see he's on the phone.

"Hey, can we talk for a second, Randall?"

Randall leans forward in his seat, furrowing his brows as he speaks into the phone. "Yeah. Let me call you back. I gotta help my dancer with something."

Did he say dancer? That's a first.

He sets the phone back on its receiver and gestures for me to have a seat. "You look upset."

"Um... I am. And... I don't know who to talk to. I don't have anybody else to go to right now..." My voice cracks, and tears start flowing.

Randall reaches behind him and hands me a box of tissues. "Thanks."

He gives me some time to dry my eyes before speaking again. "What's up, Chevy? I don't think I've ever seen you cry before."

"I just feel like I try to do the right things in my life but shit just doesn't work out for me. I don't understand that," I respond, folding the tissues neatly.

"You might as well stop thinking like that. That ain't the point of life anyway."

I should have just stayed downstairs and kept to myself. "Never mind, Randall. I'm not going to sit here and listen to you say mean shit to me like always. Sorry to bother you." I stand up.

"Relax. Sit back down. You just want me to tell you what you wanna hear, and it ain't gonna happen like that. Yeah, you mostly a decent person, but you expect rewards from life just for doing what you're supposed to do or for not doing things you shouldn't be doing."

After pondering for a few moments, I return back to my seat. He said a mouth full just now. "I don't understand that. I don't expect rewards."

"Yeah, you do. You expect to be given an easier life by doing shit by the book written by somebody else, but in reality, it's just about doing the best you can out here. Okay so you do a good thing but that doesn't mean tomorrow you're gonna wake up and have everything you want. That's not how that works. I wish it did. Maybe I would make better decisions. But now? I don't really give a fuck. I just do me."

"Okay. I hear you. I just believe in karma, good and bad, and I feel like I have yet to see any real good returned to me."

"Yeah, karma is something, I guess, but it's not enough to live by. Not for me, at least. It's just there for a balance, really. That's what I always heard, so maybe something good will happen, Ion really know. You supposed to help out if you can."

"Yeah, I know that. I don't expect anything back when I help people. Mainly just to be respected, but that's it."

Randall shakes his head. "Nah, Chev, that's you still expecting something back. But life is life, Chev. If somebody comes to you for help, and you help them, I hate to say it, but they don't owe you shit. They can leave you in the dust if they wanted to. You helped them because it was the right thing to do, and you wanted to do it. Whether they return the favor, it doesn't even matter."

"I hate that." My head shakes at the realization.

"Listen, being 'good' doesn't put you higher than anybody else. You're just gonna be known as a good person who does the right things, and that people can trust. You still gotta work hard to get what you want and need out here just like anybody else."

Whew. I think I'm able to follow. I tried to tell Omar that he and Randall are a lot alike. They both think like this.

I suddenly think of my daddy. "How come it seems like people who try to do right can't catch a break? Even if they don't expect nothing back?"

"Nobody's immune to getting fucked over. Anybody who tries to do any kind of good in this world has gotten fucked over. What makes you think it ain't gonna happen to you?"

I nod in understanding. It makes sense when he puts it like that.

"Ain't none of us getting out of this alive, so that's why you gotta live your life, Chev. Do what you wanna do and be proud about it. Whatever's got you upset is only temporary. You don't gotta let it change who you are you though."

"That's the realest thing you've ever told me, Randall, and I appreciate that. I'll remember that."

"I'm sure you will, Miss 'My Daddy Said'."

I burst into laughter and fall back into the chair, covering my mouth while I do so. He lets out a chuckle or two.

"Anyway, you better get your little ass back to work. I mean, it ain't little, but you know what I mean."

His wink makes me tingle, and it's one of those tingles that happens "down there."

No, Chevy. Get your butt up. I stand up and head for the door. "Thanks, Randall. I appreciate this, and I already feel a little better."

"Mhm..." He's looking over my body when I turn back to thank him. "If you're not trying to be alone tonight, you know I got space." Here he goes.

"Wait, what happened with Sheila?"

"What do you mean? I thought she lived with her grandma?"

"Oh, okay. You know Tara is here?"

He shrugs. I guess he isn't involved with either of them anymore.

"Well, I'm going back to work now."

Randall's chair squeaks when he leans back to prop his foot up. He glances at the time from his watch. "Looks like you got about an hour left."

That means I have an hour to decide if I'm going home with this man, or not.

CHAPTER 15
Silly of Me

A S SOON AS I step into Randall's place, I'm greeted by a massive fish tank right smack at the entrance. It's kind of over-the-top, but hey, it's his thing, so I can't really hate on it. After all, he's the one who dropped the cash for it.

I decided to tag along with him because we had a good vibe going earlier, and I figured we could chat some more. I'm really craving some genuine conversation right now.

Randall helps me out of my jacket and hangs it up, and that's when it hits me—I forgot to change out of my dancer getup from work. Instead of being dressed in something a bit more subtle, here I am practically in my underwear. Randall lets out a laugh as I scramble to cover up, praying he doesn't notice the extra bulge around my midsection.

"Damn, looks like you've been treating yourself, huh?" Randall gives my butt a playful pinch and leans back with a smirk.

I'm starting to regret my decision to come here with my sorry self. I hate how I get all foolish when I'm feeling down. Well, at least I'm not in full-on rage mode anymore, but still.

"Randall, I'm just here to grab a bite and chill. Nothing else, got it?" Can't believe I have to spell it out for this grown man, but maybe he got the wrong idea, considering I'm basically standing here in my undies. And this is the first time I've agreed to come home with him.

"I feel you. Fridge is that way," he points towards the kitchen, kicking off his shoes.

"Aren't you gonna get me something? I'm your guest, Randall.'

"If I was hungry, sure, but I'm not."

I cross my arms, sticking close to the door. Randall grunts and heads to the kitchen.

"I got some wine in here, want some?" he calls out.

"Nah, can't do wine."

"Why not?"

Shoot. Need to come up with a quick excuse. "Uh, I'm on some sleep meds right now, doc's orders, can't mix 'em with booze."

Randall gives me a side-eye from the kitchen, making me squirm. "Okay... how about some damn water then?"

Finally, I make my way over to the living room and flop onto the couch. Snatching the blanket folded neatly at the end, I wrap it around myself like a cocoon. Randall saunters in, handing me a glass of water and a bag of potato chips before plopping down beside me.

"Thanks," I mutter, not even bothering to complain. Getting him to do something nice seems like pulling teeth. Good thing I've already decided I could never date this guy. "So, what's the deal with you and Sheila?"

"We done," he says, shrugging like it's no big deal.

"I thought you two were getting pretty cozy, but okay." I can't help feeling relieved, maybe Sheila finally got the hint and left him alone for good. Shame it had to end in a fight and the demise of our friendship, all because she was trying to do the same thing for me, except she wanted to use me to keep Randall.

"She started acting too serious for me. We were just supposed to be messing around, nothing serious, but she wanted more. Told her I wasn't about that, and she didn't take it well, started acting crazy."

"Remember, she's young, probably one of the first guys she's been with like that."

"That's exactly why I dropped her. She can still keep her job though. I ain't firing her over that shit. She just needs to leave me alone."

"What about that girl you were supposedly seeing behind Sheila's back?"

"Behind Sheila? Nah, that's not a thing, Chevy. I don't know what she told you. I mess with whoever I want."

I just sigh and take a sip of my ice water. I'm glad Sheila still has a job, but if I were her, I'd run for the hills from The Phoenix Fire. She's just going to be reminded of her fling with Randall, making it harder to move on. I said the same about Tara, but now she's working with Omar, and I can't help but wonder if they're still fooling around. Not that either of them owes me the truth. I'm not with Omar anymore, and I've been keeping my distance to get over him.

I wish I could shake off these feelings for him, especially now. The heaviness I thought I'd pushed away creeps back in, and I have to set my water down. Grabbing the half-empty bag of chips, I munch on a few absentmindedly. Randall's zoned out in front of the TV, but having someone around does ease the loneliness a bit. I'd rather not be left alone with my thoughts right now.

"Randall?"

"Yeah?" he mumbles without tearing his eyes away from the screen.

"How do people move on from someone they love so damn fast? What's the trick?"

Randall shuts off the TV and turns to face me, stretching back against the arm of the sofa. "You really fell for that dude?"

Why did I even bother asking? I should've just kept quiet, nibbling on these stale chips and sipping this sorry excuse for water. "Forget it. Turn the TV back on."

He chuckles under his breath. "Nah, let me give you some advice. You wanna get past him? Start seeing someone else."

"No, that'd just be using someone else, and I'm not about that."

"Find someone who's down to be used then. Someone who's not looking for anything serious, so you don't catch feelings."

He thinks he's smooth, but that's not gonna fly with me. Sure, I'm feeling a bit, uh, pent up, but I need to stay on my side of this couch and mind my own business.

"Thanks, Randall, but I think I'm good without your advice now."

"Suit yourself." Randall grabs the remote and flicks the TV back on.

Just as he does, I hear my pager go off from my bag. Glancing at the clock on his fireplace, it reads four in the morning. *Damn. Not tonight.*

I jump up to grab my pager, noticing it's a callback request from Omar.

"Is that you and Tara's dopehead ex?" Randall's voice cuts through the room from the sofa.

"He's not a dopehead. He just sells it. Shut up, Randall," I shoot back, fixating on the screen. Part of me wants to dial his number and unleash all the frustration still swirling inside me, but the other part just wants to ignore him and move on for good.

But Chevy, you can't just cut ties with him completely. You're carrying his child. Well, cut romantic ties and make sure he knows there's no chance of getting back together.

"You gonna call him?" Randall's curiosity prods.

"I'm considering it. Just shush, Randall."

"If you're asking how to move on from someone, calling them when they want you to ain't the way to go," he advises.

"Chill out, alright? It might be urgent." Deep down, I know it's probably not. Omar's likely just drunk and looking for someone to talk to.

"That ain't urgent. As a matter of fact, call him and tell him you're busy. Let him feel it," Randall suggests.

Hmm, not a terrible idea. It's probably for the best anyway. Ignoring his calls might make him think something's wrong, and I don't need him sending out a search party. Plus, I'm always up at this hour, especially when I've got work. It hits me then how much Omar still knows about my life while I barely know a thing about his. I didn't even know he's got a new woman.

Anger bubbles up again, and I whirl around. "Where's your phone? I'm gonna tell him I'm busy so he can leave me alone."

"That's my girl," Randall grins, pointing to the phone sitting on the kitchen counter.

I stride over to the kitchen counter, my fingers tapping against the smooth surface as I punch in Omar's number.

"Hey, baby girl. You doing alright?" His voice, rich and smoky, spills through the phone, sending shivers down my spine. Lord knows I'm a sucker for that voice. And for him.

"I'm fine. I only called you back to let you know I'm busy and not up for talking tonight."

"Busy doing what? Still at work?" His curiosity seeps through the line.

Oh, shoot. Should've said I was hitting the hay.

"No, I mean, I'm busy getting ready for bed. About to hit the sheets."

There's a pause on the other end, and I pray he's not somehow reading my thoughts through the phone or trying to sniff out if I'm lying.

"You at home?" he finally questions.

Girl, LIE. "Yeah, I'm at home."

"You ain't hear the door? I swung by not too long ago."

My eyes squeeze shut, and I pull the phone away from my ear for a moment. Sure, I'm a single woman and shouldn't have to hide or explain myself, but look... If

Omar finds out I'm chilling at Randall's, of all places, we'll be hearing about another rampage, I just know it.

"Baby girl, you still there?"

"Yeah, still here. Um, no, I must've been in the shower. Why'd you swing by anyway?" I ask, trying to keep my tone light.

"'Cause I miss you and wanted to see you. You showing yet?"

I can hear the slur in his voice, but I know he means it. Too bad my current mood won't let me soak it in.

"Just a bit, but I gotta go. And seriously, Omar, don't just show up unannounced. You know how I feel about that."

"You sound like you still mad at me."

Damn right, I am.

"I'm just exhausted, okay? Getting calls at four in the damn morning ain't gonna fly anymore. We're done," I snap into the phone.

"A'ight," Omar responds, sounding surprisingly calm.

A brief sigh of relief escapes me, but it's abruptly cut short by Randall's booming laughter from the living room.

Oh my God!

I quickly cover the mouthpiece of the phone and start trembling uncontrollably. I might just pee myself.

"Who was that?" Omar's voice cuts through sharply.

"Huh? Oh, nobody. Probably just the TV," I lie through my teeth.

"I thought you were going to bed?"

"Omar, I must've left the TV on. Actually, let me go turn it off. Be right back," I hurriedly explain before placing the phone down on the counter and darting into the living room. Randall glances at me as I signal for him to shut up. He gives me a thumbs-up before turning his attention back to the TV. I approach the phone, trying to appear calm as I pick it up.

"Okay, TV's off. I'm about to head to bed now. Thanks for checking on me. Have a good night with your new girlfriend."

"I don't have a new girlfriend. What are you talkin' about?" Omar responds, sounding confused.

"I called earlier and heard a woman answer your phone. And someone told me you had a girlfriend. I'm glad I found out 'cause you sure as hell weren't gonna tell me."

"I don't have a girlfriend, Chevonne. Other people answer my phone all the time. You need to stop listening to gossip and accusations. That's why we're in this mess in the first place."

"You cheated on me, Omar. That's why we're here. Don't blame Janay or Curtis for your screw-ups. Yeah, I heard about that too! It's messed up!" I fire back, feeling my blood boil.

"Look, I'm not about to sit here and argue with you over the phone. I don't have a girl. I had a little gathering earlier tonight, and one of those bitches probably answered the phone. You're already lying and shit, and Ion' know why you lying if you claiming we done," Omar states firmly.

I knew he was sniffing me out. "I'm not lying, Omar."

"Where are you really at? Your car wasn't at your place," Omar's voice is sharp over the phone.

Damn. The one time I wish I didn't have a car. I completely forgot about my car sitting back at the club because I came here with Randall.

"I went home with one of my girls from the club, but that's none of your business."

"It is my business, Chevonne. That's my baby too. I got a right to know you safe and where you at in case some shit goes down. Don't forget, you're associated with me, and it ain't safe for you to just be out there anymore." Omar's words hit me hard.

Who would've thought I'd be forever connected to Omar because of his status in this city? And because of his baby. I wouldn't be surprised if he has me followed. I can't blame him for being worried, considering I'm pregnant, but he needs to chill out.

"I'm taking care of myself, alright? I'm good. If I need anything, I'll give you a shout," I assure him, trying to calm the tension.

My heart skips a beat when I see Randall snatch the phone from my hand and put it to his ear. Panic rises in me as I try to grab the phone back, but Randall's grip is too strong.

"Aye, homie, take your drunk ass to sleep. She said she busy," Randall's voice goes through the phone, and then he hands it back to me before strolling back to the living room.

My jaw drops, and my heart pounds in my chest as I pick up the phone again, only to hear the disconnected tone on the other end. This is all my fault. I should've kept my mouth shut instead of accusing Omar of having a girlfriend. Hell, I shouldn't have even come home with Randall in the first place.

I storm into the living room once more, standing in front of Randall. He glances over at me but quickly looks away.

"What?" he asks.

"You know Omar probably knows it was you, right?" I shoot him a glare.

"He can come here all he wants, Chev. What's he gonna do? You came here with me because you wanted to. You don't owe that fool anything. Remember our talk earlier?" Randall's voice is calm, but there's an edge to it.

I don't have time for this. I slip on my shoes, grab my jacket and bag, and turn to Randall.

"Can you please just take me home? Or back to my car? Either way, I need to get out of here," I plead, desperate to leave this mess behind.

"Chevonne, the moment you start acting scared of the motherfucka, he's already got control over you. If he loses it, that means he can't control you. You've got the upper hand, so keep it there," Randall asserts.

"I'm not scared of him for myself. I'm scared for *you*. Let's go. Now," I urge.

He shakes his head and remains sprawled out on the sofa. "You wanna get messed up, Randall? Omar's probably on his way by now. He's drunk and pissed, and I've heard he's been real nasty lately. Please, just come on. I don't want to see you hurt."

"Alright, damn," he relents, dragging himself off the couch, though not quickly enough for my liking.

I help by tossing over his shoes and grabbing his keys.

"You know, if he shows up here, I can put a bullet in his damn head for trespassing," Randall remarks with a smirk, taking his sweet time lacing up his shoes.

Omar doesn't live far from Randall's place, and I can't shake the feeling he could show up any minute.

"No, don't do that. Just hurry up and let's go. You shoulda known better than to snatch that phone from me like that."

"Aye, Chevy, I really don't give a damn. I'll throw hands with him if he wants. Then I'll hand his ass over to the feds."

My stomach knots tighter, and I feel like I might be sick. This stress isn't good for the baby. I take a few deep breaths, trying to stay calm as I wait for him to finish putting on his jacket.

"You could've at least let me get some action or something if we were gonna deal with all this. Damn," Randall grumbles, grabbing the remote to turn off the TV.

I roll my eyes so hard they nearly get stuck, but they snap back to normal when he glances in my direction. Probably why he's dragging his feet because he's mad I'm not giving in tonight.

"Let me just use the bathroom first. I'll be right back," he smirks.

I throw my hands up in resignation and let him go. No use arguing; it'll only waste more time.

After what feels like an eternity, Randall finally appears from the bathroom. He steps in front of me and reaches for the door handle, but before he can even touch it, there's a quick, urgent rapping on the door. I grip the corner of the wall next to me, trying to steady myself because there's no way Omar got over to Randall's place this quickly.

"Shit!" I hiss at Randall.

He peeks through the peephole. "Who the hell are you?" he demands through the door.

He knows what Omar looks like, so who could this be? I relax slightly, but I can't help asking, "Who is it, Randall?"

"Hello? Who the hell are you? Step away from my damn door," Randall commands, reaching into his pocket and pulling out a pocketknife.

Oh, God. Nausea churns in my stomach, and I clamp my hand over my mouth.

"I'm looking for Miss Chevy. Is she in there?" the person on the other side finally responds, their voice muffled through the door.

I recognize the voice. "Eddie?" In one swift motion, I shove Randall aside and peer through the peephole. "Eddie? What are you doing here?"

"I came to take you home, Miss Chevy. Omar's real concerned about your safety," Eddie explains.

Randall chuckles. "She's safe in here with me, man. Made sure we got protection, though. Tell Omar he doesn't need to worry about that."

I shoot Randall a glare that could kill if it were a laser beam. Smacking him on the chest, I scold, "Why would you say that, Randall! Eddie, I'm coming. Just stay calm, alright? I don't need any trouble."

"Okay, Miss Chevy," Eddie responds calmly.

Relief washes over me as I realize Omar sent Eddie. I know Eddie will handle things, if necessary, but he's not as hot-headed as Omar.

"Randall, I'm leaving with him, alright? Just stay cool and... go watch your show. I'll see you at work tomorrow, and thanks for hanging out with me." I watch him pocket the knife and wait until he does before opening the door.

I carefully swing the door open, greeted by Eddie's reassuring smile. It's a relief seeing him here, especially considering the tension between Omar and me. Who knows what Omar might've told him? But seeing Eddie again feels comforting. I just hate it that if Omar and I are on bad terms, it means I don't get to talk to Eddie. I don't want him feeling like he has to take sides with me and Omar. Sure, I'm still a bit annoyed he didn't tell me about Tara, but that's on Omar, not Eddie. Eddie was just doing his job as Omar's confidant and best friend.

But any sense of relief evaporates when Randall smacks my ass in front of Eddie, and both of our faces fall. I shake it off and continue toward Eddie.

"Hey, Eddie, thanks for coming—" I begin, but my words are cut off by a figure lurking in the hallway's corner. Before I can react, Eddie swiftly grabs me, and I watch in horror as Omar bursts into Randall's apartment, kicking the door wide open.

"Omar, no!" I scream, struggling against Eddie's tight grip. "Stop!"

But Omar is already raining blows down on Randall's face. *Poor Randall.* Why did he have to go and try to act tough? Didn't he know Omar always has to have the last word?

"What did you say, huh? Say it again!" Omar delivers another punishing kick to Randall's abdomen, stealing the breath from his lungs.

Tears stream down my face. This is completely unnecessary, and Omar's behavior is scaring me.

"Miss Chevy, calm down. It'll be alright. This guy had it coming," Eddie murmurs in my ear, his voice barely audible over the chaos.

Omar looms over Randall, his face contorted with rage. I continue to watch in horror as he reaches for his gun.

"Omar, please, don't," I plead, knowing my words might not make a difference. I'm probably out of a job regardless of what happens here. "Omar, please, just let him go. I want to go home."

His expression is pure fury—teeth bared, lip curled, jaw clenched. He's seeing red, and I wonder if that's what I look like when I'm angry too. Meanwhile, Randall writhes on the ground in agony, a gun pointed at him, while Omar bites down hard on his lip. He wants to end Randall, I can see it in his eyes, and he's searching for any justification to pull the trigger tonight. But it can't be because of me. It just can't.

"Omar..." I weakly call out his name.

Eddie shouts at some neighbors peeking out of their apartment to go back inside. Omar turns his neck sharply in my direction, his anger noticeable, making me shudder.

"Did you fuck this motherfucka, Chevonne?" Omar's voice is tight with fury, the gun still trained on Randall.

I meet Omar's gaze with disbelief. "No. I asked him to bring me here tonight 'cause I didn't want to be alone. You're making a big mistake, Omar. This isn't his fault."

"He's disrespectful. To you, to me, to everyone. I can't stand for that shit," Omar insists.

"It's not your place to kill him over this, Omar, especially not because of me," I reason, hoping to appeal to his better judgment.

"No, *especially* because of you," Omar counters firmly.

We lock eyes for a brief moment before I glance away, focusing on Randall once more as he wipes blood from his battered nose.

"Can we just go and leave him alone? I'm not feeling well. Please," I beg, my voice trembling.

Omar shifts his gaze back to Randall.

"If I ever catch you laying a hand on her again, you done, understand?" Omar presses his gun against the side of Randall's head.

Randall nods, finally finding his voice. "You fired, Chevy."

"Good. She pregnant anyway. She don't need to be workin' for you or your sleazy ass club no more," Omar declares on my behalf, tucking the gun behind him and covering it with his jacket before turning toward me and Eddie.

I know Omar is pleased about me losing my job. And it's not just because I'm pregnant.

Omar signals Eddie to release me from his grip, and I turn around, rolling my eyes at Eddie.

"Thanks a lot for setting me up, Eddie," I mutter.

"You don't know what you think you do about that fool, Miss Chevy," he responds, his expression apologetic.

My eyes roll once more as Omar's grip tightens around my upper arm, leading me down the steps. I honestly don't know anything about any of these people, for real. I always think I do, but it turns out I don't. I just silently wish Omar would let me walk on my own, but I don't dare say anything to risk further setting him off. But of course, Randall can't resist.

"That makes two of your hoes that came runnin' back," he taunts, laughing. "Guess you can't win 'em all, huh?"

"Randall, shut up!" I snap back.

We all come to a halt on the stairs, and I steal a glance at Omar, trying to gauge his reaction. His expression remains cold-blooded as he releases my arm, only to draw his gun once more and take aim at Randall's apartment. Eddie smoothly steps aside, making way for Omar's line of fire.

"No! Omar, stop!" I scream, lunging for his arm, but it's too late. The bullet has already left his gun, shattering the massive fish tank just inches above Randall's head, dousing him in water and sending it cascading across the floor.

I gasp, feeling Omar's grip tighten around me once more. It's all too much. He nearly killed Randall. Maybe it was to send a message which I know he likes to do and to show off his power. We all know if he wanted Randall dead tonight, he would be. *How terrifying is that thought?* I'm certain Randall must have been terrified, and I can't help but feel a bit of sympathy for him. At least he's not afraid to stand up to Omar like everyone else is.

Once outside, I break free from Omar's hold and stumble over to some bushes near the building's entrance. The bag of chips I had been munching on earlier spills out onto the ground as I double over, retching. Omar silently stands nearby while Eddie waits in the car. He says nothing, allowing me to vomit and spit in peace. The distant wail of sirens fills the air, signaling that one of the neighbors has likely called the cops on us.

"Let's get out of here, baby girl," Omar says softly, his tone unusually gentle.

"Why bother? You'll just pay them off anyway, you *crook*," I retort without thinking, pushing him away and heading towards the car. The biting wind cuts through me, causing me to shiver as I wrap my jacket tightly around myself.

———— ♥ ————

The car ride stretches on, the silence heavy. I wish Eddie would pick up the pace a bit. They made it to Randall's place in record time; why aren't we at our destination yet? Omar sits up front with Eddie, leaving me in the backseat. I made sure to lock the back doors before he could even think about joining me back here. No way am I letting that happen.

Finally, Omar glances back at me as the city blurs past us in the early morning light. I avoid his gaze, opting instead to stare out of the window, trying to discern our location from the passing street signs just in case I need to make a quick escape.

"You still feelin' sick, baby girl?" Omar's voice is soft as he reaches back, his hand hovering near my knee.

I shift my knee away from his touch. "Don't say anything to me. Something's wrong with you, Omar. You need to get your head checked out."

"If I do, then you do too, baby girl. You gotta be crazy to be over that fool's crib."

I can't help but stifle a laugh, cursing myself for finding his remark amusing. Yes, I gotta be crazy to have put myself in that situation without considering the consequences. But I won't give him the satisfaction of admitting it out loud. Tonight, he takes the trophy for being extra, that's for sure.

"Do you want to go back to your place or ours?" he asks, his tone almost playful.

"I want you to stop talking to me before I punch you."

Eddie chuckles from the front seat, joined by Omar. I don't see what's so funny. Omar needs to realize the seriousness of the situation we're in. The police will likely be waiting for us soon. Randall won't let this slide, and Omar's unbothered attitude is starting to grate on my nerves.

"Let's hit that drive-thru over there, Ed. She needs to eat," Omar decides, taking charge once again.

As much as I want to argue with him for making decisions on my behalf, I can't deny the rumbling of my empty stomach. I haven't eaten since before work, which then serves as a bitter reminder that I'm now unemployed. *Damn it.*

"Thanks for getting me fired. If that was your way of trying to get me back, it didn't work. I'll just find another job," I retort, frustration seeping into my voice.

"A'ight, baby girl. Do you, then," Omar responds, his demeanor unbothered as ever.

"I will."

"Good."

"Yup." Inside, I'm seething with anger. I have to resist the urge to kick the back of his head.

Eddie pulls up to the drive-thru speaker, rolling down his window. I watch Omar lean over to examine the menu. Even in the dim light, his profile is striking. It's my favorite look on him—casual in a tracksuit with a bucket hat and a chain or two resting on his chest. Those defined cheekbones of his are simply irresistible, and I remember the sensation of running my fingers over them as we slept side by side. I used to love watching him sleep. I catch a whiff of his scent; the same one I detected while on stage earlier to remind me that he was always there, even when he wasn't.

Soft music plays from Eddie's radio, filling the car with its gentle melody.

"Silly of me to think that I could ever have you for my guy," the song croons.

Omar shares my appreciation for this kind of music; it's all I ever hear him listen to—smooth R&B and soulful tunes.

"How I love you, how I want you," the lyrics continue.

I can't help but wonder if the song is speaking to me or if I'm just searching for an explanation of my current situation. He bobs his head to the music, and I catch him looking at me when I snap out of my thoughts. Deciding to embrace the moment, I continue to meet his gaze. He won't see me flustered. Inside, though, I'm a bundle of nerves.

"Stop makin' a fool of *meee*," Omar sings along, shooting me a wink as he does.

I can't help but feel a mixture of irritation and adoration at his playfulness. It's almost annoying how effortlessly charming he can be, especially when he knows I'm a sucker for it.

"So, is this what you think of me, huh?" he teases.

"Maybe," I respond, unable to hide a smirk.

He smiles in response. "What do you two know about this one?" Eddie chimes in.

"I know this is what she thinks of me," Omar replies confidently.

After Eddie retrieves our order from the drive-thru window, we pull away and Omar instructs him to park the car. I watch as Omar gets out and walks around to my side, gesturing for me to unlock the door. Eddie cranks up the music, and I comply, allowing Omar to open the door and lean in.

"Wanna dance with me, baby girl?" he asks, holding out his hand.

I hesitate for a moment before accepting his offer, reaching out to take his hand without overthinking it. He pulls me close, and I find myself melting into his embrace. Despite my efforts to stay mad at him, I can't deny the comfort and warmth I feel in his arms. We sway to the music, and I steal a glance up at him. It's surreal to see this tough, cool guy letting his guard down to dance with me like this.

His lips look inviting, tempting me to lean in for a kiss, but I resist the urge. I'm supposed to be mad at him, after all.

"I wish we could give it another try, baby girl," he murmurs, lifting my chin gently with his hand. "What do you think?"

"I don't know. You fooled me once, Omar," I reply, avoiding his gaze. "You said I was special, and you fooled me."

He stops moving, and I feel his hand fall to his side.

"Oh, love, oh, love, stop makin' a fool of me..." The song continues to play, filling the silence between us as Omar processes my words.

"You are special to me. I meant that when I said it. Believe me," Omar insists.

I shake my head, my expression reflecting the weight of my thoughts. "No, your words are not enough. This whole thing between us was doomed from the start 'cause of how it began, anyway. It was wrong. And things like that aren't meant to last, Omar. You didn't take me seriously 'cause I went against my better judgment."

He lets out a sigh, running a hand over his chin. "You still talkin' about going behind Tara?"

"Yeah, it's still on my heart and it's real hard for me to forgive myself, I'm realizing that."

"Even though we're grown adults and shit just happens? That ain't enough for you?"

"It's not. It was messed up 'cause she was still my friend. I stole her man," I admit, the weight of guilt heavy in my words.

"I ain't belong to her. But I did come onto you, so I'm not feeling guilty about that. I wanted you—still, do—and Ion' regret shit. Life is too temporary to be hung up on shit 'cause somebody got hurt. We all get hurt. Call me fucked up for that, but it is what it is."

I meet his gaze once more, seeing a sincerity in his eyes that urges me to believe him. And I do. I believe he desired me even while he was with Tara. But the truth remains—it was wrong, both on my part and his. And here I stand, still harboring resentment for how quickly he went back to her, even if it were for a hookup. Until I forgive myself, I'll have to accept that I probably deserved it.

"Tell you what..." Omar checks his watch before returning his attention to me, his hands still delicately placed on my waist. "It's like six in the morning. Let's go back to my place and sleep on it. We can start fresh when we wake up. What you think?"

It would be a chance for a clean slate, an opportunity to let go of the pain from what happened with Tara. I ponder his proposal, needing assurance before I can agree. "Promise me you won't hurt me again, Omar?"

"I promise, baby girl," he vows, his voice sincere.

"Don't say that if you don't mean it. 'Cause I won't be fooled twice. Do you hear me?" I assert, poking my forefinger into his chest.

His eyes trace the path of my finger before meeting mine once more. "I promise, and I'm sorry for hurtin' you, baby girl."

His words carry weight, and I hold onto them tightly. A shiver runs through me as a gust of wind sweeps by, reminding me that I'm still dressed in my dance attire. Seeking warmth, I move closer to him.

"We can sleep on it 'cause I have more questions, but this baby's mad at me because I didn't eat, and I'm tired as hell," I say, feeling the exhaustion creeping in.

There's a laundry list of things I need to address with Omar. Firstly, I want answers about this supposed new girl Tara mentioned. Then there's the matter of Janay and Curtis, not to mention Randall. He needs to hear it all before I even consider giving him a yes. *Give him a hard time, girl. Make him earn it.*

He smiles down at me, his expression softening, and plants a gentle kiss on my forehead before his hand finds its way to my bump. "A'ight. Let's get you home, then."

Silly of me to go around and brag about the love I found... I say you're the best...

CHAPTER 16
Our Family

O MAR STANDS BY MY side, his hand wrapped tightly around mine, as we eagerly wait to find out our baby's gender. Excitement courses through me, mingled with a nervousness that tightens my chest. This moment will make everything feel so much more real. However, there's an added layer of anxiety because I made the mistake of sharing my past experience with my doctor who initially confirmed my pregnancy with Omar, and now he insisted on scheduling with her again. I'm just hoping she keeps things professional for her sake.

Doctor Harper applies the gel to my belly every which way, but I avoid commenting. After all, she's the expert here. She works stiffly, guiding the wand over my abdomen, and we all fixate on the images appearing on the monitor. I can't contain my excitement, so I squeeze my toes and Omar's hand, stealing a glance at him. His half-smile and gentle touch under my chin reassure me, but I can still see the nervousness on his face.

"Alright, so it looks like your baby is, surprisingly, doing well in there," Doctor Harper begins, her tone professional but with a hint of shadiness to it.

I roll my eyes, silently urging Omar to stay quiet too.

"Why is that a surprise, though?" he interjects, anyway.

I curse myself for not insisting on seeing a different doctor, knowing full well Omar wanted to experience her treatment just so he can do something about it.

"Just based on her first visit. She was in a tough position, and it made me fear for the health of the pregnancy," Doctor Harper responds, her gaze lifting over her glasses to meet Omar's.

"And your lil' two cents wasn't necessary, but please continue," Omar retorts, irritation creeping into his voice.

"Alright, so there are no defects from what I see so far, but this fetus is a bit bashful, so their legs are together right now. I'm not sure I can provide you with a result today," Doctor Harper concludes.

My heart sinks like a stone dropped into deep water. It's a crushing disappointment. We had a playful bet going on the gender of our baby. Omar had casually chosen a daughter, probably to roll with my desire for a son as my firstborn baby. The stakes? The winner gets to pick the new car we'll get for our small family.

"Okay. That's fine. We were excited, but if you can't see anything..." I trail off, trying to mask my disappointment.

Omar's silence speaks volumes. I can practically feel the waves of irritation radiating from him without even looking in his direction.

But he eventually speaks up. "You didn't even look long enough, lady. You had just turned it on though."

"Oh, I'm sorry. Are you a certified physician, sir? I've been doing this for many years. I think I know what I'm talking about," the doctor retorts sharply.

"You barely looked at the shit," Omar snaps back. "You could see she was excited as hell."

"Omar, it's okay, boo. I'm just grateful the baby is healthy for now. We can always come back," I muscle in, trying to diffuse the tension.

Doctor Harper rises from her seat to retrieve a towel from the sink area. "Well, since you seem to know so much, I assume this isn't your first time in this situation, although it is hers. Second? Third child for you, maybe? You should know how this works."

I release an annoyed sigh, impatiently waiting for her to finish up so we can leave. With her nasty ass attitude, she's lucky I don't snag that stringy ponytail swinging from her neck.

"No. This is both of our first," I correct her. "Anyway, what now?"

"Try to keep stress levels down... and perhaps consider marriage so the baby has a safe environment and family to go home to. Too many are born out of wedlock in my opinion," she suggests, her tone bordering on judgmental.

Omar abruptly releases my hand and strides purposefully to the door. He swings it open, peers into the hallway, then shuts and locks it with a decisive click. Both the doctor and I watch him with curiosity as he moves to the front of the room and retrieves something from behind him. The doctor gasps in horror, but I can't even act surprised. I know Omar's temper all too well, especially when he feels someone has been disrespectful.

She was asking for it.

"Look again. I'll let you know when it's been long enough," Omar commands, raising the gun threateningly. Doctor Harper trembles uncontrollably, struggling to pick up the ultrasound device. "Lay back down, baby girl."

"Omar, just... it's okay, okay? We can just see another doctor. She's not a good one," I chime in.

"Nah. She's gonna learn a lil' something about respect today. Do your job right. We ain't ask for your opinion if it ain't medical," Omar says firmly, his grip tightening on the gun.

"Okay, okay, please just don't shoot me..." Doctor Harper pleads, applying more gel to my belly.

Never did I imagine that discovering the gender of our baby would unfold like this. I had envisioned a joyous moment, but instead, we're coercing the doctor to do her job properly.

We? Yes, we. I chose to be with him again, knowing his temperament, so we're in this together. Despite the situation, I can't help but smile as I gaze at him from across the room, his gun trained on the doctor's head. The fact I didn't hop off this table and take off when he flashed that gun confirms for me how sprung I am.

He looks like a complete whacko right about now, yet I'm mesmerized by him. But she must not have heard of Omar, or she wouldn't have dared to cross us the first time we met. All she had to do was ask me, but she ain't ask me.

Omar catches me admiring him and softens his gaze, laughing in response to my grin.

"You're so crazy, Omar," I remark.

"You love it though," he winks, the light above him causing his gold-capped teeth to glimmer.

"You're right. I might be a lil' too doped up," I quip. "You're the best drug though. I can't complain."

His smile fades, but his eyes remain fixed on mine.

If I were the doctor, I'd be rolling my eyes at our flirtatious exchange. Yet she's too terrified to react, and I can't help but feel a little bit concerned for her safety.

"Oh, look here... I can see something," she announces.

Omar steps forward, easing his grip on the trigger, and our attention shifts to the monitor.

"Okay, I'm seeing... something right there. It's a lot clearer than I originally thought," she observes.

"Everything's a lot clearer with a gun to your head, ain't it?" I ask her as Omar chuckles.

"Looks like a boy. You're having a boy," she concludes, pointing to a specific area on the screen.

I cover my mouth in disbelief, tears welling up in my eyes as I glance over at Omar. He's already lowered his gun, wearing that half-smile that melts me every time.

"How you feelin', baby girl?" he asks, his voice filled with warmth.

"I... I won the bet! *Ha!*" I exclaim, tears streaming down my face.

Omar chuckles and returns to my side, locking lips with me. "Congratulations," he murmurs against my lips.

"Same to you, baby daddy."

We hear Doctor Harper shifting the equipment and moving away from us on her stool. "You should be in jail for this," she states firmly.

It's the first time I've seen Omar roll his eyes. He shuts them for a moment, tilting his head back before finally settling back into his seat, his gaze locked on her. *What's he up to?* I start to feel nervous myself, watching their intense stare-down. I reach out to touch his shoulder, hoping to snap him out of it, but he remains still.

"I see you married, Doc. You got kids too?" Omar scratches his head with the barrel of the gun, his tone casual but with an edge.

"Excuse me?" she stammers, clearly unsettled.

"Okay, boo, let's just go, okay? She ain't even worth it." I tighten my grip on his shoulder.

"Nah, she owes you an apology, and we can sit our asses right here until you get it." Omar's eyes remain fixed on her, unblinking. "Apologize to my lady for the disrespect, and I'll let you keep your job, your family, and your life. And yeah, I can take all that shit and do no jail time, feel me?"

Doctor Harper squirms in her seat, clearly uncomfortable. She hands me a towel to wipe the gel off myself and stands quickly. "S-Sorry. And congrats. Paperwork will be ready at the front," she stammers, rushing to unlock the door and exit the room.

Omar turns back to me, helping me off the table.

"How do you know she's not going to call the cops now?" I ask him, a hint of worry in my voice.

"I ain't worried about her or none of them. I'm a crook, remember?" he replies confidently.

"Okay, but Omar, you can't just pull out your piece every time somebody pisses you off."

"I can and will every time, baby girl. Don't let nobody disrespect you like that, a'ight? I don't care who they are."

"Okay, I won't. Thanks for having my back," I say gratefully.

"Always. Wanna go eat and celebrate?" he suggests.

"Yes... We're having a *boy!*" I exclaim once more. I jump up, wrapping my legs around him. He catches me effortlessly, squeezing me tightly as we revel in the joy of our shared moment.

———— ♡ ————

The restaurant staff had to rearrange tables to accommodate our group. It wasn't the entire crew, just those who could make it on short notice. I didn't expect such an impromptu gathering, but after our appointment, Eddie spread the news like wildfire, rallying the family together. Now, here we are, about to indulge in some Mexican cuisine, which happens to be my favorite.

Eddie can't contain his excitement, showering me with wet kisses on the cheek. His enthusiasm is infectious, and I'm tempted to ask if he sees this baby as his first grandchild, given his age and role in Omar's life. But I hold back, not wanting to possibly hurt his feelings because of our age differences.

"Now, ain't this something? O's really about to be somebody's pops," Eddie announces across the table, capturing the moment with his camera, a gift from me. "That's gonna be one beautiful baby."

Cheers and congratulations fill the air, and I discreetly nudge Omar's foot under the table. He responds with a wink, a silent gesture of affection, before quieting the table to speak.

"Alright, thank y'all. I just wanna say thanks for working your asses off so I had time to make one," Omar says, eliciting laughter from the group. I can't help but bury my face in my hands, while Eddie's laughter only grows.

"But seriously, this is cool and all, but the boy ain't even here yet, and y'all here celebrating with me and my lady..." Omar continues, and I feel a sense of pride hearing him proudly refer to me as his lady.

"We appreciate you," someone interjects.

"That's what family does, O. You brought us together. You did that. We're always gonna be here," Eddie declares.

The sentiment resonates with everyone at the table, which only emphasizes the strong bond Omar has with the people most loyal to him. They've become a tight-knit family under his guidance, and despite the nature of their business, they're in it together for the long haul. It's reassuring to know that he'll make a wonderful father. This unexpected gathering serves as proof of his ability to nurture, provide, and bring people together. It's a realization that dawns on me as I sit among them, and I'm finding myself falling harder watching him as this family's leader. Yes, Omar may be a bit wild at times, but he's the best decision I've ever made.

Tears threaten to spill down my cheeks, and I reach for a napkin to stop the flow. Omar's hand finds mine, his touch silently comforting.

"You alright, baby girl?" he asks, his voice low in the thick of the loud chatter.

I pause, grappling with how to articulate my emotions to him in this moment. "Um, I'm good. It's just... seeing this, like a family and all. It's beautiful, even though you all are involved in some heavy stuff... dealing and whatnot. But if that's what binds you all together, I can't even be mad at that."

I catch the soft chuckles from Omar and Eddie in response. Eddie's hand finds its way to my back once more. "Well, it's long overdue, Miss Chevy, but welcome to the family," he declares warmly.

"Welcome aboard, Miss Chevy!"

"Welcome!"

"Yeah, Chevy! We're glad to have you! Thanks for making O a happy man!" Rita chimes in from across the table. "Just do us a favor and please don't leave him again, 'cause he had us all fucked up."

Laughter erupts once more, and I'm still curious about the antics Omar likely got up to during our time apart, especially after what he pulled off today.

A hand rests on my shoulder, and I turn to see Janay leaning in for a hug. "Janay!" I exclaim, rising to embrace her, with Curtis by her side, exchanging greetings with Omar.

"Hey, Chevy! Congratulations to you and O. We're thrilled for you both," Janay says, her hand gently resting on my baby bump.

Omar listened to my request and brought them back into our circle. It was one of my conditions for taking him back. I explained that true friends support each other, and I was grateful that Janay had spoken up. He initially hesitated, but I reminded him of his own actions with Tara. Eventually, he acknowledged his mistakes, and I refused to let him scapegoat Janay and Curtis. He admitted he preferred Janay over Sheila as my friend anyway, so he was receptive to rebuilding those friendships. Seeing Curtis here brings me a sense of relief; I know he's one of Omar's closest friends.

"I expected O to be on kid, like, three or four by now, if we bein' real," Curt jokes, eliciting a chuckle from the group. "Man used to get all the ladies. Sorry to break it to you, Chev."

"It's okay. I already know who I'm dealing with," I reply with a giggle as Eddie pulls up two chairs beside me and Omar. "I'm still number one."

I make sure I look my man in the eyes as I declare my place. I see no contest in his, only affirmation, so I'm content in this moment.

Janay settles into the seat next to me, eagerly eyeing the menu. "What you getting, Chevy? I love their burritos. I gotta get myself a margarita. You can't have that though."

"I'm okay with that. I'm getting some fish tacos," I inform her.

"That sounds good. I'ma get those too. How you been, girl? You so gorgeous. Glowing and shit like that," Janay compliments me with a warm smile.

"I'm doing better, Janay. Thanks for asking. I don't have a job anymore, thanks to my kooky man over here, but he's making up for it," I quip, glancing affectionately at Omar.

Even though he's engrossed in conversation with the guys, I catch a flicker of amusement in his eyes, signaling that he heard me loud and clear.

Janay bursts into laughter as she attempts to light her cigarette, her hand trembling slightly.

Noticing her struggle, I offer to help. "You okay, Janay?"

She nods quickly, exhaling a cloud of smoke away from us. "Yes, babe. Just been busy with the kids and shit like that. It was a tough couple of months, but we were glad O called. Curt missed his friend."

"And I'm sure Omar missed him too," I add, offering my support.

"I'm sure you helped with that, so thanks, Chevy. Being a part of this family is something special, so you feel it when you on the outside of it."

As Janay reaches for her water, her hand trembles, causing her to accidentally knock over the glass. "Shit! Sorry, y'all," she apologizes, flustered.

I glance at Omar while helping clean up the spill. He watches Janay with a hint of concern in his gaze, and I wonder if he noticed her trembling hands. He better not be mad about the spilled water; it was clearly an accident. He then resumes his conversation with Eddie and Curt.

This is the first time I've really taken in Janay's appearance without her sunglasses, noticing the exhaustion carved on her face. Despite her telling me otherwise, I can tell she's not okay, and I hope she's not facing any health issues. She needs to quit smoking, or maybe her struggles stem from the tough months she mentioned. Either way, I can't help but feel guilty, knowing I'm partly responsible for her distress, even though I had no idea Omar would do that to them.

As I watch Janay clean up her spilled water, sadness tugs at my heartstrings. I can't shake the feeling that something isn't right. *Maybe she and Curtis are having problems? Or perhaps the kids are stressing her out?* I've seen plenty of moms out here looking frazzled from chasing their wild kids around all day, and I hope my son doesn't drive me crazy like that. But then again, it'll just be what it is.

Once again, I catch Omar watching me with concern, and I realize I need to rein in my emotions. The last thing I want is for him to be constantly worried about me when I'm already worried about myself enough. I force a smile to reassure him without words, but his response is to turn away from me with a hint of annoyance. *Ouch.* Talk about mood swings.

Eventually, the waiters come around to take our orders, and we all dive into our food like it's our last meal. I'm particularly fond of my tacos, loaded with extra sour cream and a squeeze of lime. I catch a few disgusted faces from around the table, but I couldn't care less. They better mind their own business so I can enjoy my meal in peace.

"You ain't got enough of the sour cream yet, Chevy? Damn, you makin' my stomach hurt," Janay remarks, offering her opinion.

"Mind your business and your dry-ass tacos, Janay," I retort, taking another bite. After swallowing, I add, "All y'all better leave me alone about my tacos, or I'ma whip your asses."

"Leave her alone, y'all, 'cause I won't save you, neither" Omar chimes in, as the laughter kicks up.

Okay, so he's back in a good mood, but I decide to give him space to enjoy his time with his friends for the rest of the dinner. I can't keep up with his sudden mood swings on top of my own.

"You want more sour cream, baby girl?" Omar offers, a toothy grin spreading across his face.

"Hell yeah. Slap it right on this last taco here 'cause this about to be the one," I reply eagerly.

He spoons more sour cream onto my taco, and I devour it messily. I notice Omar watching me with a mixture of amusement and affection, and I can't resist teasing him. It's moments like these that make my heart race because I know... I've really got this man in love with me.

I lift my half-eaten taco, hoping to catch Omar's attention once more. Fish and sour cream might not be the sexiest combo, but I'm determined to make it work. With his eyes locked on mine, I take a deliberate, slow bite, allowing the creamy sauce to coat my lips before sensually licking them clean. Using my cream-covered finger, I delicately slide it between my lips, savoring the moment before pulling it out with a soft smack of my lips and a swallow.

"Looks nasty," he finally remarks, and I dissolve into fits of laughter, collapsing onto the ground. He leans over, watching me with amusement. "You supposed to do that with strawberries and cream or something, not some stanky fish tacos."

"I can't breathe, Omar," I manage to gasp between giggles.

"Aye, she tried, O. Let her be," Eddie chimes in, joining in our laughter.

"Did everybody see that?" I ask, realizing I hadn't even tried to hide my attempt at seduction.

"Yeah," Omar confirms, and I feel the embarrassment wash over me as a few others chuckle along. *Oh, hell.*

"Haha! Chevy's so damn goofy!" Janay remarks, wiping tears from her face. "I ain't never seen nothin' like that before."

"Yeah, that's 'cause you don't do that shit for me," Curtis jokes, earning a playful nudge from Janay.

Omar helps me up and once I'm back on my feet, I realize I really need to use the bathroom. I make my way down the hall, lost in a wave of contentment. It feels

amazing not to be alone anymore. Even though I've always been okay with solitude, being welcomed into a family with open arms is incredibly heartwarming.
I can only hope that this feeling of belonging lasts and my baby boy gets to
experience it too.

I stand at the basin, running my hands under the cool water as I steal a
glance at my reflection in the mirror. My fingertips trace the outline of my
burgeoning baby bump, a surreal reminder of the life growing inside me. It's
a boy, something I still struggle to grasp. The thought of holding him in my
arms feels almost otherworldly, as if it belongs to someone else's reality. A year
ago, if you had told me this would be my life now, I wouldn't have believed you.

But then, like a tidal wave crashing over me, a rush of emotions floods my
senses, and I collapse to my knees, overwhelmed by a wave of grief and longing.

Daddy.

The ache of his absence hits me with a force that steals my breath. He won't
be here to meet his grandson when he's born. He wasn't always proud of me,
especially after I was kicked out shortly before his passing, but I know having a
grandson would have made him happier.

He didn't fight hard enough to stick around for me. For *us.*

Leaning against the sink, I let the water mask the sound of my sobs, my tears
merging with the steady stream falling onto the floor.

A soft knock interrupts the solitude of my grief. "Just... Just a minute!" I call
out, hastily wiping my face with a handful of paper towels and attempting to
compose myself. I realize this restroom has only one toilet, and I wouldn't be
surprised if a line formed outside while I gave in to my emotions.

I fluff up my hair, trying to appear presentable, before pulling open the door
to find Omar waiting, concern all over his face. He straightens up as our eyes
meet, his protective instincts must be kicking in.

"What's going on, baby girl? You okay?" he inquires, pulling me close and
searching my face for answers. "Why you crying?"

"I'm okay, really. Just feeling a bit sensitive 'cause of the baby," I assure him,
though I know he sees through the facade.

He remains unconvinced. "Nah, tell me what's up. Were you sick? Did
someone say something? Was it something I did?"

I shake my head. "No, nothing like that. You didn't do anything. I was just thinking about my daddy..." My voice falters, tears threatening to spill over once more.

Without hesitation, Omar guides us back into the restroom, locking the door behind us.

"Wait, Omar, what if somebody has to use it," I protest weakly as he disregards my words, making himself comfortable on the toilet seat and pulling me onto his lap.

"What's got you all worked up?" he probes gently, his fingers tracing soothing patterns on my back.

"I was just thinking about how angry he was with me before he passed away, and how he left me here. He won't get to meet our son, or you, or any of that... And I just miss him," I confess, tears streaming down my cheeks as I bury my face in my hands.

Omar tenderly removes my hands from my face. "He's with you, baby girl," he reassures me.

"But... he left me here alone, Omar. I was so scared, you know? Our son won't even know his grandfather, besides what I tell him. I have no family here... And I can't call him anymore, hear his voice... get his advice, nothing," I choke out between sobs.

"Shh..." Omar gently brushes away a few stray tears with his thumb. "I know this may not be what you want to hear right now, but the biggest lesson is learning to accept shit as they are and move on. Like we said before, he prepared you to stand on your own out here. You doing damn well for yourself," he adds, his voice soft but firm.

I nod slowly, absorbing his words.

"I hear you talk like he didn't love you. You might not believe it, but he did. He mighta had a strange way of showing it, but he did. And I wouldn't be surprised if he's proud of you right now."

"You think he's proud of me?" I ask.

"Hell yeah. You been holdin' it down on your own, baby girl. And that mind of yours... that's something special," he says.

"Thank you, Omar. Do you wanna know why he kicked me out?" I toy with the chain around his neck, meeting his gaze.

"Why did he kick you out?"

"'Cause we got into a stupid argument about what I was doing with my life, and he started saying all sorts of hurtful things to me. I ended up telling him that I knew he was the reason my mama left, and I guess that hit a nerve 'cause he slapped me and told me to leave. So I did. I used the money I had saved from odd jobs to get my own place. But, boo, that was so mean of me to say... I know he was still hurt by my mama leaving, and I think that's why he was so angry."

"It sounds like he never really got over her leaving, then having to raise you all by himself," Omar murmurs softly, his tone gentle as he tries to comfort me. I feel guilty for staining his shirt with my tears, but he doesn't seem to mind as he wipes my face clean with toilet tissue. "That mighta set him off baby girl, but that doesn't mean he didn't love you. You was still his baby. I think what's really bothering you is that you never got to have that conversation with him. Now that he's gone, you're left wondering if you meant anything to him."

"Yeah, that's true," I admit, feeling the weight of his words sinking in.

"Part of moving on is accepting," Omar continues, his voice steady and reassuring. "Your mama leavin' was out of his control. He never accepted that. Then, with him passing away and leaving you here with no family, that's been hard for you to accept. You still hurting, and it's all good, but now your life is changin', baby. You don't gotta hold on to all that pain anymore."

"You're right, boo." I cup his face, pecking his cheek. "I don't want our son to ever question if we love him. So I'ma work through it."

"You got it."

"I guess I could believe my dad loved me if he taught me so many life lessons," I reflect, a small smile tugging at my lips. Omar mirrors my smile.

I then pause, remembering my conversation with Eddie. "Is that what you did when you found your mama? You had to accept it?" I inquire softly.

He stops rubbing my back, his thoughts seemingly drifting somewhere else. "Sorry if that's still hard for you. Eddie told me how you found your mama, holding her when she died."

There's a brief silence, and I lay my head on his shoulder, offering silent support. I hope he's okay, but if that's still a sore spot for him, maybe he hasn't fully accepted it either. It's as if he knows what needs to be done but hasn't made peace with it himself.

"I love you, boo. Thank you for everything you been doing for me," I finally express, attempting to change the subject.

"I love you too, baby girl," Omar responds, his voice a bit husky.

I sit up and cup his jaw, tracing his cheekbones with my thumbs before leaning in to kiss him. He reciprocates, and we share a tender moment, our lips moving in sync.

"Guess we've got a lot of accepting to do together, huh, boo?" I murmur against his lips.

"Yeah, we do," he agrees softly.

CHAPTER 17
Yvonne's Baby

I 'VE BEEN WADDLING AROUND like a duck lately, thanks to this big belly of mine—I'm in my ninth month of pregnancy! I've been chilling out, waiting for my little guy to pop out any day now. He's got me lugging around an extra twenty pounds, mostly in my belly and butt. It's a hilarious sight to see, I'm sure of it, but Omar thinks it's cute, even though he's bummed we couldn't get too cozy in this last month.

Omar's stuck doing thirty days in LA County for getting a bit too rough in a fight, with just a week to go. I'm crossing my fingers that our son doesn't decide to make a surprise appearance before Omar's out. As for what landed him there, well, let's just say, you don't mess with Omar without consequences. I learned that lesson when I tried to help Randall behind Omar's back.

I hate seeing Omar all worked up and angry like he was at the time the brawl broke out. I much prefer his softer side, but I guess that's just how things roll in our world. Respect means keeping folks in line, even if it means a bit of fear. As long as you're cool with Omar, you're golden, but cross him, and you're in for a world of hurt.

The situation got real when Omar got nabbed at the park, and I was freaking the hell out watching those cops slap cuffs on my man. But Omar, always the cool one, told me to chill, promising everything would be okay. He even asked Eddie to keep an eye on me, but deep down, I knew this wasn't going to blow over so easily this time. That's when he got hit with thirty days, which had me about to pass out until Rita told me that it's a slap on the wrist for Omar.

If a slap on a wrist means jailtime, I'd hate to see what an ass-whooping would look like if Omar doesn't let up. When I visited him last week, I begged Omar to lay off the rough stuff, especially now that all eyes are on him. But he remained unbothered as always.

This whole situation with Omar in the business still bothers me time to time because I'll never know when he'll end up behind bars or worse, and I can't deal with that. Seeing him in a jumpsuit on the other side of that glass messes with my head and heart. Sure, Omar says he'll do better, but I'm not stupid. His empire comes first, always has, always will. And he'll gladly serve thirty days for it, even if it's too close to the birth of his first child.

"Hey, what are you gonna name him, Chevy?" Sheila blurts out, tossing her empty wine cooler bottle in the trash as she finishes it off.

We're in the nursery, and Sheila's been a godsend, helping me get things ready for the baby's arrival. Janay pitches in when she can, and Eddie and Curt are knee-deep in business stuff while Omar is locked up, so they've been scarce lately. I had the freedom to pick who'd help out at the house, so I called up Sheila. She practically flew over, eager to lend a hand. We had a heart-to-heart, and she said I looked happy and taken care of, so she owes Omar a thanks. Little does she know, I haven't told Omar about bringing her on board yet, and we all know how he feels about Miss Sheila. Gonna have to break that news gently.

On the upside, Sheila and Eddie seem to be hitting it off, so even if it's just casual, it's nice they've got each other.

"That's a tough one 'cause I'm not sure," I reply, hanging up a painting of an angel bear over the crib.

"Well, don't you think you should figure it out, especially with the baby coming soon?" she quips.

"I was thinking I'd wait until I see him, you know, see how it feels when he's in my arms. I don't wanna just slap any old name on him." It's something I've always wanted to do. Pre-naming the baby just feels off to me.

"Fair enough. I can't wait," she says with excitement. "I know you got Eddie as the godfather 'cause him and O are tight, so maybe I can be the godmother? I'm great with babies, and you and me, we're tight."

As Sheila eagerly offers herself up as the baby's godmother, my heart sinks a bit. "Oh, um, he actually already has one. Janay," I manage to say.

Sheila rolls her eyes and accidentally splatters green paint on the carpet as she tosses the paintbrush into its tin can. "Oops. My bad, Chevy. I'll clean that up."

"Why'd you do that, Sheila? Omar's a neat freak. He'll notice that green stain on the carpet," I say, feeling a tad irritated.

"I didn't mean to," Sheila replies, delicately blotting it with a nearby rag. "Why'd you choose Janay? She doesn't seem right."

"Janay's been my friend, the closest one I've had since I got together with Omar. She's part of this family and has been so supportive of me," I explain.

"And I'm not your friend? We've been friends longer, Chevy, even if we had that fight and didn't talk. I still loved you as my friend," Sheila retorts.

"Sheila, let's be real. When we chose Janay, we had to think about who could take care of our baby if something happened to me or Omar. It's not about who's a better friend. Plus, we weren't even talking when we made that decision." I watch her attempt to blot the paint, but it only seems to make it worse, so I waddle over to help her. I know Omar would never agree to her being an option.

"I get it. Nobody wants a stripper as their baby's godmother anyway." Sheila rolls her eyes.

"That had nothing to do with it. If I wasn't pregnant, I'd still be dancing," I retort.

"I don't believe that. Omar seems like he wouldn't like you dancing."

I'm sure he doesn't, but it's my life.

"Omar can kiss the blackest part of my ass for all I care. It doesn't matter. I stopped judging him about what he does for a living," I respond firmly.

Sheila falls back, laughing. "That's probably why you've got that man so in love. He can control anybody and everything but you."

Omar always compliments me on my intelligence and independence, so I've always known he was drawn to those qualities but hearing it from Sheila makes me pause. "I could see that being the reason."

"It is the reason, Chevy. Besides you being beautiful, of course. Omar needs a powerful woman by his side, someone who can keep him in check," Sheila concludes with a smirk.

"You got that right." I ponder for a moment. "He's still scary sometimes though..."

"I'm sure. Omar's handsome and powerful and all, but I wouldn't dare. It takes somebody special to handle a man like that, and you got it, obviously."

"I guess, but Sheila, this mess isn't coming out," I grumble in frustration.

"Let's just cover it up with that rug. It's not like y'all don't have the money to replace it if it bothers him that damn bad," she suggests, her words dripping with a sense of entitlement that rubs me the wrong way, but I let it slide for now.

"How's Randall?"

"He's good, I guess. We don't really talk. I just go to work, do my thing, then leave. I'm sure he's still messing around," Sheila replies with a touch of sadness.

"Well, maybe after I talk to Omar about getting you on permanently, you can quit there. It's gonna be hard for you to get over him if you're still working for him, Sheila."

She stops scrubbing and looks up at me. "I'm not gonna lie, Chevy, I'm kinda surprised you're asking about Randall, especially after you slept with him again."

My eyes widen in shock at her words. "I didn't sleep with him again."

"Yeah, he said that's why Omar messed him up a few months ago. I was hurt, and sorry I didn't bring that up in that talk we had, but I didn't think that was cool, Chevy. You knew how I felt about him."

"I didn't sleep with Randall. That's not what happened," I insist firmly.

"He told us you went home with him that night."

"Yeah, but I didn't sleep with him. I just wanted some company and was upset 'cause I had just seen Tara, and she came with nothing but bad news, so I went to him for advice. Nothing happened. Omar beat him up 'cause he was tryna be big and bad," I explain, frustration bubbling up inside me as she refuses to believe me. It's infuriating that Randall would go back and spread lies like that, making me look like some thoughtless hoochie, but I'm not even surprised.

"It's cool, Chevy. I got over it."

"I'm bothered that you just won't believe me. Are you thinking about this whole Omar and Tara thing?" I question.

"I just think you know you're a real smart and attractive person and can get anything or anybody you want, and that's okay, Chevy. Some women just get lucky like that. You know I always said I wish I was you," Sheila says with a shrug.

I'm taken aback by her words, struggling to process what I'm hearing. I'll just chalk it up to her immaturity. She should know better than to have such a distorted image of me when I've always shown that I'm more than just my appearance and have been a decent friend to her.

"Okay, well, I think we should be done in here 'cause I gotta get some food on the stove," I finally say after an awkward silence.

"Sounds good. I gotta get going anyway, gotta work at the club tonight. I'll be at the family house this weekend, though, so I'll be close," Sheila says as she stands up and rubs her hands together to remove dried paint. It falls onto the floor, but I'll wait until she leaves to clean it up.

Just sloppy, like our friendship.

—————— ❦ ——————

The address scrawled on this crumpled piece of paper resembles chicken scratch, but somehow, I manage to match it to the house I'm standing in front of. Eddie mentioned that Omar had a surprise for me, passing me this note with a cryptic message about someone I'd want to meet. I figure it's gotta be someone from my family.

So here I am, standing on the weathered porch of an old house, with broken shingles and a tiny weed garden struggling to survive in the front. Initially, I was a bit hesitant, but I trust Omar enough to know he wouldn't put me or our baby in harm's way, so I muster up the confidence to knock on the door.

An elderly woman opens the door, her back slightly hunched, but her gaze steady as if she's expecting a door-to-door sales pitch.

"Yes?" she finally asks, her voice cautious, filtering through the screen door.

"Um, hi, I was sent here. I was told that I have family here. My name is Chevonne... Chevonne Bleu. My daddy's name is Clayton, and my mama's name is Yvonne," I explain, trying to sound as polite as possible.

Her hand flies to her mouth, eyes welling up with tears. I'm just noticing her green eyes; they're just like mine.

"Oh, my God... You're Yvonne's baby. Come in, come in," she says, her voice trembling.

She swings the door open, and I step inside, taking in the sight of the cluttered, dusty knickknacks and stacks of newspapers on the dining table. The woman turns to face me, then pulls me into a tight hug. I allow her embrace, sensing that she's familiar with me or knows of me, at least.

"I'm sorry. I just can't believe it," she starts, her voice wavering. "She told me your daddy took you away from here."

"So, you know who I am?"

"Mhm..." she nods solemnly. "I'm Yvonne's mama. I'm your grandmother, baby."

I stand there, momentarily stunned. I never even considered the possibility of meeting my grandparents. Daddy always said they were all dead anyway.

"Really?" I manage to stammer out, not quite sure what else to say.

"You favor her so much... I'm Cheryl," she offers, her eyes still moist with unshed tears as she looks me over. She then glances down at my baby belly, gently resting her hand on it.

"You real big. When are you due?" she asks, a hint of excitement in her voice.

"Any day now... I'm sorry, but this is so unreal to me. My daddy said that you were dead," I confess, still trying to wrap my head around the sudden revelation.

"Your daddy?" Cheryl scoffs. "Well, I ain't dead yet, now, am I?" She takes my arm gently and leads me toward the dining table, pushing aside the folded newspapers and grabbing two glasses from the cabinet.

"I ain't never thought I would see you again," she continues as she pours some tea into the glasses, carefully adding ice to each.

"We met before?"

"Yes. I seen you a couple times before—well before I ain't see you again," Cheryl replies. "You were just a baby then."

"Where is my mama? Is she still around somewhere?" I ask eagerly.

"Oh... no, baby. She passed on some years back. You still mighta been real young," Cheryl delivers the news gently, but it still hits me like a ton of bricks. I feel my heart sink, and I know my baby can feel it too. Now I'll never get to see my mama again. I wonder if my daddy knew. And if he did, why he kept it from me?

"What happened to her?"

" She was a real heavy drinker and was sad all the time. 'Ain't have nothin' to live' for is what she would tell me," Cheryl explain.

"Why did she leave me and my dad? He never told me why. I don't even remember what her face looks like," I express. I believe I was about five years old that last time I saw her. It's all a blur now.

Cheryl sets my glass in front of me and retrieves an overstuffed photo album covered in dust particles. She opens it and flips through a few pages. "You really only need to look in a mirror, but I see your daddy in you real good too. Here she is."

I follow her scrawny finger as she points to a photo. My mama looks so beautiful in the picture, with big, roller-set curls and a contagious wide smile that reaches her eyes. The same ones she gave me. I run my fingers over her face, feeling a sense of longing.

"She looks real happy right here," I remark, my voice barely above a whisper.

"Mhm. I believe this was right around the time she found out she was having you," Cheryl says as she carefully removes the photo from behind the film and hands it to me. "You can have this."

"Thank you, I'll keep it forever. How old was she here? She looks so young," I inquire, studying the photo of my mama.

"She was... let's see," Cheryl pauses, trying to remember. "She was fifteen. Yeah, that's right. She was fifteen when she got pregnant."

"What?" My mind begins reeling with questions.

"Your daddy ain't tell you nothin', damn," Cheryl says with a shake of her head.

He never told me that my mama was so young when she got pregnant with me. He barely told me anything about her when I asked him, but this discovery only adds another layer to the mystery of my family.

"Yeah, he didn't really say much about my mama. It hurt him bad when she left. I wish I knew what happened," I admit.

"I'll tell you now. Didn't seem that long ago. How old are you again, baby?" Cheryl asks.

"I'm twenty-two. Just turned twenty-two last month," I reply, my thoughts drifting back to my recent birthday celebration.

We celebrated my birthday by taking over one of my favorite clubs. It was an unforgettable day, feeling like royalty with Omar and the crew showering me with love and attention. Omar refrained from drinking, just because I couldn't, which I found incredibly thoughtful. It was hands down the best birthday I've ever had.

"Wow. twenty-two years old," Cheryl remarks, shaking her head and pursing her wrinkled lips. "Maybe it was that long ago. The years just fly on by. But uh, yeah, your mama and daddy wasn't supposed to be messin' around like that, but they would never leave each other alone. He was a grown man messin' wit' her. Me and her dad ain't like that shit, and we tried to put an end to it."

"Oh... Okay, so I'm guessing mama ran off with him?" I ask, finding the story amusing, especially considering my grandparents' disapproval of mama and daddy's relationship.

"Not ran off... I hate even havin' to admit this, but when she told me she was pregnant, I put her out. I always regretted doin' that, maybe she would not have been so messed up," Cheryl confesses, her voice filled with remorse.

"Messed up? What was wrong with her?"

"Drinking... dope... She used them things to get away from whatever she had goin' on in that head of hers. She was... She was such a sweet girl, and I never imagined my lil' girl to turn out the way she did. Me and her dad always did the best we could, but I learned to accept things for how they were, no matter how much I wanted to fix her."

Just like Omar would say.

"That's sad. I'm sorry to hear that. I wish I could have seen her again before she passed."

She only nods then continues. "It's also the reason Clayton wouldn't let her near you. I keep hearin' you say she left. She ain't leave willingly."

The clarification only confuses me more. He told me she left us.

"You said my daddy kept me from her? You think it's 'cause of the drugs and stuff?" I probe, trying to piece together the puzzle of my family's history.

Her face twists in emotional pain as she looks down at her veiny hands. "She was sick, baby. She wasn't right in her head. Your daddy had to let her go to protect you, and even though that made me so angry, I knew he really loved you to make a choice like that. Shoot, who was I to judge after what I did, anyway?"

Tears well up in my eyes as her words sink in. "He wanted to protect you. That's all he ever wanted to do," Cheryl affirms, her voice filled with compassion.

"So, he let her go?"

"Mhm, he just couldn't take it no more. If me and your granddad couldn't help her, if having you ain't push her to get it together, he knew he couldn't do it."

I take a moment to absorb the weight of her words before shifting the conversation. "Where is my granddad? Is he gone too?"

Cheryl nods. "Yeah. He passed on last year."

"My daddy did too. Well, maybe a lil' longer than that. I didn't really keep track. I don't like to think about it."

"I'm sorry, baby. It looks like he did real good with you though. You look so healthy. You're so smart. And now, you got you a lil' baby on the way. You married?" Cheryl inquires, her gaze softening.

I shake my head in response. "No, but I do have a boyfriend. He takes good care of me, and we love each other."

"Beautiful. As long as he treats you right, hold on to that as long as you can. It's tough being on your own out here. I spent a year just waiting to die," Cheryl admits. She takes a sip of her tea, the sound of her cough echoing through the room. "Mm. With my husband gone and my baby... What else do I gotta live for?"

"You shouldn't talk like that. You got me now. I know you don't know me like that, but we are still family. My man told me you can always create your own, and that's what he did and what we are doing together," I assure her, reaching out to gently squeeze her hand. Cheryl's weak smile melts my heart, and tears trickle down her weathered cheeks.

"You so sweet. I'm sorry I ain't do more to look for you. You ain't deserve to not know where you came from."

"I'm not upset about that. I used to be when I was little, but Daddy kept me busy and always taught me things. He also said that we come into the world alone anyway, so why are we so afraid of being alone? If we can't be in our own company, then that's a problem," I reflect, recalling my father's wisdom.

Cheryl scoffs and taps my untouched glass. "He always had some sorta explanation for something, got on my damn nerves, but he ain't wrong. Drink up."

I take a gulp of the bitter tea, suppressing a grimace at its taste. "I'm happy to have met you, Cheryl. Or I mean, Grandma. If that's okay," I express.

"That's just fine, sweetheart. You remind me so much of Yvonne. I just wanna pinch myself to see if this is real." She smiles as she reaches out to touch my belly. "What are you havin', baby?"

"A boy. I always wanted a boy first so he could protect his younger brothers and sisters," I share.

"Okay, good. And I like how you wanna break the one-child tradition."

"Yep. I wanna have more than one for sure. So they can all look out for each other just in case anything happened to me. I understand what my daddy said about being alone, but I think it's important to connect with people and experience love and stuff."

"I agree with you, baby," Cheryl responds. "I wanna give you something."

As Cheryl heads out the kitchen, I continue to flip through the photo album. My heart swells with love, knowing I have a surviving family member left. I can't wait to share everything with Omar and thank him for bringing me this unexpected gift. I love him so much.

Cheryl returns with a delicate necklace, its silver-plated cross glinting in the soft light of the room. She fastens it around my neck, the cool metal resting against my skin.

"Thank you so much. It's so pretty," I express, tracing the edges of the pendant with my fingertips.

"It was Yvonne's. I got it for her when she was baptized. She never took it off."

I glance back at the photo of my mama, noticing the necklace adorning her neck before turning back to my grandmother. "Well, I'll never take it off either. I wanna give you my number so we can stay in contact, and I want you to meet my baby when he comes."

Cheryl readily agrees, and I quickly jot down my contact information on a piece of nearby newspaper. "Here you go. There's so much for us to talk about. This number is the house phone, but this is my pager. Please don't be afraid to call me anytime. I'm almost always available."

Tears fall from Cheryl's eyes as she accepts the paper from me. "Okay, baby. Thank you for comin' to see me. This the best day I've had in a long time. I'ma give you mine too."

———— ♥ ————

"How did you find her?" I hold the phone close to my ear, excitement bubbling inside me as I visit Omar in jail. He didn't want me to keep visiting him in this place, but I couldn't contain my excitement about meeting my grandmother, so I rushed over during the visitation hours. Omar peers at me through the glass before responding.

"I know people, baby girl. I got in contact with somebody who could track down your family. Ain't take long; She been here this entire time."

"I'm so happy. Thank you so much. I love you. Thank you." I grin at him.

He returns a smile before it fades. "You know I got you, baby girl. I love you too. It feels good to see you happy."

My cheeks warm as I reach for my new jewelry piece. The necklace around my neck feels light but I know it carries so much. I hold it in my hand, leaning closer to show Omar. "Look what she gave me. It was my mama's necklace."

"That was real nice of her," Omar acknowledges.

"She also gave me a photo of my mama. It's old, but Mama had me when she was fifteen, and I look just like her. Oh, and my grandma said that she was real sick in her head, and my daddy was tryna protect me from whatever she had going on, even though it was hard for him to do that, but he did it for me. You were right, Omar. My daddy really did love me."

He nods, listening attentively. "And I'on want you to ever doubt that shit again, baby girl. He did what he had to do."

"Mhm, yep. I agree. I think I feel more at peace with him being gone now. I'm gonna go get some flowers one of these days and visit his gravesite and just thank him. I ain't never get to thank him."

"That will be good for you to do. Just know he knows it."

"I hope so. And if that's the case, I want my mama to know that I'm not mad at her either. Even though neither one was around long, they taught me a lot and I learned from them. So, I wanna give our baby everything we never had. And not just like buy him stuff but like love on him, and he will have both of us."

Omar teases a smile, enjoying my excitement. "Okay, enough about me. How are you doing in here, boo? I can't wait until you're out," I shift the focus to him.

"I'm a'ight, baby girl. You don't know how bad I wanna hold you though."

"I know how bad 'cause it's the same for me. Omar, I had to put a... a pillow next to me and I put one of your jackets on it 'cause, listen... yeah, I missed your cuddles and I had to do what I had to do!"

Omar bursts into laughter, covering his eyes with his hand. I couldn't resist sharing how much I miss him. It might be weird getting intimate with some pillows, but desperate times call for desperate measures.

"You so silly." He picks up the phone again, still chuckling. "I'm sorry I left you hangin' though but glad you figured something out. As long as it wasn't nobody else."

"Hell no, just you in spirit. I would never do that to you." I join in the laughter.

I know my boo probably needs a good laugh right now. This reminds me that it's probably the perfect time to tell him about Sheila working under him again.

As our laughter fades, I move my hand to the glass. He fists bumps it from the other side, making me smack my lips in response. "Why did you do that? Put your hand up, okay?"

"That's that goodbye shit. I'm gonna be outta here soon, baby girl. We can do it for real in a few days." Omar shakes his head and leans back in his chair.

My fingers play with the cord that comes from the wall, and I try to think of a way to bring up Sheila. I hesitate to speak each time I open my mouth but close it right back up.

"You wanna talk about something else?" Omar scoots forward again and glances at me through the glass.

"Um..." I begin, swallowing hard. "So, you know how you said that if I wanted to put somebody in the family house, I could?"

"Yep."

"Okay, so I did. I asked Sheila, and she's been helping a lot. Plus, she could use the money."

Omar's expression doesn't change one bit, so he knew already. *Thanks, Eddie.* "She gotta get to steppin'."

"Why though, Omar? She's still my friend. She apologized and everything. Even she and Eddie have been chilling out. And I know you trust Eddie's judgment over mine, so that's good, right? If he trusts her?"

His eyes scare me a bit, and I have to look away. They're cold at the moment. Empty. Piercing. *What does he have against Sheila so damn bad that it makes him this angry? What does he know that I don't?* I guess that would be a good thing to ask him.

"What's the problem you got with her? You want her or something?"

He shakes his head. "No. If I said I don't trust somebody, I expect you to listen. I don't gotta explain shit to you or anybody about that," he responds sharply.

"Why don't you wanna explain it to me, though? She's my friend."

"Just take my word for it, how 'bout that?"

"Is it 'cause of Randall? She's not even involved with him anymore. He doesn't care about her."

"I already said what I needed to say about the shit. I'm not gonna keep repeatin' myself."

"Why though?"

"Because I said so..."

The tension in the air thickens as Omar's clenched teeth barely releases the words. I draw back, as if his intensity could reach through the glass barrier between us. His anger is strong, reminding me of the boundaries even I can't push. Sheila may think Omar needs someone who isn't afraid to challenge him, but ultimately, he holds the reins, and that's a reality I can't escape. And it frustrates me. It's unfair.

I hold his gaze, rolling my eyes before pressing on with the topic. "You're so mean sometimes. You don't even know why you don't like her."

"A'ight, get up outta here. I can see you about to start your shit."

"I'm not about to start nothing. You wanna control everything about me, but you can't keep me from helping my friends in need," I retort. "She really hasn't done anything wrong to me, and she's in a hard spot in her life right now. She would do the same thing for me. I'm not saying she works here forever, but just for a little bit."

"You steady tryna save somebody that don't give a fuck about you. Look out for yourself," Omar counters. "That gullible shit is gonna get you killed out here, baby."

"I'm not gullible, Omar. I'm safe for the most part, got food to eat, and a place to lay my head. I'm in a place where I can help her," I fire back.

"Off of whose money though? *Yours?*" He smirks.

"Maybe if you didn't get me fired, I would have my own money."

"You was getting fired anyway. You pregnant."

"Omar, stop being a smartass to me."

"I'm not. I'm stating some facts, baby girl. Like the fact ol' girl got you jumped that night. You ain't know that though."

Is he implying Sheila set me up that night we fought Tara at the club? It sounds crazy, especially considering she helped me during the fight. Tara never mentioned it, either. I scoff at his accusation. He's just grasping for straws, trying to justify why he feels the way he does against her.

"Even if that's true, it's not enough to explain why you hate her so bad."

Omar shrugs, offering no further explanation. I hate it when he shuts me out like this, refusing to open up.

"Okay, well, since that's it, then oh well. She still needs help, and you gave me permission to choose. You ain't never said 'no Sheila'. You said I had the choice, so I made one. She is helping until she can get enough money in her pockets," I declare, refusing to back down.

"A'ight, baby girl. Do your thing then. I'll see you soon," Omar rises from his seat, his gaze never leaving mine, before returning the phone to its receiver with a nod to the officer.

Is Sheila worth jeopardizing our relationship? Probably not, but I need Omar to understand that he can't control everything I do. If only he could explain why he hates her so much. But until then, I'll have to see for myself.

CHAPTER 18
A Shower of Surprises

NESTLED SNUGLY INSIDE, MY baby boy seems content to wait a bit longer before making his grand entrance into the world. After visiting Grandma and Omar, I've been hunkering down at home, just in case the little guy decides it's time to make his debut. The last thing I want is to find myself unexpectedly giving birth in the middle of a grocery store checkout.

Nerves are definitely kicking in, especially after hearing stories from Janay and other moms about the pain of childbirth. Rita's tale about needing an emergency C-section sent shivers down my spine – definitely not something I want to experience.

As for Omar, I haven't heard any messages from him since our last conversation. His silence speaks volumes, and I can't shake the feeling that he's still just as mad at me as I am at him. With his release just a few days away, tensions are simmering, especially since Sheila is still around. I haven't mustered up the courage to talk to her about the situation, let alone address the supposed setup with Tara. Right now, I just need to focus on staying calm and excited for the baby's arrival.

"Come on, Chevy! You takin' too damn long!" Janay's voice echoes from downstairs.

"I can't exactly run right now, you *bitch*," I call back as I carefully navigate down the stairs.

Janay cackles but then her eyes widen as she watches me, and she rushes over to help me down the last few steps. "I can't believe he's almost here. Omar's first baby..."

I can't contain my excitement, and internally, I'm squealing with joy. "I know. But this is why I shouldn't be going anywhere either. I need to be here, next to my hospital bag."

"I am semi-psychic, and I don't think he gonna be here for at least the next few hours," Janay jokes, lightening the mood.

We share another moment of laughter before I take a seat to let Janay help me slip on my shoes. "Where are we going anyway?"

"Just... going to the family house real quick. I wanna show you the nursery I put up over there."

"Aww, Janay. I didn't know you did that. Thank you," I express my gratitude. She's so thoughtful for making time to do that for us.

"You're welcome. You either gonna be here or over there, and I'm sure you gonna have that boy attached at the hip, so it makes sense to have it in both places."

After slipping on my shoes, we head out the door, and I settle into the passenger seat of Janay's car. Despite her always lying about where she's taking me, I just go with it and hope she really did what she said she did. I'm a bit tired of being set up.

As Janay pulls up to the family house, I notice several cars parked outside. But before we can get out, she grabs my arm, pulling me back into my seat.

"I gotta tell you something, Chevy," Janay starts, reaching for her glove box and retrieving a pack of cigarettes. "I gotta tell you before Omar gets out."

My heart skips a beat, panic simmering. "What is it?" I manage to ask.

Janay lights a cigarette, exhaling smoke out the window before turning back to me. "I messed up. Been trying to fix it for months, but I might be running out of time. And I think Omar knows."

"What did you do, Janay? Tell me," I urge.

"Well, back when he cut me and Curtis off, I got real upset. Used some dope Curt was supposed to sell, but the rest I sold off quick for extra cash, just in case Omar didn't show. Got hooked on the feeling, so I kept stealing more. But I didn't put the money back. Couple months back, Curt comes home, saying Omar's been questioning him about missing stuff," Janay explains.

"So, you were using what you stole?"

"Yeah," Janay admits, taking another drag before continuing, "Got carried away, did more than I should've. Now, there's more missing than I can replace."

"That's why you've been looking rough lately, huh?" I ask, connecting the dots. It's probably why she's been so wired too.

The cigarette smoke starts to overwhelm me, so I crack open the passenger door for some fresh air. Janay notices and tosses the cigarette out the window.

"I didn't realize it was that obvious," Janay replies, sounding surprised.

"It is," I confirm. "I'm surprised Curtis hasn't said anything."

"Curt's been distant lately. We've got our own issues, so we don't talk like we used to. And he doesn't know about what I did," Janay confesses, her tone heavy with worry.

Their relationship is about to hit a whole new level of problems once Curtis finds out about Janay's antics.

"Look, you messed up, but do you really think Omar would care that much? He's got money to replace it, and they're always making money," I suggest, trying to ease her worries.

"One thing Omar doesn't tolerate is a thief, Chevy, no matter how small or replaceable it is. He'll notice something is off if he hasn't already, and you know he values trust," Janay responds, leaning back in her seat. "He's done so much for me and Curt alone... I feel so *stupid*."

As we sit in silence, her words sink in. She's right about Omar. It's his commitment to his people and his empire that's landed him behind bars. He looks after them, so stealing from him seems unfathomable. I wonder if Janay wants me to intervene on her behalf.

"I can talk to him, Janay, and try to make him understand why you did it. It was 'cause you were stressed and worried, right?" I offer, placing my hand on her shoulder.

"Yeah, I was also pissed off at him and Curtis. But saying that won't help, it'll just make me look worse. Like I can't be trusted at all," Janay admits.

"Considering how Omar's been questioning Curt like you say, he might already suspect something's up. You wouldn't want him blaming his best friend, though, right?"

She shrugs. "He's cheating on me anyway. I don't think I care, to be honest."

I knew it wouldn't last, pretending to be okay with our partners straying. It's wearing Janay down, mentally, emotionally, and physically. She's lost herself in it and it's so sad to witness.

"I'd rather talk to Omar before he finds out and approaches you both about it. That's why you told me, right?"

"I told you because you're my friend, and I needed to get it off my chest. Don't worry about me or mess up things with Omar because of this. You're good, Chevy. I'm the one who fucked up, and I'll deal with the consequences," Janay assures me.

"No, I'll help. I won't talk to Omar yet, but we can come up with the money and fix this," I insist, momentarily distracted by a cramp, I close my eyes, rubbing my belly to ease the discomfort.

"You okay, Chevy?"

"Yeah, just a cramp. I need to stretch my legs," I reply, opening my eyes.

"Alright, let's go inside. There was something else I wanted to tell you, but I don't want to add more bad news. Thanks for listening, and don't stress about me, okay? I'll figure it out," Janay says as we prepare to exit the car.

If she didn't want me to worry, she shouldn't have confided in me in the first place. I can't help but feel the weight of her troubles on my shoulders.

—————— ♡ ——————

The sudden shout of *"Surprise!"* from the tightly packed crowd as we open the front door almost sends me reeling back, my heart pounding with fear. Memories of the shooting at this very house flood back, the trauma still fresh in my mind. But Janay is behind me, gently urging me forward, so I take a deep breath and try to steady myself as I take in the surprise party. Eddie steps forward, wrapping me in a warm hug,

"It's okay, pretty lady. You safe," he reassures me.

"I'm not good with surprises, everyone," I manage to say through a nervous laugh. "Y'all scared the hell outta me. I might end up having this baby right here on the floor!"

Laughter fills the room, and I'm finally calm again. "Thank you!"

Looking around, I admire the decorations. I've always been a sucker for a well-decorated party, and this one is perfect. Green and blue streamers hang from the ceilings, a framed picture of our baby's sonogram adorns the fireplace, and balloons fill the space. A table covered in a baby-blue tablecloth holds an array of beautifully designed treats to fit the theme.

"Chevy! It's your baby shower! I can't believe you didn't want one, so I planned it and got everybody involved," Sheila announces, stepping forward to hug me tightly.

I hold onto her for a moment. "Thank you, Sheila. You didn't have to do this for me."

"But of course we did, Chevy. You deserve it, especially with Omar being away," Janay chimes in from behind me.

I nod, leaving the two ladies to their partying as I make my rounds, greeting and thanking everyone.

"Oh, he's gonna be here real soon. I can't wait to meet him!" Rita exclaims, planting kisses on my swollen belly.

"Yeah, I can't wait. I've been pregnant for too damn long. It's time for him to exit outta me, girl."

Rita pulls me into a squeeze. "I know we keep saying it, but thanks for coming into O's life and giving him a chance. We can all see how much happier he's been."

"Well, I can thank him too, 'cause he's been really good to me, making me happy too."

"Besides the cheating," Rita adds, raising her brow.

"Right, besides that," I agree. "But I mean... We didn't start off so perfect either. We're getting there though."

Rita giggles, but I can't bring myself to join in. It's not funny, and the memory of how our relationship began still lingers in the back of my mind.

"Stop it, Chevy. You beat yourself up too much over that. It's not that serious. You didn't see the way Tara was moving when she was with O anyway. That's why nobody even batted an eyelash when he dumped her ass for you." Rita snaps her fingers in front of my face, pulling me out of my thoughts.

"Maybe if y'all would tell me what she did so bad to where nobody even gives a damn, then I'd understand better. My guilt comes from me being her friend first anyway."

"Was she really your friend, though?"

That's not the first time I've heard that about Tara.

"You gotta be careful who you slap that label on, Chevy. But speaking of the devil..."

We both turn and see Tara walking in the front door, scanning the party. Her hair is black and cut short just below her ears. She's wearing a bold red lipstick that stands out against her skin and dark eyeshadow that accentuates her blue eyes. Our eyes meet, and she starts heading towards me and Rita.

"She's got some nerve..." Rita rolls her eyes and heads for the snack table as Tara approaches me.

Tara takes a long look at my baby belly, and I feel the need to cover it a bit, unsure of what her gaze means. She tucks her pocketbook under her arm and stops in front of me.

"Hey, Chevy. Congratulations," she says.

"Thanks. What are you doing here?"

"It's a party, ain't it? I heard about you and O having this... baby. You didn't even tell me last time we spoke. But I wanted to come show my face and send my congrats. I've got some gifts for the baby in the car." She drops her head, shuffling her feet a bit.

"Thank you, Tara. That's nice of you. Omar isn't here though. You know he's still locked up right now."

"I heard. He been treating you alright though? Like, with you being pregnant and all?" Tara lifts her head, smoothing out her side-swept bangs as she waits for an answer.

"Yeah."

"Good. Better than he did me, I hope. Sounds like he cares more about you, which is good, I guess."

"You weren't having his baby though. You lied to him too, Tara. Can't place all the blame on him when you weren't faithful either."

"You're the last one who should be talking... *friend*." She smiles mockingly. "And now you're pregnant by him and everything. *Damn,* that's crazy as hell, Chevonne. I really thought you were my friend."

I feel uneasy in the pit of my stomach. *Don't let her punk you, Chevy.*

"Okay, Tara. I don't wanna talk about this here, at my baby shower. I gave you plenty of opportunities to address me about how you felt, and you jumped me instead, so I'm good on this conversation. You got your lil' revenge, more than once, so we're even now. Which we discussed already."

"Okay, I was just saying what was on my heart. First Randall, then Omar. You're something else, girl, but I can't even be mad at you."

My eyes roll at Tara's attempt to paint me as some kind of hoochie, which couldn't be further from the truth. Randall slept with every girl he hired, so why is she choosing now to pick on me about it? And as for Omar... Well, I'm not going to keep justifying that situation. Like Rita said, I really need to stop beating myself up about it. We have a child on the way together, and we're officially a couple now. Omar and I can't help but love each other like this; sometimes shit just happens.

Until it happens to you... I shake off the unwelcomed thought and turn away from Tara to grab some iced water. "Okay, Tara. I'm done here."

"Alright, well, I'll go get the gifts and bring them inside before I take off. I hope we can meet up and talk after you have your baby. I really miss you... And I wanna meet him," Tara calls after me as I walk away.

"Okay. I'll let you know." Without turning around, I respond to her and pour myself a glass.

The music in the background calls for a small dance party in the middle of the living room. I hear the crowd gathering around, clapping and cheering. so I make my way into the room to watch. This is what I'm talking about. This is how I envisioned a party like this to go. I won't even let myself get upset about Janay dropping some bad news on me and then Tara popping up, knowing damn well she wasn't invited.

"I Like" by Guy blasts out of the stereo, and I hold onto my baby belly as I break down in laughter watching Eddie and Sheila on the dance floor. Eddie looks like an old noodle, and Sheila's getting wild, grinding on the man. I hope she doesn't hurt him. I know how she gets on the dance floor with her wild self.

"Chevy! Get over here, girl! Let's see some of those moves!" Janay calls from across the crowd.

My eyes widen, and I shake my head. "Hell no, girl. I can barely walk. What do I look like dancing right now?"

"Come on, Miss Chevy. We'll catch you if you fall," Eddie calls out, his face dripping in sweat.

Sheila pulls my arm until I'm in the middle of the floor, and the crowd claps along to the music. So, I nod my head a little to catch the beat before I get into my next move. Everyone convulses in laughter as I swing my way into a slow cabbage patch when "Get Down on It" by Kool & the Gang comes on next. I told them I couldn't do much with my big ole belly, but I'm glad I can make them laugh.

"Go 'head then, Miss Chevy!" Eddie shouts.

"Chevy, what the hell? Oh my God." Janay collapses to the ground, Sheila following behind her.

Well, damn, maybe I should dance more often if it brings my friends together like this. I'm sweating, knowing my hair won't stay in its bumped-up cut for much longer. They shouldn't have gotten me started because now I can't stop. I miss dancing.

But my groove is interrupted when I notice everyone's heads turning in a direction behind me. Sandalwood catches my nose. I spin around to find Omar walking into the room, weaving through the crowd. My mouth falls open a bit, and tears fill my eyes. It feels like he's been gone for an eternity. I'm loving all the surprises today.

"You look like you're having a good time, baby girl."

I reach up, wrapping my arms around his neck and squeezing him tight. I can't even remember why we were mad at each other, but it doesn't matter now. I'm just so happy he's out and here before our baby boy arrives. He pulls me close, and we hold each other there. *God*, he smells so good.

"Omar... You're out! Thank God."

"I couldn't miss this." He pulls back and scans the room. "Y'all don't gotta stop the party. Turn that music back up."

"Welcome home, O. Now, let's get back to this party!" Eddie yells out, and the volume cranks back up as Omar and I slip out to the back porch to sit.

I can't let go of his hand. Our fingers intertwine as we sit quietly, taking in the spring air. The music fades into the background, but we can still hear everyone having a good time.

"You're about big as hell," Omar says, his hand gliding across my belly. "He might be ready."

"Hell yeah. I'm ready for him to get out of there, but I'm scared 'cause I feel like he's big, and you mean to tell me I gotta push him out!"

Omar chuckles. "I'll be right there with you, baby girl. We'll get through that shit together."

We exchange smiles. Moments like these, so simple yet so meaningful, remind me why I love him so much. Even the quiet between us speaks volumes.

"Are you happy to be home? We all missed you so much, boo."

"Yeah, I'm glad I did my time and all that. There are little prices to pay for the industry I'm part of, and I know that. Sometimes we gotta do some messed-up shit. I don't regret a thing, and I'd do it again if I had to."

"Well, please don't do it again, Omar. I know you hate it when people break your trust, but you can't punish everybody," I say, thinking of Janay.

Even though she should have known better, I don't think she was trying to hurt Omar's business. She's still too loyal to him if anything.

"You're about to be a daddy now. He has to be the first thing you think of when you make decisions like that, okay?"

Omar nods and gazes out into the backyard. The grass is neatly mowed, and a row of bushes lines the freshly constructed fence, which I assume they put up during the repairs.

I trace the lines of his knuckles with my fingertip and inch closer until my chin finds a resting place on his shoulder. He peeks over and plants a gentle kiss on my forehead.

"I missed you, Omar. Thirty days might not seem like much to you, but it felt like forever to me."

"I know, baby. I missed you too."

"Were they treating you okay at least? I mean, I know it's jail, but I always hear about how bad they treat people in there."

"Yeah, it was smooth. I got a few homies in there, so they wasn't giving me a hard time," he replies casually, but I can read between the lines. Translation: he had it easy. *How will he learn his lesson if he can easily buy his way out of trouble?*

Despite wanting to savor this moment with Omar, my mind keeps drifting back to our last fight about Sheila. Then there's Janay's drama, not to mention Tara showing up.

"Omar, I'm sad that the last time we talked, we ended up fighting.'

"Yeah, and I see you still ain't listen. What is your homegirl still doin' here?"

I inwardly sigh, hoping to avoid another confrontation. "Is it such a big deal that she's celebrating our baby with us? She planned this party. Let's just leave it for now. I don't want us to fight."

His eyes narrow, and his jaw tensing slightly. *How can he be so quick to anger after just getting home from jail for acting out of anger?* It's infuriating. And I'm resisting the urge to give him a piece of my mind.

"Well, let's head back inside and join the celebration. They're probably tired of us always being the first ones to leave."

"Alright," he agrees, standing up and offering me a hand. As I rise, I feel another cramp, but it's mild compared to earlier, so I brush it off.

We step back into the party, and like clockwork, Sheila rushes over to us. I should've warned her about how Omar feels, but how do you tell your friend that? It would crush her, especially if nobody really knows why he's so hostile toward her.

"Omar! Welcome home. Chevy was lost without you, ha-ha," she chirps, but he doesn't respond. Instead, his gaze pierces through her, making me uneasy.

"Okay, Sheila... Let's go dance," I interject, tugging at her arm.

A few of Omar's guys have already surrounded him, which is a relief. I'll let him catch up with his boys. I hadn't realized Sheila was drunk until now, but she wrenches her arm away from me and turns back to Omar.

"No, wait. You got a problem with me or something, Omar? What did I do to you?"

"Sheila, no... come on," I plead, reaching for her arm again.

"No, fuck it, Chevy. I wanna know what the issue is. You said that to handle him, I gotta stand up firm to him, and that's what I'm gonna do." Her voice echoes loudly in the room.

I'm done giving her advice.

"So, Omar... What's your problem with me? I've been nothing but nice to you, and Chevy is my best friend."

I cover my face with my hand, stuck in the middle. I have no idea what he's thinking, but I wish Sheila would just stop.

"My lady out here giving out advice on how to handle me now?" Omar finally speaks, his tone oddly calm.

"No, it wasn't like that. I just... Um, she wasn't supposed to say that" I stammer, holding my hands up between them.

"I appreciate it though. Not a lot of people know how to step to me properly, including this bitch right here."

"A *bitch!*" Sheila snaps, hands on her hips. "What is the problem!"

The music comes to a halt, and all eyes are on us. This isn't how Omar's homecoming should be. He shouldn't have to come back to drama from someone I brought into the family. The tension in the air is suffocating. I hold my hands up, one against Omar's chest and the other holding Sheila back. *Where the hell is Eddie? Why isn't he stepping in?*

"The problem?" Omar begins, his voice cutting through the tension as he removes his jacket. "The first problem is you a thief."

"What?" I respond immediately, disbelief coloring my voice. *Sheila?* No way. "Omar, what are you talking about?"

"Ask her," he says, nodding towards Sheila.

I turn to Sheila, her expression mirroring my confusion. "I don't know what he's saying, Chevy. I've never stolen from anyone here. You know me."

"What did she steal? I don't understand," I ask, seeking clarification from anyone who knows.

"Janay. Speak up," Omar commands.

All eyes turn to Janay. She takes a deep breath, then stands tall, bracing herself to speak her truth.

"Um, so... I got a tip that this girl here has been stealing product and money from O. I wasn't sure, so I followed her around myself. I have proof. I know where she's been, who she's givin' it to, and she's been using the shit too."

My jaw practically hits the floor as Janay places the blame on Sheila. *How could she do that?* It's beyond messed up.

"What? I have *never!* Chevy... Omar... I didn't do it! I would never!" Sheila protests, desperately.

Everyone eyes her suspiciously. Eddie stands nearby, disappointment written all over his face. He was starting to like her, and now this situation sours everything but if his loyal ass told Omar she was working him, that's on him. I just can't believe Janay would stoop this low. She could have owned up to her mistake like she did to me in the car, but instead, she threw Sheila under the bus. My eyes dart to Janay, who mouths that she's *so sorry*.

"Now look at you... looking foolish. Tryna step to me in my own house, knowing what you did," Omar says.

Sheila grabs my arm. "Chevy... you know me. I didn't do that. Tell him."

I can't let her take the fall for someone else's actions. I care about Janay, but this is a betrayal. That shows me she's not trustworthy because she was quick to shift the blame instead of taking responsibility. I hate that, and now I see her in a whole new light. That must have been what else she wanted to tell me in the car earlier.

Suddenly, there's a collective gasp, and I look down to see a puddle forming beneath my feet.

"Hey... your water broke," Omar says, pulling me close as we both look at the floor.

My heart races with the realization that I'm going into labor.

"Our little man is on his way! Let's get you two to the hospital!" Eddie exclaims, rushing towards the front door.

As we head out, I rub my belly, silently thanking my baby boy for putting a pause on the stressful situation. He doesn't know what he just did, but he deserves all the kisses in the world when he arrives.

CHAPTER 19
Clayton

I NAMED HIM AFTER my daddy—*Clayton.*

I gaze down at my son, cradled gently in my arms. His tiny features bring me overwhelming joy—he's the epitome of perfection to me. I can't help but marvel at his sweet face. As he sleeps soundly, I whisper softly to him, "You look like your daddy... You've got his nose, his face... but I win the eyes."

My little bundle of joy is soft and delicate, and I run my fingers through his hair, feeling grateful for a healthy baby. The realization that I grew this tiny human inside of me fills me with a sense of wonder and magic. I can't stop planting kisses to his chubby cheeks.

As baby Clayton grips my finger with his tiny hand, I glance over to find Omar dozing off in a recliner in the corner of our room. He was my rock during labor, holding my hand and whispering words of comfort in my ear.

Even though the birth wasn't as terrifying as I had feared, all of that pushing was challenging for me. But the moment I heard Clayton's first cry, I knew it was all worth it. I just can't ignore the discomfort I'm still feeling down below, so I can't wait for that part to heal up. Until then, I'm well aware that I'll be wearing diapers along with Clayton.

A nurse enters the room, informing me that she'll be taking Clayton for more health assessments, and urging me to rest. I haven't closed my eyes since giving birth, but I couldn't help it. As she leaves, I lean back, closing my eyes and replaying the precious images of my baby in my mind.

"I see you finally goin' to sleep," Omar mumbles, his voice soft in the dim light of the room.

I lift my head from the pillow and find him peeking at me. "Trying to. You know, I think you were sleeping when I was feeding him."

"I'm sorry, baby girl. I ain't realize I was this exhausted," he replies, a yawn following.

"Well, you came right from jail to a party, then to the delivery room. I'm not even mad at you, so get your rest," I reassure him.

"Ion' know how you're up right now after going through all of that shit. You birthed a whole human. You win."

"*Haha*. I'm so happy, though. This is the best day of my life... Thank you so much for him."

Omar smiles toward me, then sits up. "You're welcome. Thank you too. Got a lot to teach that lil' boy. Get him in the family business and everything like that."

"Um... No, boo," I respond, shaking my head gently.

Omar chuckles. "What you mean?"

"Okay yeah, there is a lot to teach him, but like... we can teach him better 'cause we know better," I explain softly. "He won't have to struggle like we did, so that means he won't have to do certain things we had to do."

Omar stands and walks to my bedside, his hands in his pockets. "You right. We can only do the best we can though. We can't walk in his shoes, so whatever choices he makes when it comes time, it's out of our hands."

"That is the truth... I hope he makes better choices. I'm not saying we are bad or nothin' like that, but it was hard for us. Well, for me at least. I know you had it bad too, but you never talk to me about none of that," I say.

He nods, expressionless. I doubt I'll ever get him to open up about his past, and that realization saddens me. Building a stronger connection between us will require opening up, just like Eddie once suggested, and I've been open with him. It's frustrating to feel like I'm not getting the same in return.

Omar notices my withdrawal and reaches out to touch my chin, but I pull away. "What's wrong?" he asks.

"How are we supposed to be strong together and for Clayton if you can't even open up to me?"

"I have opened up to you. You are a part of my life now. You have seen everything I'm about and what I do," he insists.

"I'm talkin' about how you grew up. I don't know as much about you as you do about me, and that bothers me. How we supposed to be truly happy together if I don't know what kinds of things are weighing on your heart?"

Omar pauses and shifts away from me.

"Why does it take me havin' to open up about my childhood for you to be happy with me? Just know I came out of it better than what was expected of me and look at where I'm at now. That ain't enough for you?"

"You were the same one telling me about acceptance and all of that. What about you? You gave me that advice and didn't even take it yourself. Like when I brought up your mama at the restaurant and you froze up. Why can't you talk to me about her?" I press.

Omar heads back to the recliner in the corner of the room and pulls the hospital blanket over him. "Go to sleep."

"Fine, you don't have to tell me, *ugly*," I retort, crossing my arms against my chest in frustration. Tears threaten to spill, but I push them back, focusing instead on the images of Clayton in my mind. I long for the nurse to bring him back so I can go back to immersing myself in the presence of my baby.

"Ma was murdered. Some fool she was messing with gunned her down in the middle of the street... in broad daylight. I was supposed to be home right after school that day to help her pack and move 'cause she wanted to get away from him, but I ain't show up," Omar finally reveals.

My eyes widen in shock. "Why didn't you show up?"

"Earlier that morning, she told me I wasn't gonna be shit. That I was gonna end up dead and that she would have wasted fifteen years of her life tryna raise me to be a real man," Omar explains. "All because she found out what I decided to do with my life."

Just like daddy did me.

He pauses in long thought, before finally continuing on. "So I went to school that day, then handled business after school... like a man. I had already learned the game and was in it pretty deep by then. I understand why she ain't fuck with it, but little did she know, I was doing it all for her and for me. It's the typical story that a lot of us got... I had to watch my mama struggle. We stayed movin' around. She was fuckin' around with dudes to keep the lights on and wasn't takin' care of herself. I had enough of that shit, so I did what I had to do."

"I'm so sorry to hear about all of that and your mama. I hope you know it's not your fault," I offer, my heart aching for him.

"I ain't never took that blame. You know why?" Omar asks, his gaze intense as he locks eyes with me.

"Why?"

"Because I was out there proving her wrong. I was out bein' the man that she swore I'd never be. I ain't the one that held the gun to her, so I know it ain't on me," he shrugs.

"If that's how you feel, how come you don't like to talk about her?" I press gently.

"There ain't much to say, Chevonne. I mourned for her and kept going. Like I said before, I'm not one to hash over shit like that. Just know she was busy struggling and mad at me while I was out makin' shit happen for the both of us. I'll always love her, though."

"I understand, but she broke your heart," I murmur softly, unsure if he even hears me over the silence of the room. He did; it's just him and I in this room anyway. "And you never got to have that last conversation with her either. I know it still bothers you too."

"I mean, I won't lie; that shit she said to me hurt, but it is what it is. I still ain't wanna see her gunned down like that. She ain't deserve that shit," Omar responds. My heart breaks for the fifteen-year-old boy who had to witness such a thing.

"I'm so sorry, boo. *Mm.* That makes me so sad..." I murmur, wiping away a tear with the edge of the blanket. "Eddie said that's when he found you, right? Holding her in your arms?"

"Mhm. Eddie has always been there since that day. As much as I hate sayin' it, everything happens for a reason, and I'on know where I would be without Eddie, for real."

"And I love that you have each other."

Our conversation is disrupted when the door to the room opens, and my heart swells with anticipation as the nurse steps in, cradling our sleeping baby boy in her arms.

"*Ooo*, looks like dad is awake! Who wants baby Clayton?" the nurse teases.

"Give him to his daddy," I insist, pointing at Omar, eager to witness their first moment together.

As Omar gently takes Clayton into his arms, a warm rush of love and gratitude fills my heart. I can feel it spreading through my entire body, and for once, I'm learning to stop questioning how love comes to me.

Seeing Omar finally open up to me, even with such a heartbreaking story, shows how much he loves me and trusts me with his deepest feelings. His love is often guarded, but I know now that behind that protective wall is a boy who genuinely wants the best for himself and the people he loves. He'll do anything to protect us.

Thinking back, Daddy's love was tough, but it was also what kept me safe and made me the strong woman I am today. I remember Grandma Cheryl telling me she never stopped praying for me and Daddy, even when she thought she'd never see me again. It's amazing to realize that her prayers were lifting me up all this time, even though I didn't know they existed.

And then there's Baby Clayton. He chose me to be his mama, to be the one he gives his unconditional love to. Because of him, I've learned not to question or doubt my blessings anymore.

I'm ready to embrace it all. Just over a year ago, it was only me navigating this world alone. And now, I have my own family.

———— ♡ ————

We breezed through our hospital stay, only a couple of days long. The nurses were angels, making sure we were set to take Clayton home, especially since we are new parents.

I couldn't believe Omar stuck by my side the whole time. I half-expected him to dive back into work, but he surprised me. It's a relief knowing he's got reliable folks covering for him. Plus, with him being locked up, I knew he had work to catch up one, but the timing couldn't have been better. I owe it to Clayton for holding out for his dad.

I'm thankful the Janay and Sheila drama hasn't reared its ugly head yet. Omar's probably pushing it to the back of his mind, focusing on being a new dad. And honestly, I'm all for that distraction. The godparent discussion had me itching to strip Janay of her title, but that's a can of worms I'm not ready to open. I really should be standing up for Sheila, but it's complicated.

When everyone came to see Baby Clayton the morning after his arrival, Sheila came solo later that day. Thankfully, no fireworks went off, and Omar excused himself. He must've caught the plea in my eyes to keep the peace. I didn't spill what Janay said to me, but I assured Sheila I'd get to the bottom of things with Omar soon. She's terrified, and I can't blame her. I can't bear the thought of my friend getting shunned, especially for something she didn't do.

Eddie's here now. It's been two weeks since we got home, and we've been slowly letting the family meet Clayton. I'm finally getting the hang of this new mama lifestyle. I've even got my little man on a decent schedule already. I'm practically a pro at this mom thing already.

"Check out my lil' godson," Eddie coos as he cradles Clay in his arms. "I told you he was gonna be a looker. You two are beautiful, inside and out. This boy's gonna do great things. You just wait on it."

"I hope so, or I'm gonna have to set him straight real quick. I'm not raising a fool."

"I feel you, Miss Chevy. Look at you, all in mama mode. I know he's in good hands. Omar made a good choice starting a family with you."

A wave of warmth washes over me at his words. Clayton might not have been planned, but he's here for a reason.

"So, Eddie, what's your take on the whole Sheila situation?"

"I think she's got nothing to do with the missing cash and product but she's still a shady girl."

I spin around, disbelief written all over my face. "Really? 'Cause I feel the same way. Have you told Omar?"

"Omar chewed me out just for having her around, so no. But it don't matter, he don't mess with Miss Sheila. She's done more than enough dirt to still be around here."

"Can you tell me why he's so bent out of shape about her then? He won't tell me."

"The streets talk, Miss Chevy. And guess who always gets the scoop? The man calling the shots out here, and that's O. He knows things we don't. O doesn't just dislike someone without a good reason, you feel me? Maybe if that's your friend, you should be askin' her."

"Okay, so did someone tell him she called Tara to have me jumped?"

Eddie shrugs. "She ain't have no reason to do that. That's a dangerous position to put your 'friend' in."

"I'm about to put an end to this nonsense. Even if she did call Tara on me, that's between us. Omar shouldn't hate her for it. He didn't hate Tara, even though she fought me. And she's still around. So, he wants to ditch my friend but not the girl he slept with? That's fishy, and I won't stand for it. Plus, I know she's being framed for the missing money and drugs. I'm sure of it."

As I angrily fold the baby clothes, they end up messier than I intended. Before I can tidy them up, I notice an eerie silence in the room. I glance at Eddie, who shifts his gaze between me to the door behind me.

"Is that how you feel, baby girl?"

I turn to face Omar, crossing my arms. I won't back down. "That's exactly how I feel. So maybe you told me about Sheila to turn me against her, but it didn't work. It'll take more than that to make me abandon my friend. I appreciate you looking out for me, but I don't understand why you hate her but not Tara?"

"Because it's not really about you, that's why."

"Fine. Maybe not entirely about me, but I know how you are when it comes to me. Just ask Randall. But my point is, this whole thing is stupid."

"I don't give a damn about your point, baby girl. You don't know anything, and we're gonna keep it that way. Just know I make decisions for everyone's good in this damn family and for my business."

"That does not sit right with me."

"And it don't sit right with me that you sitting on information."

"Wait, what? So, I have to tell you stuff, but you won't tell me anything? How is that fair?" I plant my hands firmly on my hips. "Huh? How's that fair, Omar?"

"My business, my people, my money... it's got nothing to do with you. I'm not standing here arguing about it. Tell me who's framing your friend so I can deal with it."

"Oh, so none of this has anything to do with me? You want to keep me ignorant while I'm busy raising your baby? Got it. And no, I'm not telling you anything since it doesn't concern me."

Eddie finally stands and places Clayton in his bassinet while Omar and I exchange heated glares. "I'm gonna head out. You two keep it together for lil' man over there."

"No, Eddie, stay. Tell him you don't think Sheila's involved. Even Eddie thinks she's being framed."

"Ion' give a damn. Eddie was also involved with her, so that's swayed. Ed, bounce," Omar demands.

Eddie nods and leaves quietly, closing the door behind him. *Why does no one else stand up to this man?* Sure, he's intimidating, but is it respect or just plain fear?

"Since you wanna play games and keep things from me, expect the same treatment. I might bend, but I don't break for nobody!" I shout at him.

"I think... I'm tired of this," he says, his tone icy.

His words hit me like a bolt of lightning, and I snap to attention. I hope he's not talking about us. "What do you mean by that?"

He shifts his weight between each foot, hands buried in his pockets. "I'm tired of your mouth. It was kinda cute at first, but now you're talkin' a bit too crazy for me."

For the first time since he entered the room, I really notice his eyes. They're shooting daggers at me, chilling me to the bone. I shudder and turn away, focusing on folding Clayton's onesies.

"Yeah, well, I'm sick of everyone treating you like some kind of god they have to worship."

"Why does that bother you, though?"

"'Cause it's not right how you make people feel, Omar! You intimidate them into keeping quiet about how they really feel, and that's not how you're supposed to lead."

"I got the respect I do 'cause I take care of my people. Loyalty comes with it. Can't be mad that I also know how to handle my business and keep fools in line. But it still ain't about you. Still don't get why you're mad. I thought I made you feel good." He shrugs.

I shake my head, eyeing our baby boy wrapped snugly in his blanket. I try to picture a future where all of this is okay to raise my son in. It terrifies me.

He continues, "You barely respect me, though. That bothers me. I let a lot of things slide when it comes to you, Chevonne. But you keep bringing around these slick bitches, training them on how to step to me. You get everything you want if I can do it for you, but you keep crossin' lines that I set down for nobody to cross. I need that respect to improve."

"I'll never respect a fool. You ain't worth shit, anyway," I say, turning back to face him.

What happens next catches me completely off guard. I didn't expect him to almost cave in my chest with his fist, but he does, knocking the wind out of me. I feel myself hit the hard wooden floor, clutching my arm to my chest as pain shoots through me.

Omar steps over me, watching as I gasp for air and cry, not just from the pain, but from disbelief. *He hit me.* He really laid his hands on me.

He turns me onto my back and sits on top of me, pinning my arms above my head.

"Damn, baby girl," he mutters, as he watches me from above. "I ain't wanna have to do that shit."

"You hit me," I sob, tears streaming down my face, almost filling my ears. "Why would you do that, Omar?"

"I let you get too comfortable. Can't have that."

"Don't get too comfortable," Tara's words echo in my mind. "So, you hit me because I'm not afraid to call you out when you're wrong?"

"Did it hurt?"

"Duh, it fucking hurt!" I scream into his face.

"That's how it feels when you talk to me like that, Chevonne. Like a punch to the chest. You don't give a damn how I feel when you say shit. You just mean about it. You see why I don't open up to folks? 'Cause when I do, it gets used against me. I don't like that shit. I let you get too comfortable with the disrespect. That's my fault."

"You're so crazy, Omar," I say, forming my mouth to spit at him. His eyes lock onto mine.

"You gonna spit on me? Is that what I deserve for demanding my respect?"

He doesn't deserve that, but I sure as hell didn't deserve a fist to my chest either. I'm not eager to find out what he'll do next, so I swallow hard and turn my head away, tears still streaming down my face. There's probably a puddle underneath my head by now. I'm sure there is.

"So we're gonna sit right here, like this, until you tell me what you gotta tell me. I got all day."

I hear Clayton coo softly, hoping he'll start crying so I have an excuse to get off this damn floor, but he doesn't.

"I told you... Somebody lied on Sheila."

"Who?" he asks, still not looking away from me. "And be careful who you choose to ride for, baby girl."

He knows. He knows it was Janay. My pulse quickens. He's making me choose, and I hate it. I don't want to admit to him it was Janay, because I can't help but think of her kids. I hated seeing her so messed up after Omar kicked her and her man out of the family. It's why she did what she did anyway, besides the fact that Curtis is always cheating on her. She confided in me. I saw the dread and regret in her face when she said it.

I have no idea what Omar would do, and that's what scares me the most. He was proud to spend time in jail for beating a man down, so I'd really hate to see what happens to someone he's trusted but betrayed him.

On the other hand, I don't believe in pinning shit on somebody to save somebody else who has more to lose. Sheila messes up like we all do, but I wouldn't be able to live with myself knowing she had to take the fall for something like that. Just because I haven't seen Omar in full-blown action—besides him shooting somebody in the damn head—I know he'd kill for his first love. *His empire.* It doesn't matter who you are.

Omar exhales and loosens his grip, using one hand to turn my head to him. "I can't protect and provide for you and our son if you work against me, baby. We said whatever it takes, and I stand by that, but do you?"

"Yeah, but..." I sniffle, trying to find the words. "If you know the truth, then why are you forcing me to say it? That's messed up."

"I gotta know if you're working with me or against me, baby girl," he says, his voice low but firm. "You were just screaming about us being upfront with each other about shit. I know you loyal. That's one thing I admire about you. But who are you loyal to? It can't be me if you keep shit from me. I do that shit to protect you at the end of the day."

"I am loyal to you. I do respect you. I just have morals. I'm not scared to tell you how I feel, Omar. I'm not scared to tell you when you're wrong, and you are *wrong*."

He leans back slightly, allowing me to prop myself up on my elbows.

"You want me to make a hard decision to prove to you that I respect you, but I can't do that. You would rather me give you 'respect' instead of being true to me. I'm not gonna turn on either of my friends, 'cause that's who I am. I would never do it to you either, Omar. We're both doped up on each other. You already know where I stand, but for you to force me to say what you already know or to go against the truth is messed up. You're trying to change who I am and what I believe in for this, but if

I change, then I won't be the same person you fell in love with. I won't be ethereal. I won't even recognize myself anymore. So how am I supposed to raise Clay to always be true to himself, knowing that I wasn't? If none of that is my business, like you said, then it ain't my damn business and I'm staying out of it. But I am working with you, never against you."

He hangs his head in defeat. I hope my message got through to him. I may never understand why he really hates Sheila and I know he wanted it to be her, but I saved her life without betraying Janay. As sad as this situation may be, we're all responsible for our own choices, and Janay made hers. Like Omar said in the hospital, we can't walk in anybody else's shoes.

I love Omar, and I know he has to make the final decisions in this family. But once again, he chose this. He set the standards for his empire, and he has to uphold them. That ain't my problem.

I'll be praying for Janay, though.

CHAPTER 20
Still A Dancer

C LAYTON'S SOFT COOS FILL the air as we sit at my favorite café, enjoying our little outing. Omar was a bit worried about us venturing out so soon, but I needed a change of scenery and some fresh air. I wanted Clayton to start getting used to the world around him, you know? Plus, things have been kind of tense between Omar and me since our big fight a couple of weeks back. My chest still twinges from the blow it took, but what really stung was finding out that Omar decided to cut ties with Curtis and Janay for good.

He told me Curtis had no clue Janay was up to no good. But hey, they're like a package deal, and Janay only had access to stuff because of him. I talked to her, though, assured her I didn't spill anything, and she believed me. She even apologized for what she did to Sheila, which was pretty big of her. I asked her what her plan was now that she and Curtis are on their own again, and she said they're going to figure it out. I just hope they don't do anything shady to Omar after all he's done for them. But you know Omar, he's always got eyes on everything.

He's like the king of this city, and he's not even from around here. And it's like I've been thrown into the lead role of some movie, just like the ones I used to watch back in my old apartment. Omar somehow convinced me to let go of that place, saying it's like I'm expecting something to go wrong between us if I keep it. And you know what? He had a point. It felt liberating, like I was leaving behind my old life and stepping into this new one with him.

Amidst all the drama, I'm finding peace in this new life. Sure, I miss dancing like crazy, but I'm thinking about talking to Omar about it soon. It'll be something just for me, something to keep me well balanced. And maybe, just maybe, it'll help me feel more like myself again.

Tara finally arrives and settles across from me. She takes off her jacket and leans in to say hi to Clay.

"Oh my goodness... hi, baby boy," she says with a smile, melting at the sight of him.

I asked Tara to meet me here because I realized I need to make things right. To move forward and find real happiness, I have to let go of the hurt I caused her. It's important for both of us to heal, and I want to offer her that chance too.

"Hey. I've already ordered waffles and coffee for myself. Did you want anything?" I ask, trying to break the ice.

"I'll just grab a coffee. He's adorable, by the way. You guys did a great job," Tara replies warmly, her eyes still fixed on Clay's face.

"Thank you, Tara... So how are things going?" I ask, trying to keep things casual.

She leans back, crossing her arms. "I'm hanging in there. Still helping out Omar... but from a distance, you know? I'm hardly around anyway. How about you?"

"I'm doing alright. Just loving being a mama."

Tara nods, a small smile on her lips. "Yeah, you always had that nurturing vibe, Chevy. Me, not so much."

I remember Tara's carefree attitude, especially when she continued smoking despite finding out she was pregnant. Yeah, we're different in that department.

"Look, I asked you here 'cause I owe you an apology, Tara. I know I hurt you, and it must be weird seeing me here with his baby."

She shrugs, but I can see the pain in her eyes. "You can't control who you love, right?"

"No, you can't," I agree, feeling that stab of guilt. "I'm still sorry for breaking your heart too."

Tara takes a sip of her coffee, seeming unfazed. "It is what it is, Chevy. I threw you at him, and he took the bait. You're young, pretty, got an attitude... What fool wouldn't go for that, whether he's taken or not? I'm actually real proud of you, bitch. You're secured for life now."

I swallow, uneasy with her words. "I don't know if I like how you make it sound. I like to think it's more to it than that."

"It's just the way it is, Chevy. You two have a connection... there's chemistry there, even I can't deny that. But trust me, the excitement won't last forever. Eventually, you two will get bored of each other 'cause we all know who his first love is, anyway."

I stare into my coffee, feeling conflicted. *Is this even worth it?* Tara's bitterness is defendable, but her words sting. "Okay, Tara. I know you're still hurt, but you don't have to wish us ill. We have a son now."

"Look. What I say shouldn't affect you if you think you and Omar are meant to be. It's not about hurting me; it's about facing the reality of it. You think he'll choose you over his empire? You're just a pawn in his game, Chevy. And you're playing your part perfectly," she says, tapping her temple.

Her words hit me like a punch to the gut, and I glance at Clay in his bassinet. "His legacy," she continues. "You're just adding to it. He may love you to death, but you'll never come first. The sooner you realize that the sooner you'll know if this is the life you want."

"Alright, that's enough," I blurt out, throwing my hands up in exasperation. "I didn't come here to be talked down to about my family. If you're not up for a mature conversation like grown women, let's just call it quits."

"My bad, Chev. We're cool," Tara responds sheepishly. "You're still a good friend to have around."

There's a brief pause as Tara fidgets, eyeing her pack of cigarettes but refraining from reaching for them in Clayton's presence. I'm still working out the meaning of friendship with what I've experienced, but I appreciate being recognized as a good friend, because I truly tried to be one for her at one point.

"Can I ask you something?" I question, breaking the silence. "It's about Sheila."

She rolls her eyes but nods, indicating she's willing to entertain my question. "Go ahead."

"I've noticed Omar's been acting hostile towards Sheila, saying she's not to be trusted. Is it 'cause he's into her or 'cause he knows something I don't?"

Tara scoffs. "Chevy, she's trouble. Plain and simple."

"Trouble how?" I press.

"She's a setup bitch. She and her broke friends hustle fools for fun, taking them for all they're worth. Omar caught wind of her past and made Eddie cut ties with her real quick. Probably why he trips on you about her, but you still call her your 'friend.' Wouldn't be surprised if she's still up to her old tricks. Actually, I know she is.

I'm taken aback. *Why couldn't Omar just tell me himself?* And I had no idea about Sheila's past, though I wouldn't judge her for trying to survive. Just like I've stopped judging Tara and the others for their choices. "Neither of them told me any of this. Neither did you. which I find real funny if she is the one that called you that night."

Tara smirks. "I'm proud to see you finally caught up."

"Whatever, Tara."

She shrugs. "I'm still not the one that set you up, she did. I've always kept my distance from her for a reason, though. Sheila's not someone you want to rely on when push comes to shove. I might not be the best friend, but at least I'm honest."

"I didn't know a lot about you either, Tara. You can't preach about being real when you used me. Let's be real about that."

Tara shakes her head, moving over to Clay's stroller. "Still pointing fingers, huh? Can I hold him?"

"Yeah," I reply, surprised by her request. Despite everything, I trust her with my baby, especially since she's been trying so hard not to smoke around us.

Tara cradles Clay gently, cooing at him. As she does, I wonder how different things would be if she had chosen motherhood. But knowing her lifestyle, I doubt kids are in her future anytime soon.

"...And if you ever need anything, you know where to find me," Tara adds softly, still holding Clay.

I smile, grateful for her presence in my life. I may not agree with her choices, but I appreciate the impact she's had. It's reassuring to know we can still be civil; despite everything life throws our way.

After all, as Eddie would say, everything happens how it's supposed to.

Clay melts into his great-grandma's embrace, his tiny fingers curling around her sweater as she rocks him gently. "What a precious little angel," she coos, tucking his pacifier back into his mouth. "You look good, dear, especially for just having a baby. Lord knows I was a mess after your mama came along. Of course, I had her a bit later than you did."

Cheryl's visit was a welcomed change, especially after seeing Tara earlier in the day. I'm glad things went well, but I've accepted there will always be some sort of unspoken bitterness between us. I'll have to keep her at a distance.

"Thank you," I reply, my gaze fixed on my sleeping baby. "Yeah, I was worried at first, but I figured It won't be too bad. Having Omar by my side makes it a lot easier."

"Just make sure you carve out some time for yourself and your man," Cheryl advises, her eyes finally meeting mine. "Babies are precious, but they'll demand every ounce of your time, especially if you have more than one. But you got plenty of time ahead of you, Chevonne."

I can't help but admire Cheryl's eyes, the same vibrant hue passed down through generations. "I will," I assure her. "I've heard all about how demanding babies can be, but my man says it's all about making time."

"Sounds like you got a good one," Cheryl remarks with a warm smile. "As long as he respects you and treats you right, hold on to him. You deserve to be taken care of, dear. That's all I want for you and this little one."

Omar has been eager to meet Cheryl, but his busy schedule has made it difficult. Still, he's expressed his happiness for me and the connection I've found with her. Knowing my roots, especially after losing Daddy, adds a deeper layer of meaning to my life.

As Cheryl stands, cradling Clay close to her chest, she offers unexpected advice. "You should find a church."

Church was never part of my upbringing; Daddy had a strong distaste for it, believing it was filled with hypocrites. "I don't really know much about church. Daddy never took me," I admit.

Cheryl nods knowingly. "Find one and take yourself. It can be a sanctuary in times of need."

"Alright, I'll give it a shot when I'm ready," I respond, a sense of reluctance in my voice. I slide my chair back and make my way to the sink to wash my hands, ready to lend a hand with dinner.

"Too bad your boyfriend couldn't join us," Cheryl remarks as she follows me into the kitchen. "What's his name again?"

"Omar," I reply, turning on the faucet and letting the warm water cascade over my hands.

"And his last name?"

"Spence. Omar Spence," I say, grabbing a nearby towel to dry my hands.

"Alright, *Chevonne Spence*. It's got a nice ring to it," Cheryl says with a grin, catching me off guard. I turn to face her, surprised by her comment.

"We're not married."

"Not yet, but you're planning on it, right? You can't just be having this man's babies and not be married to him," Cheryl insists, her tone firm but caring.

"We haven't really talked about marriage," I admit.

Cheryl's expression softens as she sets Clay down in his stroller, proceeding to wash her hands quietly. "Don't be a wife to him as a girlfriend, Chevonne. That's not how it's supposed to go. If he loves you and has you having his babies, he needs to be gettin' down on one knee for you. It's about protecting yourself and your baby too, honey. That's what he's supposed to do as your man."

I bristle slightly at Cheryl's words. Tara's words earlier had already cut deep, and I didn't need Cheryl echoing the same sentiments.

"I know this might sound crazy, but I'm not really big on marriage," I offer cautiously, hoping to steer the conversation away from Omar.

"You not big on it because you haven't seen it, baby," Cheryl counters gently. "Your mama and daddy never got married, and now your poppa long gone. You haven't seen a marriage, that's all. If he loves you, he needs to make you his wife. Otherwise, this is temporary, baby."

I swallow hard, feeling the weight of Cheryl's words sinking in. "Married people break up though," I protest weakly.

"I'm not talking about other people. I'm talking about you and Omar Spence," Cheryl insists, her tone unwavering. "If he loves you, he'll stand with you before God and declare that. Don't have any more of his babies without a ring. Do you hear me?"

I nod slowly.

"What does he believe in? The same as you, I hope?" Cheryl asks, her tone softening slightly as she changes the subject.

"I don't know, ma'am. We haven't talked about it," I admit.

Cheryl chuckles to herself and shakes her head. "Sounds like you both have a lot to talk about then," she remarks. As I hand her the bowl she requested, my mind drifts off, realizing just how much Omar and I need to discuss – things we've never broached before, like religion and marriage. It's a conversation long overdue.

———— ♡ ————

Since Omar had been tied up all week with his "business," he promised to take me and Clay to the park today. It shouldn't have surprised me that he kept his word; he usually does. But maybe Tara's words about his empire being his priority are still lingering in my mind. Plus, Grandma Cheryl's advice is weighing heavy on my heart too.

But there is something else I need to discuss with him first.

We found shade from the blazing Los Angeles sun under a tree at a picnic table. I was almost afraid to keep Clay out too long, sweating like crazy in the heat. But he seemed comfortable, peacefully dozing off in his stroller.

"Omar... can we talk?"

"What's on your mind, baby girl?" he responds promptly, settling Clay's stroller beside the table and joining me on the bench.

"I know this might sound crazy, but... I wanna dance again. I miss it."

Omar absentmindedly flicks at a lighter, his eyes focused on me. "So... you like dancing for the money, or..."

"Yeah, the money's nice. I like having my own money. But I miss being on stage, moving my body," I confess, holding my breath, waiting for his response.

He finally stops flicking the lighter and turns to face me, surprising me with a chuckle. I tense up, not sure what to expect.

"I'm cool with that," he says simply.

"Oh, um, I wasn't really asking for your permission. Sorry."

He chuckles again. "So why run it by me then?"

"I wanted to hear your thoughts. I respect you; I promise I do. And Boo I love you, but even if you had said no, I was still gonna do it anyway. Maybe not as confidently as I would if you were completely okay with it, but still. I gave up my place and everything. You gotta let me have this one."

"I feel you. I mean, do what you do, baby girl. I'm surprised you thinking about that after just having Clay. I know how you are about being away from him, but hey, whatever floats your boat," he says, his tone casual.

I frown slightly. "Okay... Do you not want me to?"

"I don't got a real problem with it."

"So, what's the problem then? Because there's something bothering you. I can tell. Do you not trust me?"

"It's not you Ion' trust. I was just thinking that you don't have to do that anymore. You don't have to, 'cause I got you," he explains.

"I know you do, Boo. But I said I miss dancing. I'm not going to do it just for the money."

"I understand, then."

"I'm kinda disappointed that you're not fully on board with it," I admit.

"I am on board with it."

"I won't go back to Randall's spot. I'll find another if that makes you feel better." I offer, trying to reassure him. But deep down, I know Randall wouldn't hire me back anyway. "I like doing it 'cause it feels good for me. I love being blessed with the body I got, and I gotta embrace it."

"You good at what you do, baby girl, and I respect it. It don't make you any less of a person. But just 'cause I know that and I know you well enough don't mean that other fools out here will. I know the way y'all are treated. It don't feel right knowing you gettin' that kind of treatment and you don't have to," Omar responds, his concern is evident.

He's been in the game long enough to know how dancers are often treated, and I'm sure he's witnessed his fair share of disrespect. He's obviously attracted to them.

"I'm not thinking about none of those people. I know I got a good man, and I know how I deserve to be treated. You're not saying this 'cause you don't want me to embarrass you, right?"

"No. Why would I be embarrassed?" Omar responds, looking genuinely puzzled.

"I don't know... You are so big; people find out I'm dancing and then wonder what the hell is going on over here."

"It wouldn't be their business. I just don't nobody tryna hurt you either 'cause of me. Being in the spotlight like that... Ion' know, baby girl," Omar admits, shaking his head.

"I kinda love the spotlight. You love the spotlight, don't you? You're always in the spotlight."

"It's not always a good feeling though," he admits with a sigh.

"I understand. But dancing is a good feeling for me. It really makes me feel good.".

"Just 'cause something makes you feel good doesn't mean it's good for you."

"It's better than passing out dope to make people feel good, even though it's bad for them."

Omar shakes his head and exhales.

"Okay, sorry for saying that, but do you understand what I mean? Like... I love you and everything, but you don't think about how what you sell hurts people?" I push, knowing it's a sensitive topic.

"People have a hand in their own demise," he responds, glancing at Clayton in his stroller. "I ain't never said that what I did was right. I said I did what I had to do. Maybe if everybody thought like you did, I would be outta business."

He's right. It sucks that he's a dope dealer and consistently pumps it into the community for money, power, and respect. I also have always thought about the easy access I would actually have, yet I have no desire to fill my body with that mess, so people don't have to, but they want to. I won't judge though, because it makes me sad that sometimes drugs are all what some people have to turn to make them feel good... To make life worth living.

It makes me think about my mama.

Omar glances over at me, his gaze softening. "Dance, if that's what you wanna do for yourself. I'ma support whatever you got goin' on, baby girl."

My smile widens, mirroring his. "Thank you, boo. I appreciate the support. I'm glad you're not telling me what to do."

"Yeah, I ain't out here tryna control you either. You are your own person, and I gotta respect that 'cause I'm the same way. Can't nobody tell my ass nothin'."

"Except now we're a team, Omar. We gotta listen to each other," I remind him gently.

"You right."

"Okay, so how come we ain't never talk about getting married?" I broach the topic, but he falls silent, his attention drawn to a family playing with frisbees nearby.

The silence stretches, making me uneasy. I wish he'd just tell me if he doesn't want to marry me. But then again, I have to remind myself of my own doubts about marriage. Still, I can't help but wonder if he'd consider making me his wife.

"Never mind," I finally say, breaking the tense silence.

Omar looks over at me once again, his expression blank.

"You coulda just said that you don't wanna marry me," I add, unable to mask my disappointment.

"You gotta stop talkin' for me. Relax," he responds, setting his lighter down. "Is that what you want?"

I shrug, feeling conflicted, but then I nod softly.

He stands up and stretches, casting a shadow over me as he blocks out the sun. "Stop worrying so much. I got you, baby girl. I ain't even know you wanted to go that far with me, if I'm bein' honest with you."

I raise my head to meet his gaze, feeling a mixture of surprise and hurt. "You didn't think I wanted to marry you?"

"I feel like I'm gonna wake up one day to you gone, baby girl. You've done it before," he admits, his words hitting me hard.

His assumption stings because I have walked away once before. And I can't say that I wouldn't again if I had to. "This isn't just you saying that to avoid my question?"

"No, I'm tellin' you how I feel. I get it. You want a ring, and you deserve one. But for me? I gotta feel you really for me too, baby girl. You don't trust me all the way yet, and I can feel it."

His words continue to cut through me, revealing a truth I've been avoiding. He's right, as much as I hate to admit it. Trust is still a bridge we're building, one brick at a time. There's still a lingering sense of doubt, and I can't shake it off. Maybe it's the influence of others' opinions or my own fears, but whatever it is, it's holding me back too.

"Why is it that when I talk to you, I feel good? I feel safe, and I can trust you. But then I talk to somebody else, and it makes me think extra hard about you and us," I express, searching his eyes for understanding.

"How about you get to know me your damn self and stop listening to what other fools gotta say about me? Don't nobody know me but me. I ain't out here askin' about you," Omar responds firmly.

His response hits me like a wake-up call. I need to consider his feelings too; not just what others say or expect. I understand that it's not fair to pressure him into marriage just because we have Clay now. It's a decision we both need to make when we're ready.

"I understand, Omar. I think I'm just thinking about a timeline of things. Like we have Clay now. So maybe I'm just thinkin' that we should be getting married next. Really before him, but he's here now, so whatever," I admit, trying to convey my thoughts honestly.

"We don't gotta follow what other people are doing or do what somebody else thinks is the right way. We move at our own pace, baby girl. You feel me?" Omar reassures me, his voice softer now, his hand gently caressing my thighs.

"Yes. I agree with that. I struggled to even believe in marriage myself, so I shouldn't have pushed it on you, and I'm sorry, boo."

"You good. I'm not even mad that it came up in conversation. It's a good thing in my opinion. You thinkin' about us."

As we sit together in the park, I feel a sense of peace wash over me. Right now, all that matters is being with Omar and our baby, cherishing these simple moments together while we have them.

"I do want you though. Always will, so don't even question that," he adds.

"Okay, I won't question it. I'll always want you too. I think we should take our time like you said and get to know each other some more. I know there's more to Omar Spence than people think. You ain't getting no more babies out of me yet though, so don't try it," I tease, lightening the mood between us.

Omar chuckles, his laughter adding to the warmth of the air. I can't help but admire his genuine smile, the one that lights up his face and melts my heart every time.

"You wanna know somethin'?" I ask, tracing my finger underneath his chin.

"What's that?"

"My empire is better than yours. I got the best there is."

"How you figure that, baby girl?" he questions, his brow furrowing in amusement.

"'Cause I have you and... You're the best drug, Omar," I whisper, and without hesitation, our lips meet in a sweet, passionate kiss, sealing our bond under the scorching LA sun.

———— ♡ ————

Epilogue

As I step out of the car, the club's neon lights flicker to life, and the usual bass-heavy music echoes throughout the walls. I take a deep breath, smoothing my outfit and hair. It's been two years since I last danced, having spent that time raising our son, Clayton. The thought of leaving him tonight tugs at my heart, but I've missed dancing too much to stay away any longer. My soul craves it.

I appreciate Omar for not protesting, even though I can tell he's struggling with it. He got me this job, and I didn't want to go back to the Phoenix Fire under Randall, so I let him help me out. Before I returned to the stage, he made sure I was safe, and he was satisfied with my new boss. I'm also relieved that my new boss is a woman and she's been very sweet. *So far.*

Inside, the club feels like any other nightclub I can remember—dark, smoky, and heavy with the aroma of expensive booze mixed with cheap perfume. New faces meet me as I head to the changing room, but I'm not sweating these new coworkers. I still couldn't care less about what they have going on because I've had my fair share of lessons on minding the business that pays me. I just hope they do the same.

As I prepare for the stage, my thoughts drift to Clay, with his contagious laugh and big, Bleu eyes. For the next several hours, I'll miss him, but at least I have something to look forward to and that's coming home to my baby boy every night and snuggling with him.

The music and action of the night fly by, yet I feel oddly disconnected, as if my head is somewhere else. It's only when the music starts to fade and the crowd thins out that I notice Omar standing near the bar, staring at me with that intense gaze of his. He's always had this confident yet dangerous vibe that draws me to him, and tonight, he's dressed more sharply than usual.

He calls me over after my set. I walk up to him, happy that he came to see me on my first night back. His empire has been growing, but it hasn't yet bled into the life Omar promised me and Clayton. I don't really know how much power and influence he has to keep the chaos away, but I'm impressed. It gets complicated, but it always works out.

He pulls me close, his hand warm on my back. "That was sexy. You still got it," he murmurs, his breath hot against my ear.

"Thank you, boo," I say, barely audible above the music. "But what are you doing here, Omar?"

"I wanted to see you," he says, his eyes searching mine. "And I have something important to ask you."

He leads me to a quieter corner of the club, away from prying eyes. My heart pounds so hard it feels like it might burst out of my chest. He reaches into his pocket and pulls out a small, velvet box. The moment he opens it, I see an emerald ring inside. It matches the color of my eyes, sparkling even in the dim light. I can hardly breathe, my mind racing with a thousand thoughts.

"Chevonne... baby girl," he begins, his voice steady, as if he's practiced for this moment. "I know our lives are complicated and whatnot, and we face challenges most people can't really understand. But it ain't for them to understand. You get me, and I think I got you down. Through it all, you've been my strength, my reason. I wanna show you that you're not just a good time, you've always been here for the long time. I want us to be a family for the long time. And I want, with you by my side, to give Clay the life he deserves, even if it means he doesn't follow in my footsteps. We still gotta discuss that, but I'm okay with it for now. Will you marry me, baby?"

Tears fill my eyes as I look at him, at the ring, and think of our son. "Yes!" I whisper, my voice trembling. "Yes, I'll marry you, Omar!"

He slips the ring onto my finger, and as he pulls me into his arms, the noise of the club fades away, leaving just us and the promise of a future together.

Future *Mrs. Chevonne Spence* has a nice ring to it. I can dig it.

I can't wait to tell Grandma Cheryl.

Stay tuned for "A Dancer's Drug, Part Two" by Mille Anne
Chevy & Omar's story isn't quite over yet . . .

Acknowledgments

This book would not exist without the incredible support and encouragement I have received along the way.

To my family and friends: Your unwavering support and constant push to keep going have been the backbone of this journey. Your belief in me has been my greatest source of strength, and I am eternally grateful.

To my Love & War family: Your faith in me and your companionship on this journey have meant the world. Thank you for always believing in me and for walking beside me through every twist and turn as I build this career from the bottom up.

To my ARC Reader team: Your feedback, enthusiasm, and love for my writing have been invaluable. Your encouragement has fueled my passion and inspired me to strive for greater heights.

To the souls I've met in passing: Your brief yet impactful words of motivation have been like whispers of hope, reminding me to persevere. Thank you for your unexpected but deeply appreciated inspiration.

And above all, to God: Thank you for absolutely everything. Your guidance and blessings have been my anchor and my light.

With all my heart,

Mille Anne

A STORYTELLER FOR THE SOUL

Mille Anne is a captivating voice in contemporary fiction, romance, and urban literature, weaving gripping narratives and meaningful stories with relatable characters. Her journey as a published author began in 2020, and since then, she has enchanted readers with her fictional work.

Having mastered various aspects of business from EMU while dedicating herself to her craft, Mille Anne brings a unique blend of creativity and insight to her writing. From her early days as a young girl, she knew that writing was her calling, and she has been honing her craft ever since.

Mille Anne's writing style is as dramatic and entertaining as her stories, characterized by vivid descriptions and attention to detail that appeal to all reader senses. She takes a soulful approach to her writing, aiming to captivate readers with a passion for thought-provoking tales.

Beyond her role as an author, Mille Anne is the visionary founder of Purple Soul Publishing. As both a business owner and an author under the brand, she channels her creativity into both crafting her own art and providing a platform for other talented writers to share their stories with the world.

———— ♡ ————

www.ingramcontent.com/pod-product-compliance
Lightning Source LLC
Chambersburg PA
CBHW031608240626
47153CB00002B/682